CW00402889

Etzwane turned back
the hedge bounded
ahulphs made grinning disavowals, loping helpfully in one direction, then another. The boys
gave a caw of rage at the helplessness of the
ahulphs; then one saw the carriage and pointed.
All began to run in hot pursuit.

Etzwane said anxiously, "Can't you drive somewhat faster? Otherwise they will kill me."

The man looked stonily ahead as if he had not
heard. Etzwane gave a despairing glance behind,
to find his pursuers gaining rapidly. His life was
coming to an end. The ahulphs, with license to
kill, would rend him apart at once, then carefully
tie the parts into parcels to take home,
quarrelling over this and that as they did so.
Etzwane jumped from the carriage, to tumble
head over heels into the road. Scraped and
bruised but feeling nothing, he sprang down the
river bank, bursting through the alders and into
the swift yellow Lurne. What now? He had never
swum a stroke in his life. . . .

Also by Jack Vance in VGSF

BIG PLANET

JACK VANCE

Durdane

Book I THE FACELESS MAN
Book II THE BRAVE FREE MEN
Book III THE ASUTRA

VGSF

VGSF is an imprint of Victor Gollancz Ltd
14 Henrietta Street, London WC2E 8QJ

First VGSF edition 1987

First published in one volume
in this edition 1989

The Faceless Man Copyright © 1971 by Jack Vance
The Brave Free Men Copyright © 1972 by Jack Vance
The Asutra Copyright © 1973 by Jack Vance

British Library Cataloguing in Publication Data
Vance, Jack, *1916-*
    Durdane.
    I. Title
    813'.54 [F]

ISBN 0-575-04576-0

Printed in Great Britain by
Richard Clay Ltd, Bungay, Suffolk

The Faceless Man

CHAPTER ONE

At the age of nine Mur heard a man in his mother's rest cottage call out a jocular curse in the name of the Faceless Man. Later, after the man had gone his way, Mur put a question to his mother. "Is the faceless Man real?"

"He is real, indeed," replied Eathre.

Mur considered the matter for a period, then asked, "How does he eat or smell or talk?"

Eathre, in her calm voice, replied, "I suppose one way or another he manages."

"It would be interesting to watch," said Mur.

"No doubt."

"Have you ever seen him?"

Eathre shook her head. "The Faceless Man never troubles the Chilites, so you need not concern yourself for the faceless Man." She added as a musing afterthought: "For better or worse, such is the case."

Mur, a child thin and sombre, knit the black brows that had come as a legacy from his unknown blood-father. "Why should such a case be better? Or worse?"

"What a vexatious child you are!" declared Eathre without heat. Her lips twitched: perhaps a twinge of *chsein*.* But she said, "If a person breaks Chilite law, the Ecclesiarchs punish him. If he runs away, the Faceless Man takes his head." Eathre's hand went to her

---

* *Chsein:* (1) Conditioned recoil from a forbidden thought. (2) Blindness or obliviousness to the actuality of unfamiliar, forbidden, or unorthodox circumstances.

torc, a mannerism common to all the folk of Shant. "If you obey Chilite law, you need never fear the loss of your head. This is the 'better'. In such a case, however, you are a Chilite, and this is the 'worse'."

Mur said no more. The remarks were unsettling. Were his soul-father to hear, Eathre would incur at least a reprimand. She might be transferred to the tannery, and Mur's world would be shattered. The time left him "on mother's milk" (to use the Chilite idiom) was short enough in any event: three or four years. . . . A wayfarer entered the cottage. Eathre put a garland of flowers around her brow and poured a goblet of wine.

Mur went to sit in the shade of the great rhododendrons across the Way. To some such encounter he owed his existence, so he was aware; an Original Guilt that he must expiate when he became a Chilite Pure Boy. The whole process taxed his mind. Eathre had borne four children. Delamber, a girl of sixteen, already maintained a cottage at the west end of the Way. The second child, Blink, three years older than Mur, had already put on the white robe of a Pure Boy and had assumed the name Chalres Gargamet, combining the virtues of Chalres, the Chilite ascetic who had lived and died in the branches of the Holy Oak, four miles up Mirk Valley, and Bastin Gargamet, the master tanner who (while fuming ahulph* hides) had discovered the sacramental qualities of galga.† The fourth child, born two years

* Ahulph: a half-intelligent biped autochthonous to Durdane, ranging wild in the backlands and wildernesses, on occasion tamed, bred and crossbred for a variety of uses, from unskilled labour and portage to house pets. When sick, the ahulph exudes a detestable odour that excites even itself to complaint.

† Galga: Dried leaves of the easil bush, pulverized, bound with easil gum and ahulph blood: an important adjunct to the spasmic Chilite worship of Galexis.

after Mur, had been adjudged defective and drowned in the tannery sump, with prejudice towards Eathre, sexual eccentricity being held the cause of fetal defects.

Mur sat under the rhododendrons scratching patterns in the white dust and appraising those who passed: a mercantilist driving a pacer-trap rented at the balloon-way station in Canton Seamus, then three young vaga-bonds; agricultural workers by the green-brown verti-cals of their torc-badges.

Mur stirred himself. His plot of fibre-trees wanted tending; if the bobbins were allowed to run slack, the thread became lumpy and coarse. . . . A steam-powered dray came past, loaded with fine long black-wood tim-bers. Mur, forgetting fibre-trees, gave chase and hung dangling from the end timber all the way to Mirk Bridge where he dropped onto the road and watched the dray rumble along the far wild road to the east. For a period he dropped pebbles into the Mirk; just above the bridge turned a waterwheel to grind galls, alum, dye-stone, all manner of herbs, roots, and chemicals for the tannery.

Mur idled back along Rhododendron Way, and found the traveller departed. Eathre set out bread and soup for his lunch. As Mur ate, he asked the question that all morning had been tugging at a corner of his mind. "Chalres resembles his soul-father, but I do not; isn't this strange?"

Eathre paused for knowledge to well up into her mind: a wonderful elemental process, like the flower-ing of trees or juice oozing from bruised fruit. "Neither you nor Chalres have blood-connection with Grand Male Osso or any other Chilite. They have no knowl-edge of real women. Chalres's father I do not know. Your blood-father was a wanderer, a music-maker, one of those who travel alone. I was sorry when he went his way."

7

"He never came back?"

"Never."

"Where did he go?"

Eathre shook her head. "Such as Dystar wander all the cantons of Shant."

"And you could not go with him?"

"Not while Osso holds my indenture."

Mur ate his soup in thoughtful silence.

Into the cottage came Delamber, a cloak over her striped gown of green and blue. Like Mur, she was slender and serious; like her mother, she was tall and as softly even as a flowing river. She sank into a chair. "Already I am tired; I have had three musicians from the camp. The last was most difficult and full of talk as well. He decided to tell me of certain barbarians, the Roguskhoi: great drunkards and great lechers. Have you heard of them?"

"Yes," said Eathre. "The man who just now departed regards them with great respect. He described their lust as beyond the usual, from which no woman is safe, nor do they pay."

"Why doesn't the Faceless Man drive them away?" demanded Mur.

"Wild folk wear no torcs; the Faceless Man can't deal with them. In any event they have been beaten back and are no longer considered a threat."

Eathre served tea; Mur took two nut-cakes and went out into the garden behind the cottage where he heard the voice of Chalres, his soul-brother.

Mur looked around without enthusiasm. Down the hillside sauntered Chalres, halting at the edge of the garden where he dared not venture for fear of defilement. Chalres, who bore no resemblance to Mur, was thin and tall, with small sharp features in constant agitation. His eyes blinked, bulged, screwed up, rolled right and left; his nose twitched; he grinned, grimaced, sneered, showed his teeth, licked his lips, guffawed when a chuckle might have sufficed; he scratched his nose, rubbed his ears, made wide, ungainly gestures. Mur had long wondered why he and Chalres differed in so many attributes. Did they not share the same mother, the same soul-father? To some extent Chalres resembled their mutual soul-father Great Male Osso, who was himself tall, sallow, and thin as a bell-ringer.

"Come along," said Chalres, "you are to pick berries."

"I to pick berries? Who said I must?"

"I say so, and to ensure purity from woman-taint, I have brought sacramental gloves for you. Take care to breathe off to the side and all will be well. What is that you are eating?"

"Nut-cakes."

"Hmmf . . . I have had nothing this morning but biscuit and water. . . . No. I dare not. Osso would learn. He has a nose like an ahulph. Here, take this." He tossed Mur a basket containing white gloves: Chalres's own, Mur suspected, which even as a Pure Boy he was required to wear while handling food. Chalres, it seemed, valued his ease more than he feared defiling the food, which was for the Chilites' table, in any event.

Mur, while not overly fond of Chalres, felt a certain sympathy for his privations; in so short a time they would be inflicted on Mur himself. He took the basket without protest: if the fraud were discovered it was Chalres who would pay. He asked grudgingly, "Do you want a nut-cake? Or not?"

Chalres searched the hillside, the white bulk of Bashon Temple, the row of dark bays under the walls where the Pure Boys made their dens. "Come over to the apar tree."

Behind the apar tree Chalres ceremoniously donned the white gloves. Taking the nut-cake, he devoured it in a gulp. Then, licking the crumbs from his cheeks, he performed a set of uneasy grimaces, coughing, twitching his nose, peering up the hillside. At last, reassured, he made a grand gesture to wipe the whole affair from memory.

The two set off towards the berry patch at the western end of Rhododendron Way, Chalres pointedly maintaining a distance between himself and his unpurified soul-brother.

"Tonight the Ecclesiarchs meet in Doctrinal Conclave," Chalres told Mur with the air of one imparting important news. "They make a dessert of berries, and a great basket is required. Would you believe it? I have been sent forth alone to pluck this massive quantity. For all the delicacy of their ideals and the rigour of their determination, they consume every bite put before them."

"Hah," said Mur in saturnine deprecation. "How long until your own assumption?"

"A year. Already I grow body hair."

"Do you realize that once they clap a torc around your neck, you may never again roam or wander?"

Chalres sniffed. "That is like saying: Once a tree is grown, it may not become a seed again."

"Then you don't care to wander?"

Chalres gave a grumbling elliptical answer. "Wanderers wear torcs as well. Show me a wanderer without a torc and I will show you an outlander."

Mur had no ready response. Presently he asked: "The Roguskhoi: are they outlanders?"

"The what? I've never heard of them."

Mur, with little more knowledge than Chalres, judiciously said no more. Passing the tree-silk plantation, where Mur tended a plot of two hundred bobbins, they descended to the berry patch. Chalres halted and glanced back up towards the temple. "Look now; you go yonder, around and below to the low patch; I'll harvest above, where those of the temple can observe and approve, should they feel the inclination. Mind you, wear the gloves! This is the minimum precaution I can countenance."

"What of Osso's minimum?"

"As to that we can only speculate. I need at least two basketfuls, so work at speed. Don't forget the gloves! The Chilites detect woman-taint farther than an ordinary man smells smoke."

Mur descended to the lower verge of the berry patch where he made a further detour to inspect the camp of the musicians. This was an unusually large troupe, comprising seven wagons, each painted in patterns of meaningful colours: light blue for gaiety, pink for innocence, dark yellow for *sunuschein*,* grey-brown to affirm technical competence.

The troupe was busy with camp routine: tending the draft animals, cutting vegetables into cauldrons, flaping out shawls and blankets. As a group they were considerably more effusive and volatile than the Chilites; their gestures were abrupt and often flamboyant; when they laughed, they threw back their heads; even the chronically surly evinced their ill nature in unmistakable poses. An old man sat on the steps of a wagon fitting new pegs to a small crooknecked khitan. Nearby a boy about Mur's own age practised the gastaing, striking runs and arpeggios while the old man called gruff advice.

Mur sighed and, turning away, climbed the slope into

* *Sunuschein:* reckless, feckless gaiety, tinged with fatalism and tragic despair.

11

the berry patch. Ahead of him a blotch of pale brown shifted and flickered; there was a sound of rustling leaves. Mur stopped short, then slowly advanced. Peering through the foliage, he discovered a girl a year or two older than himself picking berries with great deftness, filling the basket slung over her arm.

Indignant at the girl's trespass, Mur strode forward, tripped on a dead branch, and crashed down into a hag-bush. The girl turned half a startled glance over her shoulder, dropped her basket, and ran pell-mell through the berry patch, skirt hiked up to her thighs. Mur hoisted himself foolishly to his feet. He looked after the girl. He had not meant to frighten her, but since the deed was done, so be it! Scratched legs or not, she had no business among the Chilite berries. He picked up the basket she had dropped and with careful malice poured the berries into his own basket. Here were berries for the Conclave!

Thrusting the gloves into his pocket, he picked for a period, working up the slope. Presently Chalres hailed him. "Boy! Where are the berries? Have you toiled or loitered?"

"See for yourself," said Mur.

Chalres peered into the basket, pointedly ignoring the fact that Mur wore no gloves. "Hmm. You've done quite well. Surprising. Well, then, pour them in here. I'll say that's all there were to be had. . . . Excellent. Ah yes, the gloves. You are exceedingly neat." Chalres crushed a berry between the fingers of the glove. "That looks somewhat better. Now, then, no tales." He shoved his thin face fiercely into Mur's. "Remember, when you're a Pure Boy, I'll be a Chilite – and much sterner than I am now, for I can see that this is how the tide runs!" He returned up the hill to the temple.

With nothing better to do, Mur picked a few more

12

berries for his mother, eating as many as he dropped into the basket. Presently, as he had half-expected, the pale brown smock of the wanderer girl appeared somewhat down the slope. He approached slowly, making sure that she heard him, and this time she showed no disposition to flee. Instead, she came running forward, face glowing with rage. "You little weirdling, you frightened me; you took my berries! Where are they now? Give them here before I pull those ridiculous ears of yours!"

Mur, somewhat taken aback, strove to maintain an imperturbable Chilite dignity. "You need not call names."

"I need to do so very much! How else should I address a thief?"

"You are the thief; these are Chilite berry grounds!"

The girl threw up her hands and gave a petulant exclamation. "Who the thief and who not the thief? It's all one, so long as I have my berries." She snatched away Mur's basket, looked askance at the handful she found there. "Was that all I had picked?"

"There were more," declared Mur with stately candour. "I gave them to my soul-brother. Don't be annoyed; they go to the Chilite Conclave. Isn't it a great joke? A woman has defiled the food!"

The girl once again became angry. "I defiled no food! What do you take me for?"

"Perhaps you don't understand that –"

"Indeed not, and I never will! Not the Chilites! I know your dirty ways! You drug yourselves with smoke and dream lewd dreams; there never was so odd a sect!"

"The Chilites are not a sect," stated Mur, reciting the doctrine he had heard from Chalres. "I can tell you little because as of yet I am not even a 'Pure Boy' and

13

won't have full control of my soul for another three or four years. The Chilites are the single emancipated and high-cultured folk of Durdane. All other folk live by emotion; the Chilites maintain an abstract and intellectual existence."

The girl gave an offensive laugh. "You infant! What do you know of other folk? You haven't set foot a hundred yards down the road in either direction."

Mur could not refute the jibe. "Well, I have learned from the men who come to my mother's cottage. And never forget, my blood-father was a musician!"

"Indeed? What was his name?"

"Dystar."

"Dystar ... Come over to the wagons. I'll learn the truth about your father, what manner of musician he was."

Mur's heart beat faster; he drew back. "I'm not sure I want to know."

"Why not? What are you afraid of?"

"I'm afraid of nothing. I am a Chilite, and consequently –"

"Yes, yes; come along, then."

On leaden legs Mur followed, trying to strike upon some convincing reason why he should not go into the musician's camp. The girl looked back, showing a bold and saucy grin, and finally Mur became annoyed. She took him for a liar and a freak, did she? Nothing could dissuade him now.... They entered the musician's camp. "Azouk, Azouk!" cried a woman. "Are there berries? Bring them here."

"No berries," stated Azouk in disgust. "This little thief took them from me. I brought him here for a hiding."

"Come now," said the woman. "Do you have berries or no?"

14

The girl gave over the near-empty basket with a flourish. "It is as I said. This freaklet took them and claims beside his father was a musician – a certain Dystar."

"Well, and why not? Are musicians unlike other men? Beget and forget, that's how it goes." And she added, "His mother must be a methodical woman."

Mur essayed a timid question. "Did you know my father Dystar?"

The woman jerked her finger. "Ply the old man with the broken khitan. He knows every drunken musician of Shant. Come, you Azouk! Must you idle away your life, you hussy? Fetch twigs and foster the fire!" The woman went off to stir a cauldron; with a saucy toss of the head, the girl disappeared behind a wagon. Mur stood alone. No one needed him. All the folk of the troupe worked with intense concentration, as if their immediate task were the most important act they would ever undertake. In all the camp the old man seemed the most relaxed, and even he worked with zestful flourishes of his elbows and intermittent pauses to scowl down at his handiwork. Step by step Mur approached. The old man flicked him a cool glance and began to fit a string to the crooknecked khitan.

Mur watched in respectful silence. As the old man worked, he hissed a tune through his teeth. He dropped his awl; Mur picked it up and handed it to him, and received another side glance. Mur moved a step closer.

"Well, then," demanded the old man in a challenging voice, "do you consider the job well done?"

After a moment's hesitation Mur said, "I would think so. However, at Bashon we see few musical instruments. The Chilites prefer what they call a 'clear, cold silence'. My soul-father, Osso Higajou, is disturbed by the tinkle of a bell-bug."

15

The old man paused in his work. "That seems a peculiar circumstance. What of yourself? Are you a Chilite?"

"No, not yet. I live with my mother Eathre, half along the Way. I'm not sure I want to be a Chilite."

"And why not? They live easy enough, in 'clear, cool silence', with all their women to toil for them."

Mur nodded sagely. "Yes, I suppose that's true . . . But first I'd have to be a Pure Boy, and I don't really want to leave my mother. Also my blood-father was a musician. His name was Dystar."

"Dystar." The old man tautened the new string and gave it a touch. "Yes; I know of Dystar. A druithine."

Mur moved closer. "What is a druithine?"

"He is one who does not go with a troupe. He wanders by himself; he carries a khitan, such as this, or perhaps a gastaing; thus he is able to import his wisdom and the circumstances of his life."

"He sings?"

"Ah no, no indeed! No singing. That is for minstrels and balladeers. We do not reckon singing to be music; it is another matter entirely. Ha ha, what would Dystar have said to that!"

"What kind of a man is Dystar?"

The old man thrust his face forward; Mur jumped a step back. The old man demanded: "Why do you ask this, you who are to become a Pure Boy?"

"I have often wondered about my father."

"Very well, I will tell you. He was a strong, harsh-faced man. He played with passion, and there was never any doubt as to his feelings. And do you know how he died?"

"I did not know he was dead."

"This is how the story goes. One night he became

16

furiously drunk. He played* the gastaing, and all who heard were deeply moved. Afterwards, so it is told, he ran out into the street, raving that his torc choked him, and some saw him wrenching at it. Whether he broke it and took his own head, or whether the Faceless Man came by and disapproved, it is not known; but in the morning his body was found, and the wonderful head, so full of tunes, was gone." The old man gave a fretful tug at his own torc. Mur noted his colours: horizontals of purple and rose, indicating lack of cantonal affiliation; verticals of grey and brown, musicians' colours; a personal code of blue, dark green, dark yellow, scarlet, blue and purple. Mur felt his own neck, as yet naked. How would it feel to be clamped with a torc? Some said that for months, or even years, a person felt stifled, in constant dread; Mur had heard of cases where the person clamped became frantic and broke the torc apart, taking his own head. Mur licked his lips. The torcs were necessary, but sometimes he wished he might remain a child and live with his mother in a pleasant cottage far from Bashon and never be troubled by torc or Chilite or Faceless Man or anyone.

The old man stroked the Khitan, producing a wistful set of chords. Mur watched the agile fingers with fascination. The tempo increased, the melody jumped this way and that.... The old man stopped playing. "That was a jig of Barbado, which is a seaport to the south of Canton Enterland. How did you like it?"

"Very much."

The old man grunted. "Take this khitan for your own. Tomorrow, steal me a pelt of good leather, or pick me

* *Played:* a feeble rendering of the Shant verb *zuweshekar:* to use a musical instrument with such passion that the music takes on a life of its own.

17

a bucket of berries, or send me only your good wishes – I do not care."

"I'll do all three!" cried Mur. "And more, if you ask! But how can I learn the sleight?"

"No great matter if you strive. To alter key, bend the neck; you need learn but a single set of chords; the complete schedule is carved on the back. As how to use the chords, that is a different matter and derives from skill and long experience of music and life." He raised his finger portentously high. "When you become a great druithine, remember that your first khitan came from Feld Maijesto."

Mur held the instrument awkwardly. "I know no tunes; at Bashon there is no music."

"Contrive your own tunes!" snapped the old man. "Further, don't let soul-father Osso hear you; don't ask him to sing to your music or you'll learn the meaning of trouble!"

Mur departed the musicians' camp, his head effervescent with joy and wonder and disbelief for the marvellous thing that had happened to him.

Stepping into the Way, he came to his senses and stopped short. To carry this khitan home in full view was to start gossip along a route leading to his soul-father. Osso would instantly order the instrument destroyed as an article at odds with the spare Chilite doctrines.

By a devious route behind the rhododendrons, Mur returned to the cottage of his mother. She showed no surprise at the sight of the khitan, nor did Mur expect any of her. He told her all that had happened to him and reported the death of Dystar. She looked off into the dusk, for the suns had set, and the sky was purple. "Just such a way Dystar was fated to die; and after all it was not so bad." She touched her own torc and, turn-

18

ing away, prepared Mur's supper, taking special pains to please him.

Even so, Mur was distraught. "Must we always wear torcs? Couldn't folk agree to behave well so that there was no need?"

Eathre shook her head sadly. "I have heard that only lawbreakers resent the torc; as to this, I can't say. On the day the torc clamped my neck, I felt cramped and broken and awry. Perhaps there are better ways; I don't know. Soon you will be gone from me; I would not hinder you, whatever the way of your life, but to bless Saccard I must damn Saccume.* I hardly know what to tell you."

At Mur's expression of bewilderment Eathre said, "Very well, listen then. I counsel you to resourcefulness: defeat adversities rather than accept them! Strive for excellence! You must try to do better than the best, even if it means a lifetime of dissatisfaction for your own inadequacy!"

Mur tested the ideas. "I must learn rites and rotes better than anyone else? Better than Chalres? Better than Neech when he becomes a Pure Boy? So that I will become an Ecclesiarch?"

Eathre was a long time answering. "If you are eager to become an Ecclesiarch, this is what you must do."

Mur, who knew every subtle intonation of his mother's voice, nodded slowly.

"But now you must go to bed," said Eathre. "Mind when you play the khitan! Muffle the strings, take the fibres from the rattle-box. Otherwise Osso will have me at the tannery before my time."

In the darkness Mur stroked the strings, shivering at

* Saccard and Saccume: protagonists of a thousand Shant fables, always at odds, or working against each other, or the victims of antithetical circumstances.

19

the soft sounds. He would never be a Pure Boy; he and his mother would run away, they would become musicians! But, ah no, Eathre could not run away! She was indentured. How could he go without her? Never! So then – what? He clutched the khitan to his breast.

The morning brought news of a terrible circumstance. Face down in the tannery sludge, the body of Chalres Gargament was discovered. How he had died was uncertain, though his arms and legs were peculiarly twisted, like those of an antic dancer.

Somewhat later, whispers seeped from cottage to cottage. On the previous day Chalres had picked berries for the Conclave. Among the berries, after he had eaten, Great Male Osso had found a long black woman-hair. And those who whispered to each other felt quivering chills of that curious emotion that is half horror and half appreciation of some grotesque absurdity. As for Mur, he became deathly pale and slumped into the darkest corner of the cottage where he lay limp, with only the twitch of his narrow shoulder blades to indicate that he was alive.

At dusk Eathre covered Mur with a quilt and allowed him to lie quiet, though all night both lay awake. In the morning she brought him gruel. He turned up his thin face, lips trembling, hair matted. Eathre blinked back her tears and hugged him. Mur began to keen: a low wailing sound deep in his throat that slowly rose in pitch. Eathre shook him gently. "Mur, Mur, Mur!"

Later in the day Mur touched the khitan: an uninterested stroke of the fingers. He could not slip into the tannery warehouse for a pelt; he could not pick a basket of berries; he tried to transmit a complement of kind thoughts, but they seemed pallid and weak.

At sunset Eathre brought him stewed fruit and tea;

Mur at first shook his head, then listlessly ate. Eathre stood looking down at him – for so long a period that Mur raised his eyes. She said, "Before you assume to Soul, if you go from Bashon, they can't denounce you to the Faceless Man. If you like, I will find a kind man to take you for apprentice."

"They would set ahulphs after us."

"The matter could be arranged."

Mur shook his head. "I don't care to leave you."

"When you become a Chilite, you leave me, and worse."

"Even then I won't leave you! They can kill me, but still I won't."

Eathre stroked his head. "Chilite or dead, we would still be apart. Is this not true?"

"I will see you secretly. I can arrange that you need not work so hard."

"The work is not all that dreadful," said Eathre softly. "Everywhere women must work."

"The Faceless Man must be a monster!" cried Mur in a husky voice.

"No!" exclaimed Eathre with as much agitation as her temperament allowed. She reflected for a moment, composing her limpid thoughts. "How can I explain? You are so young! Human beings change with the minute! The man who praises Saccard may rage like a sick ahulph at Saccume. Do you understand? Men are perverse and cannot be predicted. To love without dissension they blind themselves by rules. Each of the sixty-two cantons uses a different set of rules. Which are the best, which the worst? No one knows, and perhaps it doesn't matter if only men abide by any one of these sets. If they don't – the others call out his colours to the Faceless Man. Or perhaps a monitor files a derogation. Or sometimes the Faceless Man comes wandering, or

21

he sends his Benevolences, as quiet as the Faceless Man himself. Do you now understand? The Faceless Man merely enforces the laws of the folk of Shant: those they have made for themselves."

"I suppose this is so," said Mur. "Still, if I were the Faceless Man, I would abolish fear and hardship, and you would never work at the tannery."

Eathre stroked his head. "Yes, dear Mur, I know. You would force men to be kind and good and cause a great disaster. Go to sleep now; the world will be much the same tomorrow."

CHAPTER TWO

On a cool morning in the fall of the year a Pure Boy came down to the boundary and called for Mur. "Your soul-father will see you at noon, at the portal to the under-room. Cleanse yourself well."

With leaden motions, Mur bathed, dressed in a clean smock. Eathre watched from the far side of the room, not wishing to contribute womantaint to Mur's nervousness.

At last she could not restrain herself and came to brush down his stubborn black hair. "Remember, he only wants to gauge your growth and speak to you of Chilite doctrine. There is nothing whatever to fear."

"That may be so," said Mur. "Still, I am afraid."

"Nonsense," said Eathre decidedly. "You are not afraid; you are the brave Mur. Listen carefully; obey exactly; answer cautious words to his questions; do nothing eccentric."

At the cottage door she brought an ember from the fire and blew smoke through Mur's clothes and hair so at least not to prejudice Osso with woman-taint.

Ten minutes before noon Mur set out for the temple, taut with foreboding. The road seemed a lonely place; white dust rose in his footsteps to eddy in the lavender sunlight. Above bulked the temple: a set of squat convex cylinders, gradually filling the sky. With the flow of cool air down the hill came the reek of stale galga.

Mur circled the base of the temple to a stall-like half-room open to the sky: a place known as the under-room, now empty. Mur arranged himself primly by the wall and waited.

Time passed. The suns climbed the sky, the blaze of white Sasetta passing across the plum-red haunch of Ezeletta, blue Zael on the roundabout: three dwarf stars dancing through space like fireflies.

Mur mused across the countryside. He could see far, far, far, in all directions: west to Canton Seamus; north to Shimrod Forest and beyond to Canton Ferriy where the folk made ironweb on their red hillsides.

A sound startled him. He jerked around to find Osso frowning down from a high pulpit. Mur had made a poor beginning; rather than waiting in a crouch of timorous reverence, here he stood gazing over the panorama.

For a minute or longer Osso looked down at Mur, who stared back in fascination. Osso spoke in a voice of sepulchral gravity: "Have the girls made ignoble play with you?"

The language was ambiguous; Mur understood the semantic content. He swallowed harder, recalling incidents that might be construed as ignoble play. He said, "No, never."

"Have you suggested or initiated vile concatenations with the female girls?"

"No," quavered Mur. "Never."

Osso gave a curt nod. "From your present age forward you must take care. You will shortly become a Pure Boy, thereafter a Chilite. Do not complicate the already rigorous rituals."

Mur gave an acquiescent mumble.

"You can expedite your passage into the temple," spoke Osso. "Devour no greasy food, drink no syrups nor baklavy. The bond between child and mother is
24

strong; now is the time to start the solvent process. Gently disengage yourself! When your mother offers sweetmeats or attempts fond caresses, you must say, 'Madam, I am on the verge of purification; please do not add to the rigours I must endure.' Is this clear?"

"Yes, soul-father."

"You must start to forge the strongest of all bonds, the holy link to the temple. Galexis, the nervous essence, corresponds to female women as the candy of unmel to tannery sludge; you will learn more of this. Meanwhile, strengthen yourself!"

"How am I to do this?" Mur ventured.

Osso turned down a frightening glance; Mur shrank back. Osso spoke. "You know the nature of animal appetites. Philosophically – this is a doctrine you are not yet prepared to receive – they are First Order gratifications. Your belly is empty; you fill it with bread: the most crude reply to a crude sensation. The second Order response is to consume a varied meal; at the Third Order the viands are prepared in a subtle and expert fashion to an exacting set of standards. At the Fourth Order the demands of the stomach itself are ignored; the taste nerves are stimulated by essences and extracts. At the Fifth Order the sensations occur cerebrally, completely by-passing the glottal and olfactory apparatus. At the Sixth Order the Chilite is in a state of unconscious exaltation, and sublime Galexis Achiliadnid deals directly with the soul. Is all clear? I use the simplest and most obvious example as a basis for discussion."

"I understand this all very well," said Mur. "But I am puzzled. When Chilites put food into their mouths, what is the correct doctrine on this?"

"We sustain the energy of our bodies," intoned Osso. "The style of victual, coarse or fine, is a matter of indifference. Be firm with yourself. Direct your mind from the assault of the brute appetite; find some abstract occupation upon which to focus your attention. I tied heraldic knots with imaginary cords; another Ecclesiarch, a Six Spasm, memorized prime numbers. There are many such occupations to which you can put your mind."

"I know just the thing," said Mur with something like enthusiasm. "I will consider musical sounds."

"Use whatever device you find helpful," said Osso. "So, then, be guided. I can counsel, but progress must be made by yourself. Have you given thought to your male name?"

"Not yet, soul-father."

"It is not too early to do so. A proper name can be inspirational and exalting. In due course I will offer a list of suggestions; but for today, that is all."

Mur returned down the hill. Eathre was busy in the cottage; he wandered west along Rhododendron Way to the camp that the musicians had long vacated. Feeling hungry, he went up into the berry thicket, picked and ate berries with no thought for Osso's adjurations to abstraction. Then he looked up the hill to the temple complex and stared a full five minutes. Somewhere in his mind cogitation occurred; he was aware of no train of ideas, but presently he made a sound in his throat, something between a laugh and a contemptuous snort.

When he returned to the cottage, Eathre was drinking tea. Mur thought that she seemed tired and wan. She asked, "How went the meeting with soul-father Osso?"

Mur grimaced. "He told me to practice purity. I am not to play with girls."

Eathre silently sipped her tea.

"He told me to curb my appetites. I am also to take a name."

.26

Eathre acquiesced. "You are old enough to name yourself a name. What will it be?"

Mur gave a glum shrug. "Soul-father will send me down a list."

"He did the same for Glynet's son Neech."

"Did Neech take a name?"

"He called himself Geacles Vonoble."

"Hmf. And who were they?"

Eathre said tonelessly: "Geacles was the architect of the temple; Vonoble composed the Achiliadnid Dithyrambs."

"Hmf. So I must call fat Neech Geacles."

"That is now his name."

Four days later a Pure Boy pushed a long stick across the boundary with a paper in its cleft end. "A missive from Great Male Osso."

Mur took the paper into the cottage and with occasional help from Eathre puzzled out the sense of the characters. His face grew longer and longer as he read: "Bougozonie, the Seven-Spasm Ecclesiarch. Narth Homank, who ate but one nut and one berry each day. Higajou, who reorganized Pure Boy training. Faman Cocile, who allowed himself to be gelded by Shimrod Forest bandits rather than alter his creed of nonviolence and peace. Borgad Polveitch who denounced the Ambisexual Heresy." At last Mur put aside the paper.

"What is your selection?" asked Eathre.

"I can't make up my mind."

Three months later Mur was summoned to a second conference with his soul-father at the under-room. Osso again advised Mur on particularities of conduct. "It is not too early to begin carrying yourself in the style of a

Pure Boy. Each day put aside one adjunct of your old child's life. Study the child's Principary, with which you will be supplied. You have selected a name for yourself?"

"Yes," said Mur.

"And what is your male name to be?"

"I now call myself Gastel Etzwane."

" 'Gastel Etzwane!' Where in the name of everything extraordinary did you derive this nomenclature?"

Mur spoke placatingly. "Well – naturally I considered your suggestions, but I thought I would like to be someone different. A man who passed along Rhododendron Way gave me a book called *Heroes of Old Shant*, and here I found my names."

"And who is 'Gastel'? And who is 'Etzwane'?"

Mur, or Gastel Etzwane, as was now his name, looked uncertainly up at his soul-father, in whom he had expected familiarity with these magic personalities. "Gastel built a great glider of withe and web and launched himself from Mount Haghead, intending to fly the breadth of Shant, but when he came to Cape Merse, rather than alighting, he sailed on over the Purple Ocean towards Caraz* and was never seen again. . . . Etzwane was the greatest musician ever to wander Shant."

Osso was silent for half a minute, seeking words. At last he spoke, in ponderous opprobium: "A crazy aeronaut and a tune-twanger: these are then your examplars. I have failed to inculcate in you the proper ideals; I have been remiss, and it is clear that I must, in your case, exert myself more energetically. Your name is not to be Gaswane Etzel, or whatever. It shall be Faman

* Caraz: (1) A colour, mottled, of black, maroon, plum, with a dusting or sheen of silver-grey; symbolic of chaos and pain, macabre events in general. (2) The largest of Durdane's three continents.

28

Bougozonie, whose attributes are immeasurably more relevant and inspiring. That is all for today."

Mur – he refused to think of himself as Faman Bougozonie – returned downslope, past the tannery, where he loitered to watch the old women at their tasks, then slowly proceeded home.

Eathre asked, "Well, then, and how did it go today?"

Mur said, "I told him my name was Gastel Etzwane; he said, no, it was Faman Bougozonie."

Eathre laughed, and Mur looked at her in melancholy accusation.

Eathre became sober. She said, "A name means nothing; let him call you what he wants. You'll quickly get used to it. And to the life of a Chilite."

Mur turned away. He brought out the khitan and touched the strings. After a few moments he attempted a melody, with accents from the rattle-box. Eathre listened approvingly, but presently Mur halted and inspected the instrument with disfavour. "I know so little, so few tunes. I can't strike the side-strings or use the brilliancy buttons or the slurs."

"Skill doesn't come easily," said Eathre. "Patience, patience. . . ."

CHAPTER THREE

At the age of twelve, Mur, Faman Bougozonie, Gastel
Etzwane – the names mingled in his mind – underwent
Purification. In company with three other boys,
Geacles, Morlark, and Illan, he was shorn skin-bald,
then washed in the bitterly cold water of the sacred
stream that welled up below the temple. After the first
submersion the boys lathered themselves with aromatic
tincture and once again submitted themselves to the
bone-wrenching chill. Clammy, naked, shivering, the
boys marched into a room heavy with the smoke of
burning agapanthus. From holes in the stone floor
steam arose; in a mixture of steam and smoke the boys
gasped, sweated, coughed, and presently began to tot-
ter. One by one they stumbled to the floor; when the
doors opened, they barely were able to raise their heads.

The voice of the Chilite supervising the Purification
rang through the air: "To your feet, back to the clean
water! Are you of such soft fibre? Let me see who wants
to make a Chilite of himself!"

Mur struggled erect. One other boy, Geacles Vonoble,
did likewise and, swaying, clutched at Mur. Both fell.
Mur brought himself once more erect and helped
Geacles to his feet. Geacles pushed Mur aside and loped
splayfooted to the pool. Mur stood gazing with numb
horror at the other two boys. Morlark lay with eyes
bulging, a trickle of blood leaking from his mouth. Illan
seemed unable to control his movements. Mur leaned
forward, but the bland voice of the monstrator halted

him. "To the pool as fast as possible! You are being watched and gauged."

Mur tottered to the pool and gave himself to the chill. His skin felt dead; his arms and legs were heavy and stiff as iron posts. He dragged himself up on the stone an inch at a time and somehow stumbled along a white-tiled passage into a chamber lined with benches. Here sat Geacles, swathed in a white robe, well satisfied with himself.

The monstrator tossed a similar robe to Mur. "Your skins are flushed of stain; for the first time since the necessary depravity of birth you are clean. Attention then to Argument One of the Chilite Procourse! Man enters the world through the genital portal: an original taint which by cleansings and attitudes the Chilite casts aside, like a serpent moulting a skin, but which ordinary men carry like a stinking incubus all the way to their graves. Drink!" He handed each boy a beaker of thick liquid; they drank. "Your first purge...."

Mur spent three days in a cell, with cold sacred water for sustenance. At the end of this time he was required to enter the sacred well, lather himself with tincture, and rinse. More dead than alive, he crept out into the sunlight a Pure Boy.

The monstrator gave him succinct instructions. "I need not detail the strictures; you are familiar with them. If you taint yourself, you must undergo a new Purification. I advise against it. Osso Higajou is your soulfather and not the least rigorous of the Chilites. He deplores the most trivial contact with the Female Principle. I have known him to berate a Pure Boy for enjoying the fragrance of a flower. 'The flower is a female procreative organ of the plant' – so Great Male Osso exclaimed – 'and there you stand with your nose pushed into it.' Trust Osso Higajou to guide you in the Rotes.

31

Think purity, live purity, and make sure that Great
Male Osso recognizes your purity! So now – to your
bay in the lower compound. You will find there wafers
and porridge. Eat in moderation; tonight, meditate."

Mur went to the bay – an alcove in an open ended
chamber under the temple walls – and gulped down the
food. The suns danced below the horizon; the sky became purple, then star-shot black. Mur lay down on
his back, wondering what to make of his new existence.
He felt intensely alert; by some unnamable faculty he
seemed to know the precise condition of every person
of Bashon.

Geacles Vonoble sat across the chamber in his own
bay and pretended not to notice Mur. The two were
alone. Morlark and Illan had not yet completed their
purification; the more advanced Pure Boys were at the
evening Beatitudes. Mur considered going across to
Geacles's bay for conversation but was deterred by
Geacles's posture, one of pious reverie. Geacles was at
once brittle and devious, affable and intent. He was not
a handsome lad, with puffy cheeks and a plump torso
on long thin legs. His yellow-brown eyes were round as
a bird's and avid for sight, as if Geacles could never
have all the seeing he wanted. Mur decided definitely
against seeking Geacles's company.

He left his bay and went out to sit at the base of the
temple wall. Halfway up the sky glistened a great irregular clot of light, sparked with fifty first-magnitude
stars, the night sky's most notable object. It cast a pallid
light and created shadows blacker than black: the
Skiaffarilla, which figured in the history of Durdane.
Some said that Earth, the legendary home of men, lay
beyond the Skiaffarilla. From within the chamber came
Geacles's voice reciting aloud an Achiliadnid ode. Mur
listened a moment. In spite of his fatigue, in spite of the

32

monstrator's warnings, in spite of Great Male Osso, Mur would have slipped off down the hill to visit his mother, had it not been for Geacles. Geacles saw everything, knew everything. Still, where was the harm in stretching his legs a bit? Mur sauntered forth, around the hill. He passed above the tannery, now dark and quiet but reeking with a hundred odours in conflict. From behind him came a small noise. Mur looked back, then stepped into the shadow of the chemical shed. He waited. A furtive sound. Footsteps: hastening, pausing, hastening again. A figure came past, peering ahead with mischievous intensity: Geacles.

Mur watched him sidle around the angle of the tannery. Geacles worked on the principle that what was bad for others was good for himself and hoped to gain advantage of some unspecified sort by spying. So much was clear. Mur stood quiet in the dark, not particularly surprised nor even angry; it was what he expected of Geacles ... Not too far away was the meditation chamber where young Chilites gathered before entering the temple for nocturnal communion with Galexies. Mur slipped through the shadows to a soaking vat. Holding his breath against the stench, he prodded and pulled with a turning prong and succeeded in lifting a hide. At a gingerly half trot he carried it up and around to the meditation chamber. Through the window came a mumble of voices: "... Galexis of a million beatific forms, individual but universal, for all but each alone, submissive but magnificent in your forward search; we avert our souls from sordid stuffs, the greases and taints, the First Order Palpabilities!"

Then voices a half octave lower in response: "Tonight, all will be well; tonight, all will be well."

Then the start of a new declamation: "Galexis of the myriad colours, the infinite graces –"

Through the open window Mur tossed the hide. A startled curse interrupted the declamation. Mur trotted back to his bay. Minutes later three of the young Chilites came to look into the chamber. Mur, in the recommended invocative posture, feigned sleep. At Geacles's bay a Chilite gave a low hoarse call, "One is gone; make search, make search! The Pure Boy Geacles!"

They ran back through the pale starlight and discovered Geacles lurking below the tannery. He protested innocence with every degree of fervour; he claimed the virtue of vigilance in following Pure Boy Mur whose erratic behaviour had engaged his attention. In their outrage the Chilites paid no heed; one Pure Boy convenient to hand was better than another not demonstrably guilty. Geacles was treated to a thrashing, then forced to remove the hide and give the meditation chamber a ritual cleansing: a process occupying three nights and two days. Next, Geacles went before the Development Committee where he was asked a number of searching questions. He had now toiled three nights and two days without sleep; in a half hysteria he babbled the first words that came into his head: a hysterical demonstration that impressed the Committee favourably, rather than otherwise. Geacles was basically good substance, they decided; his astonishing act must be ascribed to an ecstatic predisposition. Geacles received a cursory reprimand and was ordered to restrain his volatility.

During the examination Geacles identified Mur as the source of the mischief, to which information the commission presented faces of indifferent scepticism; nonetheless, they took note of the name. Geacles sensed something of the committee's mood and was heartened, though his skin crawled with detestation for Mur. Alter-

34

nately giggling in jubilation and groaning in fury, he returned to the Pure Boy chambers where the scandal had been discussed from every possible aspect. In silence the Pure Boys watched Geacles as he crossed the chamber. He went to his bay and lay himself upon the pallet, too tired to sleep, his mind crawling with malice. Through slitted eyes he watched Mur, wondering how he would take revenge. Some way, somehow, by one means or another ... Geacles fermented with emotion. His hate became so great that he began to shudder. He gave a small animal moan and quickly turned his back, lest others should notice his precious hate and use it for derision. Then it would be soiled and spoiled ... A peculiar condition overcame Geacles, wherein his body slept but his mind seemed to remain awake. Time foreshortened; about ten-minutes passed, or so he estimated; he turned to look around the chamber, and found that the suns had wheeled far across the sky. The hour was well past noon; Geacles had missed his lunch: cause for new anguish! He noticed Mur sitting on a bench at the open end of the chamber. He held a copy of the Analytical Catechism, but his attention was fixed across the landscape. He seemed distraught. Geacles raised his head, wondering what went on in Mur's mind. Why did his fingers twitch, why did he frown so intently? Mur gave a peculiar jerk, as if at a message from his subconscious. He rose to his feet and, as oblivious as a somnambulist, departed the chamber.

Geacles groaned in doubt and indecision. He still ached with fatigue. But Mur's conduct was not that of a Pure Boy. He heaved himself from his couch and went to peer after Mur. Was he off to tend his silk? Conceivably. But again – Mur's gait was not that of a truly consecrated Pure Boy. Geacles drew a deep breath. His curiosity had only just brought him to grief, in circumstances exactly

35

similar. He dragged himself back to his bay where he immersed himself in his own Analytical Catechism:

"Q: In how many guises may Galexis appear?
"A: Galexis is as protean as the face of the ocean . . ."

A week passed. Geacles behaved with easy cordiality towards all; the Pure Boys treated him with cautious reserve. Mur paid him no heed whatever. But Geacles gave a great deal of quiet attention to Mur. And one day while Geacles sat in his bay memorizing Exclamations, Mur went to sit on the bench at the open end of the chamber. Geacles instantly became interested and over the top of his book watched Mur's every move. Mur seemed to be talking to himself. Hmf, grunted Geacles to himself, he merely recited a litany or Exclamations. But why did his finger tap with so regular a beat on his knee? Peculiar. Geacles watched even more intently. Mur returned to his bay; Geacles instantly frowned down into his Exclamation. Shelving his Catechism, Mur went back to the front of the chamber. Here he paused a moment or two, looking out over the sweep of the landscape. After a single backward glance into the chamber, he set off along the hillside. Geacles instantly left his bay and went to look after Mur, who marched purposefully along the path to the north. Towards his plot of fibre-trees, thought Geacles with a sniff. Mur, or rather Faman Bougozonie, had always been assiduous with his trees. Still, why the backward glance into the chamber? Geacles rubbed his pale cheeks. Interesting, interesting. To learn he must look, with his round yellow-brown eyes; to look he must move himself within range of vision. After all, there was no reason why he should not tend his own silk; it had been sorely neglected over the last few weeks. Geacles disliked the routine of winding bobbins, weeding, propping branches, drawing down new strands; but now duty offered a pretext upon which he might follow Mur with out fear of challenge.

Geacles set off along one of the paths that curved around the parched hillside. He tried to contrive a sedate and purposeful gait and simultaneously maintain stealth: no mean feat; had Mur been other than lost in his brooding, Geacles would have been forced to relinquish one or the other of his attitudes.

But Mur went unheeding down into the silk-tree brake, and Geacles, ducking and sidling, followed.

From the age of eight Mur had tended eighteen full-size trees, with over a hundred bobbins. He knew the angle of each twig, the cast of each leaf, the sap that each branch might be expected to provide. Each bobbin had its idiosyncrasy; in some, if the glass spring were wound too tightly, the ratchet would jam; others refused to turn unless tilted; a few worked flawlessly, and these Mur used under the highest beads.

Geacles watched from concealment while Mur made the rounds of his bobbins, winding the mechanisms, replacing full spools with empty ones, pinching suckers from the trunks. A dozen branches had gone dry; Mur cut into fresh shoots. The beads of sap oozed forth; Mur drew down filaments, which hardened at once into strands of silk. Mur attached the ends to bobbins, assured himself that the rotating spools drew down the strands at a steady rate. Geacles watched in glum disappointment; Mur's conduct was that of an industrious, innocent, and responsible Pure Boy.

Mur began to move at purposeful speed, as if he were anxious to finish. Geacles ducked back out of sight as Mur stepped forward to make a careful scrutiny of the hillside. Geacles grinned; Mur's conduct was no longer that of an innocent Pure Boy.

Mur set off downhill, moving so quickly that Geacles was hard put to follow. Mur reached the path that skirted the boundary behind Rhododendron Way and set off to the east. Geacles was now at something of a disadvantage. If he followed along the path, he must disclose himself. He darted through the berry patch, blundering into a nettle patch. Cursing and hissing, he took shelter among the rhododendrons. Mur was well along the patch, almost out of sight. Geacles followed crouching, dodging, running. He gained a spot where he could look along the path. Mur was nowhere to be seen. Geacles deliberated a moment, then pushed down into Rhododendron Way, highly questionable territory for a Pure Boy, not precisely tainted but still ground to be walked on gingerly. No Mur. Puzzled now, Geacles returned to the path. Where was Mur? Had he gone into one of the cottages? Geacles licked his lips in horror, trotted along the path towards the cottage of Eathre. He paused to listen: Eathre was entertaining a musician. But where was Mur? Geacles looked this way and that. Surely not in the cottage with his mother and the musician. Geacles walked past, angry and uncomfortable. In some unfathomable manner Mur had evaded him. . . . The music halted, then, after a few runs and arpeggios, began again. It seemed to be coming not from the cottage but the garden. Geacles crept close, peered through the foliage. He turned. Fleetly, soundlessly, bounding like a hare, Geacles ran up the hill toward the temple. Eathre, glancing from her window, saw him go.

Fifteen minutes passed. Down the hill on long pointfooted strides came Great Male Osso, followed by two other Chilites, all three red-eyed from their galga-induced spasms. At the back came Geacles. The group marched down into Rhododendron Way.

At Eathre's cottage the group halted. The midday air was warm; the three suns rolled overhead, projecting triple images in the dust of the road. No sound could be heard but the drone of the spiral-bugs in the foliage and a far thumping from the tannery.

Standing well back from the door, Osso signalled to a nearby child. "Summon forth the woman Eathre."

The child timidly went around to the back of Eathre's cottage. A moment later the door opened; Eathre looked forth. She stood quietly, passive but alert.

Great Male Osso demanded, "The Pure Boy Faman Bougozonie – is he here?"

"He is not here."

"Where is he?"

"So I should guess, elsewhere."

"He was seen here not fifteen minutes ago."

Eathre had no comment to make. She waited in the doorway.

Osso spoke in a ponderous voice. "Woman, you would do well not to obstruct us."

Eathre smiled faintly. "Where do you see obstruction? Search as you will. The boy is not within; nor has he been, today or any other day since his rite."

Geacles darted behind the cottage where he signalled. The Chilities, clutching their robes to themselves, went to look. Geacles pointed in excitement. "He sat on yonder bench. The woman evades."

Osso spoke portentously: "Woman, is this true?"

"Why should he not sit there? The bench does him no taint."

"Are you a keen judge of this? Where is the boy?"

39

"I don't know."

Osso turned to Geacles. "Try the Pure Boy quarters. Fetch him here."

With great zeal Geacles sprang away, arms and legs pumping. He returned in five minutes, grinning and panting like a dog. "He is coming, he comes."

Mur stepped slowly forth into the road.

Osso stood back. Mur, wide-eyed and somewhat pale, asked, "Why did you wish to see me, soul-father?"

"I call to your attention," said Osso, "the sorry face that you came here mother-milking and playing idle music."

"With utmost respect, soul-father, you have been misled."

"There is the witness!"

Mur looked towards Geacles. "He has not told the truth."

"Did you not sit on this bench, a woman's thing? Did you not take a musical instrument from this woman's hand? You are female-foul and not on good footing."

"The bench, soul-father, is from outside the under-temple. Notice, it stands away from the cottage, across the garden boundary. The khitan is my own property and was given me years ago by a man. Before my rite I took it into the temple and passed it through agapan-thus smoke; you can still smell the reek. Since then, it has been kept in the play-hut I built with my own hands yonder; there it is now. I am guilty of no defilement whatever."

Osso looked blinking up at the sky while he gathered his thoughts. He was being made ridiculous by two Pure Boys. Faman Bougozonie with great cleverness had avoided any act of flagrant defilement, but this very cleverness indicated corruption. . . . Geacles Vonoble, while inaccurate in his assertions, had correctly diagnosed impurity. If anything was certain, it was that Faman Bougozonie's sophistries should not put truth and orthodoxy to rout. Osso said, "This seems a peculiar retreat for a Pure Boy, the yard behind his mother's cottage."

"It seemed as good as any other, soul-father, and here at least I would disturb no one while I meditated."

"Meditated?" croaked Osso. "Playing jigs and kestrels while the other Pure Boys performed devotions?"

"No, soul-father; the music helped fix my thoughts, exactly as you recommended."

"What? You claim that I recommended such an affair?"

"Yes, soul-father. You declared that you found the construction of imaginary knots helpful to your austerities and permitted that I employ musical tones to the same end."

Osso stood back. The other two Chilites and Geacles looked at him expectantly. Osso said, "I envisioned different tones, in a different environment. Your conduct stinks of secularity! And woman, what of you? Are you slack-witted? Surely you must know such conduct to be incorrect?"

"I hoped, Great Male, that the music would assist him in his future life."

Osso chuckled. "The mother of Pure Boy Chalres, the mother of Pure Boy Faman. What a pair! You shall spawn no more such prodigies. To the tannery." Osso swung around, pointed a finger at Mur. "As for you, we shall test the erudition you claim to have achieved."

"Soul-father, if you please, I only aspire to erudition!" cried Mur, but Osso already had turned away. Mur looked towards Eathre, who gave him a smiling shrug and went into the cottage. Mur whirled towards

41

Geacles, but the Chilites stood in his way. "To the temple with you; did you not hear your soul-father?"

Mur marched up the path to the temple. He went to his bay. Geacles followed and went to his own alcove where he sat looking across the room at Mur.

An hour passed; a chime sounded. The Pure Boys trooped into the refectory. Mur hesitated, then turned a look back over the landscape, across road and cottages and off into the purple distances.

Geacles was watching. Mur heaved a sigh and went down the passage towards the refectory.

At the entrance stood the Chilite monstrator. He signalled Mur aside. "This way."

He led Mur around the temple to a disused under-chamber. He swung open an old timber door and signalled Mur to enter. Holding high a glow-bulb, the monstrator led the way along a passage rich with the reek of old galga fume into a large circular chamber at the very heart of the temple. The limestone walls were dank and gave off the odour of mould; the floor was dark brick. From the ceiling hung a single light globe. "What is this place?" Mur quavered.

"It is a place of solitary study where you will remain prior to your Repurification."

" 'Repurification'!" cried Mur. "But I am not defiled."

"Come, come," said the monstrator. "Why dissemble? Do you believe you can outwit your soul-father Osso, or myself for that matter? If you did not physically defile yourself, you committed a hundred acts of spiritual defilement." He waited, but Mur was silent. "Notice," the monstrator went on, "there are books on the table yonder: Doctrines and Exclamations, an Analytical Catechism. These will give you comfort and wise counsel."

42

Mur scowled around the chamber. "How long must I stay here?"

"A proper time. In the cabinet is food and drink; to the side is a sump. Now a final word: submit and all will be well. Do you hear?"

"Monstrator, I hear."

"Life is a choice of paths. Make sure you choose correctly because you may never return to choose again. Call for Galexis!"

The monstrator departed into the corridor. Mur looked after him, half of a mind to follow.... But he had been brought here to meditate; if he departed, he would incur something worse than Repurification.

He listened. Nothing but the secret murmur of underground places. He went to stand in the gap and peered down the corridor. Surely someone watched. Or an alarm or a trap had been set. If he tried to follow the monstrator, he might encounter something unpleasant. "Submit," the monstrator had told him. "Submit and all will be well."

Submission might well be the wisest course.

Soberly Mur turned away from the opening. He went to look at the table and, seating himself, examined the books. The Doctrines were hand-printed in purple ink on alternate sheets of red and green paper; they were inordinately difficult to read and contained many strange expressions. Nonetheless, thought Mur, it would be wise to study them carefully. The Exclamations, to be uttered during nocturnal worship, were not quite so important, adding only elegance, as they did, to the spasms.

Mur recalled that he had eaten no lunch and, jumping up, went to the cabinet. He found a dozen packets of dried berries: enough to nourish him for as many days, or even longer, were he frugal, as common sense dictated. Three dark green glass jugs held ample water. There was no cot or couch; he must sleep on the bench. He returned to the table, took up the Analytical Catechism, and began to read:

Q: How long have Chilites known Galexis?

A: Four thousand years ago the Great System was initiated by Hakcil, who was prompted to the use of galga by an overbearing and malodorous spouse.

Q: How many guises does Galexis assume?

A: Galexis is as protean as the face of the ocean and is at once singular to each and universal to all.

Q: Where was Galexis before the Chilites discovered the sacred herb?

A: Galexis, sempiternal and immanent, has given umbral revelation to men of all eras, but only the Chilites, by performing the Absolute Dichotomy, have made Galexis real.

Q: What is the Absolute Dichotomy?

A: It is that act of perception that, on designating Corporeal Female as dross and taint, celbrates the Beatitude of Galexis.

Q: What is the purpose of the Holy Receptacle?

A: In the dueness of time, a perfection will be yielded: the fruit of Galexis and the males.

Q: What will be Perfection's Role and Destiny?

A: He shall take news of Galexis across the worlds. Where he walks the females shall cry woe . . .

Mur put down the catechism, which he found unutterably boring. He noticed marks on the table: dozens of marks. Names carved into the wood, some worn by time, others comparatively fresh. ... What was this one? "Chalres Gargamet." Something cold gripped the pit of Mur's stomach. Here they had brought Chalres. How had he died? Mur rose slowly to his feet. He stared around him. Were there other entrances? He made a circuit of the room, testing the damp limestone that everywhere seemed solid. He slowly returned to the table and stood under the lamp. His skin crawled as he considered the bleak shape of his future. The Repurification rite might well be more rigorous than the original rite. The open door held a horrible fascination. It indicated the way to the outdoors where Mur dearly longed to be; on the other hand, it threatened a terrible penalty. He thought of Chalres, dead, broken, face down in the tannery sump.

Desolation seeped over Mur's spirit. The light cast a weird glare, illuminating the pitiful scratchings on the table. He must submit.

Time passed: an hour. Mur listlessly chanted passages from the Catechism, words without meaning. He studied the Doctrine: Hakcil's Original Elucidations. The volume was old, dog-eared, a fixture of the chamber. Mould had blurred the writing; the pages adhered to each other. The purple characters blurred into the red and green pages. Mur put down the book and studied the doorway: so appealing and so baleful. He speculated. Suppose he were to run down the passage, so swiftly that his feet skimmed the ground. He might gain the open air by sheer audacity. No. It would not be done so easily. By some means he would be trapped. The timber door might be locked. For his insubordination he would meet Chalres's fate. This was the Chilite way. If he made ignoble and utter submission, abasing himself before soul-father Osso with fervent declarations of purity and disavowals of all and any mother-milking, past, present, and future, he could preserve his status as a Pure Boy.

Mur licked his lips. It was better than the sump. He bent over the Doctrine, committing whole paragraphs to memory, working till his head swam and his eyes smarted. On the fourth page mould obscured the characters across fully half a page; the fifth and sixth pages were likewise blotched. Mur peered at the pages in dismay. How could he learn the Elucidations when they were illegible? Osso would never accept any such glib excuse. "Why were you not prepared with your own copy of Hakcil? When I was a Pure Boy, it was my constant companion!" Or, "These pages are elementary. You should have known them long ago." On the other hand, reflected Mur, the marred volume offered a valid pretext for him to try the corridor. If someone were on guard, he could display the illegible pages and ask for an "Elucidations" in better condition. Mur half-rose to his feet. The corridor showed as a sinister dark rectangle.

Mur sat down once more. The time must be well into the night; no Chilite would be standing on guard, certainly ! Nor any Pure Boy. Might there be an alarm of some sort? Mur thought the prospect unlikely. The Chilites would not care to be disturbed at their spasms.

The outer door had not been locked; perhaps the corridor was open! Mur licked his lips. More likely the passage held its own protection : a pitfall, a snare, a booby trap. A net or a cage might drop to imprison him. The way might be altered to lead into a cul de sac or a return loop with sand or mud on the floor to trace his prowling. Or the passage might lead to a brink and send him tumbling to his death.

Mur glanced furtively sidelong at the dark portal, which now seemed to have secret eyes of its own. He sighed and returned to the mildewed books. But he could not concentrate; absently, with a stone chip, he he scratched his name on the table top with the others: in sad consternation he saw that he had carved "Gastel Etzwane". Another evidence of contumacy, should anyone see. He raised his hand to scratch it out but in sudden anger threw the stone chip into the corner. He glared defiantly at the name. This was himself; he was Gastel Etzwane; they could kill him a thousand times before he'd become anyone else! His small flare-up of defiance waned. The facts were as before. He must remain here in the study chamber an unknown period, then face Repurification. Or, despite the cold crawling up and down his back, he could test the passage.

Slowly he rose to his feet and crossed the room, one furtive step at a time. He looked down the passage as far as the overhead bulb cast a glimmer – ten or fifteen feet. He looked back up at the bulb, it hung ten feet over his head. He stood the bench on the table and climbed up; the bulb still hung three feet out of reach. Mur descended to the floor, awkward and lumpish as an old man; once more he went to look into the dark passage.

Beyond all reasonable doubt it was locked off – or it held a trap. Mur tried to remember the way of the passage. As the monstrator walked ahead, he had held his light bulb high, revealing a vaulted ceiling of dank stone. Mur had seen neither cages nor dangling nets, though these might easily have been arranged after his passage. The trip in such a case must be a thread across the corridor, or perhaps an electrical contact, though the Chilites had small electrical expertise and in fact distrusted both electricity and biomechanisms. The trap, if it existed, would be simple and more than likely activated by a trip close to the floor.

Mur's heart rose up in his mouth as he contemplated

the dark tunnel. It was the most important moment of his life. As Faman Bougozonie he could remain at the table to study Catechism and the incomplete Elucidations; he could become a fervent Chilite. As Gastel Etzwane he could grope along the passageway and hope to reach the open night.

Chalres's pitiful soiled body rose up in front of his eyes. Mur made a thin high-pitched sound of desperation. He had another vision: the face of his soul-father Osso; the high receding forehead with hair clinging in sparse locks, the intent, red-rimmed eyes carefully scrutinizing. Mur gave another thin whimper; dropping to his hands and knees, he crept into the dark.

The light went dim behind him. Mur began a careful investigation of the darkness, feeling out with great delicacy and caution for thread, string, rod, or tripboard. The passage, so he recalled, would turn first left, then right; he kept close to the left wall.

Darkness was complete. Mur tested the air as if searching for cobwebs. When nothing perceptible was evident, he felt the floor with equal care, probing every inch before he pulled himself forward.

Foot by painful foot he advanced, darkness pressing upon him like a palpable substance. He was too tense to feel fear; past and future were out of mind; there was only now, with grinding danger close at hand. With fingers like moth antennae he searched the darkness: on these fingers his life depended. To his left he lost contact with the wall; the first turn. He stopped short, feeling the walls on both sides, testing the joints of the stone blocks. He turned the corner, anxious to advance but reluctant to leave safe tested territory. He could still return to the study chamber. Ahead lay the area where danger most likely might be expected. With the most exquisite care he searched the darkness, feeling the air,

48

the walls, the floor. Inch by inch, foot by foot he moved
forward. His fingers felt a strange texture along the
floor: a rasp, a grain, not so cold as stone. Wood.
Wood on the floor. Mur felt for the joint between stone
and wood. It ran across the passage at right angles to
the walls. With his knees on the stone Mur reached
ahead, feeling first for thread, then testing the floor, now
wood. He discovered no thread; the wood seemed
sound. He discovered no brinks, no lack of solidity.
Laying flat on his face, Mur reached forward as far as
his arms could stretch. He felt only wood. He wriggled
ahead a few inches and felt again. Wood. He pounded
down with his fist and thought to hear a hollow boom
rather than the dullness of a plank on soil or mortar.
Danger, danger. He inched forward. The floor began to
tilt, elevating his feet. Hastily he retreated. The floor
dropped back into place. The wooden section was
pivoted near the centre. Had he been walking, groping
along the walls, he could not have recovered. Once past
the balance point, with the back half of the trap rising
into the air, he would have been gone, to fall toppling
and sprawling through the darkness to whatever lay below. Mur lay quiet, his lips drawn back in a wolfish grin.
He measured from stone to pivot-place: the length of
his body, five feet. Ahead, after the pivot, was presumably another five feet of unsupported surface. Had he
carried a light, he might have risked a running leap.
But not in the dark. Suppose he miscalculated and
jumped short. Mur's grin became so tight the muscles
of his cheeks ached. He needed a plank, a ladder, something of the sort. He thought of the bench, back in the
study chamber, which was six feet long. Rising to his
feet, feeling along the wall he returned much faster than
he had come. The chamber was quiet, almost somnol-
ent. Mur took up the bench and carried it back into the

dark passage, which now he knew so well. He reached the turn and, once again cautious, dropped to his hands and knees and dragged the bench beside him, upside down. He came to the wood section; bringing the bench past him, he thrust it ahead until he estimated that the near end rested over the pivot and the far end, hopefully, on solid stone. With the utmost care and precision he rested his weight on the bench, ready to scramble back at a quiver.

The bench held steady. Mur crossed and at the far end felt stone under his fingers. He grinned, this time in relief and pleasure.

He was not yet free of the passage. He proceeded as cautiously as before, and presently came to the second turn. A few yards ahead glimmered a wan bulb. It shone on a door: the old timber door giving upon the unused underroom. Heart in throat once more, Mur stepped forward. The door was locked – not so much to keep him in, he suspected, but to prevent some unwary Chilite or Pure Boy from blundering upon the trap.

Mur made a sad sound and went to look at the door. It was built of solid planks, doweled and glued, with hinges of sintered ironweb. The frame was wood, somewhat soft and rotten, thought Mur. He pushed against the door, bracing himself and thrusting with the trifling weight of his immature body. The door stood firm. Mur hurled himself at the door. He thought the latch creaked slightly. He battered himself again and again at the door, but other than causing a creaking of old wood he achieved nothing. Mur's body became bruised and sore, though the pain meant nothing to him. He stood back panting. He remembered the bench and ran back down the passage, around the turn, and slowly forward until he felt the end of the bench. He dragged it across the trap-section and carried it back to the door. Aiming it, he ran forward and thrust the end against the latch. The frame splintered. The door burst back, and Mur was out into the under-room, echoing and empty.

He placed the bench along one of the walls where it would never be noticed. Closing the door, he pressed the splintered wood into place. It might well escape notice, and the Chilites would have cause for perplexity!

A moment later he stepped out into the night and looked up at the blazing Skiaffarilla. "I am Gastel Etzwane," he muttered in exultation. "As Gastel Etzwane I escaped the Chilites; as Gastel Etzwane I have much to do."

He was not yet free and away. His escape would be discovered in due course: perhaps in the morning, at the latest within two or three days. Osso could not call upon the Faceless Man, but he might well send up into the Wildlands for ahulph trackers. No trail was too old or too faint for the ahulphs; they would follow until their quarry mounted a wheeled vehicle, a boat, or a balloon. Gastel Etzwane must once again use his ingenuity. Osso would expect him to flee, to put all possible distance between himself and Bashon. Hence, if he remained close for a day, until the ahulphs had cast about fruitlessly and had been sent with a curse back to their master, he might be able to go his way unhindered – wherever the way might lie.

A hundred yards below and around the hill lay the tannery, its sheds and outbuildings with dozens of secure nooks and crannies. Gastel Etzwane stood to the side of the portal, hidden in the shadow, listening to the night sounds. He felt as strange and subtle as a ghost. Above in the temple the Chilites lay in the galga smoke worshiping Galexis; their gasps of adoration were stifled in the heavy darkness.

Gastel Etzwane stood several moments in the

shadows. He felt no urgency, no need for haste. His first concern was the ahulphs, which almost certainly would be called on to track him by signs invisible to human senses. He slipped back into the temple and presently found an old cloak, that had been cast aside in a corner. Taking it to the portal, he tore it in half. Throwing down first one half on the stony ground, then the other, and jumping forward, he made his way away from the temple and down the slope, leaving neither track nor scent for the ahulphs. Gastel Etzwane laughed in quiet exultation as he reached the first of the tannery outbuildings.

He took refuge under one of these sheds. Pillowing his head on the torn cloak, he fell asleep.

Sasetta, Ezeletta, and Zael came dancing up over the horizon, to shoot shifting beams of coloured light from the east. From the temple sounded a throbbing chime, summoning the Pure Boys to the temple kitchens where they must boil up gruel for the Chilites' breakfast. Into the eastern courtyard came the Chilites themselves, haggard and red-eyed, their beards stinking of galga smoke. They staggered to benches and sat looking drearily off into the wan sunlight, still somewhat bemused. The tannery women already had taken bread and tea; they trudged forth for roll call, some surly, others voluble. The task-mistresses called out names for special assignments; the women specified went off in various directions. A select few, all matriarchs of the Sisterhood,* sauntered to the chemical shed to compound herbs and powders, dyes and astringents. Another group went to the vats to scrape, trim, soak, steep, drain. Others worked new hides delivered by the Wild-

* The *Zoriani nac Thair nac Thairi*. In loose translation: Female Agents of Desperate Deeds.

52

land ahulphs: pelts of all the wilderness animals, ahulph hides as well. After sorting, they were laid out on circular wooden tables, where they were given a rough cleaning, trimmed and shaped, then slid down a chute into a vat of lye. To the cleaning tables Eathre had been assigned; she had been issued a brush, a glass knife, a small, sharp spoon-scraper. Jatalie, the work-mistress, stood over her, giving instructions. Eathre worked quietly, hardly taking her eyes from the work. She seemed apathetic. Etzwane's hiding place was no more than a hundred feet distant; he wriggled and squirmed to where he could peer through a niche in the foundation; upon seeing his mother, he could barely restrain himself from calling out. His gentle mother in such vulgar conditions! He lay biting his lips and blinking. He could not even offer consolation!

From the direction of the temple came a small commotion. Pure Boys ran out in excitement to peer across the valley; Chilites appeared on the upper terrace, talking in some agitation, pointing here and there. Etzwane guessed that his absence had been discovered somewhat earlier than he had expected. He watched in a discordant blend of dread and glee. Amusing to see the Chilites in such perturbation; horrifying as well! If he were tracked down and captured ... His flesh crawled at the thought.

Shortly before noon he observed the arrival of the ahulphs: two bucks with red adept ribbons tied up and down the coarse black fur of their crooked legs. Great Malc Osso, standing austerely on a pedestal, explained his needs in dadu*; the ahulphs listened, laughing like foxes. Osso dropped a shirt that Etzwane presumed to be one of his own. The ahulphs seized the shirt in their

* Dadu: a language of finger signs and the syllables *da, de, di, do, du*.

manlike hands, pressed it to the odour-detectors in their feet, tossed it into the air in a display of the raffish heedlessness that the Chilites found completely detestable. They went to Osso and gave him vehement, waggish reassurance; Osso at last made an impatient gesture. The ahulphs, after looking this way and that for something worth stealing, went to the Pure Boys' under-room. Here, detecting Etzwane's scent, they leapt into the air and called back to Osso in vast excitement.

The Pure Boys watched in horrified excitement, as did Etzwane himself, for fear that some trace of his odour might waft itself to the ahulphs.

The two cast about the temple, and Etzwane was relieved when they crossed his trail and discovered nothing. Somewhat dampened, with earflaps hanging dolefully low, they traced around Eathre's old cottage, again without success. Raging at each other in ahulph fashion, snapping, kicking out with the white talons concealed in their soft black feet, swirling their fur in spiral bristles, they returned to where Osso stood waiting and explained in dadu that the quarry had gone off upon wheels. Osso turned on his heel and stalked into the temple. The ahulphs ran south, back up Mirk Valley into the Hwan Wildlands.

Peering through his cranny, Etzwane watched the community take up its normal routine. The Pure Boys, disappointed at being deprived of a terrifying spectacle, resumed their duties. The tannery women worked stolidly at the vats, tubs, and tables. Chilites sat like thin white birds on benches along the upper terrace of the temple. Sunlight, tinted noontime lavender, struck down at white dust and parched soil.

The tannery workers went to the refectory. Etzwane directed urgencies towards his mother: *Come this way, come closer!* But Eathre moved off without turning her

54

head. An hour later she returned to her table. Etzwane crawled back under the floor and worked up into the shed itself: a storage place for kegs of chemical, tools, and the like.

Etzwane found a lump of sal soda and, cautiously approaching the doorway, tossed the lump towards his mother. It dropped almost at her feet. She seemed not to notice. Then, as if suddenly interrupted from her thoughts, she glanced at the ground.

Etzwane tossed another lump. Eathre raised her head, looked blankly around the landscape, finally towards the shed. From the shadow Etzwane made a signal. Eathre frowned and looked away. Etzwane stared in puzzlement. Had she seen him? Why had she frowned?

Past the shed and into Etzwane's range of vision stalked Great Male Osso. He halted halfway between between the shed and the table where Eathre worked. She seemed lost in another dimension of consciousness.

Osso signalled the task-mistress and muttered a few words. The woman went to Eathre, who without comment or surprise left her work and walked towards Osso. He made a peremptory signal to halt her while she was still fifteen feet distant and spoke in a low burning tone. Etzwane could not distinguish his words nor Eathre's calm responses. Osso jerked back and turned on his heel. He stalked back past the shed, so close that had Etzwane reached forth, he might have touched the cold face.

Eathre did not instantly return to her work. As if pondering Osso's words, she wandered over to the shed and stood by the door.

"Mur, are you there?"

"Yes, mother. I am here."

"You must leave Bashon. Go tonight, as soon as the sun goes down."

55

"Can you come with me? Mother, please come."

"No. Osso holds my indenture. The Faceless Man would take my head."

"I will find the Faceless Man," declared Etzwane fervently. "I will tell him of the bad things here. He will take Osso's head."

Eathre smiled. "Don't be too sure. Osso obeys canton law – only too well."

"If I go, Osso will abuse you! He'll make you work at all the hardest jobs."

"It is all the same. The days come and go. I am glad you are leaving; it is what I wanted for you, but I must stay and help Delamber through her birth-times."

"But soul-father Osso may punish you, and all on my account!"

"No, he will not dare; the women are able to protect themselves, as I have only just put forward to your soul-father.* I must return to my work. After dark go forth. Since you wear no torc, be careful of the work-jobbers, especially in Durrume and Cansume and in Seamus as well, where they will put you into a balloon-gang. When you become of age, get a musician's torc; then you may travel without hindrance. Do not go to

* Eathre alluded to the *Zoriani nac Thair nac Thairi*, which derived power from its ability to defile the temple or any particular Chilite. There were six degrees of defilement, the first being a touch of a female finger, the sixth a drenching with a bucketful of unmentionable substances. The Sister, or Sisters, who executed the defilements were volunteers, usually old, sick, and quite willing to end their lives dramatically by poison wads ingested immediately after achieving their goals.

Defilement impelled the Chilites to a month-long ritual of the most onerous Purification during which no galga was burnt; if the ecstatic trance were attempted previous to complete Purification, Galexis Achiliadnid appeared in horrid guise. During the period of Purification the Chilites became surly and restless. The Pure Boys were often victimized in one fashion or another.

the old house, nor to Delamber's. Do not go for the khitan. I have a few coins put aside, but I can't get them for you now. I will not see you again."

"Yes you will, you will!" cried Etzwane. "I'll petition the Faceless Man, and he'll let you go with me."

Eathre smiled wistfully. "Not while Osso holds my indenture. Good-bye, Mur." She went back to the work table. Etzwane retreated into the shed. He did not watch his mother.

The day waned; the women trooped off to their dormitories. When darkness came, Etzwane emerged from the shed and stole off downhill.

Despite Eathre's warning he went down to the old cottage on Rhododendron Way, already occupied by another woman. He slipped to the rear, found the khitan, and went off through the shadows, down the road. He travelled west, towards Garwiy, where the Faceless Man lived – or so went the rumour.

CHAPTER FOUR

Shant, an irregular oblong thirteen hundred miles long and six hundred miles wide, was separated from the dark bulk of Caraz by a hundred miles of water: the Straits of Pagane flowing between the Green Ocean and the Purple Ocean. South across the Great Salt Bog, Palasedra hung down between the Purple Ocean and the Blue Ocean like a three-fingured hand or an udder with three teats.

A thousand miles east of Shant appeared the first islands of the Beljamar, a vast archipelago dividing the Green Ocean from the Blue Ocean. The population of Caraz was unknown; there were relatively few Palasedrans; the Beljamar supported a few scanty blotches of oceanic nomads; most of Durdane's population inhabited the sixty-two cantons of Shant, in loose confederation under the rule of the Faceless Man.

The cantons of Shant were alike only in their mutual distrust. Each regarded as Universal Principle its own customs, costumes, jargon, and mannerisms and considered all else eccentricity.

The impersonal, unqualified rule of the Anome – in popular usage, the Faceless Man – exactly suited the xenophobic folk of the cantons. Governmental apparatus was simple; the Anome made few financial demands; the laws enforced, for the most part, were those formulated by the cantons themselves. The Anome's justice might be merciless and abrupt, but it was even-handed and adhered to a simple principle, clear to all: *He who breaks the law dies.* The Faceless Man's authority derived from the torc, a band of flexite coded in various shades of purple, dark scarlet or maroon, blue, green, grey, and rarely, brown.*

The torc contained a strand of explosive; dexax, which the Faceless Man, if necessary, could detonate by means of a coded radiation. An attempt to remove the torc worked to the same effect. Usually, when a person lost his head, the cause was well known: he had broken the laws of his canton. On rare occasions, detonation might take a person's head for reasons mysterious and inscrutable, whereupon, folk would move with great care and diffidence lest they, too, excite the unpredictable wrath of the Faceless Man.

No area of Shant was too remote; from Ilwiy to the Straits of Pagane detonations occurred and felons lost their heads. It was known that the Anome employed deputies, somewhat tartly known as Benevolences, who subserved the Anome's will.

Garwiy, where the Faceless Man made his headquar-

* By the usual Shant symbology blue, green, purple, and grey carried optimistic attributes. Browns were unfavourable, tragic, elegant, authoritative, according to context. Yellow was the hue of death. Red, signifying invisibility, was used to paint objects meant to be ignored. Thieves wore red caps. White indicated mystery, chastity, poverty, anger, dependent on circumstances. Colours in combination changed significance.

In connection with colour symbolism, the ideograms of Canton Surrume might be mentioned. Originally each word was represented by colour strokes in correct symbolic combination; the scribe wrote with as many as seven brushes in his fist. In due course a secondary system came into effect, employing monochromatic dots at various heights, indicative of colour, that in turn evolved into a jointed line tracing the position of the colour indicators, and at last the sign for each word became a cursive ideogram from which all reference to colour had been lost.

ters, was the largest city of Shant, the industrial node of all Durdane. Along the Jardeen River and in the district known as Shranke on the Jardeen Estuary were a hundred glassworks, foundries and machine shops, biomechanical fabricating plants, bioelectric works where the organic monomolecules of Canton Fenesq were stranded into null-ohm conductors, bonded to semi-living filters, valves, and switches, to produce fragile, temperamental, and highly expensive electronic gear. Bio-engineers commanded high prestige; at the opposite end of the social scale were the musicians, who nevertheless excited pangs of romantic envy in the settled folk of Shant. Music, like language and colour symbology, transcended the canton boundaries, affecting the entire population.*

In Canton Amaze a thousand, two thousand musicians took part in the annual seiach: a vast wash of sound swelling and subsiding like wind, or surf, with occasional tides, vague and indistinct, of clear little waif-bells. More general was the music played by wandering troupes: jigs and wind-ups; set-pieces and sonatas; shararas, sarabands, ballads, caprices, quick-steps. A druithine might accompany such a troupe; more often he wandered alone, playing as he fancied. Lesser folk might sing words or chant poetry; the druithine played only music, to express his total experience, all his joy and grief. Such a person had been Etzwane's blood-father, the great Dystar. Etzwane had never credited the account of Dystar's death as related by Feld Maijesto; in his childhood daydreams Etzwane had seen himself wandering the roads of Shant, taking his khitan to fests and gatherings until at last the two met; from here the daydream went in various directions. Sometimes Dystar wept to hear music so lovely; when Etzwane identified

* A notable exception: the Chilites of Canton Bastern.

60

himself, Dystar's wonder exceeded all bounds. Sometimes Dystar and the indomitable youth found themselves opposed in a battle of music; in his mind Etzwane heard the glorious tunes, the rhythms and counter-rhythms, the clink of the jingle-bar, the gratifying rasp of the scratch-box.

The daydreams at last had taken on a ghost of substance. Khitan slung over his narrow back, Etzwane trudged the roads of Shant, and all his future lay before him.

Unless he were captured and taken back to Bastern.

It was not beyond possibility that Osso would suspect the true state of affairs and call in the ahulphs once again. The thought put spring into Etzwane's steps. He jogged along at his best speed, slowing to a walk only when his lungs began to labour. Rhododendron Way lay far behind; he journeyed under the stars, with the great black hulk of the Hwan rising to his left.

The night wore on. Etzwane, no longer jogging, walked as fast as his aching legs would carry him. The road climbed a hill, rounded a spur. Behind spread a starlit landscape, grey and black, with a few far lights Etzwane could not identify.

He sat on a stone to rest and looked westward into Canton Seamus, which he had never seen before, though from men who passed along Rhododendron Way he knew something of the folk and their habits. They were stocky, ruddy-blond, and quick tempered; they brewed beer and distilled poteen, which men, women, and children alike consumed without apparent effect. The men wore suits of good brown cloth, straw hats, gold rings in their ears; the women, who were stout and boisterous, dressed in long pleated gowns of brown and black and wore combs of aventurine quartz in their hair. They never espoused men larger than themselves; in the event that fisticuffs took place after an evening at the tavern, the husbands held no physical advantage.

The North Spur of the balloon-way passed through Seamus, connecting Oswiy on the north coast with the Great Transverse Line; the road Etzwane followed met the balloon-way at Carbade. As he looked off to the west, over the country he planned to travel, he fancied to see far away a red glimmer moving slowly across the sky. If his eyes were not at fault, the light marked the course of the balloon-way – though the time was late and the wind was still. He thought of his mother's warning against the work-jobbers; alone, without a torc, he had no identity, he had claims to no one's protection, and whoever so chose could do as they liked with him. The work-jobbers would clamp a torc and an indenture upon him, ship him off to a balloon-gang. In the morning he would contrive a torc of withe or bark or leather, which would help him evade attention.

The time was late, and the night was still. So still that as he sat quietly he thought to hear coming down from the Wildlands a far, faint howling. Etzwane huddled down upon the stone, feeling clammy and cool. The ahulphs were at one of their macabre revelries, which came on them like a madness; in some remote valley of the Hwan they danced and howled around a fire.

The thought of ahulphs urged him to his feet. When sure of a trail, they moved swiftly; he was not yet beyond their reach.

He found that his legs had become stiff, and his feet ached. He should never have seated himself to rest. As fast as he was able, he limped on down the road into Seamus.

An hour before dawn he passed a village: a dozen cottages around a small neat square paved with slabs of slate. To the rear stood silos, a warehouse, and the bulbous tanks of a small brewery. A three-storey building beside the road was evidently an inn. Folk were already astir in the cook shed to the rear; Etzwane saw the blink of a fire. Beside the inn waited three large vans loaded with fresh white butts and tubs of Shimrod Forest larch destined for one or another of the distilleries. From the stable behind the inn a groom was bringing draft animals: bullocks derived from terrestrial beef stock, placid and dependable but slow.* Etzwane dodged past, hoping not to be seen in the predawn murk.

The road ahead crossed a flat waste strewn with rocks. No shelter was visible, nor any plantation from which he might have gleaned a bite or two of nourishment. His spirits dropped to their lowest ebb; he felt as if he could walk no more; his throat was parched, and his stomach ached with hunger. Only fear of the ahulph restrained him from seeking a hidden spot among the rocks in which to make himself a bed of dry leaves. Finally fatigue overcame the fear. He could walk no longer. He stumbled to a spot behind a ledge of rotten shale. Wrapping himself in his robe, he lay down to rest. He lapsed into a numb daze, something other than sleep.

A grating, grumbling sound aroused him: the passage of the vans. The suns were an hour into the sky; though he had not slept, or thought he had not slept, daylight had come without his notice.

The vans passed by and rumbled away into the west.

* The fragmentation of Shant into cantons can be attributed both to the quality of the original settlers and the lack of metal for efficient engines.

Etzwane jumped up to look after them, thinking that here was an opportunity to confuse the ahulphs. The teamsters rode on the forward benches and could not see to the rear. Etzwane ran to catch up. He swung himself aboard the last van and sat with his feet hanging over the bed. After a few moments he drew himself farther back into a convenient crevice. He intended to ride only a mile or two, then jump down, but so convenient and comfortable was his seat, so restful and secure seemed the dark nook, that he became drowsy and fell asleep.

Etzwane awoke and blinked out from his cranny at a pair of unrecognizable rectangles, one impinged on the other. The first blazed lavender-white; the second was a panel of striated dark green. Etzwane's mind moved sluggishly. What was this odd scene? He crawled slowly to the back of the van, his mind still fuzzy. The white was the wall of a whitewashed building in the full glare of noon sunlight. The dark green panel was the side of a van thrust across his field of vision. Etzwane remembered where he was. He had been asleep; the cessation of motion had wakened him. How far had he come? Probably to Carbade, in Seamus. Not the best place to be if the oddments of information he had picked up along Rhododendron Way were to be believed. The folk of Seamus reputedly gave nothing and took whatever might be had. Etzwane climbed stiffly from the van. Best to be on his way before he was discovered. No more fear of the ahulphs, at any rate.

From not too far away came the sound of voices. Etzwane slipped around the van, confronting a black-bearded man with hollow white cheeks and round blue eyes. He wore a teamster's black canvas trousers, a dirty white vest with wooden buttons; he stood with legs apart, hands held up in surprise. He seemed pleased rather than angry. "And what have we here in this young bandit? So this is how they train them, to raid the cargo hardly before the wheels come to a stop. And not even a torc around his neck."

Etzwane spoke in a tremulous voice, that he tried to hold grave and earnest. "I stole nothing, sir; I rode only a short way in the van."

"That's theft of transportation," declared the teamster. "You admit the fact yourself. Well, then, come along."

Etzwane shrank back. "Come along where?"

"Where you'll learn a useful trade. I'm doing you a favour."

"I have a trade!" cried Etzwane. "I'm a musician! See! Here is my khitan!"

"You're nothing without your torc. Come along."

Etzwane tried to dodge away; the teamster caught him by the gown. Etzwane kicked and struggled; the teamster cuffed him, then held him off. "Do you want worse? Mind your manners!" He pulled at the khitan; the instrument fell to the ground where the neck snapped away from the box.

Etzwane gave a stifled cry and stared down at the tangle of wood and string. The teamster seized his arm and marched him into the depot to a table where four men sat at a gaming board. Three were teamsters; the fourth was a Seam, the conical straw hat pushed up from his round red face.

"A vagabond in my van," said Etzwane's captor. "Looks to be bright and lively; no torc, notice; what should I do to help him?"

The four gave Etzwane a silent inspection.

65

One of the teamsters grunted and turned back to the dice. "Let the lad go his way. He doesn't want your help."

"Ah, but you're wrong! Every citizen of the realm must toil; ask the job-broker here. What do you say, job-broker?"

The Seam leaned back in his chair, pushed his hat back at a precarious angle. "He's undersized; he looks unruly. Still, I suppose I can get him a post, perhaps up at Angwin. Twenty florins?"

"For the sake of quick business – done."

The Seam rose ponderously to his feet. He signalled to Etzwane. "Come along."

Etzwane was confined in a closet for the better part of a day, then marched to a wagon and conveyed a mile south of Carbade to the balloon-way depot. Half an hour later the southbound balloon *Misran* appeared, wind on a broad reach, the dolly singing up the slot. Observing the semaphore, the wind-tender eased his forward cables, allowing the *Misran* to fall broadside to the wind and lose way. A quarter mile down the slot from the depot the tackle-man hooked a drag to the dolly, brought it to a halt, pinned the after trucks with an anchor-bolt. The spread-bar was detached; the balloon-guys were slipped into snatch-blocks on the front trucks; now the Judas dolly was hauled south along the slot, pulling the balloon to the ground.

Etzwane was taken to the gondola and put into the charge of the wind-tender. The Judas-dolly was rolled back along the track and engaged with the spreader-bar, the balloon rising once more to its running altitude. The anchor-pin was removed from the after trucks. Front trucks, thirty-foot spreader-bar, and after trucks constituted the working-dolly; the *Misran* once more rode free. The wind-tender winched in the forward guys, warping the balloon across the wind; off and away up the slot sang the dolly, gathering speed, and Carbade was left behind.*

For Etzwane, the world of his daydreams was gone and lost irrevocably, like last year's flowers. He knew something of the balloon-way work-gangs; their lots were drudgery and compulsion. Technically free men, in practice they were seldom able to pay off their indentures. The condition of Etzwane was even worse; without a torc he had no status; he could appeal to no one; the work-master could set any value he chose on Etzwane's indenture. Once clamped with a torc, the Faceless Man would enforce the terms of his contract.

* The typical balloon, carrying four to eight passengers and a wind-tender, was a semiflexible slab one unit of dimension wide, eight units long, four units high. The skeleton might be bamboo, tempered glass tubing, or rods of cemented glass fibre. The membrane was the dorsal skin of a gigantic coelenterate, nurtured and forced until it completely filled a large shallow tank, whereupon the skin was lifted and cured. Hydrogen provided buoyancy.

The slots in which the dollies ran were precast members of concrete reinforced with glass fibre, attached to foundation-sleepers. The usual dolly consisted of two sets of trucks separated by a truss thirty feet long, at the ends of which the guys were attached. The wind-tender used trimming winches to shorten or lengthen bow and stern lines, thus controlling wind-aspect, and the canting winch, to alter the shape of the bridles at bow and stern and thus control the angle of heel.

Under optimum circumstances velocity reached sixty or seventy miles an hour. The routes made purposeful use of prevailing winds; where the route consistently encountered adverse winds or calm, motive power was applied to the dollies at ground level by an endless cable driven by water wheels or a work-gang at a windlass; by a gravity-cart loaded with stone; by teams of pacers. Balloons passed each other at sidings or traded dollies.

Where the route crossed gorges, as at Angwin Junction, or met otherwise unfavourable terrain, a cable of ironweb strands formed a link in the slot.

Foreboding lay like a stone in his stomach; he felt numb and confused.

Deep inside his mind a voice began to yell. He would run away. He had escaped the Chilites; he would evade the work-gang. What had his mother told him? "Defeat adversities rather than accept them." Never would he let himself be victimized; after they clamped on his torc, he would win his way to Garwiy and there make a case to the Faceless Man: both for himself and his mother. He would ask a terrible punishment for the teamster who broke his khitan; he had neglected to notice the teamster's torc, but never would he forget the pale, black-bearded face!

Stimulated by his hate and his resolve, he began to take an interest in the balloon and the landscape: low rolling hills rippling with ripe barley, cylindrical stone farm places, round grain towers, and, at intervals, the breweries, with their curious bulging tanks.

During the middle afternoon the wind shifted forward; the wind-tender winched in his forwards guy, to close-haul the balloon; driven closer to the ground, he canted the bridles to provide lift, to raise the *Misran* into a clear stream of air.

The rolling barley fields gave way to rocky hills splotched with thickets of blue and dark orange fester-shrub, from which the ancient ahulphs had cut their weapons. To the south rose the Hwan, the great central spine of Shant, across which ran the Great Transverse Route. Late in the afternoon the *Misran* rushed up the last steep ten miles of slot and reached Angwin North Station where a work-gang shifted the guys to a shackle on a mile-long endless cable suspended across a gorge. The work-gang turned a windlass, the *Misran* was guided sedately up to Angwin Junction where the North Spur joined the Great Transverse Route. The guys were shifted to another endless loop, reaching across an even more stupendous gorge to Angwin proper, and here the *Misran* descended. The wind-tender took Etzwane to the Angwin superintendent, who at first grumbled. "What kind of whiffets and sad bantlings are they sending me now? Where can I use him? He lacks weight to push a windlass; also, I don't like the look in his eye."

The wind-tender shrugged and glanced down at Etzwane. "He's a bit under the usual standard, but that's no business of mine. If you don't want him, I'll take him back down to Pertzel."

"Hmmf. Not so fast. What's his price?"

"Pertzel wants two hundred."

"For a creature like that? I'll give a hundred."

"That's not my instructions."

"Instructions be damned. Pertzel's using us both for fools. Leave the creature here. If Pertzel won't take a hundred, pick him up on your next trip. Meanwhile, I'll hold off his torc."

"A hundred is cheap. He'll grow; he's nimble; he can switch as many shackles as can a man."

"This I realize. He'll go across to Junction, and I'll bring the top man over here for the windlass."

The wind-tender laughed. "So you're getting a windlass-man for the price of a hundred-florin boy?"

The superintendent grinned. "Don't tell Pertzel that."

"Not I. It's between the two of you."

"Good. Ride him back to Junction; I'll flash over a message." He frowned down at Etzwane. "What's expected of you, boy, is brisk, accurate work. Do your stint and the balloon-way is not so bad. If you shirk or perform, you'll find me harsh as hackle-bush. . . ."

Etzwane rode back across the gorge to Angwin Junction. The *Misran* was hauled down by a hand-winch, a blond stocky youth not much older than Etzwane turning the crank.

Etzwane was put down; the *Misran* rose once more into the gathering dusk and was hauled down over the gorge to North Station, on the North Spur.

The blond youth took Etzwane into a low stone shed where two young men sat at a table eating a supper of broad-beans and tea. The blond youth announced: "Here's the new hand. What's your name, lad?"

"I am Gastel Etzwane."

"Gastel Etzwane it is. I am Finnerack; yonder is Ishiel the Mountain Poet, and he with the long face is Dickon. Will you eat? Our fare is not the best: beans and bread and tea, but it's better than going hungry."

Etzwane took a plate of beans, which were barely warm. Finnerack jerked his thumb to the east. "Old Dagbolt rations our fuel, not to mention our water, provisions, and everything else worth using."

Dickon spoke in a surly voice: "Now I'll have to go grind windlass under Dagbolt's very nose. No talk, no chaffer; quiet, orderly work, that's Dagbolt for you. Here at least a man can spit in any direction he chooses."

"It's the same for all of us," said Ishiel. "In a year or two they'll bring me across, then it will be Finnerack's turn. And in the course of five or six years Gastel Etzwane will make the change, and we'll be reunited."

"Not if I can avoid it," said Dickon. "I'll put in for slot-cleaning duty and at least be on the move. If Dagbolt turns me down, I'll become the premier gambler of the Junction. Never fear, lads, I'll be out of my indenture before ten years have passed."

"My good wishes," remarked Finnerack. "You've won all my money; I hope you get the service of it."

In the morning Finnerack instructed Etzwane in his duties. He would stand shifts in turn with Finnerack and Ishiel. When a balloon passed along the Great Transverse Route, he must ease the clamp and shackle around the idler sheave. When a balloon came up the North Spur, or returned, the man on duty, using a claw-lever chained to the floor, hooked into the guys and switched the balloon from one cable to the other. As the youngest member of the crew, Etzwane was also required to oil the sheaves, keep the hut swept out, and boil the morning gruel. The work was neither arduous nor complicated; the crew had ample leisure, which they spent crocheting fancy vests for sale in the town and gambling with the proceeds to earn enough to pay off their indenture. Finnerack told Etzwane, "Over at Angwin, Dagbolt forbids gambling. He says he wants to stop the fights. Bah. From time to time some lucky chap wins enough to buy himself free, and that's the last thing Dagbolt wants."

Etzwane looked around the station. They stood on a bleak windswept ledge fifty yards across, directly below the stupendous mass of Mount Mish and between two gorges. Etzwane asked, "How long have you been here?"

"Two years," said Finnerack. "Dickon has been here eight."

Etzwane studied Mount Mish and was daunted: impossible to scale the crag that beetled over the station. The precipices that descended into the gorges were no less baleful. Finnerack gave a sad, knowing laugh. "You'd like to find a way down?"

"Yes, I would."

Finnerack showed neither surprise nor disapproval. "Now's the time, before they clamp on your torc. Don't think I haven't considered it, torc and all."

71

At the edge of the precipice they looked down and off across a gulf of air. "I've stood here by the hour," said Finnerack wistfully, "tracing how I'd climb down to the valley. From here down to that nose of red granite a person would need a length of rope, or he might scramble down that fissure, had he the nerve. Then he'd have to work himself across the face of that scarp – it looks worse than it is, I dare say. From there to that tumble of scree should not be impossible, and only hard work thereafter down to the valley floor. But then what? It's a hundred miles to a village, with no food nor water. And do you know what you'd find along the way?"

"Wild ahulph."

"I wasn't thinking of ahulph, but you'd find them, too, the wicked Phag brood." Finnerack searched the valley floor. "I saw one just the other day." He pointed. "Look! By that needle of black rock. I think there's a cave or a shelter there. It's where I saw the other."

Etzwane looked and thought to see a stir of movement. "What is it?"

"A Roguskhoi. Do you know what that is?"

"It's a kind of mountain savage that can't be controlled except by its yearning for strong drink."

"Great womanizers, as well. I've never seen one close at hand, and I hope I never do. What if they took it into their heads to climb up here? They'd chop us to bits!"

"Much to Dagbolt's horror," suggested Etzwane.

"Too right! He'd have to buy in three new indentures. He'd rather we'd die of overwork or old age."

Etzwane looked wistfully down the valley. "I had planned to be a musician. . . . Does anyone ever earn enough to buy off their indentures?"

"Dagbolt does his best to prevent it," said Finnerack. "He operates a commissary where he sells Seam beer, fruit, sweetmeats, and the like. When the men gamble, it always seems to be one of the career ratings who wins the money, and no one knows how they achieve such luck. One way or another, it's not all so bad. Perhaps I'll make a career myself. There are always jobs opening up below – on the windlass or as a slot-cleaner or motive man. If you learn electrics, you might get into communications. As for me, I'd like to be a wind-tender. Think of it!" Finnerack flung back his head, looked around the sky. "Up in the balloon, running the winches, with the dolly skirring along the slot below. There's sheer fun! And one day it's Pagane and Amaze, the next Garwiy, then off over the Great Transverse Route to Pelmonte and Whearn and the Blue Ocean."

"I suppose it's not a bad life," said Etzwane dubiously. "Still –" he could not bring himself to finish.

Finnerack shrugged. "Until they torc you, you're free to run off. Be sure I won't stop you, or Ishiel. In fact we'll lower you down the cliff. But it's terrible country, and you'd be going to your death. Still – were I you, without my torc, perhaps I'd try." He raised his head as a horn sounded. "Come along; a balloon is crossing over from Angwin."

They returned to the station. The shift was technically Etzwane's; Finnerack was standing by to break him in. The approaching balloon hung aslant the sky, lurching and bobbing as the cable drew it against the wind. The guys, fore and aft, were shackled to an iron ring, which in turn was chained to a grip on the drive-line. The ring bore a black marker, indicating that it must be switched down the North Spur. The grip entered the sheave and passed halfway around the circumference. Finnerack pushed an electric signal to the windlass chief at Angwin and threw a brake that halted the drive-line. He hooked the claw-lever into the ring,

73

worked the arm to pull down the ring and loosen the grip. Etzwane transferred the grip to the North Spur line; Finnerack disengaged the lever-jack; the balloon now hung on the North Spur drive-line. Finnerack pushed the electric signal to the windlass at North Station; the drive-line tautened, the balloon drifted away on the south wind.

Half an hour later another balloon arrived from the east, lurching and straining to the breeze blowing down from Mount Mish. The grip passed across the idler sheave without attention from Finnerack or Etzwane; the balloon continued across the gorge to Anwin, thence on towards Garwiy.

Not long after, another balloon came in from the west, destined as before to the North Spur. Etzwane said to Finnerack, "This time let me do the whole transfer. You stand to the side and watch that I do everything correctly."

"Just as you like," said Finnerack. "I must say you're very keen."

"Yes," said Etzwane. "I'm very keen indeed. I plan to take your advice."

"Indeed? And make a balloon-way career?"

"I plan to give the matter thought," said Etzwane. "As you have remarked, I am not yet clamped and not yet committed."

"Tell that to Dagbolt," said Finnerack. "Here comes the grip; be handy with the signal and the brake."

The grip entered the sheave; as it reached the circumference, Etzwane pressed the signal and braked the wheel.

"Quite right," said Finnerack.

Etzwane brought up the claw-jack, hooked it into the ring, drew down slack, and detached the grip.

74

"Exactly right," said Finnerack. "You've learned the knack, no question of it."

Etzwane caught the grip on the edge of the sheave, released the lever-jack, shook away the hook. He stepped up into the ring and kitcked free the grip. Finnerack stared in bewilderment. "What are you doing?" he gasped. "You've set free the balloon!"

"Exactly," called Etzwane. "Give my regards to Dagbolt. Good-bye, Finnerack."

The balloon swept him away on the wind from Mount Mish, while Finnerack watched open-mouthed from below. Etzwane perched with one foot in the ring and, clutching the guy lines, waved his hand; Finnerack, standing foreshortened with head turned back, raised his arm in dubious farewell. Etzwane felt a pang of regret; he had never met anyone he liked so well as Finnerack. Someday they might meet again . . .

In the balloon the wind-tender realized that something had gone amiss but knew no remedy for the situation. "Attention all," he cried out to the passengers. "The guys have slipped; we are floating free in a northwest direction, which will take us safely across the Wildlands. There is no danger! Everyone please remain calm. When we approach a settled community, I will valve gas and lower us to the ground. For the unavoidable change of schedule I extend the official apologies of the balloon-way."

CHAPTER FIVE

The balloon floated down from the Hwan in the halcyon quiet of the upper air. Etzwane rode surrounded by lavender-white radiance; so unreal and peaceful were the circumstances, he felt no fear. Underneath passed the great forests of Canton Trestevan: parasol darabas, dark maroon and purple, soft-seeming as feather dusters, returning ripples of wincing greenish bronze to the touch of the wind. In the dank lower valleys stood redwoods, hoary giants five hundred feet tall, half as old as the coming of the human race. Lower still, along the piedmont, were hangman trees, black oaks and green elms, the unique syndic trees whose seeds sprouted legs and poisonous pincers. After walking to a satisfactory location, each seed roved within a ten-foot circle, poisoning all competing vegetation, then dug a hole and buried itself.

The forests persisted into Canton Sable, then gave way to a region of small farms and a thousand small ponds where crayfish, eels, whiteworm, a dozen other varieties of water-food were produced, packed, frozen, and shipped to the metropolitan markets of Garwiy, Brassei, Maschein. The villages were tiny toys exuding minuscule wisps of smoke; along the roads moved infinitesimal wagons and traps drawn by insect-size bullocks and pacers. Etzwane would have enjoyed the landscape, had he been comfortable. He rode with first one foot in the ring, then the other, then one foot on top of the other. He tried to sit in the angle between the two guy lines, but the cables cut into his hips. His perch became more uncomfortable by the minute. His feet were knobs of pain; his arms and shoulders ached from the strain of clinging to the guys. Still, his exhilaration persisted; he had no fault to find with circumstances.

The wind had died to a murmur; the balloon drifted with great deliberation into Canton Frill, a green, dark blue, brown, white and purple checkerboard of fields and orchards. A meandering river, the Lurne, was a casual insult of nature to the human geometry of hedges and roads; ten miles to the west the river passed through a market town, built in the typical Frillish style: tobacco-brown panels of pressed gum-leaves between posts of polished iban, rising two or even three storeys. Above the town rose a forest of poles, flying good-luck banners, prayer-flags, secret omens, tender and sometimes illicit signals between lovers. Looking over the countryside, Etzwane thought Frill an agreeable place, and he hoped that the ballon would land here, if for no other reason than to ease his aching body.

The wind-tender, for his part, had hoped to drift on into Canton Cathriy where the trade winds blowing in from Shellflower Bay would take him southwest to meet the Great Transverse Route somewhere in Canton Mai, but he had to reckon with his passengers. They had divided into two factions. The first had become impatient with hanging motionless in the still air and demanded that the balloon be put down; the second, to the contrary, feared that the wind would rise and sweep them to perdition out over the Green Ocean; they insisted even more emphatically that the balloon be lowered.

The wind-tender at last threw up his arms in vexation and valved out a quantity of gas until his altimeter indicated gradual descent. He opened his floor panel to inspect the terrain below and from the first time noticed Etzwane. He peered down in shock and suspicion, but he could be sure of nothing. And in any event he was powerless to act unless he chose to slide down one of the guy lines to confront the unauthorized passenger, which he did not care to do.

The guys sank into the thick blue grass of a meadow. Ezwane jumped gratefully out of the ring; the balloon, relieved of his weight, swung back aloft. Etzwane ran like a wild creature for the hedge. Heedless of cuts and scratches, he burst through the brambles and into a lane where he ran pell-mell until he came to a copse of yapnut trees. He plunged into the shadows and stood till he caught his breath.

He could see nothing but foliage. Selecting the tallest tree in sight, he climbed until he could see over the hedge and across the meadow.

The balloon was down, anchored to a stump. The passengers had alighted and stood arguing with the wind-tender, demanding immediate fare rebates and expense money. This the wind-tender refused to pay over, in the certain knowledge that the main office clerks would not casually refund these sums unless he were able to produce detailed vouchers, invoices, and receipts.

The passengers began to grow ugly; the wind-tender at last resolved the matter by breaking loose the anchor and scrambling into the gondola. Relieved of the passengers, the balloon rose swiftly and drifted away, leaving the passengers in a disconsolate cluster.

For three weeks Etzwane roamed the countryside, a gaunt harsh-featured lad in the rags of his Pure Boy gown. In the heart of the yapnut grove he built a little den of twigs and leaves in which he maintained a tiny fire, blown up from a coal stolen at a farmhouse hearth. He stole other articles: an old jacket of green homespun, a lump of black sausage, a roll of coarse cord and a bundle of hay with which he planned to make himself a bed. The hay was insufficient; he returned for a second bundle and stole as well an old earthenware bowl with which the farmer fed his fowl. On this latter occasion, as he jumped from the back window of the barn, he was sighted by the boys of the farm, who gave chase and harried him through the woods until at last he went to cover in a dense thicket. He heard them destroying his den and exclaiming in anger at the stolen goods as they blundered past: "Yodel's ahulphs will winkle him out. They can take him back upland for their pains." Cold chills coursed down Etzwane's back. When the boys left the wood, he climbed the tall tree and watched them return to their farm. "They won't bring in ahulphs," he told himself in a hollow voice. "They'll forget all about me tomorrow. After all, it was just a bit of hay . . . An old coat . . ."

On the following day Etzwane kept an anxious watch on the farmhouse. When he saw the folk going about their normal duties, he became somewhat less fearful.

The next morning when he climbed the tree he saw to his horror three ahulphs beside the barn. They were a lumpy dwarfish variety, with the look of hairy goblin-dogs: the Murtre Mountain strain. In a panic Etzwane leapt from the tree and set off through the woods towards the river Lurne. If luck were with him, he would fine a boat or a raft; for he could not swim.

Leaving the forest, he crossed a field of purple moy; looking back, his worst fears were realized: the ahulphs came behind.

So far they had not sighted him; they ran with their

79

eyes and foot-noses to the ground. With pounding legs and bumping heart, Etzwane ran from the field, up the highroad that paralleled the riverbank.

Along the road came a high-wheeled carriage drawn by a prime pacing bullock, the result of nine thousand years breeding. Though capable of a very smart pace, it moved in a leisurely fashion, as if the driver were in no great hurry to reach his destination. Etzwane pulled up the old jacket to hide his bare neck and called to the man who drove the carriage: "Please, sir, may I ride with you for a little bit?"

The man, reining the pacer to a halt, gave Etzwane a sombre appraisal. Etzwane, returning the inspection, saw a lean man of indeterminate age with a pallid skin, a high forehead and austere nose, a shock of soft white hair neatly cropped, wearing a suit of fine grey cloth. The verticals of his torc were purple and grey; the horizontals were white and black, neither of which Etzwane could identify. He seemed very old, knowing and urbane, yet, on the other hand, not very old at all. He spoke in a voice of neutral courtesy: "Jump aboard. How far do you go?"

"I don't know," said Etzwane. "As far as possible. To be quite frank, the ahulphs are after me."

"Indeed? What is your crime?"

"Nothing of any consequence. The farmer boys consider me a vagabond and want to hunt me down."

"I can't very well assist fugitives," said the man, "but you may ride with me for a bit."

"Thank you."

The cart moved down the road, Etzwane keeping a watch behind. The man put a toneless question: "Where is your home?"

Etzwane could trust no one with his secret. "I have no home."

"And where is your destination?"

"Garwiy. I want to put a petition to the Faceless Man to help my mother."

"And how would he do this?"

Etzwane looked over his shoulder; the ahulphs were not yet in sight. "She is under unjust indenture and now must work in the tannery. The Faceless Man could order her indenture lifted; I'm sure she has paid it off and more, but they keep no reckonings."

"The Faceless Man is not likely to intervene in a matter of canton law."

"I've been told so. But perhaps he'll listen."

The man gave a faint smile. "The Faceless Man is gratified that canton law functions effectively. Can you believe that he'll disrupt old customs and turn everything topsy-turvy, even at Bashon?"

Etzwane looked at him in surprise. "How did you know?"

"Your gown. Your way of speech. Your mention of a tannery."

Etzwane had nothing to say. He looked over his shoulder, wishing the man would drive faster.

Even as he looked, the ahulphs bounded out into the road. Crouching down, Etzwane watched in sweating fascination. Through some peculiar working of their brain, a loss of scent confused them, and no amount of training or exhortation could persuade them to seek their quarry visually. Etzwane looked around at the man, who seemed more distant and austere than ever. The man said, "I won't be able to protect you. You must help yourself."

Etzwane turned back to watch the road. Over the hedge bounded the farmer's boys. The ahulphs made grinning disavowals, loping helpfully in one direction, then another. The boys gave a caw of rage at the helplessness of the ahulphs; then one saw the carriage and pointed. All began to run in hot pursuit.

Etzwane said anxiously, "Can't you drive somewhat faster? Otherwise they will kill me."

The man looked stonily ahead as if he had not heard. Etzwane gave a despairing glance behind, to find his pursuers gaining rapidly. His life was coming to an end. The ahulphs, with license to kill, would rend him apart at once, then carefully tie the parts into parcels to take home, quarrelling over this and that as they did so. Etzwane jumped from the carriage, to tumble head over heels into the road. Scraped and bruised but feeling nothing, he sprang down the river bank, bursting through the alders and into the swift yellow Lurne. What now? He had never swam a stroke in his life.... He clutched to the twigs, shuddering uncontrollably, torn between dread of the water and a desire to immerse himself away from view. The ahulphs came crashing down the river bank, trying to push their hairy faces through the thicket. Etzwane eased himself downstream, clinging to the twigs, letting his legs float. The green jacket weighed on him; he slipped it off. Catching a bubble of air, it moved downstream, attracting the attention of the farm boys who could see only indistinctly through the brush. They ran shouting along the bank; Etzwane waited. Fifty yards downstream they discovered their mistake and stood arguing: Where was their quarry? They ordered one of the ahulphs to swim across the stream and range the opposite bank, to which the ahulph made whining protests. The boys drew back up the bank. Etzwane floated with the current, hoping to pass them unseen and presently pull himself to shore.

Silence on the bank: a sinister absence of sound. Etzwane's legs began to feel numb; cautiously he edged himself into the thicket. The disturbance attracted attention; one of the boys set up a hallo. Etzwane fell back into the water and, missing his grip on the twigs, was carried off into the stream. Straining to hold up his head, beating down with his arms, thrashing with his legs, Etzwane floundered out into midstream. His breath came in harsh gasps; water entered his mouth to choke him; he felt himself going down. The opposite bank was not too far away. He made a desperate final effort; one of his feet touched bottom. He pushed, thrust himself, hopping and lurching towards the bank. Kneeling in the shallows, clinging to the alders, he hung his head and gave himself up to hoarse racking coughs. From the far bank the boys jeered at him, and the ahulphs began to thrust down through the alders. Etzwane wearily tried to push through the brush, but the bank beyond loomed high and steep above him. He waded with the current. One of the ahulphs jumped into the stream and paddled directly towards Etzwane; the current carried him past. With all his force Etzwane threw a chunk of water-sodden timber. It struck the hairy dog-spider head; the creature keened and moaned and retreated to the opposite bank. Etzwane half-waded, half-hopped with the current, the boys and ahulphs keeping pace along the other bank. Suddenly they all ran forward pell-mell; looking down the stream, Etzwane saw a five-arched stone bridge and, beyond, the town. His pursuers intended to cross the bridge and come down the bank at him. Etzwane gauged the stream; he could never swim back across. He made a ferocious attack on the alders, ignoring scratches, jabs, cuts; at length he pulled himself to the bank, a vertical rise of six feet overgrown with fern and thorn-grass. He scrambled halfway up, to fall moaning back into the alders. Once again he tried, clinging with fingernails, elbows, chin, knees. By the most precarious of margins he crawled up and over, to lie flat on his face at the edge of the riverside lane. He could not rest an instant. Glassy-eyed, he heaved himself first to his hands and knees, then to his feet.

Only fifty yards away the town began. Across the lane, in a wooded park, he saw a half-dozen carts painted in gay symbols of pale pink, white, purple, pale green, blue.

Etzwane staggered forward, flapping his arms; he ran up to a short sour-faced man of middle-age who sat on a stool sipping hot broth from a cup.

Etzwane composed himself as best he could, but his voice was tremulous and hoarse. "I am Gastel Etzwane; take me into your troupe. Look; I wear no torc. I am a musician."

The short man drew back in surprise and irritation. "Get along with you; do you think we clasp every passing rascal to our bosoms? We are adepts; this is our standard of excellence; go dance a jig in the market square."

Down the road came the ahulphs and behind the farm boys.

Etzwane cried, "I am no rascal; my father was Dystar the druithine; I play the khitan." He searched wildly about; he saw a nearby instrument and seized it. His fingers were weak and water-soaked; he tried to play a run of chords and produced only a jangle.

A black-furred hand seized his shoulder and pulled; another took his arm and jerked another direction; the ahulphs fell to disputing which had touched him first.

The musician rose to his feet. He seized a length of firewood and struck furiously at both ahulphs. "Goblins, be off; do you dare touch a musician?"

The peasant youths came forward. "Musician? He is a common thief, a vagabond. We intend to kill him and protect our hard-earned goods."

The musician threw down a handful of coins. "A musician takes what he needs; he never steals. Pick up your money and go."

The farm boys made surly sounds and glared at Etzwane. Grudgingly they picked the coins out of the dirt and departed, the ahulphs yelping and dancing sideways. Their work was for naught; they would receive neither money nor meat.

The musician once more settled upon his stool. "Dystar's son, you say. What a sorry letdown. Well, it can't be helped. Throw away those rags; have the women give you a jacket and a meal. Then come let me see what is to be done."

CHAPTER SIX

Clean, warm, full of bread and soup, Etzwane came cautiously back to Frolitz, who sat at a table under the trees, a flagon of liquor at his elbow. Etzwane sat down on a bench and watched. Frolitz fitted a new reed to the mouthpiece of a wood-horn. Etzwane waited. Frolitz apparently intended to ignore his presence.

Etzwane hitched himself forward. "Do you intend to let me stay with the troupe, sir?"

Frolitz turned his head. "We are musicians, boy. We demand a great deal from each other."

"I would do my best," said Etzwane.

"It might not be good enough. String up that instrument yonder."

Etzwane took up the khitan and did as he was bid. Frolitz grunted. "Now tell me how Dystar's son runs the fields in rags?"

"I was born at Bashon in Canton Bastern," said Etzwane. "A musician named Feld Maijesto gave me a khitan, which I learned to play as best as I could. I did not care to become a Chilite, and I ran away."

"That is a lucid exposition," said Frolitz. "I am acquainted with Feld, who takes a rather casual attitude towards his craft. I make serious demands upon my folk; we are not slackers here. What if I send you away?"

"I will go to Garwiy and ask the Faceless Man to give me a musician's torc and to help my mother as well."

Frolitz looked up at the sky. "What illusions the young harbour nowadays! So now the Faceless Man indulges every ragamuffin who comes to Garwiy with a grievance!"

"He must heed grievances; how else can he rule? Surely he wants the folk of Shant to be content!"

"Hard to say what the Faceless Man wants. But it's not good policy talking. He might be listening from behind that wagon, and he's said to be thin-skinned. Look yonder on the tree. Only last night, while I slept fifty feet away, that placard was posted! It gives an eerie feeling."

Etzwane examined the placard. It read:

> The ANOME is Shant!
> Shant is the ANOME!
> Which is to say: The ANOME is everywhere!
> Sly sarcasm is folly.
> Disrespect is sedition.
> With benevolent attention! With fervent zeal!
> With puissant determination!
> The ANOME works for Shant!

Etzwane nodded soberly. "This is exactly correct. Who posted the placard?"

"How should I know?" snapped Frolitz. "Perhaps the Faceless Man himself. If I were he, I'd enjoy going about making guilty folk jump. Still it's not wise to attract his notice with petitions and demands. If they are right and reasonable – so much the worse."

"What do you mean?"

"Use your head, lad! Suppose you and the canton have come into conflict, and you want matters altered. You go into Garwiy and present a petition which is right and proper and just. The Faceless Man has three choices. He can accommodate you and put the canton

87

into an uproar, with unknown consequences. He can deny your just petition and expect sedition every time you get drunk in a tavern and start to talk. Or he can quietly take your head."

Etzwane pondered. "You mean that I shouldn't take my grievance to the Faceless Man?"

"He's the last man to take a grievance to!"

"Then what should I do?"

"Just what you're doing. Become a musician and make a living complaining of your woe. But remember: Complain of your own woe! Don't complain of the Faceless Man! ... What's that you're playing now?"

Etzwane, having strung the khitan, had touched forth a few chords. He said, "Nothing in particular. I don't know too many tunes. Only what I learned from the musicians who came along the road."

"Halt, halt, halt!" cried Frolitz, covering his ears. "What are these strange noises, these original discords?"

Etzwane licked his lips. "Sir, it is a melody of my own contriving."

"But this is impertinence! You consider the standard works beneath your dignity? What of the repertory I have laboured to acquire? You tell me now that I have wasted my time, that henceforth I must attend only the outpourings of your natural genius?"

Etzwane at last was able to insert a disclaimer. "No, no, sir, by no means! I have never been able to hear the famous works; I was forced to play tunes I thought up myself."

"Well, so long as it doesn't become an obsession – Not so much thumb there. What of the rattle-box? Do you think it's there for show?"

"No sir. I hurt my elbow somewhat today."

88

"Well, then, why scratch aimlessly at the khitan? Let's hear a tune on the wood-horn."

Etzwane looked dubiously at the instrument, which was tied together with string. "I've never had the sleight of it."

"What?" Frolitz gaped in disbelieving shock. "Well, then, learn it! The tringolet, the clarion, the tipple as well. We are musicians in this troupe, not, like Feld and his scamping cronies, a set of theorizing dilettantes. Here, take this wood-horn; go play scales. After a bit I'll come by and listen."

A year later Master Frolitz brought his troupe to Garwiy, Etzwane now wearing a musician's torc. This was a locality the wandering troupes visited but seldom, for the urbane folk of Garwiy enjoyed novelty, style, and topical substance in preference to music. Etzwane, paying no heed to Frolitz's advice, went to the Corporation Plaza and stood in line at the booth where petitions to the Faceless Man might be filed for five florins. A placard reassured those who waited:

All petitions are seen by the ANOME!
The same scrupulous judgment is applied to the problems of all, if their petition costs five or five hundred florins. Be concise and definite, state the exact deficiency or hardship, specify the precise solution you propose. Merely because you are filing a petition does not indicate that your cause is just; conceivably you are wrong and your adversary right. Be instructed, rather than disappointed, should the ANOME yield a negative response.
The ANOME administers equity, not bounty!

Etzwane paid his five florins, received a form from the desk. In the most careful language he stated his case, citing the cynicism of the Chilites in respect to the indentures of the women. "In particular, the lady Eathre has more than paid her obligation to the Ecclesiarch Osso Higajou, but he has assigned her to work in the tannery. I pray that you order this injustice terminated, that the lady Eathre may be free to select the future course of her life without reference to the wishes of Ecclesiarch Osso."

Occasionally the five-florin petitions encountered slow responses; Etzwane's, however, received a verdict on the following day. All petitions and their responses were deemed in the public interest and posted openly on a board; with trembling fingers Etzwane pulled down the response coded with his torc colours.

The response read:

The ANOME notes with sympathy a son's concern for the welfare of his mother. The laws of Canton Bastern are definite. They require that before an indenture can be considered paid, the indentured person must display a receipt and balance sheet for all monies paid over by the person and all charges incurred and debited against the same person's account. Sometimes a person consumes food, lodging, clothing, education, entertainment, medicine, and the like, in excess of his or her earnings, whereupon the payment of an indenture may be delayed. Such is possibly true in the present case.

The judgment is this: I command the Ecclesiarch Osso Higajou, upon presentation of this document, to render free the person of the lady Eathre, provided that she can show a favourable balance of one thousand five hundred florins, or if some person pays in cash to Ecclesiarch Osso Higajou

90

one thousand five hundred florins, when it will be assumed that a previous balance between credit and debit exists.

In short, take this document and one thousand five hundred florins to Ecclesiarch Osso; he must deliver to you your mother, the lady Eathre.

With hope and encouregement,
THE ANOME

Etzwane became furiously angry. He instantly purchased a second petition and wrote: "Where can I get one thousand five hundred florins? I earn a hundred florins a year. Eathre has paid Osso twice over; will you lend me one thousand five hundred florins?"

As before, the response was prompt. It read:

The ANOME regrets that he cannot lend either private or public funds for the settlement of indentures. The previous judgment remains the definitive verdict.

Etzwane wandered back to Fontenay's Inn where Frolitz made his Garwiy headquarters and wondered how or where he could lay his hands on one thousand five hundred florins.

Five years later, at Maschein in Canton Maseach, on the south slope of the Hwan, Etzwane encountered his father Dystar. The troupe, coming into town late, was at liberty for the evening. Etzwane and Fordyce, a youth three or four years older – Etzwane was now about eighteen – wandered through town, from one tavern to the next, gathering gossip and listening with critical ears to what music was being played.

At the Double Fish Inn they heard Master Rickard

Oxtot's Grey-Blue-Green Interpolators.* During an intermission Etzwane fell into a discussion with the khitan-player, who minimized his own abilities. "To hear the khitan played in proper fashion, step across the way to the Old Caraz and hear the druithine."

Fordyce and Etzwane presently crossed to the Old Caraz and took goblets of effervescent green punch. The druithine sat in a corner gazing moodily at the audience: a tall man with black-grey hair, a strong nervous body, the face of a dreamer dissatisfied with his dreams. He touched his khitan, tuned one of the strings, struck a few chords, listened as if displeased. His dark gaze wandered the room, rested on Etzwane, passed on. Again he began to play: slowly, laboriously working around the edges of a melody, reaching here, searching there, testing this, trying that, like an absent-minded man raking leaves in a wind. Insensibly the music became easier, more certain; the lank themes, the incommensurate rhythms, fused into an organism with a soul: every note played had been preordained and necessary.

Etzwane listened in wonder. The music was remarkable, played with majestic conviction and a total absence of effort. Almost casually, the druithine imparted heartbreaking news; he told of golden oceans and unattainable islands; he reported the sweet futility of life, then, with a wry double beat and an elbow at the scratchbox, supplied solutions to all the apparent mysteries.

His meal, hot pickled land crab with barley, melon

* The language of Shant allows exquisite discrimination between colours. Against red, scarlet, carmine, maroon, pink, vermilion, cerise, Shant could set sixty descriptive degrees, with as many for every other colour. In Grey-Blue-Green Interpolators, the qualities of "grey", "blue", and "green" were precisely specified in order to express by symbological means the exact emotional point of view from which Master Oxtot's troupe performed their variations.

balls dusted with pollen, had been splendid but not copious; payment* had long been made. He had taken a flask of Gurgel's Elixir; another stood at his elbow, but he seemed uninterested in further drink. The music dwindled and departed into silence, like a caravan passing over the horizon.

Fordyce leaned over, put a question to one who sat nearby: "What is the druithine's name?"

"That is Dystar."

Fordyce turned marvelling to Etzwane. "It is your father!"

Etzwane, with no words to say, gave a curt nod.

Fordyce rose to his feet. "Let me tell him that his natural son is here, who plays the khitan in his own right."

"No," said Etzwane. "Please don't speak to him."

Fordyce sat down slowly. "Why not, then?"

Etzwane heaved a deep sigh. "Perhaps he has many natural sons. A good number may play the khitan. He might not care to give polite attention to each of these."

Fordyce shrugged and said no more.

Once more Dystar struck at his khitan, to play music that told of a man striding through the night, halting

---

* Druithines, unlike the troupes, never advertised their comings and goings; after an unheralded, almost furtive arrival at some locality, the druithine would visit one of the taverns and order a repast, sumptuous or frugal, according to his whim or personal flair. Then, he would bring forth his khitan and play but would not eat until someone in the audience had paid for his meal. The "uneaten meal," indeed, was a common jocular reference. Druithines in decline reputedly employed a person to make ostentatious payment for the meal as soon as it was set forth. After the meal the druithine's further income depended on gratuities, gifts from the tavern-keeper, engagements at private parties or in the manor houses of aristocrats. A druithine of talent might become wealthy, as he had few expenses.

93

from time to time to muse upon one or another of the stars.

For a reason Etzwane could not define, he became uncomfortable. Between himself and this man whom he did not know existed a tension. He had no claim against him; he could reproach him for no fault of omission or commission; his debt to Eathre had been precisely that of all the other men who had stepped into her cottage from Rhododendron Way; like the others he had paid in full and gone his way. Etzwane made no attempt to fathom the workings of his mind. He made an excuse to Fordyce and departed the Old Caraz. In a deep depression he wandered back to camp, Eathre's image before his mind. He cursed himself for negligence, for lack of diligence. He had saved little money – though for a fact he earned little enough. This was as it should be; Etzwane had no complaint. In addition to sustenance Frolitz provided instruction and opportunity to play. Musicians other than druithines seldom became wealthy, a situation that persuaded many troupers to try their luck as druithines. A few succeeded; most, finding the cost of their meals undischarged, attempted to enliven their performances with bravura effects, eccentric mannerisms, or when all else failed, singing songs with khitan accompaniment to audiences of peasants, children, and the musically illiterate.

Back at the camp Etzwane turned dark thoughts back and forth in his mind. He had no illusions; at his present competence, with his present experience of life, he was incapable of becoming a druithine. What of the future? His life with Master Frolitz was satisfactory enough; did he want more? He went to his locker and brought forth his khitan; sitting on the steps of the cart, he began to play the slow music, pensive and melancholy, to which the folk of Canton Ifwiy liked to step

their pavannes. The music sounded dry, contrived, life-
.ess. Remembering the supple, urgent music that surged
from Dystar's khitan as if it had its own life, Etzwane
became first grim, then sad, then bitterly angry – at Dystar, at himself. He put up the khitan and laid himself
into his bunk where he tried to order his whirling young
mind.

Another five years passed. Master Frolitz and the
Pink-Black-Azure-Deep Greeners, as he now called his
troupe, came to Brassei in Canton Elphine, not a great
distance from Garwiy. Etzwane had grown into a slight,
nervously muscular young man, with a face sombre and
austere. His hair was black, his skin darkly sallow; his
mouth hung in a slightly crooked droop; he was neither
voluble, gay, nor gregarious; his voice was soft and
spare, and only when he had taken wine did he seem
to become easy or spontaneous. Certain of the musicians thought him supercilious, others thought him
vain; only Master Frolitz sought out his company, to
the puzzlement of all, for Froitz was warm where Etzwane was cold, forward where Etzwane stepped aside.
When taxed with his partiality, Frolitz only scoffed; for
a fact he found Etzwane a good listener, a wry and taci-
turn foil to his own volubility.

After establishing camp on Brassei Common, Frolitz,
with Etzwane for company, made the rounds of the
city's taverns and music halls, to learn the news and
solicit work. During the late evening they came to Zerkow's Inn, a cavernous structure of old timber and
whitewashed marl. Posts supported a roof of a dozen
crazy angles; from the beams hung mementos of all the
years of the inn's existence: grotesque wooden faces
blackened by grime and smoke, dusty glass animals, the
skull of an ahulph, three dried cauls, an iron meteorite,

95

a collection of heraldic balls, much more. At the moment Zerkow's was almost deserted, due to the weekly rigour ordained by Paraplastus, the local Cosmic Lord of Creation. Frolitz approached Loy the innkeeper and made his proposals. While the two chaffered, Etzwane stood to the side, absent-mindedly studying the placards on the posts. Preoccupied with his own concerns, he observed nothing of what he read. This morning he had received a large sum of money, an unexpected sum that had substantially augmented his savings. Sufficiently? For the twentieth time he cast up a reckoning; for the twentieth time he arrived at the same figure, on the borderline between adequacy and inadequacy. Yet where would he get more? Certainly not from Frolitz, not for a month or more. But time passed; with his goal so near he itched with impatience. His eyes focused on the placards, for the most part standard exhortations to probity:

> The BLANK, being faceless, shows the same semblance to all. Whom no man knows, no man can suborn.
> Obey all edicts with alacrity! The casual bystander may be the UNKNOWN FORCE himself!
> Lucky folk of Shant! In sixty-two cantons sing praise! How can evil flourish when every act is subject to the scrutiny of the GLORIOUS ANOME?

The posters were printed in magenta, signifying grandeur, on a field of greyed pink, the colour of omnipotence.

On the wall hung a bulletin, somewhat larger, printed in the brown and black of emergency:

> Warning! Take care. Several large bands of Roguskhoi have recently been observed along the

slopes of the Hwan! These noxious creatures may not be approached, at sure peril of your life!

Frolitz and Loy came to mutually satisfactory terms: on the following night Frolitz would bring in the Pink-Black-Azure-Deep Greeners for a two- or three-week engagement. In recognition of the understanding Loy served Etzwane a free tankard of green cider. Etzwane asked, "When was the black-brown put up?"

"About the Roguskhoi? Two or three days ago. They made a raid down into Canton Shallou and kidnapped a dozen women."

"The Faceless Man should act," said Etzwane. "The least he can do is protect us; isn't that his function? Why do we wear these torcs otherwise?"

Frolitz, conversing with a stranger in traveller's clothes who had just entered the tavern, took time to speak over his shoulder: "Pay no heed to the lad; he has no knowledge of the world."

Loy, puffing out his fat cheeks, ignored Frolitz instead. "It's no secret that something must be done. I've heard ugly reports of the creatures. It seems that they're swarming like ants up in the Hwan. There aren't females, you know, just males."

"How do they breed?" Etzwane wondered. "It is a matter I can't understand."

"They use ordinary women, with great enthusiasm, or so I'm told, and the issue is always male."

"Peculiar ... Where would such creatures come from?"

"Palasedra," declared Loy wisely. "You must know the direction of Palasedran science: always breeding, always forcing, never satisfied with creatures the way they are. I say, and others agree, that an unruly strain slipped out of the Palasedran forcing houses and crossed the Great Salt Bog into Shant. To our great misfortune."

"Unless they come to spend their florins at Zerkow's!" Frolitz called down the bar. "Since they're great drinkers, that's the way to handle them: keep them in drink and in debt."

Loy shook his head dubiously. "They'd drive away my other trade. Who wants to bump beakers with a murderous red-faced demon two feet taller than himself? I say, order them back to Palasedra without delay."

"That may be the best way," said Frolitz, "but is it the practical way? Who will issue the order?"

"There's an answer to that," said Etzwane. "The Faceless Man must exert himself. Is he not omnipotent? Is he not ubiquitous?" He jerked his thumb towards the pink and magenta placards. "Such are his claims."

Frolitz spoke in a hoarse whisper to the stranger. "Etzwane wants the Faceless Man to go up into the Hwan and torc all the Roguskhoi."

"As good a way as any," said Etzwane with a sour grin.

Into the tavern burst a young man, a porter employed at Zerkow's. "Have you heard? At Makkaby's Warehouse, not half an hour ago, a burglar got his head taken. The Faceless Man is nearby!"

Everyone in the room looked around. "Are you certain?" demanded Loy. "There might have been a swash-trap set out."

"No, without question: the torc took his head. The Faceless Man caught him in the act."

"Fancy that!" Loy marvelled. "The warehouse is only a step down the street!"

Frolitz turned to lean back against the bar. "There you have it," he told Etzwane. "You complain: 'Why does not the Faceless Man act?' Almost while you speak he acts. Is not that your answer?"

"Not entirely."

Frolitz swallowed half a tankard of the strong green cider and winked at the stranger: a tall, thin man with a head of soft white hair, an expression of austere acquiescence towards the vicissitudes of life. His age was indeterminate; he might have been old or young. "The burglar suffered a harsh fate," Frolitz told Etzwane. "The lesson to be learned is this: Never commit an unlawful act. Especially, never steal; when you take a man's property, your life becomes forfeit, as has just been demonstrated."

Loy rubbed his chain with uneasy fingers. "In a sense, the penalty seems extreme. The burglar took goods but lost his life. These are the laws of Elphine which the Faceless Man correctly enforced – but should a bagful of goods and a man's life weigh so evenly on the balance?"

The white haired stranger offered his opinion. "Why should it be otherwise? You ignore a crucial factor in the situation. Property and life are not incommensurable, when property is measured in terms of human toil. Essentially property is life; it is that proportion of life which an individual has expended to gain the property. When a thief steals property, he steals life. Each act of pillage therefore becomes a small murder."

Frolitz struck the bar with his fist. "A sound exposition, if ever I heard one! Loy, place before this instructive stranger a draft of his own choice, at my expense. Sir, how may I address you?"

The stranger told Loy: "A mug of that green cider, if you please." He turned somewhat upon his chair, towards Frolitz and Etzwane. "My name is Ifness; I am a travelling mercantilist."

99

Etzwane gave him a sour look; his rancour towards the man in the pacer trap had never waned. Ifness, then, was his name. A mercantilist? Etzwane had his doubts. Not so Frolitz. "Odd to hear such clever theories from a mercantilist!" he marvelled.

"The talk of such folk is often humdrum," agreed Loy. "For sheer entertainment, give me the company of a tavern-keeper."

Ifness pursed his lips judiciously. "All folk, mercantilists as well as tavern-keepers and musicians, try to relate their work to abstract universals. We mercantilists are highly sensitive to theft, which stabs at our very essence. To steal is to acquire goods by a simple, informal, and inexpensive process. To buy identical goods is tedious, irksome, and costly. Is it any wonder that larceny is popular? Nonetheless it voids the mercantilist's reasons for being alive; we regard thieves with the same abhorrence that musicians might feel for a fanatic gang which beat bells and gongs whenever musicians played."

Frolitz stifled an ejaculation.

Ifness tasted the mug of green cider that Loy had set before him. "To repeat: when a thief steals property, he steals life. For a mercantilist I am tolerant of human weakness, and I would not react vigorously to the theft of a day. I would resent the theft of a week; I would kill the thief who stole a year of my life."

"Hear, hear!" cried Frolitz. "Words to deter the criminal! Etzwane, have you listened?"

"You need not single me out so pointedly," said Etzwane. "I am no thief."

Frolitz, somewhat elevated by his drafts of cider, told Ifness, "Quite true, quite true! He is not a thief, he is a musician! Owing to the virtue of my instruction, he has become an adept! He finds time for nothing but study.

He is master of six instruments; he knows the parts to two thousand compositions. When I forget a chord, he is always able to call out a signal. This morning, mark you, I paid over to him a bonus of three hundred florins, out of the troupe's instrument fund."

Ifness nodded approvingly. "He seems a paragon."

"To a certain extent," said Frolitz. "On the other hand, he is secretive and stubborn. He nurtures and nurses every florin he has ever seen; he would breed them together if he could. All this makes him a dull dog at a debauch. As for the three hundred florins, I long ago had promised him five hundred and decided to stint him for his cheerlessness."

"But will not this method augment his gloom?"

"To the contrary; I keep him keen. As a musician he must learn to be grateful for every trifle. I have made him what he is, at least in his better parts. For his faults you must cite a certain Chilite, Osso, whom Etzwane claims as his 'soul-father'."

"On my way east I will be passing through Canton Bastern," said Ifness politely. "If I encounter Osso, I will convey him your greetings."

"Don't bother," said Etzwane. "I am going to Bashon myself."

Frolitz jerked around to focus his eyes on Etzwane. "Did I hear correctly? You mentioned no such plans to me!"

"If I had, you would not have paid me three hundred florins this morning. As a matter of fact I just made up my mind ten seconds ago."

"But what of the troupe? What of our engagements? Everything will be discommoded!"

"I won't be gone long. When I return, you can pay me more money since I seem to be indispensable."

Frolitz raised his bushy eyebrows. "No one is indispensable save myself! I'll play khitan and wood-horn together, if I feel so inclined, and produce better music than any four fat-necked apprentices!" Frolitz banged his mug on the bar by way of emphasis. "However, to keep my friend Loy satisfied, I must hire a substitute – an added expense and worry. How long will you be gone?"

"Three weeks, I suppose."

" 'Three weeks'?" roared Frolitz. "Are you planning a rest cure on the Ilwiy beach? Three days to Bashon, twenty minutes for your business, three days back to Brassei: that's enough!"

"Well enough, if I travelled by balloon," said Etzwane. "I must walk or ride a wagon."

"Is this more parsimony? Why not go by balloon? What is the difference in cost?"

"Something like thirty florins each way, or so I would guess."

"Well, then! Where is your pride? Does a Pink-Black-Azure-Deep Greener travel like a dog-barber?" He turned to Loy the publican. "Give this man sixty florins, in advance, on my account."

Somewhat dubiously Loy went to his till. Frolitz took the money and clapped it down on the bar in front of Etzwane. "There you are; be off with you. Above all, do not let yourself be deceived by other troupe-masters. They might offer more money than I pay, but be assured, there would be hidden disadvantages!"

Etzwane laughed. "Never fear, I'll be back perhaps in a week or ten days. I'll take the first balloon out; my business at Bashon will be short enough; then it's the first balloon back to Brassei."

Frolitz turned to consult Ifness but found an empty chair; Ifness had departed the tavern.

102

CHAPTER SEVEN

A storm had struck in from the Green Ocean, bringing floods to Cantons Maiy and Erevan; a section of the Great Transverse Route had been washed out; balloons were delayed two days until crews were able to rig an emergency pass-over.

Etzwane was able to secure a place on the first balloon out of Brassei, the *Asper*. He climbed into the gondola and took a seat; behind him came other passengers. Last aboard was Ifness.

Etzwane sat indifferently, making no sign of recognition. Ifness saw Etzwane and after the briefest of hesitations nodded and sat down beside him. "It seems that we are to be travelling companions."

Etzwane made a cool response. "I will find it a pleasure."

The door was closed; bars were lowered to provide the passengers a grip when the balloon swayed and heeled. The wind-tender entered his compartment, tested the winches, checked valves and ballast release. He signalled the ground crew; they rolled the Judas-dolly out along the slot; the *Asper* rose into the air. The running dolly was released; the *Asper* danced and flounced in the beam wind until the wind-tender trimmed guys, whereupon the *Asper* steadied and surged ahead, with taut guys and singing dolly.

Ifness spoke to Etzwane: "You seem totally relaxed. Have you ridden the balloon-way before?"

"Many years ago."

"A wonderful experience for a child."

"It was indeed."

"I am never altogether comfortable in the balloons," said Ifness. "They seem so frail and vulnerable. A few sticks, the thinnest of membranes, the most fugitive of gases. Still, the Palasedran gliders seem even more precarious: transport, no doubt, which accords with their temperament. You are bound for Bashon, I understand."

"I intend to pay off my mother's indenture."

Ifness reflected a moment. "Perhaps you should have entrusted your business to a job-broker. The Chilites are a devious folk and may try to mulct you."

"No doubt they'll try. But it won't do any good. I carry an ordinance from the Faceless Man, which they must obey."

"I see. Well, I still would be on my guard. The Chilites, for all their unworldliness, are seldom bested."

After a moment Etzwane said, "You seem well acquainted with the Chilites."

Ifness permitted himself a faint smile. "They are a fascinating cult; the Chilite rationale and its physical projection make a most elegant pattern. You don't follow me? Consider: a group which nightly intoxicates itself into a frenzy of erotic hallucinations under the pretext of religious asceticism – isn't this sublime insouciance? A social machinery is necessary to maintain this state of affairs: it is as you know. How to ensure persistence in a group not itself regenerative? By recruiting the children of other men, by the constant infusion of new blood. How to secure so precious a commodity, which other men normally protect with their lives? By the ingenious institution of Rhododendron Way, which also turns a good profit. What marvellous effrontery! It can almost be admired!"

Etzwane was surprised to find Ifness so enthusiastic. He said coldly, "I was born on Rhododendron Way and became a Pure Boy; I find them disgusting."

Ifness seemed amused. He said, "They are a remarkable adaptation, if perhaps too highly specialized. What would happen, for instance, if they no longer could obtain galga? In a generation or less the structure of the society would alter in one of several conceivable directions."

Etzwane wondered that a mercantilist should be so apt at abstract analysis of human society. "What sort of goods do you sell?" he asked. "As a mercantilist I assume that you sell goods."

"Not quite the case," said Ifness. "I am employed by a mercantile association to travel here and there and discover possible new applications for their products."

"It seems an interesting job," said Etzwane.

"I find it so."

Etzwane glanced at the man's torc. "From the purple-green I assume your home to be Garwiy."

"That is the case." Ifness took a journal from his valise, *The Kingdoms of Old Caraz*, and began to read.

Etzwane looked out over the reaches of the landscape. An hour passed. The *Asper* halted at a siding to allow a pair of eastbound balloons to skim by, cables taut, dollies singing down the slots.

At noon the wind-tender sold tea, slabs of fruit jelly, buns, and meat sticks to those who required food. Ifness put away his journal and ate; Etzwane preferred to husband his funds, which were barely sufficient. Finishing his meal, Ifness fastidiously brushed his hands and returned to the journal.

An hour later the *Asper* arrived at Brassei Junction in Canton Fairlea and was switched onto the Great Transverse Route. The wind freshened but, coming

105

from the port quarter, blew the balloon only at its own speed; so passed the afternoon. At sunset the wind died completely, and the *Asper* stood becalmed above an upland moor, in Canton Shade.

The suns danced down behind the horizon; the sky flared violet behind four streaks of apple-green cloud. Darkness came quickly. A breeze stirred the upper air, still coming from astern; the *Asper* eased forward along the slot, no faster than a man could walk.

The wind-tender served a meal of cheese, wine, and biscuits, then rigged hammocks. The passengers, with nothing better to do, slept.

Late the next afternoon the *Asper* arrived at Angwin, at the head of the great Gorge. Here the slot terminated, and the cable swung up in a pair of great pale swags to Angwin Junction where years before – it seemed dream-time – Etzwane had been brought up from Carbade to work as an apprentice. He wondered if Finnerack still worked there.

The *Asper* was scheduled to continue along the Great Transverse Route, to the south slopes of the Hwan; at Angwin it descended to discharge those passengers who were to continue along the North Spur. There were four of these: Etzwane, a pair of commercial buyers bound for Dublay at the tip of Canton Cape, and Ifness.

The North Spur connection, which should have been waiting, had been delayed by light winds; the four passengers must put up a night at Angwin Inn.

The *Asper* climbed back into the sky, with the guys now shifted to the cable. In the wheelhouse under the inn the crew put their shoulders to the windlass; the balloon was drawn across the Great Gorge and up to Junction. Etzwane could not bring himself to go down to watch the windlass, as did the two buyers.

Later Etzwane and the buyers sat in the lounge overlooking the Great Gorge; Ifness had gone for a stroll along the rim of the chasm.

The suns toppled low, one behind the other; magenta light struck Mount Mish and the far peaks beyond. The gorge became dim with murk. Etzwane and the buyers drank spiced cider; as the steward brought a tray of preserved fruit, one of the buyers asked, "Do you see many Roguskhoi down in the gorge?"

"Not often," the steward replied. "The lads up at Junction used to see a few, but from what I hear, they've migrated east into the Wildlands."

"They raided down in Shallou not so long ago," said the second buyer. "That's to the west."

"Yes, so it is. Well, it's all beyond me. What we'd do if a band attacked Angwin, I can't imagine."

The other buyer spoke. "The gorge itself is some protection, so I should think."

The steward looked gloomily down into the blue murk. "Not enough to suit me if what I hear of the devils is true. If we had women up here, I wouldn't sleep nights. They hardly go out of their way to kill a man except for entertainment, but if they smell a woman, they climb through fire and flood. In my opinion something ought to be done."

Ifness, who had returned unobserved, spoke from the shadows. "What, in your opinion, is the 'something' that ought to be done?"

"The Faceless Man should be notified and have it driven home to him, that's what! I say, throw a cordon around the whole Hwan if it takes every man in Shant and then start closing in, driving the devils together, killing as we go. When men from the north, east, south, and west look at each other over the top of Mount Skarack, then we'll know we're rid of the vermin."

One of the buyers demurred. "Too complicated; it would never work. They'd hide in caves or tunnels. Now, my idea is to put out poison —"

The other buyer offered a lewd specification for efficacious bait.

"Well, why not," demanded his colleague, "if it'll draw them? But poison's the answer, mark my words."

The second buyer said, "Don't be too sure! These are not animals, you know. They're freak men from across the Salt Bog. The Palasedrans have been quiet too long; it's unnatural, and now they're sending in the Roguskhoi."

The steward said, "I don't care where they come from; let's clear them out, back to Palasedra for preference. According to the afternoon news, just in over the radio, a band came down from Mount Haghead to raid a village in Morningshore. Killed, raped, kidnapped. The village is a total ruin."

"So far to the east?" murmured Ifness.

"That's the report. First Shallou to the west, then Morningshore to the east. The Hwan must be crawling with them."

"That doesn't necessarily follow," said Etzwane.

"You may be sure," said the first buyer in a pontifical voice, "that the Faceless Man is ready to act. He has no choice."

The steward sneered. "He's far away in Garwiy; what's our safety to him?"

The buyers pursed their lips. "Well," said one, "I wouldn't go so far as that. The Faceless Man represents us all! By and large he does a good job."

"Still," said the other, "the time has come. He should take action."

The steward inquired, "Do you gentlemen require

more drink before supper? If so call out now before cook strikes the gong."

Etzwane asked, "Is Dagbolt still superintendent?"

"No, old Dagbolt's been dead five years of throat chancre," replied the steward. "I knew him a mere three months, more than ample. Dickon Defonso is superintendent, and affairs go tolerably well."

"Does a certain Finnerack work at Angwin?"

"Finnerack? Somewhere I've heard the name. But he's not here."

"Might he be at Junction?"

"Nor at Junction. Finnerack ... Some sort of scandal. Was he the criminal who loosed a balloon?"

"I couldn't say."

In the middle of the morning the balloon *Jano* arrived at Angwin. The four passengers climbed aboard; the *Jano* rose to the extent of its guys and was pulled back across the gorge to Junction. Etzwane gazed down in fascination at the little island in the sky. There the three great sheaves, almost in contact; there the stone shelter with the timber door and the outhouse cantilevered over the gorge. At the sheave he saw the motion of the man on duty; the balloon gave a jerk as the claw-jack drew down the guys and the grip was transferred to the North Spur cable, and another jerk as the jerk was released. Etzwane smiled as he thought of another balloon, so long ago. ...

The *Jano* was drawn down to the North Station; the guys were transferred to a dolly; then off down the slot into Canton Seamus ran the *Jano*, tacking into a brisk breeze off the starboard bow. With the balloon trimmed to best advantage, the wind-tender came into the gondola. "All here for Oswiy, I take it?"

"Not I," said Etzwane. "I'm for Bastern Station at Carbade."

"Bastern Station? I'll put you down if the landing crew is on hand. They took themselves into Carbade during the raid."

"What raid is this?"

"You wouldn't have heard. The Roguskhoi, a band of fifty or sixty, pushed out of the wildlands and plundered down the Mirk."

"How far down the Mirk?"

"That I don't know. If they turned towards Seamus, you won't find a crew at Bastern Station. Why not go on down to Ascalon? You'd find it more secure."

"I must get off at Bastern Station if I slide down the guys."

When the *Jano* reached Bastern Station, the crew had returned to duty; the *Jano* was hauled down with a nervous jerkiness. Etzwane jumped to the ground; Ifness followed. "I take it that you are travelling east?" asked Ifness.

"Yes, to Bashon."

"I propose, then, that we share a vehicle."

Etzwane calculated his probable expense. Fifteen hundred florins for the indenture, a hundred for the return to Brassei with Eathre, another fifty for unforeseen contingencies. Sixteen hundred and fifty. He carried sixteen hundred and sixty-five. "I can't afford anything expensive," he said in a somewhat surly voice. Of all the folk of Shant, he least of all wished to be under obligation to Ifness. Save perhaps his soul-father Osso.

At the hostelry Ifness ordered a fast trap drawn by a pair of prime pacers. "I'll have to take two hundred florins from you," the hostler told Ifness. "That is the deposit. Hire will be twenty florins a day."

Etzwane said flatly, "I can't afford it." Ifness made

an indifferent gesture. "It is how I choose to travel. Pay what you can; I will be satisfied."

"It's not much," said Etzwane. "Fifteen florins, in fact. Were it not for the Roguskhoi, I'd walk."

"Pay fifteen florins or nothing whatever," said Ifness. "It's all the same to me."

Nettled by the condescension, the more irritating for its absent-minded quality, Etzwane brought forth fifteen florins. "If this satisfies you, take it. Otherwise I will walk."

"Well enough, well enough; let us be off; I am anxious to inspect the Roguskhoi, circumstances offer."

The pacers, tall, rangy beasts, deep and narrow-chested, long and fine in the legs, sprang off down the road; the trap whirled after.

Etzwane glowered at Ifness from the corner of his eye. A strange man, for a fact; Etzwane had never seen another like him. Why should he want to inspect the Roguskhoi? There seemed no sensible reason for such an interest. If a Roguskhoi were dead and lying beside the road, Etzwane would pause to examine the corpse from natural curiosity; but to go about the business so purposefully – it seemed sheer lunacy!

Etzwane pondered the possibility that Ifness, for a fact, might be insane. The preoccupied placidity, the indifference to others, the bizarre predilections, all were suggestive of dementia. Still Ifness was nothing if not self-controlled; his appearance – spare, austere, otherwise nondescript save for the cropped white hair, the old-young face – seemed the very definition of sanity. Etzwane lost interest in the subject; he had other, more pressing concerns.

Ten miles they drove, up and down the rolling hills of Seamus. Along the road from the east came a man on a thrust-cycle wearing the red cap of invisibility. He rode at the best speed he could muster, lying flat on the pallet, buttocks surging and jerking as he kicked at the ratchet.

Ifness pulled the trap to a halt and watched the man's approach. A discourteous act, thought Etzwane; the man wore red. The cyclist swerved to pass by. Ifness called him to a halt, to the man's displeasure.

"Why do you molest me? Have you no eyes in your head?"

Ifness ignored his agitation. "What is the news?"

"Dreadful news; don't stay me; I'm off to Canton Sable or beyond." He made as if to hump the cycle into motion once more; Ifness called out politely: "A moment, if you please. No danger is visible. From what are you fleeing?"

"From the Roguskhoi; what else? They burnt Salubra Village; another band pillaged the Chilites. For all I know they're close on my heels! Delay me no longer; if you're wise, you'll turn about and flee west at all speed!" The man thrust his cycle into motion and was gone along the road to Carbade.

Ifness turned to look at Etzwane. "Well, what now?"

"I must go to Bashon."

Ifness nodded and without further remark whipped up the pacers.

Etzwane leaned forward, heart in his mouth. Visions crossed before his eyes. He thought of florins wasted on drink, gifts to occasional sweethearts, unnecessary garments, his costly silver-mounted wood-horn. Frolitz thought him niggardly; he considered himself a wastrel. Vain regrets. The money was spent; the time was lost. The pacers, prime beasts, ran without fatigue; miles passed under the wheels. They entered Bastern; ahead appeared the shadow of Rhododendron Way. From behind the hill rose a column of smoke. As they entered

112

Rhododendron Way, Ifness slowed the trap to a more cautious pace, inspecting the shadows under the trees, the berry coverts, the hillsides, with an alertness Etzwane had not noticed in him before. All seemed normal, save for the utter silence. The lavender-white sunlight lay in irregular sprinkles among the white dust; in the garden of the first cottage purple and magenta geraniums bloomed among spikes of lime-green ki. The door of the cottage hung askew. Across the threshhold lay the body of a man, face obliterated by a terrible blow. The girl who had lived in the cottage was gone.

A gap through the trees revealed the temple. Along the upper terraces a few Chilites moved slowly, tentatively, as if trying to convince themselves that they were alive. Ifness touched up the pacers; the trap whirled up the hill towards the temple. From the embers of the tannery and women's dormitory rose the column of smoke they had seen from far off. The temple and its conjoined structures seemed to be whole. Etzwane, standing up in the trap, looked all around. He saw no women, young or old.

Ifness halted the trap before the temple portico. From the terrace above a group of Chilites, haggard and uncertain, peered down.

Ifness called up: "What has happened?"

The Chilites stood like ghosts in their white robes. "Hello up there!" called Ifness with acerbity in his voice. "Can you hear me?"

The Chilites moved slowly back out of sight, as if toppling over backward, thought Etzwane.

Several minutes passed. The three suns performed their majestic gyrations across the sky. The stone walls baked in the glare. Ifness sat without motion. Again, with sharper puzzlement, Etzwane wondered why Ifness troubled himself to such an extent.

The iron gates moved ajar and revealed a group of Chilites. He who had opened the gate was a round-faced young man, somewhat portly, with overlarge features, scant sandy hair, and a full sandy beard. Etzwane 'on the instant recognized Geacles Vonoble. Behind stood half a dozen other Chilites, and one among them was Osso Higajou.

Ifness spoke sharply, "What has occurred here?"

Osso said in a voice that rasped as if bitter phlegm choked his throat, "We are victims of the Roguskhoi. We have been pillaged; they have done us vast harm."

"How many were there in the band?"

"No less than fifty. They swarmed at us like savage beasts! They beat on our doors; they brandished weapons; they burnt our structures!"

"In the process of defending your women and your property, you doubtless inflicted many casualties?" inquired Ifness dryly.

The Chilites drew back in indignation; Geacles gave a contemptuous laugh. Osso said in a waspish voice, "We are nonviolent folk; we advocate peace."

"Did the abducted women defend themselves?" inquired Ifness.

"Yes, many of them; it did no good, and they violated their consciences in the process."

"They must suffer doubly in that case," Ifness agreed. "Why did you not shelter them in the temple?"

The Chilites surveyed him in calm silence, making no response.

Ifness asked again: "In regard to the Roguskhoi, what weapons did they carry?"

Geacles pulled at his beard, glanced off across the hillside. He spoke in a subdued voice: "They carried cudgels studded with spikes; these swung from their wrists. They wore scimitars at their belts, which they did not use."

"How long ago did they depart?"

"No more than an hour; they herded the women into a file; young and old, infants excepted; these they threw into the tannery vats. We are now bereft."

Etzwane could restrain himself no longer. "Which way did they go?"

Geacles stared at Etzwane, then turned and muttered to Osso, who came forward three quick steps.

Ifness, coldly polite, put the question a second time: "Which way did they go?"

"Up the Mirk Valley, the way they had come," said Geacles.

Osso pointed a finger at Etzwane. "You are the Pure Boy Faman Bougozonie who committed foul acts and fled."

"My name is Gastel Etzwane. I am the son of Dystar the druithine. My mother is the lady Eathre."

Osso spoke in a menacing voice: "Why did you come here?"

"I came to dissolve my mother's indenture."

Osso smiled. "We do not engage in such casual traffic."

"I carry an ordinance from the Faceless Man."

Osso grunted. Geacles said smoothly, "Why not? Pay us our money; the woman will be released to you."

Etzwane made no response. He turned to look up Mirk Valley where he had never ventured for fear of ahulphs. The women would walk at less than three miles an hour. The Roguskhoi had departed an hour since. Etzwane thought furiously. He looked towards the tannery: destroyed, burnt to the ground. The far sheds where chemicals and dyes were stored still stood. He turned to Ifness and spoke in a low voice: "Will you lend me the trap and the pacers? If I lose them, I will pay; I carry sixteen hundred florins."

"Why do you require the trap?"

"So that I may save my mother."

"How?"

"It depends upon Osso."

"I will lend you the trap. What are a pair of pacers, after all?"

Etzwane spoke to Osso: "The Roguskhoi are great wine-drinkers. Give me two large kegs of wine. I will convey them up the valley and deliver them."

Osso blinked in bewilderment. "You intend to assist their revelries?"

"I intend to poison them."

"What?" cried Geacles. "And so provoke another attack?"

Etzwane looked to Osso. "What do you say?"

Osso calculated. "You plan to deliver the wine in the trap?"

"I do."

"What will you pay for the wine? It is our ceremonial liquor; we have none other."

Etzwane hesitated. Time was too precious to be used haggling; still, if he offered generously, Osso would ask more. "I can only offer what it is worth, thirty florins a cask."

Osso gave Etzwane a cold glance. Ifness lounged indifferently against the trap. Osso said, "That is not enough."

Ifness said, "It is ample. Bring forth the wine."

Osso examined Ifness. "Who are you?"

Ifness looked unsmilingly off over the valley. Presently he said, "In due course the Faceless Man will move against the Roguskhoi. I will inform him of your refusal to cooperate."

116

"I have refused nothing," rasped Osso. "Give me your sixty florins, then go to the door of the storeroom."

Etzwane paid over the coins. Two casks of wine were rolled forth and loaded into the back of the trap. Etzwane ran over to the chemical storehouse, looked along the lines of jugs and packets. Which would serve his purpose best? He did not know.

Ifness entered the shed. He glanced along the shelf and selected a cannister. "This will serve best. It has no remarkable flavour and is highly toxic."

"Very well." They returned to the trap.

"I will be gone at least six hours," said Etzwane. "If possible, I will bring back the trap, but as to this –"

"I paid a large deposit for the use of the trap," said Ifness. "It is a valuable piece of equipment."

With compressed lips Etzwane brought forth his pouch. "Will two hundred florins suffice? Or as many as you wish, to sixteen hundred."

Ifness climbed into the seat. "Put away your florins. I will come along to protect my interests."

Wordlessly Etzwane sprang aboard; the trap moved off up Mirk Valley. From the terraces of the temple the Chilites stood watching until the trap passed from view.

CHAPTER EIGHT

The road was little more than a pair of wheel tracks beside the Mirk River. To either side were flats overgrown with rich green bandocks, each plant raising a single pale blue spine that flicked at passing insects. Along the river grew willows, alders, clumps of stately dark blue miter-plants. Signs of the Roguskhoi were evident: odd articles of female clothing; on three occasions the corpses of old women, looking harried beyond their capacity; and in one dreary little heap, the corpses of six infants, evidently pulled from their mothers and dashed to the ground.

Ifness drove at the best pace the road allowed: The trap bounced, bumped, swung from side to side, but still moved three times the best possible speed of the Roguskhoi and the women.

Ifness asked after a few minutes, "Where does the road lead?"

"Up to Gargamet Meadow – that's what the Chilites call it. It's the plantation where they grow their galga bush."

"And how far to Gargamet Meadow?"

"Five or six miles from here, at a guess. I would expect the Roguskhoi to stop at Gargamet Meadow for the night."

Ifness pulled in the pacers. "We don't want to overtake them in this gully. Have you poisoned the wine?"

"I'll do so now." Etzwane climbed into the rear of the trap and poured half of the cannister into each keg.

The suns passed behind the western slope; the valley began to grow dim. A sense of imminence pressed down on Etzwane; the Roguskhoi could not be too far ahead. Ifness drove with great caution; to blunder into a Roguskhoi rear guard would not serve their purposes. Ahead the road passed through a notch with tall coral-trees silhouetted on the sky at either side. Ifness stopped the cart; Etzwane ran ahead to reconnoiter. The road, passing through the noch, swung around a clump of purple-pear trees, then eased out upon a flat. To the left loomed a grove of dark bawberrys; to the right the galga plantations spread: sixty acres of carefully-tended vines. Beside the bawberry grove a pond reflected back the lavender sky; here the Roguskhoi marshalled their captives. They had just arrived; the women were still moving as the Roguskhoi directed with great roaring commands and sweeps of their huge arms.

Etzwane signalled back to Ifness, who brought the trap forward to the clump of purple-pears. With pinched nostrils Ifness looked across the flat. "We can't be too transparent in our scheme," he told Etzwane. "We must contrive natural movements."

Etzwane's nerves began to draw and grate. He spoke in a high-pitched, rasping voice: "Any minute they'll start in on the women! They can hardly contain themselves."

Indeed, the Roguskhoi now surrounded the women, making tremulous motions, surging towards the shrinking huddle, then drawing back.

Ifness inquired, "Can you ride a pacer?"

"I suppose so," said Etzwane. "I've never tried."

"We will drive across the meadow furtively, as if hoping to evade attention. As soon as they see us – then you must be quick, and I as well."

Etzwane, terrified but desperately resolved, nodded

119

to Ifness's instructions. "Anything, anything. We must hurry!"

"Haste provokes disaster," chided Ifness. "We have just arrived; we must take account of every circumstance." He appraised and considered another ten seconds, then drove out on the edge of the meadow and turned towards the plantation, away from the bawberry grove. They moved in full view of the Roguskhoi, should one by chance remove his glance from the ashen-faced women.

They drove a hundred yards, attracting no attention; Ifness nodded in satisfaction. "It would seem now as if we are hoping to escape their notice."

"What if they don't see us?" asked Etzwane in a thin voice he hardly recognized as his own.

Ifness made no response. They drove another fifty yards. From the Roguskhoi came a yell, hoarse yet wild, with a peculiar crazy timber that started up the hairs behind Etzwane's neck.

"They have seen us," said Ifness in a colourless voice. "Be quick now." He jumped down from the cart with no undue haste and unsnapped the traces from one of the pacers; Etzwane fumbled with the straps of the other pacer. "Here," said Ifness, "take this one. Climb upon its back and take the reins."

The pacer jerked at the unaccustomed weight and lowered its head.

"Ride for the road," said Ifness. "Not too fast.

Twenty of the Roguskhoi lumbered across the meadow, eyes distended, arms flailing and pumping: A fearful sight. Ifness ignored them. He snapped loose the traces on the second pacer, cut short the reins, tied them deliberately, jumped upon the pacer's back. Then, kicking it in the ribs, he sent the beast loping after Etzwane.

The Roguskhoi, sighting the casks, forgot the fugitives; with hardly a pause in their stride they lifted the tongue of the trap; cavorting in particularly grotesque fashion, they drew it back across the meadow.

In the shadow of the purple-pears Ifness and Etzwane halted the pacers. "Now," said Ifness, "we must wait."

Etzwane made no reply. The Roguskhoi, abandoning the women, swarmed around the trap. The casks were broached; the Roguskhoi drank with hoarse bellows of approval.

In a strained voice Etzwane asked, "How long before the poison acts?"

"So much poison would kill a man within minutes. I hopefully assume that the Roguskhoi metabolism is similar."

The two watched the encampment. The wine had been totally consumed. With no evidence either of sickness or intoxication the Roguskhoi turned upon the women. Each rushed into the whimpering group and without regard for age or condition seized a female and began to tear away clothing.

Ifness said: "The moment has come."

Several of the Roguskhoi had stopped short to gaze uncomprehendingly at the ground. Slowly they touched their abdomens, their throats, drew their fingers across their naked red scalps. Others displayed similar symptoms; the women, gasping and sobbing, crawled away in random directions like insects poured from a bottle. The Roguskhoi commenced to writhe, to dance a strange, slow ballet; they raised a crooked leg, clamped knee against abdomen, hopped, then repeated the antic on the opposite leg. Their faces sagged, their mouths hung pendulous.

Suddenly, in terrible rage, one cried out a word in-

121

comprehensible to Etzwane. The others shouted the same word in grotesque despair. One of the Roguskhoi dropped to his knees and slowly crumpled to the ground. He began to work his arms and legs like a beetle turned on its back. Certain of the women who had almost reached the bawberry grove began to run. The movement stimulated the warriors to frenzy. Staggering, reeling, they lurched in pursuit, flailing with their bludgeons. Screaming, sobbing, the women ran this way and that; the Roguskhoi jumped among them; the women were caught and beaten to the ground.

The Roguskhoi began to topple, one after the other. Ifness and Etzwane stepped out upon the meadow; the last Roguskhoi erect noticed their presence. He snatched out his scimitar and hurled it. "Take care!" cried Ifness, and sprang nimbly back. The scimitar whirled murderously through the air but curved to the side and slashed into the dirt. With renewed dignity Ifness once more stepped forward, while the last Roguskhoi fell to the ground.

Ifness said, "The trap appears to be unharmed. Let us reclaim it."

Etzwane looked at him, face blank with horror. He made a sound in his throat, moved forward a step, then halted. The features of the women had been blurred – by motion, by distance. Almost all he had known. Some had been kind, some had been beautiful; some had laughed, some had been sorrowful. With his poison he had contributed to the massacre, still – what else, what else?

"Come along," said Ifness brusquely. "Lead your pacer." He marched across the meadow, never troubling to look back.

Etzwane followed sluggishly, forcing his feet to move. Arriving at the Roguskhoi camp, Ifness inspected the bodies with fastidious interest. The Roguskhoi still made small movements: twitches, jerks, clenched digging with the fingers. Etzwane forced himself to look here and there. He noticed the body of his sister Delamber: dead. Her face had been smashed almost beyond recognition; Etzwane recognized first the red-gold glints of her hair. He wandered across the field. There was Eathre. He fell down on his knees beside her and took her hands. He thought she still lived, though blood oozed from both her ears. He said, "It is Etzwane: your son Mur. I am here. I tried to save you, but I failed."

Eathre's lips moved. "No," he thought to hear her say, "you didn't fail. You saved me ... Thank you, Mur ..."

Etzwane dragged branches and boughs from the bawberry woods, stacked them high; he had no spade to dig a grave. He placed the bodies of Eathre and Delamber on the pyre and placed more branches to lean around and over. He needed much wood; he made many trips.

Ifness had been otherwise occupied. He harnessed the restive pacers to the trap and repaired the reins. Then he turned his attention to the Roguskhoi. He examined them closely, with frowning concentration. To Etzwane they seemed much alike: muscular, massive creatures, a head taller than the average man, with a skin hard and sleek as copper. Their features, which might have been hewn with an axe, were contorted and twisted, like those of a demon-mask: probably the effect of the poison. They grew no hair on head or body; their costumes were almost pitifully meagre: black leather crotch-pieces, a belt from which hung their bludgeons and scimitars. Ifness took up one of the scimitars and

123

examined the gleaming metal with interest. "No product of Shant here," he mused. "Who forged such metal?"

Etzwane had no answer; Ifness placed the scimitar in the back of the trap. The cudgels likewise interested him. The handles were seasoned hardwood, eighteen inches long; the heads were iron balls studded with two-inch points: terrible weapons.

Etzwane finally completed the pyre and set it afire on four sides. Flame licked up into the air.

Ifness had taken upon himself a grisly investigation. With his knife he had slit open the abdomen of one of the Roguskhoi. Blackish-red intestines rolled out; Ifness moved them aside with a stick; with nostrils fastidiously pinched, he continued his inspection of the creature's organs.

Dusk had come to the meadow. The pyre burnt high. Etzwane did not care to tarry longer. He called to Ifness: "Are you ready to leave?"

"Yes," said Ifness. "I have one small further task."

While Etzwane watched in utter astonishment, Ifness selected the corpses of six women; deftly cutting off the battered heads, he took the six torcs. Going to the pond, he washed torcs, knife, and hands and returned to where Etzwane stood by the trap, wondering as to Ifness's sanity and his own.

Ifness seemed brisk and cheerful. He stood back to watch the flames from the pyre lick high into the gathering darkness. "It is time to go," said Ifness.

Etzwane climbed into the seat of the trap. Ifness turned the pacers across the meadow. Etzwane suddenly signalled him to a halt. Ifness pulled up the pacers; Etzwane jumped to the ground. He ran back to the pyre, extracted a burning brand. This he carried to the galga plantation and fired the foliage, which was dense, dry, heavy with resin. Flames surged up through

124

clouds of black smoke. In grim delight Etzwane stood back to watch; then he ran back to the trap.

Ifness had no comment to make; Etzwane was unable to sense either approval or disapproval but did not care particularly.

Leaving the meadow, they halted and looked back at the two fires. The galga patch lit the sky; the pyre glowed ruby red. Etzwane turned away, blinking. The fires were the past; when the fires died to ashes, the past would be gone.

Down the dark valley moved the trap, by the light of the Skiaffarilla. The shuffle of hoofs, the creak of harness, and the soft scrape of wheels were the only sounds; they magnified the silence. Once or twice Etzwane looked back to watch the red glow slowly fading. At last he could see it no more; the sky was dark. He turned in the seat and gazed sombrely ahead.

In a quiet and formal voice Ifness asked, "Now that you have studied the Roguskhoi, what is your opinion?"

Etzwane said, "They must be mad or demon-possessed. In a sense they are pitiable. But they must be destroyed."

Ifness said reflectively, "I find myself in agreement with you. The cantons of Shant are highly vulnerable. The Chilites must now change beyond recognition or disappear."

Etzwane tried to see Ifness's face in the starlight. "You can't believe this is unfortunate?"

"I regret the passing of any unique organism; there has never been such a human adaptation before in all the history of the race; there may never be again."

"What of the Roguskhoi: I suppose you'd be sorry to see them destroyed!"

Ifness gave a small, quiet laugh. "Rather than the Roguskhoi themselves, I fear what they may represent.

125

To such an extent that I have been forced to compromise my principles."

"I don't understand you," said Etzwane shortly.

Ifness said in a grave voice, "As you know, I travel here and there across Shant, according to the urgencies of my profession. I see many circumstances, some happy, others grievous, but by the very nature of my affairs I may never involve myself."

Into Etzwane's mind came the memory of his first encounter with Ifness. "Not even to help a small boy escape the cannibal ahulphs?"

Ifness turned to peer through the darkness. "You were that boy?"

"Yes."

Ifness was silent for several minutes. Then he said, "You have a dark and brooding streak in your nature which persuades you against your best interests. By resurrecting an episode ten years old you risk offending me; what benefit do you derive?"

Etzwane spoke in a detached voice. "I have long resented that placid man who was willing to let me die. To express myself is a relief and a pleasure. I suppose that is the benefit which you asked about. I don't care a fig whether or not you are offended." Now that he had started talking, he found that he could not stop. "All that I have hoped and worked for is gone. Who is to blame? The Roguskhoi. Myself. The Faceless Man. The Chilites. All of us are to blame. I should have come sooner. I try to excuse myself: I had insufficient funds, I could not have anticipated the Roguskhoi raid. Still, I should have come sooner. The Roguskhoi – they are mad things; I am glad I poisoned them; I would gladly poison the entire race. The Chilites, whom you mourn: I don't care a fig for them, either. The Faceless Man:

There is another matter! We have trusted him to protect us; we pay his imposts; we wear his torc; we follow, as we must, his edicts. To what end? Why has he not acted against the Roguskhoi? It is disheartening, to say the least!"

"And to say the most?"

Etzwane only shook his head. "Why did you cut open the Roguskhoi?"

"I was curious as to their physiology."

Etzwane gave a laugh that held a shrill note of wildness. He cut the laugh short. For a period there was silence. The trap moved down the star-lit valley. Etzwane had no notion of how far they had come, how far they must go. He asked another question: "Why did you take the torcs?"

Ifness sighed. "I had hoped you would not ask that question. I cannot provide you a satisfactory answer."

"You have many secrets," said Etzwane.

"All of us keep covert certain areas of ourselves," said Ifness. "You yourself for instance: you have evinced dissatisfaction with the Faceless Man, but you do not reveal your further intentions."

"They are not secret," said Etzwane. "I shall go to Garwiy; I shall buy a Purple Petition; I shall argue my views with as much clarity as possible. Under the circumstances the Faceless Man must take notice."

"One would think so," Ifness concurred. "But let us assume the contrary. What, then?"

Etzwane squinted sidewise at the stiff yet casual silhouette against the blazing Skiaffarilla. "Why should I trouble myself with remote eventualities?"

"I agree that overplanning sometimes limits spontaneity," said Ifness. "Still, when there are but two cases

127

of equal probability, it is wise to consider contingencies in both directions."

"I have ample time to form my plans," said Etzwane shortly.

CHAPTER NINE

In the dead middle of the night they came down out of Mirk Valley. A few dim lights flickered from the terraces of the temple; a breeze brought the sweet-acrid whiff of galga mingled with vile odours of charred wood and hides.

"The Chilites will worship Galexis until their drug runs out," remarked Ifness. "Then they must cry after a new goddess."

They passed into Rhododendron Way, an avenue breathless and dark, haunted by remembered sounds. The foliage was black overhead, the road a white glimmer below. The cottages stood with doors ajar, offering shelter and rest; neither of the two suggested a halt. They continued on through the night.

Dawn came as a glorious cascade of orange and violet across the east; as Sasetta curveted into the sky, the trap entered Carbade. The pacers walked slowly, heads drooping, considerably more weary than the men.

Ifness drove directly to the hostler's and relinquished the conveyance; the torcs and the weapons he wrapped into a parcel and tucked into his jacket.

Etzwane would return westward; at Brassei Ifness had stated his destination to be in the east. Etzwane said somewhat ponderously, "We go our different ways. I can't ignore the fact that you have helped me a great deal. I give you thanks, and I must say that I leave you in a better spirit than I did on a previous occasion. So then, Ifness, I bid you farewell."

Ifness bowed courteously. "Farewell to you."

Etzwane turned and strode across the square to the balloon-way depot. Ifness followed in a more leisurely fashion.

At the ticket-seller's window Etzwane said in a crisp voice, "I want passage by the first balloon to Garwiy." As he paid the fee, he became conscious of Ifness standing behind him and gave a curt nod that Ifness returned. Ifness went to the wicket and arranged balloon passage for himself.

The balloon south to Junction would not arrive at Carbade for another hour; Etzwane paced back and forth, then crossed the square to a food-vender's stall where he found Ifness. Etzwane took his meal to a table nearby, as did Ifness, after murmuring a conventional excuse to Etzwane.

The two ate in silence. Etzwane, finishing, returned to the depot, followed somewhat later by Ifness.

The slot began to sing: a thin, high-pitched whirring that told of the approaching dolly. Five minutes later the balloon came trembling and swaying down to the loading platform. Etzwane rose to his feet, leaving Ifness looking pensively from the depot window; he entered the gondola and settled himself upon the bench. Ifness came in behind him and took a seat directly opposite. Etzwane could ignore his presence no longer. "I thought you were continuing east."

"An urgent matter takes me elsewhere," said Ifness.

"To Garwiy?"

"To Garwiy."

The balloon rose into the air; riding the fresh morning wind, it slid up the slot towards Junction.

During Etzwane's time Frolitz had taken his troupe to Garwiy but seldom, and only for short periods; the folk of Garwiy preferred entertainments more dramatic, more frivolous, more urbane. Etzwane nonetheless found Garwiy a fascinating place, if only for the marvel and grace of its vistas.

In all the human universe there was no city like Garwiy, which was built of glass – blocks, slabs, prisms, cylinders of glass: purple, green lavender, blue, rose, dark scarlet.

Among the original exiles from Earth had been twenty thousand Chama Reya a cult of aestheticians. On Durdane they vowed to build the most magnificent city the race had yet known, and so dedicated themselves. The first Garwiy persisted seven thousand years, dominated in turn by the Chama Reya, the Architectural Corporation, the Director Dynasties, the transitional superdirectors, and finally the Purple Kings. Each century brought new marvels to Garwiy, and it seemed that the goal of each Purple King was to daunt the memory of the past and stupefy the future. King Cluay Pandamon erected an arcade of nine hundred crystal columns sixty feet tall, supporting a prismatic glass roof. King Pharay Pandamon ordained a market pavilion of startling ingenuity. In a circular lake curved glass hulls were joined to form twelve floating concentric rings, each twenty feet wide, separated by bearings so that each ring floated free of those to either side. On these floating ways merchants and craftsmen established a bazaar, each booth isolated from its neighbour by a panel of coloured glass. In a sub-surface way round the lake, a hundred bullocks pulled the outside ring into slow rotation, which, through the agency of the water surrounding the hulls, gradually impelled the inner rings to rotations. Every six hours the bullocks reversed the rotational direction of the outer ring, and presently the rings all rotated at various speeds in different directions, presenting a succession of shifting colours and shadows: this the market bazaar built by King Pharay Pandamon.

During the reign of King Jorje Shkurkane, Garwiy reached its peak. The slopes of the Ushkadel glittered with palaces; at the Jardeen docks glass ships unloaded the wares of the world: fibres, silks, and membranes from North Shant, the meat-products of Palasedra, salts and oxides from the mines of Caraz for the production of glass. All sixty-two cantons contributed to the glory of Garwiy; the Pandamon Bailiff was a familiar sight in the far corners of Shant. During King Kharene's unlucky reign, the south revolted; the Palasedran Eagle-Dukes crossed the Great Salt Bog to spark the Fourth Palasedran War, which terminated the Pandamon Dynasty.

During the Sixth Palasedran War Palasedran bombardiers established themselves on the Ushkadel Ridges, from where they were able to lob air-mines into the old city. Fountain after fountain of antique glass spurted high into the sunlight. At last the War lord Viana Paizifume launched his furious uphill assault, which subsequently became the substance of legend. With his cataphracts destroyed, his Elite Pikes dazed and leaderless, his Glass Darts cramped against the base of the cliff, Paizifume destroyed the Palasedran host with a horde of crazed ahulphs, daubed with tar, set afire and directed up the Ushkadel. Victory was a poor exchange for Garwiy shattered; the deed brought the Palasedrans a permanent legacy of distrust and bitterness.

Viana Paizifume, from Canton Glirris on the east coast, refused to allow another Pandamon upon the Purple Throne and called a conclave of the cantons to form a new government. After three weeks of bickering and caprice, Paizifume's patience was exhausted. Mounting to the podium, he indicated a platform on which a screen had been arranged.

"Beyond that screen," decreed Paizifume, "sits your new ruler. I will not tell you his name; you will know him only by his edicts, which I shall enforce. Do you understand the virtue of this arrangement? When you do not know your ruler, you will be unable to plot, wheedle, or suborn. Justice at last is possible."

Did the first Faceless Man actually stand behind the screen? Or had Viana Paizifume invented an invisible *alter ego*? No one knew than or ever. However, when at last Paizifume was assassinated, the plotters were immediately apprehended, sealed into glass balls and suspended on a cable running between a pair of spires. For a thousand years the balls hung like baubles until one by one they were struck by lightning and destroyed.

For a period the Faceless Man enforced his commands by means of a coercive corps, which gradually assumed improper prerogatives and stimulated a revolt. The Conservative Counsel quelled the revolt, disbanded the Coercive Corps, and restored order. The Faceless Man appeared before the counsel in armour of black glass, with a black glass helmet to conceal his identity. He demanded and was conceded greater power and greater responsibility. For twenty years the total energies of Shant were expended in the perfection of the torc system. The Magenta Edict decreed torcs for all and stimulated further strife: the Hundred Years War, which ended only when the last citizen had been clamped into his torc.

Garwiy never regained its Pandamon magnificence but still was reckoned the first wonder of Durdane. There were towers of blue glass, spires of purple glass, green

133

glass domes, prisms and pillars, walls of clear glass glinting and glittering in the sunlight. At night coloured lamps illuminated the city: green lamps behind blue and purple glass, pink lamps behind blue glass.

The palaces up the Ushkadel still housed the patricians of Garwiy, but these were a far cry from the flamboyant grandees of the Pandamon Era. They drew their income from country estates, from shipping, from the laboratories and workshops where torcs, radios, glowbulbs, a few other electronic devices, were assembled, using components produced elsewhere in Shant: monomolecule conductor strands, semiorganic electron-control devices, magnetic cores of sintered ironweb, a few trifles of copper, gold, silver, lead, for connections and switches. No technician comprehended the circuits he used; whatever the original degree of theoretical knowledge, it now had become lore: a mastery of techniques rather than of principles. The workshops and factories were located in the industrial suburb Shranke on the Jardeen River; the workers lived nearby in pleasant cottages among gardens and orchards.

This, then, was Garwiy: a metropolis of considerable area but no great population, a place of entrancing beauty enhanced by antiquity and the weight of history.

The people of Garwiy were unique – hyper-civilized, sensitive to all varieties of aesthetic distinction but not themselves particularly creative. The Aesthetic Society, with a membership of patricians from the Ushkadel, administered civic functions, which the ordinary folk of Garwiy found right and proper. The patricians had the money; it was right that they should accept the responsibilities. The typical citizen felt no resentment towards the patricians; he was equal before the law. If by dint of cleverness or energy he acquired a fortune and bought a place, he was taken into the Aesthetic Society as a matter of course. After two or three generations as parvenus, his descendants might regard themselves as Aesthetes in their own right. This typical citizen was a complicated person: suave and civil, vivacious, fickle, frivolous, and somewhat brittle. He was voluptuous but critical; complacent but demanding; fashion-conscious but amused by eccentricity. He was gregarious but introverted; knowledgeable regarding every green facet and purple glint of his wonderful city, current with the latest entertainments, uninterested in the rest of Shant. He was not deeply moved by music and had no great patience with the traditions of the druithines or the musical troupes; he preferred facetious ballads, songs with topical references, entertainers with eccentric antics: in short, all the manifestations detested by the musician.

He regarded his torc as a necessary evil and occasionally made a satirical reference to the Faceless Man, for whom he felt a half-contemptuous awe. Somewhere along the Ushkadel the Faceless Man reputedly lived in a palace; the question of his identity was a constant titillation for the man of Garwiy. He seldom if ever exercised his right of petition; this facility was reserved for the outlander, whom Garwiy folk liked to consider a yokel. He had heard mention of the Roguskhoi and perhaps wondered at their peculiar habits, but his interest went little further. To the Garwiy man the wildlands of the Hwan were almost as remote as the centre of Caraz.

The sun toppled south towards the winter solstice; Durdane at the same time entered that sector of its orbit where the suns occulted: a situation intensifying seasonal contrasts. Cold air from Nimmir brought autumnal winds to the north of Shant.

The balloon *Shostrel*, leaving Angwin, spun down
135

the Great Transverse at extraordinary speeds, out of the Wildlands into Shade, then Fairlea, and past Brassei Junction where Etzwane turned an expressionless glance west, to where Frolitz presumably anticipated his early arrival; through Cantons Conduce, Maiy, Wild Rose, each jealous of its unique identity, and at last into Canton Garwiy. Down the Vale of Silence they veered at fifty miles an hour, along the line of clear glass tablets, each encasing the monumental effigy of a dynastic king. The poses were identical; the kings stood with right feet slightly forward, forefingers pointing at the ground, the faces wearing sombre, almost puzzled expressions, eyes staring ahead, as if in contemplation of an astounding future.

The wind-tender began to slacken his warps; the *Shostrel* sailed at an easier pace through the Jardeen Gap and into Garwiy Station. Brakes slowed the running dolly; a Judas was snatched to the guys so expertly that the balloon came to ground in a continuous even motion.

Etzwane alighted, followed by Ifness. With a polite nod Ifness walked off across the station plaza, to turn into Kavalesko Passway, which led under a tower of dark blue glass ribbed with water-blue pilasters, and into Kavalesko Avenue.* Etzwane shrugged and went his way.

Frolitz customarily made resort at Fontenay's Inn, north of the plaza, beside the Jardeen, where the management provided meals and lodging in return for a few evenings of music. To Fontenay's Inn Etzwane now betook himself. He called for stylus and paper and immediately set to work drafting the petition that he planned to submit on the following day.

* The twelve avenues radiating from the Aesthetic Corporation Plaza were named for Chama Reya avatars.

Two hours later Etzwane finished the document. He gave it a final reading and could find no fault; it seemed clear and uncompromising, with no sacrifice of calm reason. It read:

To the attention of the ANOME:

During my recent visit to the lowlands of the Hwan, in Canton Bastern, I observed the effects of a Roguskhoi raid upon the Chilite community Bashon. Considerable property damage occurred: a tannery and certain out-buildings were demolished. A large number of women were abducted and subsequently killed under distressing circumstances.

It has become well known that the Wildlands of the Hwan are a haven for those noxious savages, who therefore are free to maraud and plunder at will. Each year they wax both in numbers and audacity. It is my opinion that all Roguskhoi now resident in Shant should be destroyed by a stern and unremitting effort. I suggest that a suitable militia be recruited, trained, and armed. Coincidentally, a study should be made of the Roguskhoi, their habits, their preferred resorts. When all is prepared, the militia, using disciplined tactics, should penetrate the Hwan, attack and expunge the Roguskhoi.

In broad outline, this is my petition. I realize that I propose a major governmental operation, but in my opinion such action is necessary.

The time was late afternoon: too late to present the petition. Etzwane crossed the Jardeen and strolled through Pandamon Park where the north wind sent autumn leaves scurrying past his feet. He came to the

137

Aeolian Hall, a musical instrument of pearl-grey glass three hundred feet long. Wind collected by scoops was directed into a plenum. The operator worked rods and keys to let pent air move one, two, a dozen, or a hundred from among the ten thousand sets of glass chimes. A person who wandered the hall experienced audible dimension, with sound coming from various directions: tinkling chords, whispers of vaguely heard melody, thin, glassy shiverings, the crystal-pure tones of the centre gongs; hurried gusts racing the ceiling like ripples across a pond; fateful chimes, pervasive and melancholy as a buoy bell heard through the fog. On occasion the entire ceiling would seem to burst into sound.

With the north wind at its full weight, Etzwane heard the hall at its best; at twilight he crossed the river and dined in one of Garwiy's splendid restaurants under a hundred pink and lavender lamps – an experience he had heretofore denied himself. The money he had hoarded over the years: what was its purpose? It represented grief and futility; he would spend it as fast as possible, frivol it away. His sobre second self quickly interposed a veto. He would do no such thing. Money so hardly come by should not be lightly dissipated. But tonight, at least, he would enjoy his meal, and he forced himself to do so. The courses were set before him by a pretty waitress. Etzwane considered her with sombre interest; she seemed amiable, with a mouth that seemed always twitching on the verge of a smile. He ate: the viands were prepared and presented to perfection. The meal came to an end. Etzwane wanted to talk to the waitress but felt too shy. In any event she was of Garwiy, and he was an outlander; she would consider him quaint. He wondered as to the whereabouts of Frolitz, even of the uncommunicative Ifness. In a fretful mood he returned to the inn. He looked into the tavern, which was composed and quiet; no musicians were on hand. Etzwane took himself to bed.

In the morning he visited a haberdasher who fitted him out with new clothes: a white tunic with a high flaring collar, dark green breeches buckled at the ankles, black ahulph-leather boots with silver-wood clasps. He had never before owned an outfit so dashing. He was not altogether convinced that the figure in the carbon-fume mirror was himself. A barber trimmed his hair and shaved him with a glass razor. On a sudden impulse, as if to defy the jeers from his under-brain, he bought a rakish little cap with a medallion of coloured glass. The image of himself in the mirror aroused a complicated emotion: disgust and wonder for his own folly, with a trace of ebullience, as if whatever flamboyant traits he had inherited from Dystar were pushing to make themselves felt. Etzwane shrugged and grimaced; he had spent the money; now he must wear the cap. He stepped out into the blazing lavender noon light; the glass of Garwiy flashed and glittered.

Etzwane walked slowly to the Corporation Plaza. To buy a five-hundred-florin petition, to assert his views, must bring him to the attention of the Faceless Man. Well, what, then? His concerns were valid; his petition was legal. They expressed honest anxiety; by his own assertion the Faceless Man was servant to the people of Shant!

Etzwane crossed the Corporation Plaza to the long, low structure of magenta glass where once before he had come. The front wall supported a panel of dull purple satin to which were pinned petitions and the Faceless Man's response. Twenty or thirty folk, in a variety of cantonal costumes, stood waiting at the five-florin window. They had come from every corner of Shant with their grievances; as they stood in line, they

139

watched the passing folk of Garwiy with truculent expressions. Nearby were more dignified precincts for those earnest enough to buy a hundred-florin petition. At the far end of the building a door distinguished by a purple star opened into the chamber where the very wealthy or the very vehement bought petitions at a cost of five hundred florins.

Through this latter door marched Etzwane without slackening his stride.

The chamber was empty. He was the single petitioner. Behind the counter a man jumped to his feet. "Your wishes, sir?"

Etzwane brought forth his money. "A petition."

"Very well, sir. A matter of grave importance, no doubt."

"This is my opinion."

The clerk brought forth a magenta document, a pen, a dish of black ink; as Etzwane wrote, the clerk counted the money and prepared a receipt.

Etzwane indited his petition, folded it, tucked it into the envelope provided by the clerk, who, examining Etzwane's torc, noted the colour code. "Your name, sir, if it please you?"

"Gastel Etzwane."

"Your native canton?"

"Bastern."

"Very good, sir; that is sufficient."

"When will I have my response?"

The clerk held wide his hands. "How can I answer? The Anome comes and goes; I know no more of his movements than you. In two or three days you might expect to find your response. It must be posted publicly like all the rest; no one may claim that the Anome performs private favours."

Etzwane went off somewhat less briskly than he had

come. The deed was accomplished. He had done all he could; now he must wait upon the decision of the Faceless Man. He climbed a flight of green glass steps to a refreshment garden; the flowers, plants, fronds, and trees were all simulated of blue, green, white and scarlet glass. At a table overlooking the plaza he ate a dish of fruit and hard cheese. He ordered wine and was brought a goblet, slender and high as his lips, of pale cool Pelmonte. He felt dull, deflated. He even felt somewhat absurd. Had he been too bombastic? The Faceless Man surely understood every aspect of the problem; the petition would seem brash and callow. Etzwane glumly sipped his wine. Five hundred florins gone. For what? Expiation of guilt? So that was it. This flinging down of five hundred florins on a useless petition was the way he punished himself. Five hundred hard-earned florins!

Etzwane compressed his lips. He rubbed his forehead with his fingertips. What was done was done. At all events the Faceless Man's reply would provide information regarding counter-Roguskhoi measures now in progress.

Etzwane finished his wine and returned to Fontenay's Inn. He found the proprietor in the pot-room with a trio of cronies. He had been testing his own merchandise and had reached a difficult and captious state.

Etzwane asked politely, "Who plays the music here of evenings?"

The proprietor turned his head to survey Etzwane from head to toe; Etzwane regretted the expensive new clothes. In his old garments he looked the part of a travelling musician.

The proprietor responded curtly: "At the moment, no one."

"In that case I wish to apply for the chair."

"Aha. What are your abilities?"

141

"I am a musician. I often play the khitan."

"A budding young druithine, it seems."

"I do not present myself in such terms," replied Etzwane.

"A singer, then, with three chords and as many bogus dialects?"

"I am a musician, not a singer."

One of the cronies, seeing how the wind blew, held up his goblet and looked through the glass at the contents. "New wine is thin; old wine is rich."

"My own opinion exactly," said the proprietor. "A new musician knows too little, has felt too little; remember the great Aladar Szantho? He secluded himself fourteen years. Now, with no reflection upon either your aptitudes or potentialities, how could you interest a mature and knowledgeable company?"

"You will never know until you hear me."

"You refuse to be daunted? Very well, you shall play. I pay nothing unless you attract custom into the tavern, which I doubt."

"I expect no pay," said Etzwane, "other than my board and lodging."

"I can't even agree to that until I hear you. Garwiy is not a city which takes to outland music. If you could hypnotize toads or recite lewd verse or sing topical ballads or roll your eyes in opposite circles, that is another matter."

"I can only play music," said Etzwane. "My fee, if any, I will leave to your generosity. Is there a khitan on the premises?"

"You will find one or two such in the cupboard yonder."

Three days passed. Etzwane played in the pot-room, well enough to amuse the customers and satisfy the proprietor. He attempted no bravura and used the rattle-box with a delicate elbow.

On the third night, with the time growing late, the mood came upon him, and he struck the idle chords of the druithine commencing a reverie. He played a reflective melody and a minor retrospect. Music is the result of experience, he thought; he had had sufficient experience to be a musician. Admittedly some of his emotions were raw, and some of his chords were played with his knee too hard against the brilliancy lever. The awareness of this came to Etzwane; he changed, almost in midphrase, to soft, quiet passages. He noticed that the company had become attentive. Before he had been playing in an abstraction; now he felt self-conscious. Modulating into a set of conventional chords, he finished. He was afraid to raise his eyes and look out over the company. Might they have felt what he felt? Or were they smiling at his excesses? He put down the instrument and stepped from the chair.

To confront Frolitz. Who faced him with a queer half smile. "The sublime young druithine! Who performs his fantastic surprises at Fontenay's while his master, poor doddering old Frolitz, prays for his return at Brassei."

"I can explain everything," said Etzwane.

"Your mother is well, I hope?"

"She is dead."

" 'Dead' is a sour word," said Frolitz. He scratched his nose, drank from his mug, looked over his shoulder. "The troupe is here. Shall we play music?"

On the following morning Etzwane (again wearing his new garments) went to the Corporation Plaza and across to the Office of Petitions. To the left, grey cards gave answers to the five-florin petitions: adjudications

143

of petty disputes, actions for damage, complaints against local restrictions. In the centre, sheets of pale-green parchment, pinned to the board with emerald-glass cabochons, decided hundred-florin actions. At the far right documents of vellum with surrounding bands of black and purple announced responses to the five-hundred-florin petitions. Only three of these were posted on the board.

Etzwane could hardly restrain his strides as he crossed the plaza; the last few steps he almost ran.

He scanned the purple-and-black-bordered documents. The first read:

> Lord Fiatz Ergold, having called for the ANOME'S intercession against the unusually harsh judgement rendered in Canton Amaze against his son, the Honourable Arlet, now may hear: The ANOME has requested a transcript of the proceedings and will study the case. The cited penalty appears disproportionate to the offence. Lord Fiatz Ergold however must know that an act merely vulgar or inopportune in one canton is a capital offence in the next. The ANOME, despite sympathy for Lord Fiatz Ergold, may not in justice contravene local laws. However, if circumstances warrant, the ANOME will pray for leniency.

The second read:

> The gentlewoman Casuelda Adrio is advised that, notwithstanding her anger and concern, the punishment she urges for the man Andrei Simic will not beneficially repair circumstances as they now exist.

The third read:

144

For the attention of the gentleman Gastel Etzwane and the other worthy folk who have expressed concern for the Roguskhoi bandits in the Wildlands of the Hwan, the ANOME counsels a calm mien. These disgusting creatures will never dare to venture down from the wilderness; their depredations are not likely to molest folk who make it their business to avoid reckless exposure of themselves and their properties.

Etzwane leaned forward, gaping in disbelief. His hand went to his torc, the unconscious gesture of Shant folk when they reflected in regard to the Faceless Man. He looked again. The statement read exactly as it had originally. With a trembling hand Etzwane reached to claw the document from the display board. He restrained himself. Let it stay. In fact . . .

He brought a stylus from his pocket; he wrote on the parchment:

The Roguskhoi are murderous beasts! The Faceless Man says ignore them while they kill and plunder.

The Roguskhoi infest our lands. The Faceless Man says keep out of their way.

Viana Paizifume would have spoken differently.

Etzwane drew back from the board, suddenly abashed. His act was close to sedition, for which the Faceless Man had little patience. Anger flooded Etzwane again. Sedition, intemperance, insubordination. How could affairs be otherwise? Any man must be prompted to outrage by policy so bland and unresponsive! He looked around the plaza in trepidation and defiance. None of the folk nearby paid him any close attention. He noticed a man strolling slowly across the

145

square, head bowed as if in cogitation. It was surely Ifness. He seemed not to have observed Etzwane, though he must have passed only thirty feet from the Petitioners' Board. On a sudden impulse Etzwane ran after him.

Ifness looked around without surprise. He seemed, thought Etzwane, even more placid than usual. Etzwane said, somewhat grimly, "I saw you pass, and I thought to pay my respects."

"Thank you," said Ifness. "How go your affairs?"

"Well enough. I am back with Master Frolitz; we play at Fontenay's Inn. You should come by and hear our music."

"A pleasant thought. Unluckily I fear I will be occupied. You seem to have altered your style." His glance indicated Etzwane's garments.

Etzwane scowled. "The clothes are nothing. A waste of money."

"And your petition to the Faceless Man: Have you had a response?"

Etzwane stared at him stonily, wondering if Ifness enjoyed subterfuge for its own sake; surely Ifness had noticed him at the board! He said carefully, "I bought the petition at a cost of five hundred florins. The answer has been posted. It is yonder."

He led Ifness to the board. Ifness read with his head thrust slightly forward. "Hmm," said Ifness. Then in a sharp voice, "Who wrote the remarks at the bottom of the sheet?"

"I did."

"*What!*" Ifness's voice was vibrant. Etzwane had never before seen him exercised. "Do you realize that in the building opposite a telescope is fixed on this board! You scribble your callow and irrelevant complaints,

146

then stalk grandly over to implicate me. Do you realize that you are about to lose your head? Now we are both in danger."

Etzwane started to make a hot retort, but Ifness's gesture cut him short. "Act naturally; do not pose or posture. Cross to the Pomegranate Portal; continue slowly along. I must alter certain arrangements."

His head whirling, Etzwane crossed the plaza, moving with as natural a stride as he could muster. He looked towards the Aesthetic Corporation offices, from which, so Ifness averred, the board was telescopically monitored. The objective lens might well be that particularly lucid glass boss directly opposite the board. The Faceless Man hardly sat with his own eyes glued to the lens; a functionary no doubt kept vigil. The telescope would readily pick up the colours in Etzwane's torc; when he turned away, the man's curiosity would hold on him, and he would have observed the colloquy with Ifness.

If all were as Ifness declared. At least, thought Etzwane, he had startled Ifness from his supercilious calm.

He passed through the Pomegranate Portal, so called for festoons of dark scarlet fruit, into Serven Airo Way beyond.

Ifness caught up with him. "It is possible that your act went unnoticed," said Ifness. "But I cannot risk even one chance in ten."

Etzwane, still surly, said, "I understand none of your actions."

"Still, you would prefer not to lose your head?" asked Ifness in his most silky voice.

Etzwane gave a noncommittal grunt.

"Here is the situation," said Ifness. "The Faceless Man will shortly learn of your acts. He may well take your head; he has already taken the heads of three per-

147

sons who have pushed too hard in this connection. I propose to prevent this. Next I intend to learn the identity of the Faceless Man. Then I will urge him to alter his policy."

Etzwane looked at Ifness in awe. "Can you do this?"

"I intend to try. You may be able to assist me."

"Why have you formed such plans? They are surprising!"

"Why did you file a five-hundred-florin petition?"

"You know my motives," said Etzwane stiffly.

"Exactly," said Ifness. "It gives me reason to trust in your participation. Walk faster. We are not being followed. Turn to the right at the Old Rotunda."

Passing from the city of glass, they walked a quarter mile north along the Avenue of the Thasarene Directors, into a lane shaded by tall blue-green hedges, through a gap to a small cottage of pale blue tile. Ifness unlocked the door, ushered Etzwane within. "Take off your jacket quickly."

Etzwane sulkily obeyed the instructions. Ifness indicated a couch. "Lie down, on your face."

Again Etzwane obeyed. Ifness wheeled over a table on which rested an assortment of tools. Etzwane rose from the couch to examine them; Ifness curtly told him to lie back. "Now, on your life, do not move."

Ifness switched on a bright light and clamped Etzwane's torc in a small vice. He slipped a metal strip between the torc and Etzwane's neck, then clipped a u-shaped device to the strip. He touched a button; the device set up a soft hum; Etzwane felt a tingle of vibration. "Electron flow is impeded," said Ifness. "It is safe to open your torc." With a spinning razor-sharp wheel he sliced the flexite of the torc along its seam. Putting the tool aside, he split the torc open, then, with a long-nose pliers, he drew forth a length of black soft stuff.

148

"The dexax is removed." With a hooked rod he worked at the internal lock. The torc fell away from Etzwane's neck.

"You are no longer subject to the control of the Faceless Man," said Ifness.

Etzwane rubbed his neck, which felt thin-skinned and naked. Rising from the couch, he looked slowly from the torc to Ifness. "How did you learn to do this?"

"You will remember the torcs I salvaged on Gargament Meadow. I studied these with great care." He indicated the interior of Etzwane's torc. "These are the coded receptors; this is a trigger mechanism. If a signal comes through from the Faceless Man, this fibre jerks to detonate the explosive. Off comes your head. This is the echo relay, which allows the Faceless Man to discover your whereabouts; it is now inoperative. These nodules I believe to be energy accumulators."

He stood frowning down at the device so long that Etzwane became restless and donned his tunic.

Ifness finally said, "If I were the Faceless Man, I might well suspect a cabal, of which Gastel Etzwane was not the most important member. I would not instantly take Etzwane's head, but I would use the echo circuit to locate him and investigate his activities."

"That seems reasonable enough," said Etzwane grudgingly.

"On this basis," said Ifness, "I will attach a signal to your torc; if and when the Faceless Man tries to locate you, we will be warned." He busied himself. "When he receives no return signal, he must assume that you have left the district, and we will have verified his interest in Gastel Etzwane. Above all, I do not wish to alarm him or put him on his guard."

Etzwane asked the question that long had been at the front of his mind. "What, in fact, are your wishes?"

"I hardly know," Ifness murmured. "My perplexity is greater than your own."

Sudden illumination came to Etzwane. "You are a Palasedran! You come to observe the work of the Roguskhoi!"

"Not true." Ifness, seating himself on a couch, regarded Etzwane with a passionless gaze. "Like yourself, I wonder at the Roguskhoi and the Faceless Man's unconcern. Like yourself, I have been prompted to action. It is no less illicit for me than for you."

"What kind of action do you plan?" Etzwane asked cautiously.

"My first goal must be to identify the Faceless Man," said Ifness. "After that I will be guided by events."

"You claim not to be Palasedran," said Etzwane. "Nevertheless, this remains a possibility."

"My conduct in Mirk Valley was that of a Palasedran?"

Etzwane reflected upon Ifness's action. In no respect had Palasedran interests been advanced, or so it would seem. And the tools on the table: marvellous things! Of shining metal, of substances to which he could put no name – but not Palasedran. "If you are not Palasedran, what are you? Certainly no man of Shant."

Ifness leaned back on the couch, an expression of intense boredom on his face. "With churlish persistence you press for information I clearly do not wish to extend. Since your cooperation now becomes useful, I am forced to make certain disclosures. You have discerned that I am not a man of Shant. I am, in fact, an Earthman, a Fellow of the Historical Institute. Are you any the wiser?"

Etzwane surveyed him with a fierce gaze. "Earth is a real place?"

"Very real indeed."

"Why are you here on Shant?"

Ifness spoke in a patient voice. "The folk who came to Durdane nine thousand years ago were secretive and eccentric; they marooned themselves and sank their spaceships in the Purple Ocean. On Earth Durdane is long forgotten – except by the Historical Institute. I am the latest in a succession of Fellows resident upon Durdane – and possibly the first to ignore the First Law of the Institute: Fellows may never interfere in the affairs of the worlds they study. We are organized as a fact-gathering association, and we so restrict ourselves. My conduct in regard to the Faceless Man is absolutely illicit; in the purview of the Institute I am a criminal."

"Why, then, did you concern yourself?" Etzwane demanded. "Because of the Roguskhoi raids?"

"My motives need not concern you. Your interests, so far as they go, are concurrent with mine; I do not care to be more explicit."

Etzwane ran his hand through his hair and sank back down upon the couch opposite to that on which Ifness sat. "These are great surprises." He warily studied Ifness. "Are there other Earthmen on Durdane?"

Ifness replied in the negative. "The Historical Institute spreads its personnel thin."

"How do you move between here and Earth?"

"Again, this is information I prefer to keep to myself."

Before Etzwane could make an irritated reply, his torc produced a sharp buzzing sound. Ifness jumped to his feet; in one long stride he was at the torc. The buzzing stopped, leaving a silence that had a weighty and sinister quality of its own. Somewhere, thought Etzwane, the Faceless Man had turned away from his instruments frowning.

"Excellent!" Ifness declared. "The Faceless Man is

151

interested in you. We will persuade him to reveal himself."

"All very well," said Etzwane, "but how?"

"A tactical exercise, which we will discuss presently. At the moment I wish to resume the business which your presence in the Plaza interrupted. I was about to dine."

The two returned to the Corporation Plaza; here they kept to the peripheral arcade, beyond the purview of the observer in the Corporation Centre. Etzwane looked towards the Office of Petitions; the purple-and-black-bordered document was no longer to be seen. He informed Ifness of the fact.

"Another evidence of the Anome's sensitivity," said Ifness in an abstracted voice. "Our work will be the easier on this account."

"How so?" demanded Etzwane, ever more irritated by Ifness's condescension.

Ifness looked sidewise with raised eyebrows and spoke in a patient voice: "We must induce the Faceless Man to reveal himself. A quail cannot be seen until it moves; so with the Faceless Man. We must generate a situation which he will wish to inspect in his own person, rather than relying upon his Benevolences. The fact of his sensitivity makes such a reaction more likely."

Etzwane gave a sardonic grunt. "Just so. What situation do we generate?"

"It is a matter we must discuss. First, let us dine."

They seated themselves in the loggia of the Old Pagane Restaurant; their meal was set before them. Ifness stinted himself nothing. Etzwane, unsure whether or not he might be required to pay his own score, dined less lavishly. In the end, however, Ifness laid down money for both meals and leaned back to sip the dessert wine. "Now, to our business. The Faceless Man returned a polite response to your five hundred florins and in fact evinced interest only when you noted your dissatisfaction. This calibrates one of our parameters."

Etzwane wondered where all this was leading.

Ifness mused: "We must act within bounds of Garwiy law, to give the Aesthetic Corporation no pretext for action. Perhaps we will offer an informative lecture on the Roguskhoi and promise startling revelations. The Faceless Man has demonstrated his concern in regard to this subject; in all probability he will be interested enough to attend."

Etzwane agreed that such a contingency was possible. "But who will give such a lecture?"

"That is a matter to be carefully considered," said Ifness. "Let us return to the cottage. Again I must modify your torc so that it becomes a tool of aggression rather than a mere warning device."

In the cottage once more, Ifness worked two hours on the modification of Etzwane's torc. At last he completed his work. A pair of inconspicuous wires now led to a coil of fifty turns tied down upon a square of stiff fibre board. "This is a directional antenna," said Ifness.

"You will wear the coil under your shirt. Warning signals inside the torc will notify you when an attempt is being made either to locate you or to take your head. By turning, you will maximize the signals and thus determine their direction. Allow me now to place the torc around your neck."

Etzwane submitted without enthusiasm. "It seems," he grumbled, "that I am to function as bait."

Ifness allowed himself a frosty smile. "Something of the sort. Now listen carefully. The explosive impulse you will feel as a vibration against the back of your neck. The locator pulse will be received as a vibration at the right side. In either case, turn until you maximize

153

the vibration. The source will then be directly in front of you."

Etzwane nodded grimly. "And what of you?"

"I will carry a similar device. With luck we should be able to strike a fix upon our subject."

"And what if we are unlucky?"

"This, to be frank, is my expectation. Such facile success is too much to hope for. We may startle our quail on this occasion, but other quail may move as well and so confuse us. But I will carry my camera; we will at least have an exact record of the occasion."

CHAPTER TEN

At those places throughout Garwiy designated for the display of public announcements appeared large placards printed in brown and black on white paper with a yellow border: colours to signify dire and fateful import, with overtones of the sensationally macabre.

The ROGUSKHOI EXPOSED!

Who are these horrid savages who ravage and rape, who torment our land? Where do they come from? What is their plan?

AN ANONYMOUS ADVENTURER JUST RETURNED FROM THE HWAN WILL REVEAL STARTLING FACTS AND EVEN MORE STARTLING SUSPICIONS. WHO SHARES THE BLAME FOR THIS INFESTATION? YOU WILL HEAR AN AMAZING ACCUSATION!

MIDAFTERNOON KYALISDAY
AT THE PUBLIC PAVILION
IN PANDAMON PARK

On a hundred bulletin boards the placards were posted, and even the folk of Garwiy took notice, reading the placards once, twice, a third time. Ifness was pleased with the effect. "The Faceless Man will not ignore this. Yet we give neither him nor the Corporation cause to interfere."

Etzwane said sourly, "I'd rather that you were the 'anonymous adventurer'."

Ifness laughed – in high good humour. "What? The

talented Gastel Etzwane uncomfortable before an audience? What happens when you play one of your instruments?"

"That is different."

"Possibly so. But as the 'anonymous adventurer' I could not use my camera. You have memorized the material?"

"As much as needs be," growled Etzwane. "In all candour, I dislike acting as your cat's-paw. I do not care to be seized by the Discriminators* and clapped off to Stonebreakers' Island while you dine on pomfret and inger eggs at the Old Pagane."

"Unlikely," said Ifness. "Not impossible but unlikely."

Etzwane merely grunted. As an "anonymous adventurer" he wore a bulky cape of black fur, square and wide across the shoulders, with sand-coloured breeches and black boots: the garments of a Canton Shkoriy mountaineer. The medallion of his torc showed at his neck; the designation "musician" was not at odds with the role of "adventurer". Slender, taut, his face keen and quick-featured, Gastel Etzwane cut a gallant figure in the mountaineer's costume; insensibly it affected his stride, his mannerisms, his mode of thought. He had become in fact the "anonymous adventurer". Ifness wearing dark grey trousers, a loose white shirt, a soft grey jacket, was as usual. If Ifness felt any emotion, he gave no indication; Etzwane found it difficult to control his nervousness.

They arrived at Pandamon Park.

"A half hour to the midafternoon chime," said Ifness. "A fair number of folk are about; all idle wanderers, or

* *Avistioi:* literally, "nice discriminators": the constabulary of the Aesthetic Corporation.

156

so I suspect. No person of Garwiy is early for an event. Those who come to hear the scandal will arrive one minute before the chime."

"What if none arrive?" asked Etzwane in melancholy hopefulness.

"There will be some," said Ifness, "including the Faceless Man, who cannot be happily anticipating the occasion. He may even post a Discriminator to discourage the speech. I suspect, however, that he will listen, then act as circumstances dictate. We must stimulate him to push his 'explode' button."

"And when I retain my head?"

"The torc circuits must occasionally fail; he will conclude that such is the case and send forth other impulses. Remember the signal I have stipulated."

"Yes, yes," muttered Etzwane. "I hope he doesn't become dissatisfied with his explosive and shoot me with a gun."

"A risk we must take ... The time is still twenty minutes to the chime. Let us stand in the shadows yonder and rehearse the matter of your address."

The midafternoon chime sounded. From the foliage came the "anonymous adventurer". Looking neither right nor left, walking with something of a swagger, he approached the rostrum. He went to the rear, climbed the white-glass steps, and approached the lectern. He stopped short to study the magenta-bordered notice on the green-glass surface.

It was the Faceless Man's reaction, and it read:

> Your advertisement has excited the interest of the ANOME himself. He requests discretion, that you may not jeopardize certain very sensitive investigations. The ANOME'S opinion is this: the

157

Roguskhoi are a nuisance, a tribe of disreputable folk already on the decline. A person properly informed will stress the minor and transitory aspects of the matter, or he might even wish to discuss a subject of more general interest.

Etzwane put down the notice. He examined the faces that had collected around the rostrum. A hundred persons stood watching; as many more sat on benches. To the left stood Ifness; he had pulled a merchant's hood over his soft white hair and by some peculiar alteration of pose now seemed one with the others. Did the Faceless Man stand among the people present? Etzwane looked from face to face. There: that hollow-cheeked man with the lank black hair and burning eyes. Or that small man yonder with the high round forehead, the delicate mouth. Or the handsome Aesthete in the green cloak with the neat fringe of black beard along his jaw. Or the stern man in the plum-coloured habit of the Eclectic God-head. Others, still others.

Etzwane wasted a moment or two longer, steeling himself to immobility. The audience had now assembled. Etzwane leaned forward and began to speak, and because of the magenta-bordered notice he altered his remarks.

"In my advertisements I promised remarkable information; this I will provide – immediately." He held up the notice. "The illustrious Anome himself has demonstrated an interest in my remarks. Listen to his advice!" Etzwane read the notice in a studiously solemn voice; when he looked up, he saw that he had indeed interested his audience; they gazed at him in wonder. Ifness, so Etzwane saw, studied the crowd with care. He carried an inconspicuous camera and took many pictures.

Etzwane frowned at the document. "I am pleased

158

that the Anome considers my ideas significant, especially since his other informants have misled him. 'A minor and transitory' nuisance? The Anome should take the head of the man who so deceived him. The Roguskhoi threaten everyone who now hears me. They are not 'a tribe of disreputable folk' – as the Anome innocently believes. They are ruthless, well-armed warriors, and they are sexual maniacs as well. Do you know their habit? They do not copulate normally; instead they seed a woman with a dozen imps which are born while she sleeps, and never again can she bear a human child – though she can bear another dozen imps. Every woman alive in Garwiy now may conceivably mother a brood or two of Roguskhoi imps.

"The Hwan Wildlands swarm with Roguskhoi. In the cantons bordering the Hwan it is an accepted fact that the Roguskhoi have been sent from Palasedra.

"The situation is remarkable, is it not? Reputable folk have implored the Anome to destroy these terrible creatures. He refuses; in fact, he takes their heads. Why? Ask yourself. Why does the Faceless Man, our protector, scoff at this peril?"

Vibrations jarred at the back of Etzwane's neck: the explosive circuit. The Faceless Man was angry. Etzwane swung around to maximize the vibrations. They ceased before he could make a fix as to their direction. He clenched his left hand: the signal to Ifness.

Ifness nodded and studied the crowd with even more intense interest than before.

Etzwane spoke on: "Why does the Faceless Man deprecate so imminent a threat? Why does he write a document urging me to 'discretion?' Friends, I ask a question; I do not answer it. Is the Faceless Man –"

The vibrations struck again. Etzwane swung around but again could not decide upon the source of the pulses. He looked straight at the cold-eyed man in green, who stared back at him, gravely intent.

The directional antenna, at least with respect to the killer pulses, was a failure. It was pointless to provoke the Faceless Man to a state where he might use a weapon less subtle. Etzwane modified the tone of his discourse. "The question I wish to ask is this: has the Faceless Man become old? Has he lost his zest? Should he perhaps pass on his responsibilities to a man with more energy and decision?"

Etzwane looked around the group to see who responded to the question. Here he was disappointed; the folk in the audience all looked around as well, more interested in the others than themselves. (They knew their own ideas; how did the others feel?)

Etzwane spoke on in a voice of spurious docility. He held up the magenta-bordered notice. "In deference to the Anome, I will reveal no more secrets. I may say that I am not alone in my concern; I speak for a group of persons dedicated to the safety of Shant. I go now to make my report. In a week I will speak again, when I hope to recruit others into this group."

Etzwane jumped down from the rostrum and to avoid idle questions set off at a brisk pace in the direction from which he had come. As he walked, he touched the switch in his torc to activate the echo circuit. From the shelter of the foliage he looked back. The Aesthete in green strolled after him without haste. Behind the Aesthete, no less casual, came Ifness. Etzwane turned, hurried on. A vibration struck against the right side of his neck: someone had sent out a questing radiation.

Etzwane went directly to the blue tile cottage north of Garwiy.

As he passed along Elemyra Way, east of the Corporation Plaza, his torc vibrated a second time, again as he entered the Avenue of the Thasarene Directors, again as he turned down the hedge-shaded lane. Once within the cottage Etzwane slipped out of the clumsy black cloak, unclasped the torc and set it on the table. Leaving the cottage by the back door, he went to where he could survey the road.

Half an hour passed. Along the lane came a man in a hooded dark green cloak. His eyes were very keen; he looked constantly right and left and occasionally down at an object he held in his hand. At the gap in the hedge he stopped short, the instrument in his hand resonating to the pulse echoed from Etzwane's torc inside the cottage.

Stealthy as a thief, the man looked up and down the lane, peered along the path at the cottage; slipping quickly through the gap, he took shelter behind a lime tree. Here stood Etzwane, who sprang forward. The man was enormously strong; Etzwane clung with feet and one arm and with the other slapped the man on the side of the neck with the needle-sack Ifness had supplied.

Almost at once the man's activity lessened; a moment later he fell to his hands and knees.

Ifness appeared; the two carried the limp body into the cottage. Ifness, instantly setting to work, removed the man's torc. Etzwane switched off the echo circuit of his own torc.

Ifness gave an exclamation of dissatisfaction and drew forth a tube of black explosive, which he regarded with vast displeasure.

The man had regained consciousness to find his arms and wrists bound. "You are not the Faceless Man, after all," said Ifness.

"I never claimed to be," said the captive in a cool voice.

"Who are you, then?"

"I am the Aesthete Garstang: a Director of the Corporation."

"It seems that you serve the Faceless Man."

"As do all of us."

"You more than the rest, to judge by your conduct, and by this control box." From the table Ifness picked up the instrument he had taken from Garstang's cloak: a metal box, three inches wide, an inch deep, four inches long. From the top of the case protruded a set of studs, each a different colour. The ten squares of a read-out below displayed the colours of Etzwane's torc.

Below the read-out, on one hand, was a yellow switch, the yellow of death. On the other was a red switch, the red of invisibility – in this case the red of the invisible person being sought.

Ifness set the box on the table. "How do you explain this?"

"It explains itself."

"The yellow button?" Ifness raised his eyebrows.

"Destroy."

"The red button?"

"Find."

"And your exact status?"

"I am what you already know me to be: a Benevolence of the Faceless Man."

"When are you expected to make your report?"

"In an hour or so." Garstang's answers came easily, in a voice without intonation.

"You report in person?"

Garstang gave a chilly laugh. "Hardly. I report into an electric voice-wire; I receive my instructions by postal delivery or through the same voice-wire."

"How many Benevolences are employed?"

"Another besides myself, so I have been told."

"The two Benevolences and the Faceless Man carry boxes such as this?"

"I don't know what the others carry."

Etzwane asked, "The Faceless Man and two Benevolences – only three persons – police all Shant?"

Garstang gave a disinterested shrug. "The Faceless Man could do the job alone, had he a mind."

For a moment there was silence. Ifness and Etzwane studied their captive, who returned the inspection with eyebrows raised in debonair unconcern. Etzwane asked, "Why won't the Faceless Man move against the Roguskhoi?"

"I have no more knowledge than you."

Etzwane said in a brittle voice, "For a man so near to death, you are very easy."

Garstang seemed surprised. "I see no cause to fear death."

"You tried to take my life. Why should I not take yours?"

Garstang gave him a stare of disdainful puzzlement. "I did not try to take your life. I had no such orders."

Ifness held up his hand urgently to still Etzwane's angry retort. "What in fact were your orders?"

"I was to attend the meeting in Pandamon Park; I was to note the speaker's code and follow him to his place of residence; I was there to gather information."

"But you were not instructed to take the speaker's head?"

Garstang started to reply, then turned shrewd, quick glances first towards Etzwane, then Ifness. A change seemed to come over his face. "Why do you ask?"

"Someone attempted to take my head," said Etzwane. "If it wasn't you, it was the Faceless Man."

Garstang shrugged, calculated. "That may well be. But it has nothing to do with me."

"Perhaps not," said Ifness politely. "But now there is no more time for conversation. We must prepare to meet whomever comes to find you. Please turn your back."

Garstang slowly rose to his feet. "What do you plan to do?"

"I will anesthetize you. In a short time, if all goes well, you will be released."

In response Garstang flung himself sideways. He raised his leg in a grotesque prancing gait. "Look out!" screamed Etzwane. "He wears a leg-gun!"

Fire! Glare! Explosion through the cuffs of Garstang's elegant trousers: the tinkle of broken glass; then the thud of Garstang's dead body falling to the floor. Ifness, who had crouched, snatched and fired his hand-gun, stood looking down at the corpse. Etzwane had never seen him so agitated. "I have soiled myself," hissed Ifness. "I have killed what I swore to preserve."

Etzwane gave a snort of disgust. "Here you sob over this dead murderer; but on other occasions, when you might have saved someone, you looked aside."

Ifness turned him a yellow-eyed glare, then, after a moment, spoke in a calm and even voice. "The deed is done. What impelled him to act so desperately? He was helpless." For a moment he stood musing. "Many mysteries remain," he muttered. "Much is obscure." He made a peremptory gesture. "Search the body, drag it to the back shed. I must modify his torc."

An hour later Ifness stood back. "In addition to the 'explode' and 'echo' circuits, I discover a simple vibrator signal as well. I have installed an alarm to inform us when someone seeks Garstang. This time should not be far distant." He went to the door. The suns had rolled behind the Ushkadel; the soft dusk of Garwiy, suffused with a million coloured glooms, settled over the land.

164

"Before us now is a problem in tactics," said Ifness. "First, what have we achieved? A great deal, it seems to me. Garstang has convincingly denied all attempts to take your head, hence we may reasonably put the onus for these acts upon the Faceless Man. We may affirm, therefore, that he came to Pandamon Park and into the range of my camera. If we chose, we might attempt to identify and investigate each of the two hundred persons present – a tedious prospect, however.

"Secondly: What can we next expect of the Faceless Man? He awaits Garstang's report. In view of his failure to take the 'anonymous adventurer's' head, he will be curious, to say the least. Lacking news, he will become first annoyed, then concerned. I would guess that Garstang's report was due an hour ago; we can expect a signal to Garstang's torc in the near future. Garstang, of course, will not respond. The Faceless Man must then either send forth another Benevolence or go himself to find Garstang, using the locator-pulses.

"We have, in fact, a situation analogous to that of this morning. Instead of the 'anonymous adventurer' and his threatened sedition, we now have Garstang's torc to stimulate our quail into motion."

Etzwane gave a grudging acquiescence. "I suppose that this is reasonable enough."

Garstang's torc emitted a thin, clear sound, eerily disturbing the silence, followed by four staccato chirping noises.

Ifness gave a fateful nod. "There: the signal for Garstang to report at once. Time we were moving. The cottage gives us no advantage." He dropped Garstang's torc into a soft black case, then after reflecting a moment added a handful of his exquisite tools.

"If we don't hurry, we'll have the Discriminators around our ears," grumbled Etzwane.

165

"Yes, we must hurry. Switch off the echo circuit in your torc if you have not already done so."

"I have done so, long since."

The two departed the cottage and walked towards Garwiy's complicated skyline. Beyond, along the Ushkadel, a thousand palaces glittered and sparkled Trudging through the dark with Ifness, Etzwane felt like a ghost walking with another ghost; they were two creatures on an eerie errand, estranged from all other folk of Shant. "Where are we going?"

Ifness said mildly, "To a public house, a tavern, something of the sort. We will put Garstang's torc in a secluded spot and watch to see who goes to investigate."

Etzwane could find no fault with the idea. "Fontenay's is yonder, along the river. Frolitz and the troupe will be there."

"As good as any. You, at least, will be provided the camouflage of your instrument."

CHAPTER ELEVEN

Music came through the open door of Fontenay's. Etzwane recognized the fluid lower register of Frolitz's wood-horn, the graceful touch of Fordyce's khitan, Mielke's grave bass tones; he felt a deprivation so great that tears came to his eyes. His previous life, so miserly and pinched, with every florin into his lock-box, now seemed sweet indeed!

They entered and stood in the shadows. Ifness surveyed the premises. "What is that door?"

"It leads to Fontenay's private quarters."

"What about the hall yonder?"

"It leads to the stairs and a back door."

"And what about that door behind Frolitz?"

"It leads into a storeroom where the musicians leave their instruments."

"It should serve. Take Garstang's torc, go into the storeroom for your instrument, and hang the torc somewhere near the door. Then when you come forth –" From within the black bag Garstang's torc produced the whine of the locator circuit. "Someone soon will be here. When you come forth, take a place near the storeroom door. I will sit in this corner. If you notice anything significant, look towards me, then turn your left ear towards what you notice. Do this several times, in case I do not see you the first time, as I will be busy otherwise. . . . Again, where is the rear entrance?"

"Down the hall, past the stairs and to the right."

Ifness nodded. "You are now a musician, a part of the troupe. Don't forget the torc."

Etzwane took the torc, tucked it into his inside pocket. He sauntered up to Frolitz, who gave him an indifferent nod. Etzwane recalled that he had been parted from the troupe only a single day. It seemed as if a month had passed. He went into the storeroom, hung the torc on a peg near the door, and covered it with someone's old jacket. He found his khitan, his tringolet, and his beautiful silver-mounted wood-horn and brought them out to the musician's platform. Finding a chair, he seated himself only a yard from the door. Ifness still sat in the corner of the room; with his mild expression he might have been a merchant's clerk; no one would look at him twice. Etzwane, playing with the troupe, was merged even more completely into the environment. Etzwane smiled sourly. The stalking of the Faceless Man was not without its ludicrous aspects.

With Etzwane present, Fordyce put aside his khitan and took up the bass clarion; Frolitz jerked his head in satisfaction.

Etzwane played with only a quarter of his mind. His faculties seemed magnified, hypersensitized. Every sound in the room reached his ears: every tone and quaver of music, the tinkle of glasses, the thud of mugs, the laughter and conversation. And from the storeroom an almost petulant whine from Garstang's torc. Etzwane glanced towards the far corner of the room; catching Ifness's eye, he reached up his hand as if to tune the khitan and gave a jerk of his thumb back towards the storeroom. Ifness nodded in comprehension.

The music halted. Frolitz turned around. "We will play that old piece of Anatoly's; you, Etzwane –" Frolitz explained a variation on the harmony. The barmen brought up mugs of beer; the musicians refreshed them-

168

selves. Etzwane thought: here was a life worth living –
easy, relaxed, not a worry in the world. Except for the
Roguskhoi and the Faceless Man. He lifted his mug
and drank. Frolitz gave a sign; the music started. Etzwane let his fingers move of themselves; his attention
wandered around the room. Fontenay tonight did good
business; all the tables were occupied. The mulberry
glass bosses high in the dark blue glass wall admitted a
glow from the lights outside; over the bar hung a pair
of soft white glow-bulbs. Etzwane looked everywhere,
studying everyone: the folk coming through the door,
Aljamo with fingers tapping the marimbaboards, the
pretty girl who had come to sit at a nearby table, Frolitz
now stroking a tipple, Ifness. Who among these people
would know him now for the "anonymous adventurer"
who had so disturbed the Faceless Man?

Etzwane thought of his past life. He had known much
melancholy; his only pleasure had come from music.
His gaze wandered to the pretty girl he had noticed before: an Aesthete, from the Ushkadel, or so he assumed. She wore clothes of elegant simplicity: a gown
of dark scarlet-rose, a fillet of silver with a pair of rock
crystals dangling past her ear, a curious jewelled belt,
slippers of rose satin and pink glass. She was dark-
haired, with a clever, grave face; never had Etzwane seen
anyone so captivating. She felt his gaze and looked at
him. Etzwane looked away, but now he played to her
with new concentration and intensity. Never had he
played so richly, with such lilting phrases, such poig-
nant chords. Frolitz gave him a half-sneering side-
glance, as if wordlessly asking, "What's got into you?"
The girl leaned to whisper to her escort, whom Etzwane
had hardly noticed: a man of early middle-age, apparently also an Aesthete. Behind Etzwane the torc gave
a thin whine, reminding him of his responsibilities.

The Aesthete girl and her escort moved to a table directly in front of Etzwane, the escort glum-faced and bored.

The music halted. The girl spoke to Etzwane. "You play very well."

"Yes," said Etzwane with a modest smile. "I suppose I do." He looked towards Ifness, to find him frowning disapproval. Ifness had wished that particular table close by the storeroom left vacant. Etzwane again made the quick signal with his thumb towards the torc. Ifness nodded distantly.

Frolitz spoke over his shoulder: "The Merrydown." He jerked his head to give a beat; the music came forth, a rollicking quick-step, up and down, with unexpected halts and double beats. Etzwane's part was mainly a strong and urgent chord progression; he was able to watch the girl. She improved upon proximity. She gave off a subtle fragrance; her skin had a clean glow; she knew the uses of beauty as Etzwane knew the meaning of music. He thought with a sudden inner ferocity, "I want her; I must have her for my own." He looked at her, and his intent showed clear in his eyes. She raised her eyebrows and turned to speak to her escort.

The music ended; the girl paid no more heed to Etzwane. She seemed uneasy. She settled her fillet, adjusted her belt. Behind Etzwane came the whine of the circuit. The girl jerked to stare. "What is that?" she asked Etzwane.

Etzwane pretended to listen. "I hear nothing."

"Is someone in there making peculiar sounds?"

"Perhaps a musician rehearsing."

"You are joking." Her face was alive with – humour? Alert mischief? Etzwane wondered.

"Someone is ill," she suggested. "You had better investigate."

170

"If you'll come in with me."

"No, thank you." She turned to her escort, who gave Etzwane a glance of haughty warning. Etzwane looked towards Ifness and, meeting his gaze, turned to look fixedly towards Frolitz, who stood to his right. His left ear indicated the table in front of him.

Ifness nodded without overmuch interest, or so it seemed to Etzwane.

Into the tavern came four men wearing mauve and grey uniforms: Discriminators. One spoke loudly: "Your attention! A disturbance has been reported in this building. In the name of the Corporation, I order no one to move."

Etzwane glimpsed the twitch of Ifness's hand. Two reports, two flashes: The glow-bulbs burst. Darkness and confusion came suddenly to Fontenay's tavern. Etzwane made a lunge. He felt the girl, caught her up, carried her in front of Frolitz into the hall. She tried to scream. Etzwane clapped his hand over her mouth. "Not a sound if you know what's good for you!" She kicked and struck at him; her noises were drowned by hoarse shouts in the tavern proper.

Etzwane staggered to the back door; he groped for the latch, opened the door, carried the writhing girl out into the night. Here he paused, let her feet swing to the ground. She tried to kick him. Etzwane twisted her around, held her arms in a lock. "No noise," he growled in her ear.

"What are you doing to me?" she cried.

"Keeping you safe from the raid. Such affairs are great inconveniences."

"You are the musician!"

"Exactly."

"Let me go back. I don't fear the Discriminators."

"What idiocy!" Etzwane exclaimed. "Now that we

171

are free of that tiresome man you sat with, we can go elsewhere."

"No, no, no!" Her voice was more confident, even somewhat amused. "You are gallant and bold – but I must go back into the tavern."

"You may not," said Etzwane. "Come with me, and please make no trouble."

The girl once more became alarmed. "Where are you taking me?"

"You'll see."

"No, no! I –" Someone came behind; Etzwane turned, ready to drop the girl and defend himself. Ifness spoke, "Are you there?"

"Yes. With a captive."

Ifness approached. In the dim light of the back alley he peered at the girl. "Who do you have?"

"I can't say for sure. She wears a peculiar belt. I suggest you take it."

"No!" cried the girl in an astounded voice.

Ifness unclasped the belt. "We had best be away, and swiftly." He told the girl: "Do not make a scene of any sort; do not scream or try to attract attention or we will use you roughly. Is that understood?"

"Yes," she said huskily.

Each taking one of the girl's arms, they set off through the back streets and in due course arrived at the blue tile cottage. Ifness unlocked the door; they entered.

Ifness pointed to a couch. "Please sit."

The girl wordlessly obeyed. Ifness examined the belt. "Curious indeed."

"So I thought. I noticed her touch the red stud whenever the alarm sounded."

"You are observant," said Ifness. "I thought you were interested otherwise. Be careful of her; remember Garstang's leg-gun."

172

Etzwane went to stand by the girl. "No Faceless Man, then – but a Faceless Woman."

The girl made a scornful sound. "You are mad."

Ifness said gently, "Please turn and lay face down on the couch. Excuse me while I search for a weapon." He did so with thoroughness. The girl cried out in indignation; Etzwane looked away. "No weapons," said Ifness.

"You need only to have asked," said the girl. "I would have told you."

"You are not otherwise candid."

"You have asked no questions."

"I shall, in a few minutes." He rolled over his work table, adjusted the vice to grip the girl's torc. "Do not move or I will be forced to anesthetize you." He worked with his tools, opened her torc. Reaching with his long-nose pliers he removed a tube of explosive. "No Faceless Man, nor Faceless Woman, either," he told Etzwane. "You seized the wrong individual."

"This is what I tried to tell you," cried the girl in a voice of desperate hope. "It's all a terrible mistake. I am of the Xhiallinen; and I want nothing to do with you or your intrigues."

Ifness, making no response, worked further on the torc. "The echo circuit is dead. You cannot now be located. We can relax and test your vaunted candour. You are of the Xhiallinen family?"

"I am Jurjin of Xhiallinen." The girl spoke sullenly.

"And why do you wear this belt?"

"For the most simple reason imaginable: vanity."

Ifness went to the cupboard and returned with a small sac, which he pressed to the girl's neck: sides, nape, and front. She looked at him in apprehension. "It is wet. What did you do to me?"

"The liquid penetrates your skin and enters your

173

blood. In a moment it will reach your brain and paralyze a certain small organ. Then we will talk further."

Jurjin's face became rueful and anxious. Etzwane watched her in morbid fascination, wondering as to the details of her existence. She wore her gown with flair and ease; she used the manners of the Garwiy patricians; her colouring was that of the Garwiy race. But her features showed a trace of some foreign strain. Xhiallinen, one of the Fourteen Families, was ancient, and if anything inbred. Jurjin spoke. "I will tell you the truth voluntarily, while I still can think. I wear the belt because the Anome required service of me, and I could not refuse."

"What was the service?"

"To act as Benevolence."

"Who are the other Benevolences?"

"There is only Garstang of Allingenen."

"Might there not be others?"

"I am certain that there are none."

"You, Garstang, and the Faceless Man controlled the whole of Shant?"

"The cantons and the cities are ruled by their particular leaders. It is only necessary to work through these folk. One alone could do this."

Etzwane started to speak, then controlled his voice. These slim hands must often have pressed the yellow stud of her belt; she must often have seen the heads of men disappear. He turned away with a heavy feeling in his throat.

"Who," asked Ifness ingenuously, "is the Faceless Man?"

"I don't know. He is as faceless to me as he is to you."

Ifness asked, "The box Garstang carried, and your belt: are they guarded against unauthorized use?"

"Yes. Grey must be pressed before the colours are coded."

Ifness leaned forward, inspected her eyes, and gave a slight nod. "Why did you summon the Discriminators to Fontenay's?"

"I did not summon them."

"Who did?"

"The Faceless Man, I suppose."

"Who was your escort?"

"The Second of Curnainen, Matheleno."

"Is he the Faceless Man?"

Jurjin's face showed a flicker of astonishment. "Matheleno? How could he be so?"

"Have you received orders from the Faceless Man in regard to Matheleno?"

"No."

"He is your lover?"

"The Faceless Man said I might take no lovers." Jurjin's voice began to slur; her eyelids drooped.

"Was the Faceless Man at Fontenay's Tavern?"

"I am not sure. I think he was there and noticed something which impelled him to call in the Discriminators."

"What could that have been?"

"Spies."

"Spies from where?"

"From Palesedra." Jurjins voice came slowly; her eyes took on a curious blank stare.

Ifness spoke sharply: "Why should he fear Palasedrans?"

Jurjin's voice was an unintelligible mutter; her eyes closed.

She slept. Ifness stood looking down in annoyance.

Etzwane looked from Ifness to the girl and back to Ifness. "What troubles you?"

"Her lapse into coma came swiftly. Too swiftly."

Etzwane peered into the girl's calm face. "She could not feign such a thing."

"No." Ifness bent over Jurjin's face. He scrutinized each of her features, opened her mouth, peered within. "Hmm."

"What do you see?"

"Nothing conclusive, or even suggestive."

Etzwane turned away, his mind inhabited only by doubts and uncertainties. He straightened the girl's body on the couch and drew a shawl over her. Ifness watched with brooding detachment.

"What do we do now?" Etzwane asked. He no longer felt antagonism towards Ifness; such an emotion seemed pointless.

Ifness stirred, as if rousing from a reverie. "We return to a consideration of the Faceless Man and his identity – though for a fact other mysteries seem more cogent."

"Other mysteries?" Etzwane asked, uncomfortably aware that he must seem numb and stupid.

"There are several. First I might cite the Roguskhoi scimitars. Then Garstang for no clear or good reason attempts a desperate attack. Jurjin of Xhiallinen lapses into a coma as if her brain has been turned off. And the Faceless Man resists, not passively but actively, all demonstrations against the Roguskhoi. All seem guided by a transcendent policy beyond our present imagination."

"It is very strange," muttered Etzwane.

"Were the Roguskhoi human, we might reconcile these grotesque acts with simple treachery; but the concept of Garstang and Jurjin of Xhiallinen plotting with the Roguskhoi is sheer insanity."

"Not if the Roguskhoi are Palasedran freaks sent here to destroy us."

"The theory is arguable," said Ifness, "until someone

176

troubles to examine the physiology of the Roguskhoi and considers their reproductive methods. Then doubt is renewed. However – to the lesser mystery. Who is the Faceless Man? We have thrown two stones; the quail has made two startled motions. To recapitulate: We are told with authority that the Anome employed only two Benevolences. Jurjin was not at Pandamon Park, yet an attempt was made to take your head. We must credit this attempt to the Faceless Man. Garstang was not at Fontenay's, still someone summoned the Discriminators. Again we must hold the Faceless Man responsible. I took photographs at both locations; if we find a person common to both – well, let's see what the Laws of Probability have to tell us. I believe that I can quote precise odds. There are roughly two hundred thousand adults in this immediate area, of which two hundred heard the 'anonymous adventurer' – not a large turnout: one in each thousand persons. A similar number might have come to Fontenay's to enjoy the music of Frolitz's troupe: only about a hundred, or one in each two thousand did so. The chances of the same person being present at both locations – unless he had urgent business at both, as did you, I, and the Faceless Man – are therefore one in two million: sufficiently scant to discount. So then, let us investigate."

Ifness brought from his pocket a tube of dull black metal an inch in diameter, four inches long. Along the flattened top a number of knobs caught the light and glittered in Ifness's hand. He made an adjustment, pointed the tube at the wall beside Etzwane, and projected a cone of light.

Etzwane had never seen a photograph so detailed. He glimpsed several views of the Corporation Plaza; then Ifness made new adjustments, sending a thousand images flickering against the wall. The picture became still, to depict Pandamon Park and the folk who had come to hear the "anonymous adventurer."

"Look carefully at these faces," said Ifness. "Unfortunately I can't show these pictures and those from Fontenay's in juxtaposition; we must shift from one set to another."

Etzwane pointed: "There stands Garstang. Here – here – here – here –" he pointed to other faces. "I noticed these men; I wondered which might be the Anome."

"Study them. He will certainly know tricks of altering his appearance." Ifness projected pictures from various angles and vantages; together they scrutinized every face visible.

"Now to Fontenay's taproom."

The taproom was half-empty; the musicians sat on the dais. Matheleno and Jurjin had not yet occupied the table near Etzwane.

Ifness chuckled. "You chose a perfect disguise. You appear as yourself."

Etzwane, uncertain as to the quality of Ifness's amusement, gave a noncommittal grunt.

"We go forward in time. The young woman and Matheleno are at your table. Could Matheleno be one of the men at Pandamon Park?"

"No," said Etzwane after reflection. "He somewhat resembles Garstang, however."

"The Aesthetes are a distinctive group – a race, in fact, in the process of differentiating."

The picture changed once more. "It is now four to five minutes before the Discriminators arrived. I would suppose the Faceless Man to be in the room. He would stand where he could watch his Benevolence." Ifness expanded the cone of light, magnifying the images, sending some to the ceiling, some to the floor. Moving

178

the projector, he brought the faces one at a time to the wall beside Etzwane.

Etzwane pointed. "The man in the far corner leaning against the bar."

Ifness expanded the image. They looked at the face. It was a quiet face, broad of forehead, clever of eye, small of chin and mouth. The man himself was short, trim, compact. His age could not be guessed.

Ifness flicked back to Pandamon Park. Etzwane pointed out the small man with the pursed mouth and the clever sidelong eyes. "There he is."

"Yes," said Ifness. "That is he, unless my logic and the laws of mathematics are at fault, and one is as incontrovertible as the other."

For a period they studied the face of the Faceless Man.

"Now what?" Etzwane asked.

"For now – nothing. Go to bed, sleep. Tomorrow we will try to put a name to the fellow."

"What of her?" Etzwane indicated the dazed girl.

"She won't move for twelve to fourteen hours."

CHAPTER TWELVE

The suns tumbled up into the mauve autumn sky like rollicking kittens: Sasetta over Ezeletta behind Zael. Ifness left the cottage slowly and cautiously, like an old grey fox going forth to hunt. Etzwane sat elbows on knees, pondering Jurjin of Xhiallinen. She lay as Ifness had left her, breathing shallowly: a creature, Etzwane thought, of absolutely entrancing appearance, beautiful enough to hypnotize a man. He studied her face: the pure pale skin, the innocent profile, the dusky eyelashes. How to reconcile this Jurjin of Xhiallinen with her dark occupation? No question but what the work must be done by someone. If unlawful acts went unpunished, Shant would lapse into anarchy, as in the old days when canton feuded with canton. Etzwane's mind was a confusion, swinging between noble rationalization and disgust. She had been commanded by the Anome; she had no choice but to obey. But why had the Anome commanded her, Jurjin of Xhiallinen, to serve as his Benevolence? Surely men like Garstang were more apt for such a service. The Anome's mind was a labyrinth with many strange chambers. Like the minds of all men, including his own, Etzwane told himself bitterly.

He reached forth, arranged a lock of her soft dark hair. Her eyelids flickered and slowly opened. She turned her head and looked at Etzwane. "You are the musician."

"Yes."

She lay quiet, thinking. She noticed the light pouring through the window and made a sudden movement. "It is daytime; I can't stay here."

"You must."

"But why?" She turned him a melting glance. "I have done you no harm."

"You would, had you the chance."

Jurjin inspected Etzwane's dour face. "Are you a criminal?"

"I am the 'anonymous adventurer' that Garstang went forth to kill."

"You taught sedition!"

"I urged that the Faceless Man protect Shant from the Roguskhoi. That is not sedition."

"The Roguskhoi are nothing to be feared. The Anome has told us this."

Etzwane gave an angry ejaculation. "I saw the results of the raid on Bashon. My mother was killed."

Jurjin's face became blank and distant. She murmured, "The Roguskhoi are nothing to fear."

"How would you cope with them, then?"

Jurjin focused her eyes upon him. "I don't know."

"And when they swarm down upon Garwiy, what will you do then? Do you wish to be ravaged? Would you bear a dozen imps that creep from your body while you sleep?"

Jurjin's face twitched. She started to wail, stopped short and became placid. "It's a matter for the Anome." She raised to her elbow and, watching Etzwane, slowly slid her legs to the floor. Etzwane watched impassively. He asked, "Are you hungry, or thirsty?"

She made no direct reply. "How long will you keep me here?"

"Until we find the Faceless Man."

"What do you want with him?"

181

"We will insist that he deal with the Roguskhoi."

"You intend him no harm?"

"Not I," said Etzwane, "though he has unjustly tried to kill me."

"The acts of the Anome must always be just. What if you can't find him?"

"Then you will remain here. Could it be otherwise?"

"Not from your point of view. Why do you look at me like that?"

"I wonder about you. How many men have you killed?"

She screamed, "One less than I would wish to!" and sprang for the door. Etzwane sat watching. Ten feet from the couch she was jerked to a halt by the cord Ifness had tied from her waist to the couch. She cried out in pain, turned and tugged frantically at the cord. Etzwane watched with detachment, feeling no pity.

Jurjin found the knot too cunning for her fingers. Slowly she returned to the couch. Etzwane had no more to say to her.

So they sat for two hours. Ifness returned as quietly as he had gone. He carried a folder that he handed to Etzwane; it contained six large photographic prints, so detailed that Etzwane could count the hairs of the man's sparse eyelashes. At Pandamon Park he had worn a soft black rimless cap pulled low over his forehead; this, with his down-curving little mouth and small, almost immature, nose, gave his face a foreshortened bulldog look. At Fontenay's the dark hair of a wig was drawn straight back from his forehead to swirl down and around each ear: a style popular among the upper middle classes of Garwiy, which displayed to advantage the philosopher's forehead and diminished the pinched expression of nose and mouth. Nowhere did the eyes look directly ahead; always they bore off somewhat to right or left. In both sets of photographs he appeared humourless, determined, introspective, and pitiless.

Etzwane studied the pictures until the face was stamped into his consciousness. He returned the pictures to Ifness.

Jurjin, sitting on the couch, feigned boredom. Ifness handed her the photographs. "Who is this man?"

Jurjin's eyelids descended the merest twitch; she said in a voice rather too casual, "I haven't a notion."

"Have you ever seen him?"

Jurjin frowned and licked her lips. "I see many people; I couldn't begin to remember them all."

Ifness asked, "If you knew this man's identity, would you tell us?"

Jurjin laughed. "Of course not."

Ifness nodded and went to the wall cabinet. Jurjin watched him, her mouth sagging in dismay. Ifness asked over his shoulder, "Are you hungry or thirsty?"

"No."

"Do you care to visit the bathroom?"

"No."

"You had best consider carefully," said Ifness. "It now becomes necessary that I apply the hypnotic tincture. You will not move for twelve hours, which, added to the twelve hours you have already occupied the couch, might cause an embarrassment."

"Very well," said Jurjin in a cold voice. "Be so good as to release me; I would like to wash my face and hands."

"Of course." Ifness untied the cord; Jurjin marched to the door Ifness indicated. Ifness spoke to Etzwane, "Stand below the bathroom window."

A moment after Etzwane arrived at his post the window eased cautiously ajar, and Jurjin looked out. At the sight of Etzwane she scowled and closed the window once more.

Jurjin returned slowly to the living room. "I do not care to be drugged," she told Ifness in a flippant voice. "Dreadful dreams afflict me."

"Indeed! What do you dream about?"

"I don't remember. Frightening things. I become very sick."

Ifness was unmoved. "I will dose you more heavily."

"No, no! You want to ask me about the pictures! I'll help you any way I know!" Her bravado had disappeared; her face had melted; it was tender, beseeching. Etzwane wondered how she looked with her finger on the yellow button.

Ifness asked; "Are you concealing information regarding the pictures?"

"Suppose I were? Would you expect disloyalty of me?"

"No," said Ifness. "I use the drug and remove your options. Please return to the couch."

"You will make me sick. I will fight you; I will kick and scream and bite."

"Not for long," said Ifness.

The sobbing girl lay on the couch. Etzwane, panting, sat on her knees and pressed down on her arms. Ifness applied the solution to her neck. Almost at once her writhing halted.

Ifness asked, "What do you know of the man in the photograph?"

Jurjin lay in a coma.

Etzwane said in a hushed voice, "You dosed her too heavily."

"No," said Ifness. "An overdose has no such effect."

"Then what happened to her?"

"I am mystified. First Garstang chooses an absurd method of suicide, now this."

"Do you think she knows the Faceless Man?"

"No. But she knows the man in the photographs. The Aesthetes, after all, are not strangers to each other." Ifness studied the photographs. "Of course, he might be the green-grocer. I neglected to mention that a picture of the 'anonymous adventurer' is posted in the Corporation Plaza, with information requested by the Discriminators."

"Hmf. So now I am proscribed."

"Until we remonstrate with the Faceless Man."

"He will be on his guard, with both Benevolences missing."

"So I would imagine. The identity of his adversaries must puzzle him greatly."

"Jurjin mentioned Palasedran spies."

"Similar theories may occur to the Faceless Man." Ifness studied the photographs. "Notice his torc. Observe the colours. What do they signify?"

"The purple-green is Garwiy. Double dark green is a person without trade or craft: a landholder, an industrialist, a foreign trader, an Aesthete."

Ifness nodded placidly. "No new information. The torc will certainly not respond to an echo pulse. No doubt we could walk about the Ushkadel asking questions, but I fear that we would soon be approached by the Discriminators."

Etzwane studied the photographs. "He travels around Shant, at least to some extent. Balloonway clerks might recognize his picture."

"But would they give us information? Or would they consult the Discriminators?"

"The publishers of *Frivolity* no doubt could put a name to him, but I suppose the same objection applies."

"Precisely. Questions arouse suspicion. Before informing a pair of strangers, they would first notify the principal."

Etzwane pointed to the collar of the Faceless Man's jacket. "Notice this brooch: silver and amethyst in a clever design. The artificers of such objects occupy Neroi Square, to the west of Corporation Plaza. The maker would be certain to recognize his work. When we put forth the story that we had found the jewel, he might supply the name of the person to whom he had sold it."

"Excellent," said Ifness. "We will try this plan."

Neroi Square occupied the heart of the Old City. The paving – three-foot tiles of murky lavender glass – was worn and irregular; the fountain at the centre dated from the reign of the first Caspar Pandamon. A two-storey arcade of translucent black glass surrounded the square, each column displaying the emblem of a mercantile family extinct two thousand years. The old offices had been converted into workshops for Garwiy's jewellers and metal-crafters. Each worked jealously alone, with his sons and nephews for apprentices, barely deigning to recognize the existence of his fellows. The work of each shop reflected the temperament of the shop-elder; some were known for their opals, agates, moonstones; others carved tourmaline or beryl; others created miniatures with microscopic slivers of cinnabar, lapis, turquoise, jade. Fashions and whimsicalities were only grudgingly heeded; special orders were accepted without enthusiasm. No piece carried seal or sigil; each craftsman deemed his work instantly recognizable.

The shop of Zafonce Agabil was currently in the mode; his designs were thought quaint and endearing. Into the shop of Zafonce Agabil went Ifness and Etzwane. Upon the counter Ifness tossed a section cut from his photograph of the Faceless Man. "Someone lost such a brooch at my house; did you make it? If so can you supply me the name of its owner, that I may return it?"

The clerk, one of the four Agabil sons, examined the photograph with a contemptuous twist of the mouth. "None of our work, certainly."

"Whose might it be?"

"I could not say."

At the shop of Lucinetto, Ifness encountered a similar response, but additionally: "It is somewhat old-fashioned work and might well be an heirloom. The cabochon is cut with an overly shallow dome, as one might use a garnet. Not our work; never, never, could we so shame a stone."

From shop to shop went Ifness and Etzwane.

At Meretrice's the latest of the lineage examined the photograph. "Yes, this is one of our pieces, in the style of the Siume Dynasty. Notice the vitality of the cabochon? It comes of a secret contour, known only to us. It was lost? A pity. I do not recall the purchaser; it was crafted five years or more ago."

"I think I know the owner," said Ifness. "He came as a friend of one of my guests, and I do not recall his name." He displayed a photograph of the Faceless Man.

Meretrice glanced at it. "Yes! That is Sajarano of Sershan Palace: something of a recluse. I am surprised he came to your banquet."

CHAPTER THIRTEEN

The Sershan Palace, an intricate confection of clear and coloured glass, faced southeast across Garwiy. Ifness and Etzwane examined the premises from a discreet distance. They saw no activity on the loggia nor in that area of the garden accessible to view. The Office of Archives had yielded information of no great interest. The Sershan lineage went back to middling antiquity. Prince Varo Sershan of Wild Rose had supported Viana Paizifume; a certain Almank Sershan had raided the south coast of Caraz, returning with a vast fortune in silver corpse effigies. Sajarano was last in the direct lineage. A spouse had died twenty years before without issue; he had never taken another. He still controlled the hereditary Wild Rose estates and was a keen agriculturist. Heir presumptive was a cousin, Cambarise of Sershan.

"One possible tactic is to go to the door and ask to speak to his Excellency Sajarano," said Ifness. "Such an approach, with the virtue of utter simplicity, has much to recommend it. A pity," he said in musing afterthought, "that my mind always discovers hazards and contingencies. What if he expects us? By no means impossible. Meretrice might have become suspicious. The clerk at the Office of Archives seemed overly alert."

"I believe he would call Discriminators the instant we appeared," said Etzwane. "Were I Sajarano I would be a worried man."

Ifness said, "In this same vein, were I Sajarano, I

would not keep to my palace. I would dress inconspicuously and wander the city. We are wasting our time here. We should go where the Faceless Man is likely to go."

During the late afternoon the cafés of Corporation Plaza became crowded with folk making rendezvous; at the largest of these cafés Ifness and Etzwane seated themselves and ordered wine and biscuits.

The folk of Garwiy passed back and forth, all in greater or lesser degree imbued with the peculiar Garwiy verve and volatility.

They saw nothing of Sajarano.

The suns rolled behind the Ushkadel; shadows filled the plaza. "Time we were returning," said Ifness. "Jurjin will be rousing herself; we should be on hand."

Jurjin had already regained consciousness. Frantically, by every resource known to her, she had been trying to free herself from the cord that connected her waist to the couch. Her gown was dishevelled where she had tried to slip the loop over her hips. The wood of the couch was scarred where she had sought to fray the cord. The knots, sealed by a means known only to Ifness, now engrossed her to such an extent that she failed to notice the arrival of Ifness and Etzwane. She looked up with the face of a trapped animal. "How long will you keep me here? I am miserable; what right have you to do such a thing to me?"

Ifness made a gesture of boredom. He loosened the cord from the couch, allowed her once more the freedom of the house.

Etzwane prepared a meal of soup, bread, and dried meat, which at first she haughtily declined, then ate with good appetite.

She became more cheerful. "You two are the strangest men on Durdane. Look at you! Glum as crakes! Of course! You are ashamed of the acts you have perpetrated upon me!"

Ifness ignored her; Etzwane merely gave a sour chuckle.

"What are your plans?" she demanded. "Must I stay here forever?"

"Possibly," said Ifness. "I suspect however that circumstances may change in a day or two."

"And in the meantime? What of my friends? They are worried sick, of this I am sure. And must I wear this same gown day in and day out? You treat me like a beast."

"Patience," murmured Ifness. "Presently I will give you a drug and send you back to sleep."

"I do not want to sleep. I consider you the epitome of boorishness. And you –" she turned her attention upon Etzwane "– have you no gallantry? You sit grinning like a dogfish. Why do you not force the old man to release me?"

"So that you could report us to the Faceless Man?"

"It would be my duty. Should I be punished on this account?"

"You should not have become a Benevolence were you not willing to assume the risks."

"But I had no choice! One day I was told my destiny, and from that time my life was not my own."

"You could have refused to serve. Do you enjoy taking men's heads away from them?"

"Bah," she said, "you refuse to speak on a sensible level. What is wrong with you?" This to Ifness, who had jerked around in his chair, to sit listening.

Etzwane listened as well, but the night was quiet. "What do you hear?" he asked.

Ifness jumped to his feet. He went to the doorway and looked out into the dark. Etzwane rose as well. Still he could hear no sound. Ifness spoke in an incomprehensible language, then listened once more.

Jurjin took advantage of the distraction to coil the cord in her hand. She lunged for Ifness, hoping to push him aside and win her freedom. Etzwane, waiting for just such a move, caught her and carried her kicking and yelling to the couch. Ifness brought over his drug; the girl became quiet. Ifness tied the end of the rope to the couch, and this time taught Etzwane the secret of the lock. "The knot itself is a meaningless tangle of loops and turns." Ifness spoke in haste. "Come here to the table. I must teach you what I know of the torcs. Quickly now, quickly!"

"What is the trouble?"

Ifness looked towards the door. He spoke in a dreary voice: "I have been recalled. I am in deep disgrace. At the least I will be expelled from the Institute."

"How do you know all this?" demanded Etzwane.

"A signal has reached me. My time on Durdane is ended."

Etzwane stared with a slack jaw. "What of the Faceless Man? What shall I do?"

"Your best. It is tragic that I must go. Attend me. I will leave you my tools, my weapons, my drugs. You must listen carefully, as I can explain only once. First: the torcs. Watch how to open one safely." He demonstrated on a torc he had brought from Gargamet Meadow. "And here is how to lock it. Watch; I will reactivate the girl's torc. The dexax fits in here; this is the detonator. The echo circuit is broken; notice this loose connection ... Demonstrate what I have told you ... Good ... This is my only weapon; it shoots a needle of energy. The camera I must keep."

191

Etzwane listened with foreboding. He had not realized his dependence on the detestable Ifness. "Why must you leave?"

"Because I must! Be wary of the Faceless Man and his Benevolence here. Their conduct is aberrant, in an almost imperceptible degree."

A soft sound reached Etzwane's ears. Ifness heard it as well and turned his head; otherwise he made no move.

A polite rap-tap-tap sounded at the door. Ifness walked across the room, drew the latch. In the darkness stood two shapes. The first came a little forward; Etzwane saw a man of medium stature with a pale complexion, the blackest of hair and eyebrows. He seemed to smile, a placid, grim smile; his eyes glittered in the light. The second man was a vague shape in the gloom.

Ifness spoke in a language strange to Etzwane; the black-haired man replied curtly. Ifness spoke again; the stranger as before replied with a few dry syllables.

Ifness turned back into the cottage. He took his soft black case; without a glance, word, or gesture towards Etzwane, he stepped out into the night. The door closed.

A minute later Etzwane heard the soft sound. It faded into a sigh and was gone.

Etzwane poured himself a glass of wine and sat at the table. Jurjin of Xhiallinen lay in a coma on the couch.

Etzwane rose to his feet and explored the cottage. In the cabinet he found a wallet containing several thousand florins. In a wardrobe were garments: at need, they would fit Etzwane.

He went back to sit at the table. He thought of Frolitz, of the old days that in retrospect seemed so care-free. No more, never again. By now the "anonymous adventurer" must be identified with Gastel Etzwane.

He decided he did not wish to remain in the cottage. He slipped into Ifness's grey cape and a grey hat. Into his pocket he tucked the energy gun and Garstang's box. After a moment's deliberation he included the drug of stupefaction that Ifness had demonstrated to him: suppose he should meet Sajarano of Sershan on this autumn evening?

Etzwane turned down the lights. The cottage was dark except for the coloured loom of Garwiy through the window. Jurjin lay quiet; he could not hear her breathing. Etzwane walked softly from the cottage.

For hours he wandered the avenues of Garwiy, pausing by cafés to examine the patrons, stepping into taverns to scan the faces in the room. He dared not approach Fontenay's. At midnight he ate a meat bun and a cake of cheese at a late-hour booth.

Mist had come drifting in from the Green Ocean. It flew in wafts and tendrils among the spires, blurring the coloured lights, bringing a damp scent to the air. Few folk were abroad. Wrapping himself in the cloak, Etzwane returned to the cottage.

At the gate he halted. The dark cottage seemed to wait for him. Behind, in a shed, festered Garstang's body.

Etzwane listened. Silence, darkness. He walked through the garden and paused by the door. A slight sound? He strained his ears. Another sound: a dry scraping. Etzwane flung open the door, sidled into the room, gun in hand. He turned up the lights. No changes were evident. The back door creaked. Etzwane ran from the front door, circled the cottage. He saw nothing. The door of the shed appeared to be ajar. Etzwane stopped short, hair bristling at the nape of his neck. Slowly he approached; jumping forward, he slammed the door and threw the latch. Then he wheeled and sprang nervously aside in case the open door were a ploy to distract him.

No sound. Etzwane could not bring himself to investigate the shed. He went into the house. Jurjin lay in her coma. She had moved or been moved; an arm hung down to the floor.

Etzwane bolted the doors and drew the blinds. The cord binding Jurjin to the couch had been disturbed. The wooden frame of the couch had been abraded, rasped. Etzwane bent over Jurjin, examined her with care. He raised her eyelid. The eyeball was rolled back. Etzwane jerked around, looked over his shoulder.

The room was empty, save for the ghosts of dead conversations.

Etzwane brewed tea and went to sit in a chair. Time passed. Constellations rose and fell; Etzwane dozed. He awoke cold and stiff to find the light of dawn seeping through the shutters.

The cottage was quiet and dismal. Etzwane prepared himself a meal and planned his day. First he must examine the shed.

Jurjin awoke. She had nothing to say. He fed her and allowed her a visit to the bathroom. She returned in a dull and despondent mood, without defiance or vivacity. She stood in the centre of the room flexing her arms, which apparently were cramped. Presently she asked, "Where is the old man?"

"He is gone about his affairs."

"What may they be?"

"You'll learn in due course."

"What a strange pair you are!"

"I find you much stranger than myself," said Etzwane. "By contrast I am starkly simple."

"But still you preach sedition."

"By no means. The Roguskhoi killed my mother, and my sister as well. I say that they must be destroyed, to save all of Shant. This is not sedition. It is ordinary rationality."

"You should leave such decisions to the Anome."

"He refuses to act; hence I must force him."

"The old man's mother was likewise killed?"

"I don't believe so."

"Why is he so zealous to break the laws?"

"From sheer philanthropy."

"What? That man? He is cold as the Nimmir wind."

"Yes, in certain ways he is strange. Now I must drug you once more."

Jurjin made an airy gesture. "You need not bother. I will agree not to leave the cottage."

Etzwane gave a cynical laugh. "Please be good enough to lie upon the couch."

Jurjin approached him, smiling up into his face. "Let us be friends instead. Kiss me."

"Hmmf. At this time in the morning?"

"Would you like to?"

Etzwane dourly shook his head. "No."

"Am I so ill-favoured? Old and wrinkled?"

"No. But if you could press the yellow button and take my head, you would do so. The idea does not compel my affection. Please make haste."

Jurjin thoughtfully went to the couch. She lay supine while Etzwane applied the drug, and soon she slept. Etzwane locked the cord to a decorative ceiling bracket.

He went out to inspect the shed. The door was bolted as before. He walked around. Nothing larger than a rat could have found its way in or out.

Etzwane flung wide the door; daylight revealed garden tools, household clutter, Garstang's body where he had dragged it. The face and chest were fearfully torn. Etzwane stood in the doorway looking for the creature that had done the damage. He did not dare enter for fear the rat, if such it were, might dart forth and bite him. He closed and bolted the door.

Wearing the grey cloak, Etzwane sauntered glumly into Garwiy. He went directly to the Corporation Plaza. The Faceless Man might be walking the halls of Sershan Palace. He might be resting in solitude at his Wild Rose estate. He might have gone off to the far corners of Shant to punish malefactors. Etzwane thought otherwise. If he were the Faceless Man, he would stay in Garwiy, in contact with the Discriminators, and sooner or later he must cross the Corporation Plaza.

Etzwane stood a moment or two under the old Clockmakers' Gate. A misty, chilly morning today, the suns eclipsing each other as they sidled across the sky. Etzwane went to a nearby café and took an inconspicuous table. He ordered broth and sat sipping.

The folk of Garwiy passed across the plaza. Near the Office of Petitions three Discriminators came together and stood talking. Etzwane watched them with interest. What if they all came at him together? He could never kill them all with the metal box; there would be insufficient time. The Faceless Man must carry another weapon, thought Etzwane; a device that would explode any torc at which it was pointed. Into the café came a man in a suit of grey and purple. His forehead was broad and pallid; the small nose, the pursed down-curving mouth were undistinguished, but the eyes, which looked off to the side, were luminous and thoughtful. He signalled to the waiter for a mug of soup; a motion peremptory but polite, in the fashion of the Aesthetes.

When the broth was served, he glanced sidewise towards Etzwane, who took care to have his own mug raised before his face; but for an unsettling instant he met the gaze of the Faceless Man.

The Faceless Man frowned slightly and looked away, as if resenting a stranger's attention.

Etzwane's nervousness made careful thinking difficult. He clenched the mug and, forcing his thoughts into a channel, sorted out his options.

He carried a gun. He could step forward, press it into the Anome's back, and utter appropriate orders. The plan had a single overwhelming disadvantage: conspicuity. If the act were noticed, as it must be, the Discriminators would be summoned.

He could wait until the Anome departed and follow; but the Anome in his present condition of uncertainty might well notice and lead him into a trap. Etzwane told himself that he must not relinquish the initiative.

The Anome, if he recognized the "anonymous adventurer," might be persuaded to follow Etzwane; more likely he would summon the Discriminators.

Etzwane heaved a fateful sigh. He reached into the pocket of his cape and secured an item of the equipment Ifness had left with him. He clinked a florin down on the table to pay for the broth; scraping his chair back, he rose to his feet; then, with an exclamation, he stumbled forward to place his hand upon the Faceless Man's neck. "Sir, my apologies!" declared Etzwane. "What a disgrace! This wet napkin has fallen upon your neck!"

"No matter, no matter."

"Allow me to help you."

The Anome jerked away. "You are clumsy; what do you mean daubing my neck in such a fashion?"

"Again, my apologies! I will replace your coat if it is stained."

"No, no, no. Just be off with you, I can take care of myself."

"Very well, sir, as you wish. I must explain that this cursed chair engaged my leg and threw me forward. I'm sure the matter came as a great shock!"

"Yes, quite so. But the episode is finished; please say no more."

"Your indulgence one more moment; I must adjust my shoe. May I sit here no more than an instant?"

"As you will." The Anome turned away in his chair. Etzwane, dealing with his shoe, watched him carefully.

A moment passed. The Anome glanced about. "You are still here?"

"Yes. What is your name?"

The Anome blinked. "I am Sajarano of Sershan."

"Do you know me?"

"No."

"Look at me!"

Sajarano turned his head. His face was calm and even.

"Rise to your feet," said Etzwane. "Come with me."

Sajarano's face showed no emotion. Etzwane led him from the café.

"Walk faster," said Etzwane. They passed under the Pomegranate Portal into Serven Airo Way. Etzwane now clasped Sajarano's arm. Sajarano blinked. "I am tired."

"You will rest shortly. Who is the 'anonymous adventurer?'"

"He is a man from the east; he is at the centre of a seditious cabal."

"Who are the others of this cabal?"

"I don't know."

198

"Why do you not order soldiers against the Roguskhoi?"

Sajarano for ten seconds made no reply. Then he mumbled: "I don't know." His voice had begun to slur; he moved with an unsteady gait. Etzwane supported him and took him along the way as fast as possible, until near the Gate of the Seasons the Faceless Man could walk no more.

Etzwane conveyed him to a bench and waited until an empty fiacre came by, which he halted. "My friend has had a drop too much; we must take him home before his wife finds out."

"It happens to the best of us. Into the back with him. Can you manage?"

"Very well. Drive out the Avenue of the Thasarene Directors."

CHAPTER FOURTEEN

Etzwane undressed the Faceless Man to his undergarments and laid him on the couch across from Jurjin. The Faceless Man was not physically impressive. From the garments Etzwane removed an activating box like that carried by Garstang, an energy gun of complex design, a small case that Etzwane presumed to be a radio transceiver, a metal tube of unknown function; Etzwane thought it might be the all-torc destroyer he had hypothesized.

He brought forth Ifness's tools and ranged them carefully in a row. With intense concentration he removed Sajarano's torc as he had seen Ifness do. To his intense puzzlement the torc contained a full complement of dexax. The echo circuits were apparently operative. Etzwane stared in amazement. What could be the reason for this? A terrible presentiment struck him; had he captured the wrong man?

If not, why should the Faceless Man wear an armed torc?

The solution rose into his mind – a reason so simple and full of relief that he laughed outright. Like everyone else Sajarano of Sershan had assumed his torc at puberty. When, through circumstances shrouded and secret, he had become the Anome, he knew no method to alter the situation, except to alter the colour coding as protection against his Benevolences.

Etzwane slipped off his own torc. He restored the

explosive to its slot, reconnected the circuits. He placed this around Sajarano's neck and locked it in place.

An unpleasant task awaited him. He went out to the shed and threw open the door. The rat, if such it were, scuttled under a pile of sacks. It had, so Etzwane noted, been feeding upon Garstang's body. In revulsion Etzwane brought forth Ifness's gun and sent a spear of pale fire at the sacks. They disappeared in a gust of vile-smelling smoke, and with them the creature who had taken refuge below.

Etzwane picked up a spade and, digging a shallow grave, buried Garstang.

When he returned into the house, all was as before. He bathed, changed his clothes, then sat and waited, his mood a strange mixture of exultation and loneliness.

Jurjin awoke first. She seemed tired; her face sagged and her skin showed an unhealthy colour. Sitting up on the couch, she looked at Etzwane with undisguised bitterness.

"How long will you keep me here?"

"Not long now."

She peered across the room "Who is that man?"

"Do you know him?"

Jurjin shrugged, a brave attempt at debonair defiance.

"His name is Sajarano of Sershan," said Etzwane. "He is the Faceless Man."

"Why is he here?"

"You shall see. . . . Are you hungry?"

"No."

Etzwane thought a moment or two. Then he unlocked the cord that bound her. She stood up, free of her bonds. Etzwane faced her.

"Do not leave this house. If you do, I will take your head. The Anome is here and cannot help you. You must

201

now obey me as formerly you did the Anome. You must not obey him. Do you understand?"

"I understand well enough. But I am confused. Who are you?"

"I am Gastel Etzwane, a musician. So I was, so I hope to be again."

Hours passed. Jurjin wandered about the house, watching Etzwane with wonder, defiance, and female spite.

Towards evening Sajarano recovered his senses. He became alert very quickly and sat up on the couch. For half a minute he appraised Etzwane and Jurjin. He spoke in the coldest of voices. "Suppose you explain why you have brought me here."

"Because the Roguskhoi must be attacked; because you refused to act."

"This is solemn and deliberate policy," said Sajarano. "I am a man of peace; I refuse to bring the horrors of war to Shant."

"Worry no longer; the Roguskhoi have done the job for you."

Etzwane pointed to Sajarano's old torc. "You are wearing an active torc. It carries its full complement of dexax. I carry the detonator. You now must answer to me, and your Benevolence as well."

Jurjin, standing across the room, went to sit on the couch. "I obey the Anome."

Sajarano asked, "What of Garstang?"

"Garstang is dead."

Sajarano's hand went up to his new torc, after the manner of the folk of Shant. "What do you propose to do?"

"The Roguskhoi must be destroyed."

Sajarano spoke in a quiet voice: "You do not know

what you are saying. In Shant we enjoy peace and good fortune; we must maintain it. Why risk chaos and militarism for the sake of a few barbarians?"

"Peace and good fortune are not the natural bounties of nature," said Etzwane. "If you believe this, I will send you to Caraz where you can learn for yourself."

"You cannot wish to bring turmoil to Shant," cried Sajarano in a suddenly brassy voice.

"I wish to repel a clear and present danger. Will you obey my orders? If you refuse, I will kill you this moment."

Sajarano sank back in his chair. He seemed apathetic and watched Etzwane sidelong, in which pose his small nose and mouth seemed curiously immature. "I will obey."

Jurjin was restless; her face twitched and jerked in grimaces that under other circumstances might have been amusing. She rose to her feet, went to the table.

Etzwane asked, "The Discriminators are now searching for the 'anonymous adventurer?'"

"Yes."

"They have orders to kill him?"

"If necessary."

Etzwane gave him the transceiver. "How do you use this?"

Jurjin came forward as if interested. From behind her back flashed a glass knife. Etzwane, watching from the corner of his eye, knocked her sprawling back on the couch. Sajarano struggled up, kicked Etzwane, grappled him around the neck. Etzwane lunged ahead. The line around Sajarano's neck snapped taut, and snatched him flailing back to the couch.

"Your promises seem to mean little," Etzwane observed in a mild voice. "I was hoping that I might trust you both."

203

"Why should we not fight for what we believe?" demanded Jurjin.

"I promised to obey you," said Sajarano. "I said nothing about not trying to kill you when opportunity offered."

Etzwane grinned, a dour, sardonic grin. "In that case I order you not to try to kill or injure me in any way. Will you obey?"

Sajarano sighed in vast unease. "Yes. What else can I say?"

Etzwane looked at Jurjin. "What about you?"

"I promise nothing," she declared haughtily.

Etzwane seized her arm and pulled her towards the door.

"Where are you going?" she cried. "What are you doing?"

"I am taking you to the back yard to kill you," said Etzwane.

"No, no no!" she cried. "Please do not. I promise to obey you!"

"And will you seek to harm me?"

"No!"

Etzwane released her; she ran back to the couch.

Etzwane returned to Sajarano. "Explain the function of this transceiver."

"I press the white button," said Sajarano in a calm voice. "It transmits to the relays I designate on this dial. I speak; the orders are broadcast from the relay station."

"Call the Discriminators, order them no longer to molest the 'anonymous adventurer'. State that Gastel Etzwane must be given respectful and instant obedience, no less than you would expect for yourself."

Sajarano did so in a flat voice. He looked up at Etzwane. "What else do you require of me?"

Etzwane, standing across the room, looked from one

face to the other, from Jurjin of Xhiallinen to the Faceless Man. Both, he knew, would play him false as soon as opportunity offered. Dead, they would be no threat to him. Jurjin's eyes widened as if she read his thoughts. It might be for the best. Still, if he killed the Faceless Man, who would govern Shant? Who would organize the military apparatus necessary to his goals? The Faceless Man must live; in which case he could see no reason to kill Jurjin of Xhiallinen.

The two watched him intently, trying to divine the direction of his thoughts. Etzwane said in a fateful voice: "You are free to go. Do not leave the Ushkadel."

He untied the cord from Sajarano's waist. "A warning: if I am killed, my associates will still take both your heads."

With neither ceremony nor overmuch dignity the two departed the cottage. At the gate Jurjin looked over her shoulder; in the dark Etzwane could see only the glimmer of her face. Uneasily he sensed that Ifness would have handled the situation differently, that at some essential juncture his affairs had gone wrong.

He loaded Ifness's black case with such weapons and instruments he did not dare leave behind and departed the cottage.

At the Old Pagane he dined on the best the house offered, amused by his twinges of instinctive parsimony. Money had become the least of his concerns.

He sauntered along the river bank to Fontenay's where he found Frolitz and the troupe drinking beer. Frolitz hailed Etzwane in angry reproof mixed with relief. "What have you been up to? We've been persecuted by the Discriminators! They say you kidnapped an Aesthete girl."

"All nonsense," said Etzwane. "A ridiculous mistake. I'd rather not talk about it."

205

"Clearly you don't care to enlighten us," said Frolitz. "Well, no matter: to work. I have a sore lip; tonight I'll use the khitan; Etzwane will play wood-horn. We'll start with that Morningshore trifle 'Birds in the Surf'."

The Brave Free Men

CHAPTER ONE

In a chamber high under the dormers of Fontenay's Inn, Etzwane stirred on his couch. He had slept but little. Presently he arose and went to the window, where the stars had paled on the violet dawn. The far slopes of the Ushkadel showed only the occasional green sparkle of a street lamp; the Aesthete palaces were dark.

In one of these palaces, thought Etzwane, the Faceless Man had slept no better than himself.

He turned away from the window and went to the washstand. A carbon-fume mirror gave back his image, a face altered both by the gloom of dawn and the umbral quality of the mirror. Etzwane peered close. This unreal, somewhat menacing person might well be himself most truly: the face sardonic, drooping of mouth, hollow of cheek; the skin sallow with a leaden sheen; the eyes dark holes, punctuated by a pair of glittering reflections. He thought: here stands Gastel Etzwane, first Chilite Pure Boy, then Pink-Black-Azure-Deep Greener, now a man of enormous power. He spoke to the image: "Today is a day of important events; Gastel Etzwane must not allow himself to be killed." The image gave back no reassurance.

He dressed and went down to the street. At a booth on the riverbank he ate fried fish and bread and considered his prospects for the day.

In broad essence the job was simple. He must go to Sershan Palace and there compel Sajarano, the Anome of Shant, to do his bidding. If Sajarano demurred, Etzwane need merely press a button to explode his head, for now Sajarano wore a torc and Etzwane did not. It was work of stark and brutal simplicity – unless Sajarano divined his solitary condition, his lack of ally or confederate, in which case Etzwane's situation became precarious.

With his breakfast finished there was nothing to deter him; he set forth up Galias Avenue. Sajarano, he reflected, would desperately be seeking to escape from his intolerable predicament. Etzwane asked himself: what, in Sajarano's place, would be his own response? Flight? Etzwane stopped short. Here was a contingency he had not considered. From his pouch he brought the pulse-emitter, once Sajarano's basic tool of law enforcement. Etzwane encoded the colours of Sajarano's torc. The yellow button would now – if necessary – detonate the torc, thereby removing Sajarano's head. Etzwane pushed the red "Seek" button. The box hummed, the sound fluctuating with change of direction. At maximum the box pointed towards Sershan Palace. Etzwane proceeded, more thoughtful than ever. Sajarano had not taken to flight. He might have evolved a strategy more active.

Galias Avenue terminated at the Marmione Plaza, where a fountain of milk-white water played over artifacts of purple glass; the Koronakhe Steps opposite, constructed by King Caspar Pandamon, rose towards the terraces of the Ushkadel. At the Middle Way Etzwane left the steps and proceeded eastwards, around the sweep of the Ushkadel. The prismatic Palace Xhiallinen rose above him; here lived Jurjin, the Faceless Man's "Benevolence." Among a dozen other mysteries, this: why had Sarajano

6

selected so conspicuously beautiful a girl for his deputy?
... The mystery, in this case, might be more apparent
than real, so Etzwane speculated. The Anome, like any
man, could suffer the pangs of love. Jurjin of Xhiallinen
perhaps had reacted coolly to the attentions of Sajarano,
who was neither handsome, dashing, nor distinguished.
Perhaps she wondered when the Faceless Man had ordered her into his service and commanded her to take no
lovers. In due course the Faceless Man might have ordered her to look kindly upon Sarajano. So Etzwane con-
jectured.... He came to the Palace Sershan, neither more
nor less splendid than any of the others. Etzwane halted,
to review all circumstances. The next half-hour would determine the future of Shant; each minute carried more
weight than all the days of a normal man's life. He looked
up and down the façade of Sershan Palace. Columns of
crystal, more lucid and transparent than air itself, fractured the beams of the triple suns; the violet and green
domes beyond sheltered chambers where sixty Sershan
generations had lived, celebrated their festivals, and died.

Etzwane trudged forward. He crossed the loggia, approached the portico, and here he paused. Six doors of
inch-thick glass, each fifteen feet high, barred his way.
No light or movement appeared within. Etzwane hesitated, uncertain how to proceed. He began to feel foolish,
hence angry. He rapped on the glass. His bare knuckles
made little noise; he pounded with his fist. He saw movement within; a moment later a man came around the side
of the place. It was Sajarano himself.

"These are ceremonial doors," said Sajarano in a mild
voice. "We seldom open them; would you come this way?"

In glum silence Etzwane followed Sajarano to a side
entrance. Sajarano motioned him within. Etzwane halted

and searched Sajarano's face, to which Sajarano returned a faint smile, as if he found Etzwane's wariness amusing. With his hand on the yellow button Etzwane entered the palace.

"I have been expecting you," said Sajarano. "Have you breakfasted? Perhaps you'll take a cup of tea. Shall we go up to the morning room?"

He led the way to a sunny chamber with a floor of green and white jade tiles. The wall to the left was shrouded in dark green vines; the wall to the right was clear white alabaster. Sajarano motioned Etzwane to a wicker chair beside a wicker table, then at a sideboard served himself a few morsels of food and poured tea into a pair of silverwood cups.

Etzwane carefully seated himself; Sarajano took the chair opposite, his back to the ceiling-high windows. Etzwane studied him with sombre calculation, and Sajarano once again gave back his faint smile. Sajarno was not an imposing man physically; his features were small; under a broad high forehead his nose and mouth seemed almost immature, his chin was a nubbin. The Anome of popular conception was vastly different from this mild, reasonable man.

Sajarano sipped his tea. Best to take the initiative, thought Etzwane. He spoke in a careful monotone: "As I previously mentioned, I represent that segment of the public which is seriously concerned in regard to the Roguskhoi. We believe that if decisive steps are not taken, in five years there will be no more Shant – only a great horde of Roguskhoi. As the Anome it is your duty to destroy these creatures; such is the trust the people of Shant repose in you."

Sajarano nodded without emphasis and sipped his tea.

8

Etzwane left his cup untouched. "These considerations," Etzwane continued, "forced my friends and myself to extreme lengths, as you know."

Sajarano nodded once more: a kindly reassuring nod. "These friends: who are they?"

"Certain persons who are shocked by the acts of the Roguskhoi."

"I see. And your position: you are the leader?"

"I?" Etzwane gave an incredulous laugh. "By no means."

Sajarano frowned. "Would it be fair to assume that the others of your group are known personally to me?"

"It is a matter which really has no bearing on the issue," said Etzwane.

"Perhaps not, except that I like to know with whom I am dealing."

"You need deal with no one; you need only muster an army and drive the Roguskhoi back into Palasedra."

"You make it sound so simple," said Sajarano. "A further question: Jurjin of Xhiallinen spoke of a certain Ifness, who demonstrated remarkable abilities. I confess to curiosity regarding this Ifness."

"Ifness is a remarkable man indeed," said Etzwane. "As to the Roguskhoi: what do you propose to do?"

Sajarano ate a slice of fruit. "I have considered the matter carefully, to this effect. The Anome is what he is only because he controls the lives of all the people of Shant but is himself exempt from such control. This is the definition of the Anome. It no longer defines me; I wear a torc. I can take no responsibility for acts or policies not my own. In short I propose to do nothing."

"Nothing whatever? What of your normal duties?"

"I resign them all to you and your group. You wield the

9

power; you must bear the burdens." Sajarano laughed at Etzwane's glum expression. "Why should I go into a hysteria of effort over policies whose wisdom I doubt? What nonsense this would be!"

"Am I to understand that you no longer consider yourself Anome?"

"That is correct. The Anome must work anonymously. I can no longer do this. You, Jurjin of Xhiallinen, others in your group know my identity. I am no longer effective."

"Then who is to be Anome?"

Sajarano shrugged. "You, your friend Ifness, another member of your group. You control the power, you must accept the responsibility."

Etzwane frowned. Here was a contingency for which he had not prepared. Obduracy, threats, scorn, anger: yes. Supine relinquishment: no. It was too easy. Etzwane became wary, Sajarano's subtlety far exceeded his own. He asked cautiously, "You will cooperate with us?"

"I will obey your orders, certainly."

"Very well. First, a state of national emergency is to be proclaimed. We will identify the danger, then make it clear that an effort of major proportions must be made."

Sajarano made a polite sound. "So much is easy. Remember, however, that the population of Shant is over thirty million souls; to cry emergency to so many is a serious affair."

"Agreed; no dispute here whatever. Second, women must be evacuated from all areas adjacent to the Wildlands."

Sajarano gave him a look of polite bewilderment. "Evacuated to where?"

"To the coastal cantons."

Sajarano pursed his small mouth. "It is not all so simple. Where will they live? Will their children accompany them? What of their homes, their ordinary duties? The cantons affected would number twenty or thirty. That is a large number of women."

"Which is precisely why we want them moved," said Etzwane. "That number of women impregnated by Roguskhoi means a vast horde of Roguskhoi!"

Sajarano shrugged. "What of the other difficulties I mentioned? They are real."

"Administrative detail," said Etzwane.

"To be handled by whom? Me? You? Your group?" Sarajano's tone had become patronizing. "You must think in terms of practicalities."

His strategy becomes clear, thought Etzwane. He will not oppose, but he will not help, and will do all in his power to induce indecision.

"Third," said Etzwane, "the Anome by executive order, must call into being a national militia."

Etzwane politely waited for Sajarano's objections; Sajarano did not disappoint him. "I regret the role of the carper, the defeatist; nevertheless I must point out that it is one matter to issue fiats; it is quite another to implement them. I doubt if you realize the full complexity of Shant. There are sixty-two cantons with nothing in common but language."

"Not to mention music and colour-lore.* Additionally, every citizen of Shant, with the seeming exception of yourself, hates and fears the Roguskhoi. The cantons are more united than you think."

Sajarano gave his little finger an annoyed jerk. "Let me

---

*Ael'skian: More exactly, the symbology of colour and colour-combinations; in Shant an intensely meaningful aspect of life, adding another dimension to perception.

11

recite the difficulties; perhaps then you will understand why I have drawn back from an intolerable confusion. To integrate sixty-two distinct militias, with sixty-two versions of life itself, is a stupendous task. An experienced staff is necessary. There is only myself and my single Benevolence – a girl."

"Since you consider my proposals inept," said Etzwane, "what were your own plans?"

"I have learned," said Sajarano, "that not every problem requires a solution. Many apparently urgent dilemmas dwindle and disappear if ignored. . . . Will you drink more tea?"

Etzwane, who had drunk no tea, signalled in the negative.

Sajarano leaned back in his chair. He spoke in a reflective voice: "The army you propose is impractical for yet another reason – perhaps the most cogent of all. It would be futile."

"Why do you say that?"

"It is really obvious. When any problem must be solved, when some irksome duty must be performed, it is referred to the Faceless Man. When folk complain of the Roguskhoi – have you heard them? – they always call on the Faceless Man to act! As if the Anome need only issue an ordinance to abate all and any nuisances! He has maintained peace for two thousand years, but it is the peace of a father upon a household of children."

Etzwane was silent for a period. Sajarano watched him with peculiar intensity. His gaze dropped to Etzwane's cup of tea. An idle thought drifted into Etzwane's head, which he rejected; certainly Sajarano would not attempt to poison him.

Etzwane said, "Your opinions are interesting, but they

argue only for passivity. My group insists that definite steps be taken: first, a declaration of national emergency; second, women must be evacuated from regions surrounding the Hwan; third, each canton must mobilize and train a militia; fourth, you must designate me as your Executive Aide, with all the authority you yourself command. If you are finished with your breakfast, we will issue these proclamations now."

"What if I refuse?"

Etzwane brought out the metal box. "I will take your head."

Sajarno nibbled at a wafer. "Your arguments are convincing." He sipped his tea and indicated Etzwane's cup. "Have you tasted it? I grow it at my own plantation."

Etzwane pushed his cup across the table. "Drink it."

Sajarano raised his eyebrows. "But I have my own cup."

"Drink it," said Etzwane in a harsh voice. "Otherwise I will believe that you have tried to drug me."

"Would I attempt so banal a ploy?" demanded Sajarano in a brassy voice.

"If you believed that I would discount such a trick as banal, then it becomes subtle. You can refute me by drinking."

"I refuse to be hectored!" spat Sajarano. He tapped his finger on the table. From the corner of his eye Etzwane saw the dark green ivy tremble; he glimpsed a glinting trifle and jerked back. From his sleeve he brought the broad-impulse tube he had taken from Sajarano and pointed it at the ivy. Sajarano emitted a terrible screech; Etzwane pushed the button. From behind the ivy sounded an explosion. Sajarano sprang across the table at Etz-

13

wane. "Murderer, murderer! Oh, the horror, the murder, the blood of my dear one!"

Etzwane struck Sajarano with his fist; Sajarano fell to the rug and lay moaning. From under the ivy a red puddle began to well out across the jade.

Etzwane fought to control his stomach. His mind twisted and reeled. He kicked Sajarano, who looked up with a yellow face and a wet mouth. "Get up!" cried Etzwane hoarsely. "If Jurjin is dead, the fault is yours; you are her murderer! You are my mother's murderer as well; if you had controlled the Roguskhoi long ago, there would not be this trouble!" He kicked Sajarano again. "Get up! Or I take your head in the bargain!"

Sajarano uttered a sob and staggered to his feet.

"So you instructed Jurjin to stand behind the ivy and kill me at your signal!" said Etzwane grimly.

"No, no! She carried an impulse gun, to drug you."

"You are insane! Can you imagine I would not have taken your head? And the tea – poisoned?"

"A soporific."

"What purpose does drugging me serve? Answer!"

Sajarano only shook his head. He had totally lost his poise; he pounded his forehead as if to subdue his thoughts.

Etzwane shook his shoulder. "What do you gain by drugging me? My friends would kill you!"

Sajarano mumbled, "I act as my inner soul dictates."

"From now on I am your inner soul! Take me to your office. I must learn how to communicate with the Discriminators* and the cantonal governments."

Sajarano, round shoulders slumping, led the way

*Avistloi (literally *Nice Discriminators*): the constabulary of the Garwiy Aesthetic Corporation, and the single sophisticated police force of Shant.

through his private study to a locked door. He touched code-keys to open the door; they climbed a spiral staircase to a chamber overlooking all Garwiy.

A bench along the far wall supported a number of glass boxes. Sajarano made a vague gesture. "This is radio equipment. It sends a narrow beam to a relay station on top the Ushkadel, and cannot be tracked. I press this button to transmit messages to the Office of Proclamations; by this, to the Chief Discriminator; by this, to the Hall of Cantons; by this, to the Office of Petitions. My voice is disguised by a filtering device."

"What if I were to speak?" asked Etzwane. "Would anyone know the difference?"

Sajarano winced. His eyes were dull with pain. "No one would know. Do you plan to become Anome?"

"I have no such inclination," said Etzwane.

"In effect this is the case. I refuse all further responsibility."

"How do you answer the petitions?"

"This was Garstang's job. I regularly checked his decisions on the display board. Occasionally he found it necessary to consult; not often."

"When you use the radio, what is your routine? What do you say?"

"It is very simple. I say: 'The Anome instructs that such an act be accomplished.' That is the end of it."

"Very good. Call now the Office of Proclamations, and all the rest. This is what you must say:

'In response to the depredations of the Roguskhoi I proclaim a state of emergency. Shant must now mobilize its strength against these creatures and destroy them.'"

15

Sajarano shook his head. "I cannot say that; you must do so yourself." He seemed disoriented. His hands twitched; his eyes jerked from side to side, his skin showed an ugly yellowish tint.

"Why can't you say it?" asked Etzwane.

"It is contrary to my inner soul. I cannot participate in your venture. It means chaos! "

"If we don't destroy the Roguskhoi it means no more Shant, which is worse," Etzwane said. "Show me how to use the radio."

Sajarano's mouth trembled; for a moment Etzwane thought that he would refuse. Then he said, "Push that switch. Turn the green knob until the green light glows. Push the button of the agency you choose to call. Press the purple button to signal the monitor. When the purple light flashes, speak."

Etzwane approached the bench; Sajarano drew back a few steps. Etzwane pretended to study the equipment. Sajarano darted for the door, passed through, swung it shut. Etzwane hurled himself into the opening; the two struggled. Etzwane was young and strong; Sajarano thrust with hysterical frenzy. Their two heads, on opposite sides of the opening, were only inches apart. Sajarano's eyes bulged, his mouth hung open. His feet slipped, the door swung back.

Etzwane said politely, "Who lives here beside yourself?"

"Only my staff," muttered Sajarano.

"The radio can wait," said Etzwane. "First I must deal with you."

Sajarano stood with sagging shoulders. Etzwane said, "Come. Leave these doors open. I want you to instruct

16

your staff that I and my friends will be taking up residence here."

Sajarano gave a fatalistic sigh. "What are your plans for me?"

"If you cooperate, your life is your own."

"I will do my best," said Sajarano, in the voice of an old man. "I must try, I must try. . . . I will call Aganthe, my major-domo. How many persons will be coming? I live a solitary life."

"I'll have to take counsel with them."

CHAPTER TWO

Sajarano lay drugged in his bedchamber; Etzwane stood in the hall. What to do with the corpse? He did not know. Unwise to order the servants to remove it. Let it stay then, until he had organized matters. . . . Lovely Jurjin! What a waste of beauty and vitality! He could summon no more fury against Sajarano; such emotion seemed stale. Sajarano clearly was insane.

Now: the proclamation. Etzwane returned to the radio room, where he wrote what he considered a succinct and emphatic message. Then he manipulated the array of dials and buttons as Sajarano had instructed. He first signalled the Office of Proclamations.

The purple light flashed.

Etzwane spoke. "The Anome orders dissemination throughout Shant of the following proclamation:

"In response to the dangerous presence of the Roguskhoi in our midst, the Anome proclaims a state of emergency, effective immediately.

"For several years the Anome has attempted to deal with the invaders on the basis of peaceful persuasion. These efforts have failed; we now must act with the total force of our nation; the Roguskhoi will be exterminated or repelled into Palasedra.

"The Roguskhoi exhibit an unnatural lust, from which many women have suffered. To minimize further episodes of this type, the Anome orders that all women depart those cantons adjacent to the Wildlands. They are to travel to maritime cantons, where the authorities must prepare safe and comfortable accommodations.

"Simultaneously, the authorities in each canton shall organize a militia of able men, to the number of at least one man for each one hundred persons of population. Further orders in this regard will be forthcoming. Cantonal authorities, however, must immediately start the process of recruitment. Delay will not be tolerated.

"The Anome will make additional proclamations at an appropriate time. My Executive Aide is Gastel Etzwane. He will coordinate the separate efforts and speak with my voice. He must be obeyed in all regards."

Etzwane called the Chief Discriminator of Garwiy and once again read his proclamation. "Gastel Etzwane must be obeyed as if he were the Anome himself. Is this clear?"

The Chief Discriminator's voice returned: "Gastel Etzwane will be accorded full cooperation. I may say, your Excellency, that this policy will be welcomed throughout Shant. We are pleased that you are taking action!"

"It is not I, declared Etzwane. "The folk of Shant are taking action. I only direct their efforts. I alone can do nothing!"

"This of course is correct," came the response. "Are there further instructions?"

"Yes. I want the most able technists of Garwiy assembled tomorrow at noon in the Corporation Offices, in order that I may take advice upon weapons and weapons production."

19

"I will see to this."

"For the moment, that is all."

Etzwane explored Sershan Palace. The staff watched him askance, muttering and wondering. Never had Etzwane imagined such elegance. He found richness accumulated over thousands of years: glass columns inlaid with silver symbols; rooms of pale blue opening upon rooms of old rose; whole walls worked into vitran* landscapes; furniture and porcelain of the far past; magnificent rugs of Maseach and Cansume; a display of distorted gold masks, stolen at fearful risk from the interior of Caraz.

Such a palace, mused Etzwane, could be his own if he desired. Absurd that Gastel Etzwane, casually fathered by the druithine Dystar upon Eathre of Rhododendron Way, should be – why not admit the situation? – effectively Anome of Shant!

Etzwane gave a melancholy shrug. During his youth he had known penury; each florin he could save represented the fifteen-hundredth part of his mothers freedom. Now the wealth of Shant lay open to his hand! It held no appeal. . . . And what to do about the corpse in the morning room?

In the library he sat down to ponder. . . . Sajarano

*Vitran: a process of visual representation unique to Garwiy. The artist and his apprentice use minute rods of coloured glass a quarter of an inch long, one twentieth of an inch in diameter. The rods are cemented lengthwise against a back-plate of frosted glass. The finished work, illuminated from behind, becomes a landscape, portrait, or pattern, vital beyond all other representational processes, combining radiance, chromatic range, flexibility, refinement, detail, and scope. Inordinate effort and time is required to produce even a small work, with approximately sixty thousand individual rods comprising each square foot of finished surface.

seemed not a villain, but a figure of doom. Why could he not have expressed himself frankly? Why could they not have worked together? Etzwane reviewed the dismal circumstances. Sajarano could not be kept drugged indefinitely; on the other hand he could not be trusted in any other condition – except dead.

Etzwane grimaced. He longed for the presence of Ifness, who seemed never to lack resource. In the absence of Ifness, allies of any sort would be welcome.

There was always Frolitz and his troupe: the Pink-Black-Azure-Deep Greeners. A ridiculous idea, which Etzwane rejected at once ... who else? Two names entered his mind: Dystar, his father, and Jerd Finnerack.

Essentially he knew little of either. Dystar was not even aware of his existence. Etzwane nevertheless had heard Dystar's music, and had been provided evidence as to Dystar's inner self. As for Finnerack, Etzwane remembered only a sturdy youth with a determined brown face and sun-bleached blond hair. Finnerack had been kind to the desperate waif Gastel Etzwane; he had encouraged Etzwane to attempt escape from Angwin Junction, an island in the air. What had become of Jerd Finnerack?

Etzwane returned to the radio room. He called the Chief Discriminators office and requested that information regarding Jerd Finnerack be solicited from the balloon-way office.

Etzwane looked in upon Sajarano, who lay supine in drugged slumber. Etzwane scowled and left the room. He summoned a footman to the great parlour and sent him to Fontenays Inn, where he was to find Frolitz and fetch him to Sershan Palace.

In due course Frolitz arrived, at once truculent and ap-

21

prehensive. At the sight of Etzwane he stopped short, jerked his head back in suspicion.

"Come in, come in," said Etzwane. Waving away the footman, he led Frolitz into the great parlour. "Sit down. Will you take tea?"

"Certainly," said Frolitz. "Are you about to divulge the reason for your presence here?"

"It is a queer set of circumstances," said Etzwane. "As you know I recently submitted a five hundred florin petition to the Anome."

"Of this I am aware; more fool you."

"Not altogether. The Anome had come to share my views; he therefore asked me to assist in what will be a great campaign against the Roguskhoi."

Frolitz gaped in astonishment. "You? Gastel Etzwane the musician? What fantasy is this?"

"No fantasy. Someone must do these jobs. I agreed; additionally, I volunteered your services in this same cause."

Frolitz' grizzled jaw dropped even further. Then his eyes took on a sardonic gleam. "Of course! Precisely what is needed to send the Roguskhoi scuttling: old Frolitz and his savage troupe! I should have thought of it myself."

"The situation is extraordinary," said Etzwane. "Still you need only accept the evidence of your senses."

Frolitz gave a qualified assent. "We seem to be sitting like Aesthetes in an uncommonly luxurious palace. What next?"

"It is as I told you originally. We are to assist the Anome."

Frolitz examined Etzwane's face with renewed suspicion. "One matter must be clear beyond any reconsideration: I am not a warrior; I am too old to fight."

22

"Neither you nor I will actually wield a sword," said Etzwane. "Our duties are to be somewhat clandestine and – naturally – profitable."

"In what regard and to what degree?"

"This is Sershan Palace," said Etzwane. "We are to take up residence here: you, I, the entire troupe. We will be fed and lodged like Aesthetes. Our duties are simple, but before I tell you more I want to learn your opinion of this appointment."

Frolitz scratched his head, working his sparse grey hair into a bristle. "You spoke of profit. This sounds like the Gastel Etzwane of old, who nurtured each florin as if it were a dying saint. All else carries the flavour of hallucination."

"We sit here in Sershan Palace. Hallucination? I think not. The proposal is unexpected, but, as you know, strange things happen."

"True! The musician lives a startling life. . . . I certainly have no objection to occupying Sershan Palace, for as long as the Sershans permit. This would not be your idea of a prank, to see old Frolitz hauled off to Stonebreakers' Island, protesting innocence all the while?"

"Absolutely not, I swear it. What of the troupe?"

"Would they ignore such an opportunity? What then would be our duties – assuming the matter not to be a hoax?"

"It is a peculiar situation," said Etzwane. "The Anome wants Sajarano of Sershan kept under observation. To be blunt, Sajarano is to be held under house-arrest. That is to be our function."

Frolitz grunted. "Now I am beset by another fear: if the Anome starts to employ his musicians as jailers, he may decide to use the displaced jailers as musicians."

"The process will not go so far," said Etzwane. "Essentially, I was instructed to recruit a few trustworthy persons; I thought first of the troupe. As I say, we will all be well paid; in fact, I can requisition new instruments for everyone in the troupe: the best woodhorns, blackbirk khitans with bronze hinges, silver tipples, whatever may be needed or desired, and no thought for expense."

Frolitz' jaw dropped again. "You can do all this?"

"I can."

"If so, you may count upon the cooperation of the troupe. Indeed, we long have needed such a period of relaxation."

Sajarano occupied chambers high in a tower of pearl-glass to the back of the palace. Etzwane found him primly at ease on a green satin couch, toying with a beautiful set of puzzle ivories. His face was drawn; his skin showed the colour and texture of old paper. His greeting was reserved; he refused to meet Etzwane's gaze.

"We have acted," said Etzwane. "The force of Shant is now committed against the Roguskhoi."

"I hope that you find the problems as easy to resolve as to create," said Sajarano curtly.

Etzwane seated himself across from Sajarano on a white wood chair. "You have not altered your views?"

"When they derive from earnest study over a period of years? Of course not."

"I hope, however, that you agree to desist from adverse actions?"

"The power is yours," said Sajarano. "I must now obey."

"So you said before," noted Etzwane. "Then you attempted to poison me."

24

Sajarano gave a disinterested shrug. "I could only do as my inner voice dictated."

"Hmmf.... What does it dictate now?"

"Nothing. I have known tragedy and my only wish is for seclusion."

"This you shall have," said Etzwane. "For a brief period, until events order themselves, a company of musicians with whom I am associated will ensure this seclusion. It is the minimal inconvenience I can impose on you. I hope you will take it in good part."

"So long as they do not rehearse or indulge in destructive horseplay."

Etzwane looked out the window towards the forests of the Ushkadel. "How should we remove the corpse from the morning room?"

Sajarano said in a low voice: "Push the button yonder; it will summon Aganthe."

The major-domo appeared. "In the morning room you will find a corpse," said Sajarano. "Bury it, sink it in the Sualle, dispose of it as you like, but with all discretion. Then clean the morning room."

Aganthe bowed and departed.

Sajarano turned to Etzwane. "What else do you require?"

"I will need to disburse public money. What procedure do I follow in this regard?"

Sajarano's lips twitched with bitter amusement. He put aside the ivories. "Come."

They descended to Sajarano's private study, where for a moment Sajarano stood in cogitation. Etzwane wondered if he planned another grim surprise, and ostentatiously put his hand into his pouch. Sajarano gave the slightest of shrugs, as if dismissing from his mind what-

25

ever idea had entered. From a cabinet he extracted a packet of vouchers. Etzwane cautiously came forward, finger on the yellow button. But Sajarano's defiance had waned. He muttered, "Your policies are far too bold for me. Perhaps they are right; perhaps I have buried my head in the sand.... Sometimes I feel as if I have been living a dream."

In a dull voice he instructed Etzwane in the use of the vouchers.

"Let us have no misunderstandings," Etzwane told Sajarano. "You must not leave the palace, use the radio, send the servants on missions, or entertain friends. We intend you no inconvenience so long as you do nothing to provoke our suspicion."

Etzwane then summoned Frolitz and made him known to Sajarano. Frolitz spoke with a waggish cordiality. "This for me is unfamiliar employment I trust that our association will be placid."

"It will be so on my part," said Sajarano in a bitter voice. "Well then what else do you require?"

"At the moment nothing."

Sajarano went off to his chambers in the pearl-glass tower Frolitz said in a quizzical voice, "Your duties appear to exceed the simple jailing of Sajarano."

"Quite true," said Etzwane. "If you are curious –"

"Tell me nothing!" cried Frolitz. "The less my knowledge the greater my innocence!"

"As you wish." Etzwane showed Frolitz the stairs leading to the radio room. "Remember! Sajarano must definitely be barred from this area!"

"A bold restriction," said Frolitz, "in view of the fact that he owns the palace."

"Regardless, it must be applied. Someone must remain on guard here at all times, day and night."

"Inconvenient when we wish to rehearse," grumbled Frolitz.

"Rehearse here in front of the stairs." He pushed the call-button; Aganthe appeared.

"We will be disrupting your routines for a certain period," said Etzwane. "To be candid, the Anome has ordained a mild form of house-arrest for Sajarano. Master Frolitz and his associates will be in charge of arrangements. They are anxious to obtain your complete cooperation."

Aganthe bowed. "My responsibility is to his Excellency Sajarano; he has instructed me to obey your orders; this I will do."

"Very good. I now instruct you not to listen to any orders Sajarano may utter in conflict with our official duties. Is that clear?"

"Yes, your Excellency."

"If Sajarano gives such an order, you must consult me or Master Frolitz. I cannot emphasize this too strongly. In the morning room you have seen the consequence of incorrect conduct."

"I understand completely, your Excellency." Aganthe departed.

Etzwane told Frolitz: "From now on you must control events. Be suspicious! Sajarano is a resourceful man."

"Do you consider me any the less so?" demanded Frolitz. "Remember when we last played *Kheriteri Melanchine?* Who instantly transposed to the seventh tone when Lurnous embarrassed us all? Is not this resource? Who locked Barndart the balladist in the privy when he persisted in song? What then of resource?"

27

"I have no fears," Etzwane replied.

Frolitz went off to inform the troupe in regard to their new duties; Etzwane returned to Sajarano's study and there drew up a voucher against public funds to the sum of twenty-thousand florins – enough, he calculated, to cover ordinary and extraordinary expenses for the near future.

At the Bank of Shant the sum of twenty thousand florins was paid over without question or formality; never in his life had Etzwane thought to control so much money!

The function of money was its use; at a nearby haberdashery Etzwane selected garments he deemed consonant with his new role: a rich jacket of purple and green velour, dark green trousers, a black velvet cape with a pale green lining, the finest boots to be had.... He surveyed himself in the haberdasher's massive carbon-fume mirror, matching this splendid young patrician with the Gastel Etzwane of earlier days, who never spent a florin on other than urgent need.

The Aesthetic Corporation was housed in the Jurisdictionary, a vast construction of purple, green, and blue glass at the back of the Corporation Plaza. The first two levels dated from the Middle Pandamons; the next four levels the six towers and eleven domes, had been completed ten years before the Fourth Palasedran War, and by a miracle had escaped the great bombardment.

Etzwane went to the office of Aun Sharah, Chief Discriminator of Garwiy, on the second level of the Jurisdictionary. "Be so good as to announce me," he told the clerk. "I am Gastel Etzwane".

Aun Sharah himself came forth: a handsome man

with thick silver hair worn close to his head, a fine aquiline nose, a wide, half-smiling mouth. He wore the simplest of dark grey tunics, ornamented only by a pair of small silverwood shoulder-clips: a costume so distinguished that Etzwane wondered if his own garments might not seem over-sumptuous by comparison.

The Chief Discriminator inspected Etzwane with easy curiosity. "Come into my rooms, if you will."

They went to a large, high-ceilinged office overlooking the Corporation Plaza. Like Aun Sharah's garments, the furnishings of his office were simple and elegant. Aun Sharah indicated a chair for Etzwane and settled upon a couch at the side of the room. Etzwane envied him his ease; Aun Sharah was distracted by no trace of self-consciousness. All his attention, so it appeared, was fixed upon Etzwane, who enjoyed no such advantage.

"You know of the new state of affairs," said Etzwane. "The Anome has committed the power of Shant against the Roguskhoi."

"Somewhat belatedly" murmured Aun Sharah.

Etzwane thought the remark a trifle insouciant. "Be that as it may, we must now arm ourselves. In this regard, the Anome has appointed me his Executive Aide; I speak with his voice."

Aun Sharah leaned back into the couch. "Isn't it strange? Only a day or so ago a certain Gastel Etzwane was the object of an official search. I assume you to be the same person."

Etzwane regarded the Chief Discriminator with pointed coolness. "The Anome sought me; he found me. I put certain facts at his disposal; he reacted as you know."

"Wisely! Or such is my opinion," said Aun Sharah. "What, may I ask, were the 'facts'?"

29

"The mathematical certainty of disaster unless we gave instant battle. Have you arranged the assembly of technists?"

"The arrangements are being made. How many persons did you wish to consult?"

Etzwane glanced sharply at the Chief Discriminator, who seemed bland and relaxed. Etzwane feigned perplexity. "Did not the Anome issue a specific command?"

"I believe that he left the number indefinite."

"In that case, assemble the most expert and well-regarded authorities, from whom we can select a chairman or director of research. I want you to be on hand as well. Our first objective is to create a corps of capable men to implement the Anome's policies."

Aun Sharah nodded slowly and thoughtfully. "How much progress has been made along these lines?"

Etzwane began to find the casual gaze somewhat too knowing. He said, "Not a great deal. Names are still under discussion. . . . In regard to the person Jerd Finnerack, what have you learned?"

Aun Sharah picked up a slip of paper. He read: " 'Jerd Finnerack: an indentured employee of the balloon-way. Born in the village Ispero in the eastern region of Morningshore. His father, a berry grower, used the child's person as security against a loan; when he failed his obligation the child was seized. Finnerack has proved a recalcitrant worker. On one occasion he criminally loosed a balloon from the switching wheel at Angwin Junction, resulting in extensive charges against the company. These costs were added to his indenture. He works now at Camp Three in Canton Glaiy, which is an accommodation for refractory workers. His indenture totals somewhat over two thousand florins.' " He handed the paper to Etzwane.

"Why, may I ask, are you interested in Jerd Finnerack?"

More stiffly than ever Etzwane said, "I understand your natural interest; the Anome, however, insists upon total discretion. In regard to another matter: the Anome has ordered a movement of women to the maritime cantons. Unpleasant incidents must be minimized. In each canton at least six monitors should be appointed to hear complaints and note down particulars for subsequent action. I want you to appoint competent officers and station them as quickly as possible."

"The measure is essential," Aun Sharah agreed. "I will dispatch men from my own staff to organize the groups."

"I leave the matter in your hands."

Etzwane departed the Office of the Chief Discriminator. On the whole, matters had gone well. Aun Sharah's calm visage undoubtedly concealed a seethe of clever formulations, which might or might not persuade him to mischief. More than ever Etzwane felt the need of a completely trustworthy and trusted ally. Alone, his position was precarious indeed.

He returned by a roundabout route to Sershan Palace. For a period he thought that someone followed him, but when he stepped through Pomegranate Portal and waited in the crimson gloom behind the pillar, no one came past, and when he continued, the way behind seemed clear.

CHAPTER THREE

Exactly at noon Etzwane entered the main conference hall of the Jurisdictionary. Looking neither right nor left he marched to the speaker's platform; placing his hands on the solid silver rail, he looked out over the attentive faces.

"Gentlemen: the Anome has prepared a message, which by his instructions I will read to you." Etzwane brought forth a sheet of parchment. "Here are the words of the Anome:

'Greetings to the technical aristocracy of Garwiy! Today I solicit your counsel in regard to the Roguskhoi. I have long hoped to repel these creatures without violence, but my efforts have been in vain; now we must fight.

'I have ordered formation of an army, but this is only half the work; effective weapons are needed.

'Here is the exact problem. The Roguskhoi warrior is massive, savage, fearless. His principal weapons are a metal cudgel and a scimitar: this latter both a cutting and a throwing weapon, effective to a distance of fifty yards or more. In hand-to-hand combat an ordinary man is helpless. Our soldiers therefore must be armed with weapons useful to a range of one hundred yards, or preferably more.

'I place this problem in your hands and direct that you immediately concentrate your efforts upon this single task. All the resources of Shant will be at your disposal.

'Naturally it is necessary that the effort be organized. So now I wish you to choose from among your present number a chairman to supervise your efforts.

'For my Executive Aide I have appointed the person who reads this message, Gastel Etzwane. He speaks with my voice; you will make your reports to him and follow his recommendations.

'I reiterate the urgency of this matter. Our militia is gathering and soon will need weapons.' "

Etzwane put down the paper and looked out over the ranked faces. "Are there any questions?"

A stout and somewhat florid man rose ponderously to his feet. "The requirements are less than clear. What sort of weapons does the Anome have in mind?"

"Weapons to kill the Roguskhoi, and to drive them back, at minimal risk to the user," said Etzwane.

"This is all very well," complained the stout man, "but we are afforded no illumination. The Anome should provide a general set of specifications, or at least basic designs! Are we required to grope in the dark?"

"The Anome is no technist," said Etzwane. "You people are the technists! Develop your own specifications and designs! If energy weapons can be produced, so much the better. If not, contrive whatever is practical and feasible. All over Shant the armies are forming; they need the tools of war. The Anome cannot ordain weapons out of thin air; they must be designed and produced by you, the technists!"

The florid man looked uncertainly from right to left, then sat down. In the back row Etzwane noticed Aun Sharah, with a musing ruminative smile on his face.

A tall man with black eyes burning from a waxen face rose to his feet. "Your remarks are to the point, and we will do our best. But remember: we are technists, not innovators. We refine processes rather than create concepts."

"If you can't do the work, find someone who can," said Etzwane. "I delegate to you the responsibility for this task. Create or die."

Another man spoke: "A matter to affect our thinking is the size of the proposed army. This controls the number of weapons required. Elegance might well be less important than availability and effectiveness."

"Correct," said Etzwane. "The army will number between twenty thousand and one hundred thousand, depending upon the difficulty of the campaign. I might add that weapons are only the most urgent need. We want communication equipment so that the commanders of various groups may coordinate their efforts. Your chairman should appoint a team to develop such equipment."

Etzwane stood waiting for further inquiries, but a glum and dubious silence persisted. Etzwane said, "I will leave you to your work. Select a chairman, a man whom you know to be competent, decisive, and, if necessary harsh. He will designate work groups as he deems practical. Questions or recommendations will reach me through the Chief Discriminator, Aun Sharah."

Without further words Etzwane bowed and departed the way he had come.

In the pavilion before the Jurisdictionary Aun Sharah

approached Etzwane. "The processes go into motion," he said. "I hope efficiently. These folk have no experience in creative work, and if I may say so, the Faceless Man seems in this case indecisive."

"How so?" asked Etzwane in a neutral voice.

"Ordinarily he would request dossiers and evaluations of each man; he would then appoint a chairman and give precise orders. The technists are now puzzled and uncertain; they lack a sure initiative."

Etzwane gave a disinterested shrug. "The Anome has many calculations to make. It is essential that other men share the load."

"Of course, if they are capable, and given a programme."

"They must develop their own programme."

"It is an interesting idea," admitted Aun Sharah. "I hope that it will work."

"It must work, if we are to survive. The Anome cannot fight the Roguskhoi with his own hands. I presume that you have examined my background?"

Aun Sharah assented without embarrassment. "You are, or were, a musician with the well-considered troupe of Master Frolitz."

"I am a musician. I know other musicians in a way you could not know them, if you prepared a hundred dossiers."

Aun Sharah rubbed his chin. "So then?"

"Suppose the Anome wished to organize a troupe of Shant's best musicians. No doubt you would compile dossiers and he would make a selection: would these musicians play well; would they complement each other? I suspect otherwise. My point is this: no outsider can effectively organize a group of experts; they must organ-

35

ize themselves. Such is the Anome's present conviction."

"I will be interested in the progress made by the group," said Aun Sharah. "What weapons do you expect from them?"

Etzwane turned Aun Sharah a cold side-glance. "What do I know of weapons? I have no expectations, any more than the Anome."

"Natural enough. Well then, I must return to my office to reorganize my staff." Aun Sharah went his way.

Etzwane crossed the plaza and stepped down into the Rosewalk. At a secluded table he sipped a cup of tea and considered his progress to date. It was, he thought, significant; important forces had been set into motion. Women were moving to relative safety in the maritime cantons; at best there would be no more breeding of new Roguskhoi, at worst the Roguskhoi would raid further afield. The militia had been ordained; the technists had been instructed to produce weapons. Sajarano was guarded by Frolitz; Aun Sharah, an uncertain quantity, must be dealt with gingerly.

For the moment he had done all in his power. . . . Someone had left a copy of *Aernid Koromatik** on a nearby chair; Etzwane picked it up and scanned the coloured patterns. Pale blue and green characters informed of social events and trivial gossip, with pink and old rose titillations; these columns Etzwane ignored. He read the lavender proclamation of the Anome. In various shades of indigo and green† opinions of well-known persons

---

*Literally "Chromatic Envelope," to signify an inclusive range of every kind of news.

†The exact quality of blue or green measured the quoted person's prestige: Reputation, vanity, ridicule, popularity, pomposity: all were implicit in the depths, variations, and overtones of the colours employed – a symbology of great subtlety.

36

were set forth: all evinced approval. "At last the Anome turns his vast power against the savage hordes," declared the Aesthete Santangelo of Ferathilen, in ultramarine symbols. "The folk of Shant can now relax."

Etzwane's lip curled; he gave the journal a shake. At the bottom of the page a border of brown enclosed an ochre-yellow message: news of morbid and dreadful nature. The Roguskhoi had moved in a strength estimated at over five hundred into the Farwan Valley of Canton Lor-Asphen, killing many men and enslaving a large number of women. "They have established a camp; they show no signs of retreating into the Hwan. Do they then regard the valley as conquered territory?

"The women of Lor-Asphen are now being evacuated into Cantons Morningshore and Esterland as rapidly as possible. Unfortunately, the Anome has not yet mustered sufficient strength to deal a counterblow. It is hoped that there will be no more such terrible acts."

Etzwane laid the paper aside, then on second thought folded it into the pocket of his cape. For a space he sat watching the folk at nearby tables. They chatted; they were charming; their sensibilities were subtle.... Into the garden now came the florid technist, he who had arisen first to ask questions. He wore a pale green cloak over his black and white; he joined a group of his friends at a table near where Etzwane sat: two men and two women, wearing rich robes of blue, green, purple, and white. They leaned forward as the stout man spoke in an animated voice. Etzwane listened: "— insane, insane! This is not our function; what do we know of such things? The Anome expects miracles; he wants bricks without furnishing straw! Let him provide the weapons; is he not the power of Shant?"

37

One of his companions spoke a few words, to which the florid technist made an impatient retort: "It is all nonsense! I intend to draw up a petition of protest; the Anome will surely see reason."

Etzwane listened in a rigidity of disbelief that dissolved into fury. Only minutes before he had enjoined selfless exertion upon this fat, stupid man. Already he spread defeatism! Etzwane brought out the pulse-emitter; he punched the studs to the man's code. .... He stopped short of touching yellow; instead he went to glare down into the man's suddenly blank face. "I heard your remarks," said Etzwane. "Do you know how close you came to losing your head? One eighth of an inch, the press of a button."

"I spoke idly, no more," cried the man in a plaintive rush of words. "Must you take everything at face value?"

"How else? It is how I intend my words. Say goodbye to your friends; you have suddenly become a member of the Garwiy militia. I hope you fight as well as you talk."

"The militia! Impossible! My work—"

"'Impossible'?" Etzwane ostentatiously made a note of the man's colour code. "I will explain circumstances to the Anome; you had best set your affairs in order."

Stunned, white-faced, the man slumped back in his chair.

Etzwane rode a diligence to Sershan Palace. He found Sajarano in the rooftop garden, playing with a prismatic toy. Etzwane stood watching a moment. Sajarano moved coloured spots of light along a white bar, small mouth pursed, eyes studiously averted from Etzwane.

Under that poet's forehead what occurred? What impulses actuated those small hands, once so quick and pow-

38

erful? Etzwane, already in a grim mood, found the bafflement intolerable. He brought forth the newspaper and placed it in front of Sajarano, who put aside the toy to read. He glanced up at Etzwane. "Events rush together. History occurs."

Etzwane pointed to the brown and yellow. "What do you make of this?"

"Tragedy."

"You agree that the Roguskhoi are our enemies?"

"It cannot be denied."

"How would you deal with them, had you power once again?"

Sajarano started to speak, then looked down at his toy. "The avenues of action all lead into dark mist."

Sajarano might well be the victim of mental affliction, thought Etzwane; in fact, this almost certainly was the case. He asked, "How did you become Anome?"

"My father was Anome before me. When he grew old he passed on the power." Looking off into the sky, Sajarano smiled in sad recollection. "The transfer was in this case simple; it is not always so."

"Who was to have been Anome after you?"

Sajarano's smile faded; he frowned in concentration. "At one time I inclined towards Arnold of Cham, whom I considered qualified by birth, intellect, and integrity. I reconsidered. The Anome must be clever and harsh; he can afford no qualms." Sajarano's fingers gave a convulsive twitch. "The terrible deeds I have done! In Haviosq to alarm the sacred birds is a crime. In Fordume the apprentice jade carver must die if his masterwork cracks. Arnold of Cham, a reasonable man, could not enforce laws so grotesque. I considered a man more flexible: Aun

39

Sharah, the Chief Discriminator. He is cool, clever, capable of detachment. . . . I rejected Aun Sharah for reason of style, and settled upon Garstang, now dead. . . . The whole subject is irrelevant."

Etzwane pondered a moment. "Did Aun Sharah know that he was under consideration?"

Sajarano shrugged and picked up the toy. "He is a perceptive man. It is hard to conceal the exercise of power from a person in his position."

Etzwane went to the radio room. He adjusted the filter to disassociate himself from the previous message; he then called Aun Sharah. "This is Gastel Etzwane. I have taken counsel with the Anome. He has ordered that you and I go forth as plenipotentiaries to all regions of Shant. You are required to visit the cantons east of the Jardeen and north of the Wildlands, including Shkoriy, Lor-Asphen Haghead, and Morningshore. I am assigned the cantons to west and south. We are to stimulate and, if necessary coerce the mobilization and training of the various militias. Do you have any questions?"

There was a brief silence. "You used the word 'coerce'. How is this to be effected?"

"We are to note particulars of recalcitrance; the Anome will inflict penalties. Conditions vary. I can offer no explicit instructions; you must use your best judgment."

Aun Shara's voice was a trifle bleak: "When am I to leave?"

"Tomorrow. Your first cantons should perhaps be Wale Purple Fan, Anglesiy, Jardeen, and Conduce; then you can take the balloon-way at Brassei Junction for the far west. I go first to Wild Rose, Maiy, Erevan, and Shade, then take balloon for Esterland. For funds we are

40

to issue drafts against the Bank of Shant, and naturally stint ourselves nothing."

"Very well," said Aun Sharah without enthusiasm. "We must do what is required."

CHAPTER FOUR

The balloon *Iridixn*, requisitioned by Etzwane, swayed at the loading platform: a triple-segmented slab of withe, cord, and glossy film. The winch-tender was Casallo, a young man of airs and graces, who performed the sensitive acts of his trade with bored disdain. Etzwane stepped into the gondola; Casallo, already in his compartment, asked: "What, sir, are your orders?"

"I want to visit Jamilo, Vervei, Sacred Hill in Erevan, Lanteen in Shade. Then we will proceed directly across Shant to Esterland."

"As you wish, sir." Casallo barely stifled a yawn. Over his ear he wore a sprig of purple arasma, souvenir of last night's revelry. Etzwane watched with suspicion as Casallo checked the action of his winches, tested gas valves and ballast release, then dropped the semaphore. "Up we go."

The station gang walked the judas dolly down the slot, allowing the balloon a medium scope. Casallo negligently adjusted cant and aspect to lay the balloon on a broad reach across the wind. The guys were detached from the sheave on the judas dolly, the running dolly was released from its clamp; the balloon slid away; the dolly whirred cheerfully down the slot. Casallo adjusted the guys with the air of a man inventing a new process; the balloon per-

42

ceptibly accelerated and sailed east through Jardeen Gap. The Ushkadel became a dark blur to the rear, and presently they entered Wild Rose, where among wooded hillocks, vales, ponds, and placid meadows the Aesthetes of Garwiy maintained their country estates.

Approaching the market town Jamilo, the balloon showed its orange semaphore and luffed; the station gang trapped the running dolly and diverted it onto a siding, where they clamped it to the slot. They caught the guys in the sheaves of the judas dolly and, hauling the judas dolly up the slot towards the depot, drew the balloon to the ground.

Etzwane went to the canton Moot-hall, which he found quiet and unoccupied. The Anome's proclamation had been posted, but no person of authority had come past to see it.

In a fury Etzwane went to the clerk's cubicle, where he demanded an explanation. The clerk hobbled forth and blinked without comprehension as Etzwane criticized his conduct. "Why did you not summon the councilman?" stormed Etzwane. "Are you so ignorant that you cannot understand the urgency of the message? You are discharged! clear out of this office and be grateful if the Anome does not take your head!"

"During all my tenure events have moved with deliberation," quavered the clerk. "How was I to know that this particular business must go at the speed of lightning?"

"Now you know! How do you summon the councilmen to an emergency session?"

"I don't know; we have never experienced an emergency."

"Does Jamilo boast a brigade for the control of fires?"

43

"Yes indeed. The gong is yonder."

"Go sound the gong!"

The folk of Maiy were commerciants: a tall, dark-haired, dark-skinned people, suave and quiet of demeanour. They lived in octagonal houses with tall, eight-sided roofs; from the centre of which projected chimneys, each taller than the one before; and indeed the height of a man's chimney measured his prestige. The canton's administrative centre, Vervei, was not so much a town as an agglomeration of small industries, producing toys, wooden bowls, trays, candelabra, doors, furniture. Etzwane found the industries working at full speed and the First Negociant of Maiy admitted that he had taken no steps to implement the Anome's proclamation. "It is very difficult for us to move quickly," he stated with a disarming smile. "We have contracts which limit our freedom; you must realize that this is our busy season. Surely the Anome in his power and wisdom can control the Roguskhoi without turning our lives upside down!"

Etzwane ostentatiously noted the code of the Negociant's torc. "If a single one of your concerns opens for business before an able militia is formed and at drill, you will lose your head. The war against the Roguskhoi supersedes all else! Is so much clear?"

The Negociant's thin face became grave. "It is difficult to understand how —"

Etzwane said: "You have exactly ten seconds to start obeying the Anome's orders. Can you understand this?"

The Negociant touched his torc. "I understand completely."

In Conduce Etzwane found confusion. Looming above

44

the horizon to the southeast stood the first peaks of the Hwan; an arm of Shellflower Bay extended almost as close from the north. "Should we send our women north? Or should we prepare to receive women from the mountains? The Fowls say one thing, the Fruits* another. The Fowls want to form a militia of young men, because old men are better with the flocks; the Fruits want to draft old men, because young men are needed to harvest the fruit. Only the Anome can solve our problems!"

"Use young Fowls and old Fruits," Etzwane told him, "but act with decision! If the Anome learned of your delay he'd take heads from Fowls and Fruits alike."

In Shade, under the very loom of the Hwan, the Roguskhoi were a known danger. On many occasions small bands had been glimpsed in the upper valleys, where now no man dared to go; three small settlements had been raided. Etzwane found no need to stress the need for action. A large number of women had been sent north; groups of the new militia were already in the process of organization.

In the company of the First Duke of Shade Etzwane watched two squads drilling with staves and poles, to simulate swords and spears, at opposite ends of the Lanteen Arena. The squads showed noticeable differences in costume, zeal, and general competence. The first wore well-cut garments of indigo and mulberry, with green leather boots; they sprang back and forth; they lunged, feinted, swaggered; they called jocular comments back and forth as they exercised. The second group, in work clothes and sandals, drilled without fervour and spoke only in surly mutters. Etzwane inquired as to the disparity.

*Fowls and Fruits: the rival factions of Conduce, representing the poultry industry and the fruit growers.

"Our policy has not yet been made firm," said the First Duke. "Some of those summoned to duty sent indentured bondsmen, who show no great zest. I am not sure if the system will prove feasible; perhaps persons who find themselves unable to drill should send two bondsmen, rather than one. Perhaps the practice should be totally discouraged. There are arguments for all points of view."

Etzwane said, "The defence of Shant is a privilege accorded only to free men. By joining the militia the indentured man automatically dissolves his debts. Be so good as to announce this fact to the group yonder; then let us judge their zeal."

The balloon-way led into the Wildlands, the *Iridixn* now sailing at the full length of its guys, the better to catch the most direct draughts of wind. At Angwin an endless cable drew the *Iridixn* across Angwin Gorge to Angwin Junction, an island in the sky, from which Etzwane had escaped long ago with the unwitting assistance of Jerd Finnerack.

The *Iridixn* continued southeast, across the most dramatic regions of the Wildlands. Casallo scrutinized the panorama through binoculars. He pointed down into a mountain valley. "You're concerned with the Roguskhoi? Look there! A whole tribe before your eyes!"

Taking the binoculars Etzwane observed a large number of quiet dark spots, perhaps as many as four hundred, beside a stockade of thorn bush. From under a dozen great cauldrons came wisps of smoke, to drift away down the valley. Etzwane examined the interior of the stockade. Certain ambiguous bunches of rags he saw to be huddles of women, to the number of possibly a hundred. At the back of the stockade, under the shelter of a rude shed, were perhaps others.... Etzwane examined other areas of the camp. Each Roguskhoi squatted alone and self-sufficient; a few mended harness, rubbed grease on their bodies, fed wood into the fires under the cauldrons. None, so far as Etzwane could detect, so much as glanced up at the passing balloon or towards the dolly which rolled whirring through the slot not a quarter-mile distant.... The *Iridixn* passed around a crag of rock; the valley could no longer be seen.

Etzwane put the binoculars on the rack. "Where do they get their swords? Those cauldrons are metal – a fortune wouldn't buy them."

Casallo laughed. "Metal cauldrons and they cook grass, leaves, black worms, dead ahulph, and live ones too, anything they can get down their throats. I've watched them through the binoculars."

"Do they ever show any interest in the balloon? They could cause trouble if they meddled with the slot."

"They've never bothered the slot," said Casallo. "Many things they don't seem to notice. When they're not eating or breeding, they just sit. Do they think? I don't know. I talked to a mountain man who walked past twenty sitting quietly in the shade. I asked: 'Were they asleep?' He said, no; apparently they felt no urge to kill him. It's a fact; they never attack a man unless he's trying to keep them from a woman, or unless they're hungry – when he'll go into the cauldron along with everything else."

"If we were carrying a bomb, we could have killed five hundred Roguskhoi," said Etzwane.

"Not a good idea," said Casallo, who tended to contest or qualify each of Etzwane's remarks. "If bombs came from balloons, they'd break the slot."

47

"Unless we used free balloons."

"So then? In a balloon you can only bomb what lies directly below; not often would you drift over a camp. If we had engines to move the balloons, there's a different story, but you can't build engines from withe and glass, even if someone remembered the ancient crafts."

Etzwane said, "A glider can fly where a balloon can only drift."

"On the other hand," Casallo troubled himself to point out, "a glider must land, when a balloon will drift on to safety."

"Our business is killing Roguskhoi," snapped Etzwane, "not drifting safely back and forth."

Casallo merely laughed and went off to his compartment to play his khitan, an accompliment of which he was very proud.

They had reached the heart of the Wildlands. To all sides ridges of grey rock humped into the sky; the slot veered first this way, then that, compromising between vertical and horizontal variations, the first of which made for an uneasy ride and the second for continuous exertion on the part of the winch-tender. As much as possible the slots led across the prevailing winds to afford a reach to balloons in either direction. In the mountains the winds shifted and bounced, sometimes blowing directly along the slot. The winch-tender then might luff and cant to warp his balloon off the side and low, thus minimizing the reverse vector. In worse conditions he could pull the brake cord, wedging the wheels of the dolly against the side of the slot. In conditions worse yet, when the wind roared and howled, he might abandon the idea of progress and drift back down the slot to the nearest station or siding.

Such a windstorm struck the *Iridixn* over Conceil

Cirque: a vast shallow cup lined with snow, the source of the river Mirk. The morning had shown a lavender-pink haze across the south and high in the east a hundred bands of cirrus, through which the three suns dodged and whirled to create shifting zones of pink, white, and blue. Casallo predicted wind, and before long the gusts were upon them. Casallo employed every artifice at his command: luffing, warping high and low; braking, swinging in a great arc, then releasing the brake at a precise instant to eke out a few grudging yards, whereby he hoped to reach a curve in the slot a mile ahead. Three hundred yards short of his goal the wind struck with such force as to set the frame of the *Iridixn* groaning and creaking. Casallo released the brake, put the *Iridixn* flat on the wind, and drifted back down the slot.

At Conceil Siding the station gang brought the balloon down and secured it with a net. Casallo and Etzwane rested the night in the station house, secure within a stockade of stone walls and corner towers. Etzwane learned that the Roguskhoi were very much in evidence. The size of the groups had increased remarkably during the last year, the Superintendent reported. "Before we might see twenty or thirty in a group; now they come in bands of two or three hundred, and sometimes they surround the stockade. They attacked only once, when a party of Whearn nuns were forced down by the wind. There wasn't a Roguskhoi in sight; then suddenly three hundred appeared and tried to scale the walls. We were ready for them – the area is sown thick with land mines. We killed at least two hundred of them, twenty or thirty at a time. The next day we hustled the nuns into a balloon and sent them off, and had no more trouble. Come; I'll show you something."

At the corner of the stockade a pen had been built from

49

ironwood staves; two small red-bronze creatures peered through the gaps. "We took them last week; they'd been rummaging our garbage. We strung up a net and baited it. Three tore themselves free; we took two. Already they're as strong as men."

Etzwane studied the two imps, who returned a blank stare. Were they human? derived from human stock? organisms new and strange? The questions had been raised many times, with no satisfactory answers. The Roguskhoi bone structure seemed generally that of a man, if somewhat simplified at the foot, wrist, and rib cage. Etzwane asked the Superintendent, "Are they gentle?"

"To the contrary. If you put your finger into the cage, they'll take it off."

"Do they speak, or make any sound?"

"At night they whine and groan; otherwise they remain silent. They seem little more than animals. I suppose they had best be killed, before they contrive some sort of evil."

"No, keep them safe; the Anome will want them studied. Perhaps we can learn how to control them."

The Superintendent dubiously surveyed the two imps. "I suppose anything is possible."

As soon as I return to Garwiy I will send for them, and of course you will benefit from your efforts."

"That is kind of you. I hope I can hold them secure. They grow larger by the day."

"Treat them with kindness, and try to teach them a few words."

"I'll do my best."

Down from the Wildlands drove the *Iridixn*, and across the splendid forests of Canton Whearn. For a period the wind died completely; to pass the time Etzwane watched forest birds through the binoculars: undulating air-anenomes, pale green flickers, black and lavender dragonbirds. . . . Late in the afternoon the wind came in a sudden rush; the *Iridixn* spun down the slot to the junction city Pelmonte.

At Pelmonte water of the river Fahalusra, diverted by flumes, provided power for six huge lumber mills. Logs floating down the Fahalusra from the forests were cleaned, trimmed, ripped into planks by saws of sintered ironweb. In seasoning yards the lumber dried in clamps, underwent surfacing, impregnation with oils, stains and special ointments then was either loaded aboard barges or cut to patterns for distant assembly. Etzwane had visited Pelmonte twice before as a Pink-Black-Azure-Deep Greener; he well remembered he redolence of raw sap, resin, varnish, and smoke which permeated the air. The canton Superintendent gave Etzwane an earnest welcome.

The Roguskhoi were well known in North Whearn; for years the lumbermen had kept a watch along the Fahalusra, turning back dozens of minor incursions, using crossbows and pikes, which in the forests were weapons more advantageous than the thrown scimitar of the Roguskhoi.

Recently the Roguskhoi had been attacking by night and in larger bands; the Whears had been driven back beyond the Fahalusra, to their great disturbance. Nowhere in Shant had Etzwane found so much zeal. The women had been sent south; the militia drilled daily. "Take this message to the Anome!" declared the Superintendent. "Tell him to send weapons! Our pikes and crossbows are futile in the open country; we need energy darts, flashing lights, death-horns, and dire contrivances. If the Anome

51

in his power and genius will provide our weapons, we will use them!"

Etzwane could find no words. The Anome, insofar as the office had meaning, was himself: a man with neither power or genius. What to say to these brave people? They should not be deceived; they deserved the truth. He said: "There are no weapons. At Garwiy the best technists of Shant are hard at work. They must be designed, tested, produced. The Anome can only do all he can."

The Superintendent, a tall harsh-faced man, cried out: "Why so tardy? He has known of the Roguskhoi for many years; why is he not ready with the means to protect us?"

"For years the Anome hoped for peace," said Etzwane. "He negotiated, he thought to contain. The Roguskhoi of course have no ears for persuasion."

"This again is no subtle or refined deduction; anyone could have seen it from the first. Now we must fight and we have none of the tools; The Anome, whatever his reasons – softness, indecisiveness, fear – has betrayed us. I say this; you may report my words; the Anome can take my head, nevertheless it is the simple wicked truth."

Etzwane gave a curt nod. "Your candour does you credit. I will tell you a secret. The Anome who so diligently hoped for peace is Anome no longer. Another man has assumed the burden and now must do everything at once. Your remarks are precisely to the point."

"I am overjoyed to hear this!" declared the Superintendent. "But in the meantime what shall we do? We have men and skill and the energy of outrage. We cannot throw ourselves away; we want to give our best: what shall we do?"

"If your crossbows kill Roguskhoi, build bigger crossbows, with greater range," said Etzwane. He remembered the Roguskhoi encampment high in the Hwan. "Build gliders: one-, two-, and six-man carriers; train flyers. Send to Haghead and Azume; demand their best gliders. Take these apart and use the pieces for patterns. For fabric and film send to Hinthe, Marestiy, Purple Stone; require their best in the name of the Anome. For cordage obtain the finest from Cathriy and Frill. In Ferriy the iron workers must set out new tanks; even though they lose their secrets, they must train new men. . . . Call on the resources of all Shant in the name of Anome."

From Pelmonte the *Iridixn* floated at speed to Luthe; from Luthe into Bleke a passenger barge towed the *Iridixn* down the Alfeis River against the sea wind. From Bleke back into Luthe the *Iridixn* drove ahead of a long-keeled coracle, which followed the river Alfeis as a dolly followed the slot. From Luthe to Eye of the East in Esterland, whence Etzwane took sailing packet to Morningshore and Ilwiy, this last canton actually in the territory assigned to Aun Sharah. Etzwane, however, thought to inspect conditions so that he might have a gauge by which to check Aun Sharah's care and accuracy.

From Ilwiy Etzwane returned to Eye of the East, again by ship. The gap in the balloon-way between Ilwiy and Eye of the East was one of several which must be closed as soon as possible! Likewise the long-planned link between Brassei in Elphine and Maschein in Maseach. The distance in each case was not great – perhaps two hundred miles – yet the balloon-way route between, in each case, extended more than sixteen hundred miles. Another loop might well be extended from Brassei west to Pagane, then through Irreale to Ferghaz at the far north of Gitanesq, then southeast through Fenesq to Garwiy. The isolated cantons Haviosq, Fordume, and Parthe had small need for balloon-way service now, true, but what of the future?

From Eye of the East the *Iridixn* drove back to Pelmonte, then swung out along the Great Southern Line, through those wild cantons fronting on the Salt Bog. In each canton Etzwane found a different situation, a different point of view. In Dithibel the women, who owned and managed all shops, refused to leave the mountain areas, out of the certain knowledge that the men would loot their stocks. At the town Houvannah Etzwane, hoarse with rage, cried: "Do you then encourage rape? Have you no sense of perspective?"

"A rape is soon; a loss of goods is long," stated the Matriarch. "Never fear, we have pungent remedies against either nuisance." But she craftily refused to spell out the remedies, merely hinting that "bad ones will rue the day. The thieves, for instance, will find themselves without fingers!"

In Burazhesq Etzwane encountered a pacifist sect, the Aglustids, whose members wore only garments fashioned from their own hair, which they argued to be natural, organic, and deleterious to no other living organism. The Aglustids celebrated vitality in its every aspect and would eat no animal flesh, no vegetable seed or kernel, no nut, and fruit only when the seed might be planted and afforded a chance to exist. The Aglustids argued that the Roguskhoi, more fecund than man, produced more life and were hence to be preferred. They called for passive resistance to "the Anome's war." "If the Anome wants war, let the Anome fight," was their slogan, and wearing their garments of matted hair they paraded through the streets of Manfred, chanting and wailing.

Etzwane was at a loss as to how to deal with them. To temporize went against the grain of his temperament. Still, in what direction should he act? To take the heads of so many tattered wretches was an intolerable idea: on the other hand, why should they be allowed to indulge themselves in recalcitrance while better men suffered for the common good?

In the end Etzwane threw up his hands in disgust and went his way into Shker, where he encountered a condition once more new and distinct, though with haunting echoes of the situation in Burazhesq. The Shker were diabolists, worshipping a pantheon of demons known as *golse*. They espoused an intricate and saturnine cosmology, whose precepts were based on a syllogism, thus:

Wickedness prevails throughout Durdane.
The *golse* are evidently more powerful than
    their beneficient adversaries.
Therefore it becomes the part of simple
    logic to appease and glorify the *golse*.

The Roguskhoi were held to be avatars of the *golse* and creatures to be revered. Arriving at the town Banily Etzwane learned that none of the Anome's orders had been heeded, much less acted upon. The Vay of Shker said with doleful fatalism: "The Anome may well take our heads; still we cannot range ourselves against creatures so sublime in their evil. Our women go willingly to them: we offer food and wine to their appetites; we make no resistance to their magnificent horror."

"This must stop," declared Etzwane.

"Never! It is the law of our lives! Must we jeopardize our future simply for your irrational whims?"

55

Once more Etzwane shook his head in bafflement and went on into Canton Glaiy: a region somewhat primitive, inhabited by a backward folk. They offered him no problems: the regions near the Hwan were uninhabited save for a few feudal clans, who knew nothing of the Anome's instructions. Their relationship with the Roguskhoi was not unequal; whenever possible they waylaid and killed single Roguskhoi, in order to obtain the precious metal in bludgeon and scimitar.

At the principal town, Orgala, Etzwane taxed the three High Judges with their failure to commission a militia; the Judges merely laughed. "Any time you wish a band of able men for your purposes, give us two hours' notice. Until you can provide weapons and definite orders, why should we inconvenience ourselves? The emergency may pass."

Etzwane could not dispute the logic of the remarks. "Very well," he said. "See that when the time comes you are able to perform as promised.... Where is Camp Three, the balloon-way's work agency?"

The Judges looked at him curiously. "What will you do at Camp Three?"

"I have certain orders from the Anome."

The Judges looked at each other and shrugged. "Camp Three is twenty-five miles south, along the Salt Bog Road. You plan to use your fine balloon?"

"Naturally; why should I walk?"

"No reason, but you must hire a tow of pacers; there is no slot."

An hour later Etzwane and Casallo in the *Iridixn* set forth to the south. The balloon guys were attached to the ends of a long pole, which counteracted the buoyancy of the balloon. One end of the pole was attached to the backs

56

of two pacers; the other end was supported by a pair of light wheels, with a seat on which the driver rode. The pacers set off down the road at a fast trot, with Casallo adjusting the aspect of the balloon to produce as little strain as possible. The ride was noticeably different from the movement of a balloon on the wind, a rhythmic impulse being communicated up the guys to the balloon.

The motion and a growing tension – or perhaps he felt guilt? By dint of no great effort he might have come sooner to Camp Three – put Etzwane into a dour, dyspeptic mood. The airy Casallo, with no concerns other than the abatement of boredom, brought forth his khitan; assured of his own musicianship and Etzwane's envious admiration, he attempted a mazurka of the classical repertory which Etzwane knew in a dozen variations. Casallo played the tune woodenly and almost accurately, but on one of the modulations he consistently used an incorrect chord, which presently exasperated Etzwane to a state where he cried out in protest: "No, no, no! If you must pound that instrument, at least use the correct chords!"

Casallo raised his eyebrows in easy amusement. "My friend, you are hearing the Sunflower Blaze; it is traditionally rendered thus and so; I fear you have no ear for music."

"In rough outline, the tune is recognizable, though many times I have heard it played correctly."

Casallo languidly extended the khitan. "Be so good as to instruct me, to my vast gratitude."

Etzwane snatched the instrument, tuned the thumb-string,* which was a pinprick sharp, played the passage

---

*The five prime strings of the khitan are named for the fingers of the right hand; the four second strings have names of unknown significance: Ja, Ka, Si, La.

correctly, with perhaps unnecessary brilliance. Then, working through a second modulation, he played an inversion of the melody in a new mode; then modulating again, he performed an excited staccato improvisation upon the original strain, more or less in accordance with his mood. He struck a double-handed coda with off-beats on the scratch-box and handed the khitan back to the crestfallen Casallo. "So goes the tune, with an embellishment or two."

Casallo looked from Etzwane to the khitan, which he now sombrely hung on a peg, and set about oiling his winches. Etzwane went to stand by the observation window.

The countryside had become wild, almost hostile: patches of white and black rainforest stood like islands on a sea of saw grass. As they travelled south the jungles grew darker and denser, the saw grass showed patches of rot, and presently gave way to banks of blue-white fleshmolt. Ahead gleamed the Brunai River; the road swung somewhat away and to the west, up and across a volcanic flow of rotten grey rocks, then detoured a vast field of overgrown ruins: the city Matrice, besieged and destroyed by the Palasedrans two thousand years before, now inhabited by the huge, blue-black ahulphs of South Glaiy, who conducted their lives in a half-comic, half-horrifying travesty of human urbanity. The ruins of Matrice overlooked a peneplain of a thousand ponds and marshes; here grew the tallest osiers of Shant, in clumps thirty and forty feet tall. The workers of Camp Three cut, peeled, cured, and bundled the withe, barged it down the Brunai to Port Palas, whence coastal schooners conveyed it to the balloon factories of Purple Fan.

Far ahead appeared a dark blot, which through the binoculars became Camp Three. Within a twenty-foot high stockade Etzwane discerned a central compound, a line of work sheds, a long two-storey dormitory. To the left stood a complex of small cottages and administration offices.

The road forked; the pacer team swung towards the administration offices. A group of men came forward and, after a word with the driver, tugged the balloon guys down to sheaves anchored to concrete posts; the pacers, moving forward, drew the *Iridixn* to the ground.

Etzwane stepped from the gondola into a world of humidity and heat. Above him Etta, Sassetta, and Zael whirled through zones of colour; the air over the wasteland quivered; mirages could not be differentiated from the myriad sloughs and ponds.

Three men came slowly forward: one tall, full-fleshed, with bitter grey eyes; the second stocky, bald, with an enormous chin and jaw; the third somewhat younger, lithe and supple as a lizard, with inappropriate black ringlets and flint-black eyes. They were part with the landscape: harsh humourless men without ease or trust. They wore wide-brimmed hats of bleached saw-grass cord, white tunics, grey trousers, ankleboots of chumpa*-hide; at their belts hung small crossbows, shooting gandlewood splints. Each stared coldly at Etzwane, who could not understand the near-palpable hostility and so for a moment was taken aback. More than ever he felt his youth, his inexperience, and, above all, the precariousness of his position. He must assume control. In a neutral voice he said:

**Chumpa:* amphibious creatures of the Salt Bog, cousin to the ahulph, but larger, hairless, and somewhat more sluggish of habit. The chumpa, combining the subtlety and malice of the ahulph with a hysterical obstinacy, were proof against domestication.

"'I am Gastel Etzwane, Executive Aide to the Anome. I speak with the Anome's voice."

The first man gave a slow ambiguous nod, as if at the confirmation of a suspicion. "What brings you here to Camp Three? We are balloon-way people, responsible to balloon-way control."

Etzwane, when he sensed hostility, had developed a habit of pausing to inspect the face of his adversary: a tactic which sometimes upset the other's psychological rhythm and sometimes gave Etzwane time to choose among options. He paused now to consider the face of the man before him, and then chose to ignore the question altogether. "Who are you?"

"I am Chief Custodian of Camp Three, Shirge Hillen."

"How many men work at Camp Three?"

"Counting all personnel: two hundred and three." Hillen's tone was surly, at the very edge of truculence. He wore a torc with the balloon-way code; the balloon-way had been his life.

"How many indentured men?"

"One hundred and ninety."

"I want to inspect the camp."

The corners of Hillen's grey lips pulled back. "It is inadvisable. We have hard cases here; this is a camp for recalcitrants. Had you notified us of your coming, we would have taken proper precautions. At this moment I cannot recommend that you take your inspection. I will give you all relevant information in my office. This way, if you please."

"I must obey the Anome's instructions," said Etzwane in a matter-of-fact voice. "By the same token you must obey me or lose your head." He brought out his pulse-

60

emitter and punched buttons. "Candidly, I do not like your attitude."

Hillen gave the brim of his hat a twitch. "What do you want to see?"

"I'll start with the work area." Etzwane looked at the other two men: the one bald and somewhat short, with immensely wide shoulders and long, knotted arms, which in some particular seemed twisted or deformed. This man's face was curiously still and composed, as if his thoughts occupied an exalted level. The other man, with the black ringlets and black eyes, was not ill-favoured, save for a long, crooked nose, which gave him a devious, dangerous look. Etzwane addressed the two together: "What are your functions?"

Hillen allowed no opportunity for reply. "They are my assistants; I give orders which they carry out."

As Etzwane confronted the three men, his purposes underwent a change. Shirge Hillen apparently had received advance warning of his coming. If so – from whom, to what effect, and why? First, a precaution. Turning on his heel, Etzwane went to where Casallo lounged beside the *Iridixn*, studying a blade of saw grass. "Something is very wrong here," said Etzwane. "Take the balloon aloft; don't bring it down unless I signal with my left hand. If I'm not back before sunset, cut your guys and trust to the wind."

Casallo's aplomb was disturbed by not so much as a raised eyebrow. "Certainly; indeed; just as you wish." He turned a glance of supercilious distaste over Etzwane's shoulder. Etzwane swung around to find Hillen standing with his hand close at his dart gun, his mouth twitching. . . . Etzwane took a slow step back, to where he could now hold Casallo in view. In a sudden, frightening dazzle came

61

a new realization: Casallo had been assigned to the *Iridixn* by officials of the balloon-way. Etzwane could trust no one. He was alone.

Best to maintain the face of trust; Casallo after all might not be party to the plot. But why had he not warned of Hillen's hand so close to his dart gun? Etzwane said in a voice of calm explication: "Be on your guard; if they kill both of us they'd blame one of the workers, and who could prove otherwise? Get into the balloon."

Casallo slowly obeyed. Etzwane watched him closely and could not read the meaning of Casallo's backward glance. Etzwane signalled the hostler: "Let the balloon go aloft." He waited until the *Iridixn* floated three hundred yards overhead, then walked back to the three men.

Hillen grunted a few words over each shoulder to his assistants, then faced Etzwane, who halted at a distance of twenty feet. To the younger of the assistants Etzwane said: "Go, if you please, to your office and bring me here the roster of workers, with the record of their indentures."

The young man looked expectantly towards Hillen, who said: "Please address yourself to me; I alone give orders to camp personnel."

"I speak with the Anome's voice," said Etzwane. "I give orders as I choose, and I must be obeyed, otherwise heads leave necks."

Hillen showed no trepidation. He gestured to his assistant. "Go fetch the records."

Etzwane spoke to the short man. "What are your duties?"

The man looked towards Hillen, his face bland and placid.

Hillen said, "He acts as my bodyguard when I walk

62

among the workers. We deal with desperate men at Camp Three."

"We won't need him," said Etzwane. "Go to the office and stay there until you are summoned."

Hillen made an indifferent gesture; the short man departed.

Hillen and Etzwane waited in silence, until the younger of the assistants returned with a thick grey ledger, which Etzwane took. "You may now return to the office and wait there; we will not need you."

The aide looked questioningly at Hillen, who gave his head a shake and signalled the man to the office. Etzwane watched with suddenly narrowed eyes: the two had betrayed themselves. "Just a moment," he said. "Hillen, why did you shake your head?"

For a moment Hillen was nonplussed. He shrugged. "I meant nothing particular."

Etzwane said in a measured voice: "At this moment we reach a critical phase in your life. Either you cooperate with me, to the exclusion of all else, or I will impose a harsh penalty. You have your choice; which is it to be?"

Hillen smiled a patently insincere smile. "If you are the representative of the Anome, I must obey you. But where are your credentials?"

"Here," said Etzwane, handing over a purple protocol bearing the Anome's sigil. "And here." He displayed the pulse-emitter. "Tell me, then: why did you shake your head to this man? What did you warn him against?"

"Insolence," said Hillen in a voice so neutral as to be an insult in itself.

"You were notified of my coming," said Etzwane. "Is this not correct?"

63

Hillen gave the brim of his hat a twitch. "No such notification reached me."

Around the corner of the stockade came a group of four men carrying rakes, shovels, and leather sacks of water. What if one threatened with his shovel and Hillen, in aiming his dart gun, struck Etzwane instead?

Etzwane, who held absolute power in Shant, was also absolutely vulnerable.

The garden gang shambled across the compound without menace. No threat here. But perhaps on another occasion?

Etzwane said, "Your dart guns are unneeded. Drop them to the ground, if you please."

Hillen growled, "To the contrary, they are constantly necessary. We live and work among desperate men."

Etzwane brought forth the broad-impulse tube, a destructive weapon of cruel potential, which exploded every torc within its range and could as easily destroy a thousand as one. "I make myself responsible for your safety, and I must see to my own. Drop the dart guns."

Hillen still hesitated.

"I will count to five," said Etzwane. "One –"

With dignity Hillen placed his weapon on the ground; his assistant followed suit. Etzwane moved back a pace or two and glanced into the ledger. Each page detailed the name of a worker, his torc code, a resumé of his background. Figures indicated the fluctuating status of his indenture.

Nowhere did Etzwane see the name *Jerd Finnerack*. Odd. "We will visit the stockade," he told Hillen. "You may return to the office." This last was for Hillen's assistant.

They marched through the afternoon glare to the tall

64

stockade, the portals of which stood open. Flight would have little appeal for a man in this soggy land of chumpa, blue-black ahulph, swamp vermin.

Inside the stockade the heat was concentrated and rose in shimmering waves. To one side were tanks and racks, to the other was a great shed where the withe was peeled, scraped, graded, hardened, and packed. Beyond were the dormitories, the kitchens and refectory. The air smelled sour: a rancid odour which Etzwane assumed to derive from withe processing.

Etzwane went to the shed and looked along the line of tables. About fifty men worked here, with a peculiar listless haste. They watched Etzwane and Hillen from the side of their faces.

Etzwane looked into the kitchens. Twenty cooks, busy at various tasks – peeling vegetables, scouring earthenware pots, boning the carcass of a grey-fleshed beast – turned aside expressionless glances which implied more than glares or hoots of derision.

Etzwane slowly returned to the centre of the compound, where he paused to think. The atmosphere at Camp Three was oppressive in the extreme. Still: what else could be expected? Indenture and the threat of indenture guaranteed that each man fulfilled his obligations; the system was acknowledged to be a useful social force. No denying, however, that under extreme circumstances, great hardship was the result. Etzwane asked Hillen, "Who cuts the withe?"

"Work parties go out into the thickets. When they cut their quota they come back in."

"How long have you been here yourself?"

"Fourteen years."

"What is the turnover in personnel?"

"They come, they go."

Etzwane indicated the ledger. "Few of the men seem to diminish their obligations. Ermel Gans, for instance, in four years has reduced his debt only two hundred and ten florins. How is this possible?"

"The men run up irresponsible charges at the canteen – drinking, for the most part."

"To the extent of five hundred florins?" Etzwane pointed to an entry.

"Gans committed an unruly act and was put into a disciplinary cell. After a month Gans decided to pay a fine."

"Where is the disciplinary annex?"

"It is an annex behind the stockade," Hillen's voice had taken on a rough edge.

"We will inspect this annex."

Hillen strove to keep his voice pitched in a tone of calm rationality. "This is not a good idea. We have serious disciplinary problems here. The interference of an outsider can create a turmoil."

"I am sure this is true," said Etzwane. "On the other hand, abuses, if such exist, come to light only when someone notices them."

"I am a practical man," said Hillen. "I merely enforce company regulations."

"Conceivably the regulations are unreasonable," said Etzwane. "I will inspect the annex."

Etzwane said in a stifled voice: "Get these men out into the air at once."

Hillen's face was like a stone. "What are your plans here at Camp Three?"

"You'll learn in due course. Bring the men up from those holes."

66

Hillen gave a terse order to the guards. Etzwane watched as fourteen haggard men came forth from the annex. He asked Hillen: "Why did you remove the name *Jerd Finnerack* from the roster?"

Hillen apparently had been waiting for the question. "He is no longer on the work force."

"He paid out his indenture?"

"Jerd Finnerack has been transferred to civil custody."

In a mild voice Etzwane asked, "Where is he now?"

"In criminal detention."

"And where is that?"

Hillen jerked his head towards the south. "Yonder."

"How far?"

"Two miles."

"Order a diligence."

The way to the detention house led across a dreary flat, mounded with rotting waste from the withe processing, then entered through a grove of enormous grey shagbarks. After the stockade, and in anticipation of the detention compound, the beauty of the way seemed weird and unreal. Masses of pale green foliage floated far overhead, ethereal as clouds; the cool spaces below were like grottoes. A few thin beams of sunlight impinged in a trefoil of circles upon the dust of the road: pale blue, pearl white, pink.

Etzwane broke the silence: "Have you seen Roguskhoi in the neighbourhood?"

"No."

The forest dwindled into a thicket of aspen, tape leaves, and stunted similax, the road broke out upon a soggy, black heath, steaming with aromatic vapours. Insects

67

glinted past, whining like darts. Etzwane at first tended to flinch and duck; Hillen sat sternly erect.

They approached a low concrete structure almost windowless. "The detention house," said Hillen.

Etzwane, noticing a peculiar aliveness to his expression, became instantly suspicious. "Stop the diligence here."

Hillen turned him a burning, narrow-eyed glance. He looked in angry frustration towards the detention hall, then hunched his shoulders. Etzwane jumped quickly to the ground, now certain that Hillen had planned mischief. "Get to the ground," he said. "Walk to the hall, call forth the guards. Have them bring out Jerd Finnerack and send him here to me."

Hillen gave a fatalistic shrug; stepping down to the road, he trudged to the blockhouse, halting a few yards from the entrance. He called brusquely. From within came a short, fat man with unkempt wads of black hair hanging down past his cheeks. Hillen made a sharp, furious motion; the two looked back at Etzwane. The fat man asked a sad question; Hillen gave a terse reply. The fat man returned within.

Etzwane waited, his mind charged with tension. At Angwin Junction Finnerack had been a sturdy blond youth, mild and trusting. From sheer goodness, so it then had seemed, Finnerack had urged escape upon Etzwane and had even offered assistance. Certainly he had never envisioned Etzwane's dramatic act, which after the event had cost Finnerack dearly. Etzwane now realized that he had bought his own freedom at the cost of Finnerack's suffering.

From the house stumbled a thin, crooked man of indeterminate age. His yellow-white hair hung in snarls past his ears. Hillen jerked his thumb towards Etzwane. Finnerack turned to look, and across fifty yards Etzwane felt the hot, blue-white gaze. Slowly, painfully, as if his legs ached, Finnerack came down the road. Twenty feet behind strolled Hillen arms casually folded.

Etzwane called out sharply: "Hillen! go back to the house!"

Hillen appeared not to hear.

Etzwane pointed the pulse-emitter. "Go back!"

Hillen turned and, still holding his arms folded, went slowly back to the house. Finnerack looked back and forth, with a puzzled half-grin, then continued towards Etzwane.

Finnerack halted. "What do you want of me?"

Etzwane searched the corded brown face, seeking the placid Finnerack of old. Finnerack clearly did not recognize him. Etzwane asked, "You are the Jerd Finnerack who served at Angwin Junction?"

"I am and I did."

"How long have you been here?" Etzwane indicated the detention house.

"Five days."

"Why were you brought here?"

"So they could kill me. Why else?"

"But you are still alive."

"True."

"Who is inside?"

"Three prisoners and two keepers."

"Finnerack, you are now a free man."

"Indeed. Who are you?"

"There is a new Anome in the land of Shant. I am his executive assistant. What of the other prisoners? What are their crimes?"

"Three assaults on a guard. I have assaulted only twice; Hillen no longer can count to three."

Etzwane turned to consider Hillen, who hulked morosely in the shade of the detention house. "Hillen carries a dart gun under his arms, or so I suspect. Before my arrival, what was the conduct of the guards?"

"An hour ago they received a message from Camp Three and went to stand by the window with their weapons. Then you arrived. Hillen called to put me out. The rest you know."

Etzwane called to Hillen. "Order the guards outside."

Hillen spoke over his shoulder; two guards came forth, the first fat, the second tall and sallow with docked ears.

Etzwane moved a few slow paces forward. "All three of you — turn your backs and put your hands in the air."

Hillen stared woodenly, as if he had not heard. Etzwane was not deceived. Hillen calculated his chances, which were poor, from any aspect. Hillen disdainfully dropped the dart gun he had somehow managed to obtain. He turned and put his hands into the air. The two guards did likewise.

Etzwane moved somewhat closer. He told Finnerack: "First check the guards for weapons, then release the other prisoners."

Finnerack went to obey. Moments passed, silent except for the whine of insects and a few muffled sounds from within the detention house. The prisoners came forth: pallid, bony men blinking curiously towards Etzwane. "Pick up the dart gun," Etzwane told Finnerack. "Take Hillen and the guards to the cells; lock them up."

With ironic calm Finnerack signalled the three officials — gestures no doubt modelled upon those the officials themselves employed. Hillen, appreciating this, smiled grimly and walked into the detention house.

Whatever his faults, thought Etzwane, Hillen accepted adversity without loss of dignity. Today, from Hillen's point of view, had proved an adverse day indeed.

Etzwane consulted with Finnerack and the other two erstwhile prisoners, then went into the fetid detention house. His stomach jerked at the filth of the cells, in which Hillen and his minions hunched grim and disconsolate.

Etzwane spoke to Hillen: "Before arriving at Camp Three I bore you no ill will, but first you sought to thwart me, then to kill me. Beyond doubt you received instructions from another source. What was that source?"

Hillen only stared with eyes like lead balls.

Etzwane said, "You have made a bad choice." He turned away.

The fat guard, already streaming with sweat, called plaintively: "What of us?"

Etzwane spoke dispassionately, "Neither Finnerack, Jaime, nor Mermiente argues for your release. Each feels that clemency would be a mistake. Who should know better than they? Jaime and Mermiente have agreed to act as your jailers; henceforth you must deal with them."

"They will kill us; is this the justice of the Anome?"

"I don't know where justice lies," said Etzwane. "Perhaps it will come of itself, for you surely will get as much mercy as you gave."

Finnerack and Etzwane went to the diligence, Etzwane ill-at-ease and looking back over his shoulder. Where was justice indeed? Had he acted wisely and decisively? Had

71

he taken the weak, maudlin easy course? Both? Neither? He would never know.

"Hurry," said Finnerack. "Towards sunset the chumpas come up from the swamp."

Through the declining light they set out to the north. Finnerack began to study Etzwane from the side of his eyes. "Somewhere I have known you," said Finnerack. "Where? Why did you come for me?"

Sooner or later the question must be answered. Etzwane said, "Long ago you did me a service, which I finally am able to repay. This is the first reason."

In Finnerack's corded brown face the eyes glinted like blue ice.

Etzwane went on. "A new Anome has come to power. I serve as his executive assistant. I have many anxieties; I need an assistant of my own, a confederate on whom I can rely."

Finnerack spoke in a voice of awe and wonder, as if he doubted either Etzwane's sanity or his own. "You have chosen me for this position?"

"This is correct."

Finnerack gave a chuckle of wild amusement, as if his doubts were now resolved: both he and Etzwane were mad. "Why me, whom you hardly know?"

"Caprice. Perhaps I remember how you were kind to a desperate waif at Angwin."

"Ah!" The sound came up from the depths of Finnerack's soul. The amusement, the wonder were gone as if they had never existed. The bony body seemed to crouch into the seat.

"I escaped," said Etzwane. "I became a musician. A month ago the new Anome came to power and instantly called for war against the Roguskhoi. He required that I enforce this policy and I myself was given power. I learned of your condition, though I did not realize the harshness of Camp Three."

Finnerack straightened in his seat. "Can you guess your risk in telling this tale? Or my rage towards those who have made my life? Do you know what they have done to me to make me pay debts I never incurred? Do you know that I consider myself mad: an animal that has been made savage? Do you know how taut is the film that halts me from tearing you to pieces and running back to do the same for Hillen?"

"Restrain yourself," said Etzwane. "The past is the past; you are alive, and now we have work to do."

"Work?" sneered Finnerack. "Why should I work?"

"For the same reason I work: to save Shant from the Roguskhoi."

Finnerack uttered a harsh gust of laughter. "The Roguskhoi have done me no harm. Let them do as they like."

Etzwane could think of nothing to say. For a period the diligence rolled north along the road. They entered the shagbark grove, and the sunlight, now noticeably lavender, cast long green shadows.

Etzwane spoke. "Have you never thought how you would better the world, had you the power?"

"I have indeed," said Finnerack in a voice somewhat milder than before. "I would destroy those who had ravaged me: my father, Dagbolt, the wretched boy who took his freedom and made me pay the cost, the balloon-way magnates, Hillen. There are many."

"This is the voice of your anger," said Etzwane. "By destroying these people you do nothing real; the evil continues, and somewhere other Jerd Finneracks will ache to destroy you for not helping them when you had power."

"Correctly so," said Finnerack. "All men are bags of vileness, myself as well. Let the Roguskhoi kill all."

"It is foolish to be outraged by a fact of nature," Etzwane protested. "Men are as they are, on Durdane even more so. Our ancestors came here to indulge their idiosyncrasies; an excess of extravagance is our heritage. Viana Paizifiume understood this well and put torcs around our necks to tame us."

Finnerack tugged at his torc so viciously that Etzwane shrank away for fear of an explosion.

"I have not been tamed," said Finnerack. "I have only been enslaved."

"The system has faults," Etzwane agreed. "Still, across Shant the cantons keep peace and laws are obeyed. I hope to repair the faults, but first the Roguskhoi must be dealt with."

Finnerack gave only an uninterested shrug. They rode on in silence: out of the shagbark forest across the saw-grass meadow, now silent and melancholy in the twilight.

Etzwane spoke pensively, "I find myself in a peculiar position. The new Anome is a man of theories and ideals; he relies on me to make the hard decisions. I need help. I initially thought of you, who had helped me before and to whom I owed gratitude. But your attitude discourages me; perhaps I must look elsewhere. I can still give you freedom and wealth – almost anything you want."

Finnerack tugged again at the torc, which hung loosely around his taut brown neck. "You can't remove my noose; you can't give me real freedom. Wealth? Why not? I have earned it. Best of all give me the governance of Camp Three, if only for a month."

"What would you do if this were the case?" asked Etzwane, hoping to gauge the exact condition of Finnerack's mind.

"You would see a new Finnerack. He would be calm and judicious and calculate each act to an absolutely just proportion.

"Hillen now will die in a week or so, but he is far more guilty. His policy has been to goad the workers into insolence, or insubordination, or careless work, whereupon they are fined the labour of three months, or six months, or a year. No man in memory has paid off his indenture while working at Camp Three. I would keep him alive at least the month I was in power, in a cage where the men he has abused could come to look at him and speak to him. At the end of a month I would give him to the chumpas. The assistants, Hoffman and Kai, are unspeakable; they deserve the worst." Finnerack's voice began to vibrate. "They would work withe through the lye vats by day and go to the annex at night: this for the rest of their lives. They might live two or three months; who knows?"

"What of the guards?"

"There are twenty-nine guards. All are strict. Five are fair and inclined to leniency. Another ten are detached and mechanical. The others are brutes. These would go at once to the detention house and never return. The ten would go to the annex for an indefinite period – perhaps three months – and thereafter work withe for five years. The five good guards –" Finnerack knit his sun-bleached brows. "They offer a problem. They did what they could, but took no personal risks. Their guilt is not precise; nevertheless it is real. They deserve expiation – a year at working withe, then discharge without pay."

"And the indentured men?"

Finnerack looked around in surprise. "You talk of indenture? Everyone has paid ten times over. Each man goes forth free, with a bonus of ten times his original indenture."

"And who then is to cut withe?" asked Etzwane.

"I care nothing about withe," said Finnerack. "Let the magnates cut their own withe."

They rode on in silence, Etzwane reflecting that Finnerack's dispensations were not disproportionate to the conditions that had prompted them. Ahead, black on the violet dusk, stood the shape of the Camp Three stockade. The *Iridixn* floated above.

Finnerack indicated a crumble of rotten rock beside the road. "Someone waits for us."

Etzwane pulled the diligence to a halt. For a few seconds he considered. Then he brought forth the broad-impulse tube, pointed it towards the rocks, and pressed the button. A pair of explosions pounded against the evening calm.

Etzwane walked behind the rock, followed by Finnerack; they looked down at the headless bodies. Finnerack gave a grunt of disgust. "Hoffman and Kai. They are lucky men indeed."

At the entrance to the stockade Etzwane drew up the diligence. Camp Three was an outrage; justice must be done. But how? to whom? by whom? by which set of laws? Etzwane became confused and sat staring through the portal to where men stood in muttering groups.

Finnerack began to fidget and shiver and hiss through his teeth. Etzwane was reminded of Finnerack's set of judgments, which while harsh had seemed appropriate. He now discerned a principle which, he told himself, he should have apprehended before, since it formed the basic ethos of Shant.

For local grievance, local redress. For Camp Three crimes, Camp Three justice.

CHAPTER FIVE

Etzwane had gone aloft in the *Iridixn*. In fascination he looked down through binoculars into the stockade. The portal had been closed; the guards were confined in a storage shed. By the light of wall lanterns and a crackling bonfire men wandered back and forth, as if dazed. The best food the camp had to offer was spread out on tables – including all the delicacies of the commissary. The men ate as if at a banquet, regaling themselves with dried eel and the thin, sour wine Hillen had sold so dearly. Certain of the men began to grow agitated; they walked back and forth talking and gesticulating. Finnerack stood somewhat to the side; he had eaten and drunk sparingly. Outside the stockade Etzwane saw the furtive movement of dark shapes: ahulphs and chumpas, attracted by the unusual activity.

The men could eat no more; the cask of wine was dry. The men began to pound on the table and chant. Finnerack came forward; he called out; the chanting dwindled and ceased. Finnerack spoke at some length, and the crowd became dull and quiet, with restless motions of the shoulders. Then three men almost simultaneously jumped forward and in great good nature hustled Finnerack off to the side. Finnerack shook his head in disgust but said no more.

The three men held up their arms for quiet. They conversed among themselves and listened to suggestions from the crowd. Twice Finnerack thrust forward to make a passionate point, and on each occasion he was respectfully heard. It appeared to Etzwane that the differences concerned tactics rather than substance.

The colloquy became intense, with a dozen men pounding on the table at once.

Again Finnerack came forward, and his proposals halted the argument. One of the men took paper and stylus and wrote to Finnerack's dictation, while others in the crowd called out suggestions and emendations.

The bill of indictments – such it appeared to be – was complete. Finnerack once more moved aside and watched with a brooding gaze. The three men took charge of proceedings. They designated a group of five, who went to the storage shed and returned with a guard.

The crowd surged forward, but the three men spoke sternly and the crowd drew back. The guard was placed up on a table to confront the men so recently under his authority. One of the workers came forward and recited an accusation, punctuating each charge with a dramatic stab of the forefinger. Finnerack stood apart with lowering brows. Another man came forward and uttered his own complaints, and another and another. The guard stood with a twitching face. The three men spoke a verdict. The guard was dragged to the gate of the stockade and thrust outside. Two blue-black ahulphs came to take him; as they argued, a mottled grey chumpa lumbered up and dragged the guard off into the darkness.

Fourteen of the guards were brought forth from the

storage shed. Some came indolent and resigned, some glared in defiance, some hung back and jerked at the grip of the men who conveyed them, a few came hopefully smiling and jocular. Each was lifted up to stand on the table, in the full glare of the firelight, where he was judged. In one case Finnerack lunged forward to protest, pointing up towards the *Iridixn*. This man evaded the dark grounds beyond the stockade, where latecoming chumpas moaned. Instead he was directed to the long vats, where new withe steeped in a caustic solution, and forced to strip bark.

The remaining guards were brought forth and charged. One of these, after considerable debate, and with the guard pleading his own case, was thrust out into the night; the others were put to working withe.

All the guards had now been judged. Another cask of Hillen's wine was carried forth; the men drank and revelled, and jeered at the erstwhile guards who now worked withe. A few became torpid and sat lounging around the fire. The guards stripped bark and cursed the destiny which had brought them to Camp Three.

Etzwane put down the binoculars and went to his hammock. Events, he told himself hollowly, had gone about as well as could be hoped.... Somewhat after midnight he went again to look down into the stockade. The men sat around the fire, dozing or asleep. A few stood watching the guards work withe, as if they could never get enough of the spectacle. Finnerack sat hunched on a table to the side. After a few minutes Etzwane returned to his hammock.

Etzwane spent a tiresome morning cancelling indentures and signing indemnity vouchers for more or less arbitrary sums.—Most of the men wanted no more withe cutting; in small groups they departed the camp and trudged north towards Orgala. About twenty agreed to remain as supervisors; their ambitions extended no farther. For years they had envied the guards their perquisites, now they could enjoy them to the utmost.

The *Iridixn* was brought down; Etzwane entered, followed by Finnerack, whom Casallo regarded with shock and fastidious dismay; for a fact Finnerack was somewhat unkempt. He had neither bathed nor changed his clothes; his hair was tangled and overlong; his smock was torn and filthy.

The *Iridixn* lifted into the air, the pacers set off to the north. Etzwane felt like a man awakening from a nightmare. Two questions occupied his mind. How many more Camp Threes existed in Shant? Who had warned Shirge Hillen of his visit?

At Orgala the *Iridixn* returned to the slot and, reaching on a fresh breeze, spun off into the north-west. Late in the following day they entered Canton Gorgash, and the morning after put down at the city Lord Benjamin's Dream. Etzwane found no fault with the Gorgash militia, though Finnerack made sardonic criticisms in regard to the pompous leadership, almost equal in numbers to the uninterested and sluggish soldiers themselves. "It is a start," said Etzwane. "They have no experience in these matters. Compared with the folk of Dithibel or Buraghesq or Shker, these folk are proceeding with intelligence and urgency."

"Perhaps so – but will they fight the Roguskhoi?"

"That we will learn when the time comes. How would you alter matters?"

"I would strip the uniforms and plumed hats from the officers and make cooks of the lot. The troops I would

81

split into four corps and skirmish them daily against each other, to anger them and make them vicious."

Etzwane reflected that a similar process had altered a placid blond youth into the corded brown recalcitrant now in his company. "It may come to that before we're done. At the moment I'm content to see so earnest a turn-out."

Finnerack gave his jeering laugh. "When they find out what they're up against, there'll be less."

Etzwane scowled, not liking to hear his secret fears verbalized so openly. Finnerack, he thought, was by no means tactful. Additionally, he was less than a savoury travelling companion. Etzwane looked him over critically. "Time we were repairing your appearance, which at the moment is a cause for adverse comment."

"I need nothing," Finnerack muttered. "I am not a vain man."

Etzwane would not listen. "You may not be vain but you are a man. Consciously or unconsciously you are affected by your appearance. If you look untidy, unkempt, and dirty, you will presently apply the same standards to your thinking and your general mode of life."

"More of your psychological theories," growled Finnerack. Etzwane nonetheless led the way to the Baronial Arcades, where Finnerack grimly allowed himself to be shorn, barbered, bathed, manicured, and attired in fresh garments.

At last they returned to the *Iridixn,* Finnerack now a wiry, taut-muscled man with a square, deeply lined face, a head of tight bronze curls, a bright, ever-shifting gaze, a mouth clenched back in what at first view seemed a good-natured half-smile.

At Maschein, in Canton Maseach, the *Iridixn* reached the terminus of Calm Violet Sunset* Route. Casallo, allowing himself a final extravagance, swept the *Iridixn* in a great swooping arc around and into the wind, a fine flourish which pitched Etzwane and Finnerack to the floor of the gondola. A station gang drew the *Iridixn* to the landing dock. Without regret Etzwane jumped down from the gondola, followed by the unsmiling Finnerack, who had not forgiven Casallo his intemperate manoeuvre.

Etzwane bade Casallo farewell, while Finnerack stood sombrely to the side, then the two set forth into the city.

A passenger punt, which plied the many canals of Maschein, took them to the River Island Inn, which, with its terraces, gardens, arbours, and pergolas, occupied the whole of a rocky islet in the Jardeen. During his visits to Maschein as a penurious Pink-Black-Azure-Deep Greener, Etzwane had long and often gazed across the water at this most agreeable of hostelries; he now commanded a suite of four chambers giving on a private garden banked with cyclamen, blue spangle, and lurlinthe. The rooms were panelled in fine-grained wood, stained ash-green in the sleeping chambers, a delicate aelsheur* in the drawing

---

*The language of Shant discriminates between various types of sunsets. Hence:

feovhre – a calm, cloudless violet sunset.

arusch'thain – a violet sunset with horizontal apple-green clouds.

gorușurhe – a flaring, flamboyant sunset encompassing the entire sky.

shergorszhe – as above; additionally with cumulus clouds in the east, illuminated and looking towards the west.

heizen – a situation where the sky is heavily overcast except for a ribbon of clarity at the western horizon, through which the sun sets.

Aelsheur: literally air-colour.

room, with the subtlest films of pale green, lavender, and dim blue to suggest meadows, and water vistas.

Finnerack looked around the chambers with a curled lip. He seated himself, crossed one leg over the other, stonily gazed out over the slow Jardeen. Etzwane allowed himself a small, private smile. Had the amenities at Camp Three been so superior?

In a limpid garden pool Etzwane bathed, then donned a white linen robe. Finnerack sat as before gazing out at the Jardeen. Etzwane ignored him; Finnerack would have to adjust in his own way.

Etzwane ordered an urn of frosted wine and copies of the local journals. Finnerack accepted a goblet of wine but showed no interest in the news, which was grim. Paragraphs by turns black, brown, and mustard-ochre reported that in Cantons Lor-Asphen, Bundoran, and Surrume the Roguskhoi were on the move, that Canton Shkoriy had fallen entirely under Roguskhoi control. Etzwane read:

> The Anome's policy of evacuating women to the maritime cantons is doubtless correct; the effect however has been to stir and stimulate the Roguskhoi to ever more ferocious depredations, that they may gratify their apparently insatiable lust. Where will this dreadful process end? If the Anome in his might cannot thrust the fearful hordes back from whence they came, in five years Shant will be a solid seethe of Roguskhoi. Where will they turn next? To Caraz? It must be so assumed, since the Palasedrans would not loose so fearful a weapon upon the folk of Shant without reserving for themselves a means of control.

84

Another article, surrounded in dark scarlet and grey, described the Maseach militia in sufficient detail that Etzwane decided to make no personal representations. With an uncomfortable grimace he read the final sentences:

> Our brave men have come together; they now familiarize themselves with military minutiae, long put aside and almost forgotten. With eagerness and hope they await the powerful weapons the Anome prepares; inspired by his majestic leadership they will smite the vicious red bandits and send them howling like scalded ahulphs.

"So they await my 'powerful weapons,' my 'majestic leadership,'" muttered Etzwane. If they knew him as he was – a bewildered musician, without competence, experience, or aptitude – they would be less sanguine.... His eye fell on a notice bordered in grey and ultramarine. Etzwane read:

> Last night at the Silver Samarsanda the druithine Dystar made his appearance. His meal was paid for long before he ordered it and anonymous gifts were pressed upon his uninterested attention. As usual he rewarded the company with astonishing hurusthra* and told of places where few are privileged to go. Dystar may return tonight to the Silver Samarsanda.

Etzwane read the notice a second and a third time. Recently he had thought nothing of music; now a wave of longing came over him: what had he done to himself?

Hurusthra: roughly, musical panoramas and insights.

Must he pass all his life in these sterile circumstances? Luxury, frosted wine, four-room garden suites – what were they to the life he had known with Frolitz and the Pink-Black-Azure-Deep Greeners?

Etzwane put the journal aside. In contrast to the life Finnerack had led he had been lucky. He turned to examine Finnerack, wondering what went on behind the taut brown countenance. "Finnerack!" Etzwane called out, "have you seen the news?" He handed the journal to Finnerack, who scanned the page with a scowl of unguessable import. "What are these mighty weapons the Anome is preparing?" asked Finnerack.

"To the best of my knowledge, they are non-existent."

"Without weapons, how do you expect to kill Roguskhoi?"

"The technists are at work," said Etzwane. "If weapons are forthcoming, the men will be armed. If not they must fight with dart guns, bows and arrows, dexax grenades and bombs, lances and pikes."

"The decision to fight comes tardily."

"I know this. The former Anome refused to attack the Roguskhoi, nor will he now explain his reasons."

Finnerack evinced a degree of interest. "He is not dead then?"

"No, he was deposed and replaced."

"Who performed this remarkable feat?"

Etzwane saw no reason to withhold the information. "Do you know of Earth?"

"I have heard it mentioned: the human home world."

"On Earth is an organization known as the Historical Institute, where Durdane is remembered. By chance I met a man named Ifness, a Fellow of the Historical Institute, who had come to study Durdane. Together we learned the identity of the Faceless Man and urged him to take steps against the Roguskhoi. He refused, so we deposed him and set new processes into motion."

Finnerack inspected Etzwane with glittering eyes. "An Earthman is Anome of Shant?"

"I wish he were," said Etzwane. "Unfortunately he refuses the job.... The Anome is someone else. I assist him; I myself need an assistant: perhaps yourself, if you have the will to serve Shant?"

"Shant has done me nothing but harm," said Finnerack. "I must live for myself alone."

Etzwane grew impatient. "Your bitterness is understandable, but should you not focus it more carefully? Working with me, you could help other victims. If you don't do this you become no better than Hillen, and far worse than the ordinary people, whom you despise so much. Who here in Maschein, for instance, knew of Camp Three? No one."

Finnerack shrugged and stared wooden out over the Jardeen, on which violet evening light was falling.

Etzwane presently spoke, in a voice he tried to keep even: "Tonight we dine at the Silver Samarsanda, where we will hear a great druithine."

"And what is that?"

Etzwane looked around in astonishment. Nothing could have better dramatized the scope of Finnerack's deprivation. Etzwane spoke more warmly, "A druithine is a musician who wanders alone. He may play the gastaing, or the khitan, or even the darabence, and his music is usually of high quality."

"I don't know one note of music from another," said Finnerack in a flat voice.

Etzwane controlled a new sense of impatience. "You will at least enjoy your meal; the Maseache are famous for their fine restaurants."

The Silver Samarsanda stood above the Jardeen, behind a line of tall pencil cypress; an irregular bulk of masonry, plastered and whitewashed, with a wide, many-slanted roof of mossy tiles. Beside the entrance five coloured lanterns hung in a vertical line: deep green, a dark, smokey scarlet, a gay light green, violet, and once more dark scarlet; and at the bottom, slightly to the side, a small, steady yellow lamp, the purport of all being: *Never neglect the wonder of conscious existence, which too soon comes to an end!*

Through a pair of tall timber doors Etzwane and Finnerack passed into the foyer, where a small boy served each a phial of grass wine and a morsel of crystallized fish, tokens of hospitality. A smiling maiden came forward, wearing the plum-coloured flounces of an ancient Maseach maenad; from each young man she clipped a trifle of hair and touched their chins with yorbane wax: a quaint survival of the olden times when the Maseach were notorious for their immoderate pleasures.

Etzwane and Finnerack entered the vaulted hall, still almost empty, and took a table close beside the musician's bench. A dish of sharp, bitter, pungent and salt pastilles was set before them. Partly from a malicious desire to confound Finnerack, Etzwane commanded the traditional Feast of Forty-Five Dishes, and also instructed the steward to lay out the best for Dystar, when and if he appeared.

The meal was served, one dish after another, with Finnerack at first grumbling at the smallness of the portions, which he considered over-dainty, until Etzwane reminded him that so far he had consumed only twelve of forty-five dishes.

Dish after dish was brought, conforming to the theoretical absolute of a gastronome dead four thousand years. Texture against texture, aroma contrasting with flavour, the colour and placement of each morsel to the ancient stipulation upon the ritually correct bowl, plate, or board. With each dish came a specified wine, tincture, essence, or brew. Finnerack's complaints dwindled; he became fascinated, or perhaps subdued.... At the twenty-eighth dish Dystar appeared in the entrance: a tall, spare man with well-shaped features, wearing grey trousers and a loose grey-black tunic. He stood a moment looking across the hall, then turned and made a fretful remark to the man standing behind him, Shobin the proprietor. For a moment Etzwane wondered if Dystar might not simply depart the premises, but Shobin went off to correct whatever deficiency Dystar had pointed out.... The lights in the arched alcoves near the musician's bench were bright; Dystar disliked illumination too strong or emphatic. Shobin made the adjustments; Dystar came forward, still not in the best of moods. He carried a khitan and a darabence with a green jade fingerplate; he placed these on the bench and then settled at a table only six feet from Etzwane and Finnerack. Etzwane had seen him on a single previous occasion, and had then been fascinated by Dystar's ease, strength, certainty.

The steward announced that his meal had been spoken for, to which Dystar gave an indifferent nod. Etzwane studied him sidelong, trying to read the flow of Dystar's thoughts. Here was his father, half of himself. Perhaps it was his duty to announce himself.... Dystar might have a dozen sons, here and there across Shant, reflected Etzwane. The revelation might only irritate him.

The steward brought Dystar a salad of leeks in oil, the crust of a loaf, a dark sausage of meats and herbs, a jug of wine: a modest meal. Dystar had been sated with fine food, thought Etzwane; richness was no novelty to him, nor the attention of beautiful women. . . .

Dish after dish after dish. Finnerack, who perhaps never in his life had tasted good wine, had become more relaxed and examined the surroundings with a lessening of reserve.

Dystar finished half his food, pushed the rest away, and sat back, fingers around the stem of his goblet. His eyes passed across Etzwane's face; with a faint frown he looked back, as if troubled by a fleeting recollection. . . . He took up his khitan and for a moment examined it as if surprised to find such an ungainly and complicated instrument in his hands. He touched it lightly here and there, bringing all the unlikely parts into consonance, then put it aside for the darabence. He played a soft scale, adjusted whines and drones, then played a merry little jig, first with simple harmony, then with two voices, then three: a bit of virtuosity which he managed without effort or even any great interest. He put the darabence down and mused over his wine. . . .

The tables nearby were now crowded, with the most discriminating and perceptive folk of Maschein on hand to gain enlightenment.

Etzwane and Finnerack examined their thirty-ninth dish: pith of marrow tree, slivered, crisped, salted, in a pale green syrup, with a ball of purple jelly flavoured with maroes and ernice, barley sweet. The accompanying wine, a subtle quick liquid, tasted of sunlight and air. Finnerack looked doubtfully at Etzwane. "Never in my life have I eaten so much. Yet – my appetite remains."

"We must finish the forty-five dishes," said Etzwane. "Otherwise they are not allowed to accept our money, the pleasant fiction being that the cooks have incorrectly prepared the dishes, or served in a crude manner. Eat we must."

"If such be the case I am the man for it."

Dystar began to play his khitan: a soft lilt, with no obvious pattern, but as he proceeded, the ear began to anticipate and hear the pleasant corroboration. So far he had played nothing which Etzwane could not easily duplicate. . . . Dystar struck a set of soft strange chords, then began to play the melody with the chords tolling below like mournful sea bells. . . . Etzwane wondered as to the nature of Dystar's talent. Part, he thought, derived from ease and simplicity, part from profundity, part from a detachment which made him indifferent to his audience, part from a sleight which allowed him to play as the whim took him. Etzwane felt a pang of envy; for his part he often avoided passages whose resolution he could not foresee, knowing well the fragile distinction between felicity and fiasco. . . . The music came to an end, without notable accent or emphasis, the sea gongs fading into mist. Dystar put the instrument aside. Taking up his goblet he gazed across the hall; then, as if in sudden recollection, he again lifted the khitan and tested a set of phrases. He played them again with an alteration of harmony and they became a twitching, eccentric melody. He modulated into another mode and the melody altered; effortlessly Dystar played the first and second together in wry counterpoint. For a moment he seemed to become interested in the music and bent his head over the neck of the khitan.

... He slowed the tempo, the doubled tunes became one, like a pair of coloured images joining to create the illusion of perspective. . . .

The last of the forty-five courses was served to Etzwane and Finnerack: a sour-sweet frost in shells of purple lacquer, with thimble-size goblets of Thousand Year Nectar.

Finnerack consumed the frost and tasted the nectar. His brown face seemed less gaunt; the mad, blue glitter was gone from his eyes. Suddenly he asked Etzwane: "How much must be paid for this meal?"

"I don't know. . . . Two hundred florins, I suppose."

"At Camp Three a man might not reduce his indenture two hundred florins in a year." Finnerack seemed rueful rather than angry.

"The system is archaic," said Etzwane. "The Anome will make changes. There will be no more Camp Threes, or Angwin Junctions, for that matter."

Finnerack turned him a glance of dour appraisal. "You seem very sure of the Anome's intentions."

For want of an appropriate reply, Etzwane let the remark go by. He raised a finger to the steward, who brought a tall earthenware flask, velvet with dust, from which he poured a cool pale wine, soft as water.

Etzwane drank; Finnerack cautiously followed suit.

Etzwane made an oblique reference to Finnerack's remark. "The new Anome in my opinion is not a man hidebound by tradition. After the Roguskhoi are destroyed important changes will be made."

"Bah!" said Finnerack. "The Roguskhoi are no great problem; the Anome need only hurl the might of Shant against them."

Etzwane chuckled sadly. "What might? Shant is feeble

as a baby. The last Anome turned his face away from danger. It is all very mysterious; he is neither a wicked nor a stupid man."

"No mystery," said Finnerack. "He enjoyed ease above exertion."

"I might agree," said Etzwane, "were there not other mysteries as well: the Roguskhoi themselves, in the first instance."

"Again no mystery: they derive from Palasedran malice."

"Hmm ... Who informed Hillen of my coming? Who gave orders that I be killed?"

"Is there any doubt? The balloon-way magnates!"

"Possible again. But there are other mysteries less easily explained." Etzwane recalled the Benevolence Garstang's suicidal attack and the peculiar mutilation worked upon his corpse, as if a rat had gnawed a hole in his chest."

Someone sat at their table. It was Dystar. "I have been studying your face," he told Etzwane. "It is a face I know, from the far past."

Etzwane collected his thoughts. "I have heard you play at Brassei; there perhaps you chanced to notice me."

Dystar glanced at Etzwane's torc to read the locality code. "Bastern, a strange canton."

"The Chilites no longer worship Galexis," said Etzwane. "Bastern is not so strange as before." Dystar, he noted, wore the rose and dull blue of Shkoriy. He asked, "Will you share our wine?"

Dystar gave a polite acquiescence. Etzwane signalled the steward, who brought another diorite goblet: eggshell thin, polished to the colour and sheen of pewter. Etzwane poured. Dystar raised a finger. "Enough ... I no longer enjoy food or wine. An innate fault, I suppose."

Finnerack gave his sudden harsh laugh; Dystar glanced at him with curiosity. Etzwane said, "For long years my friend has laboured under indenture at a camp for recalcitrants, and has known bitter times. Like yourself, he has no taste for fine food or wine, but for exactly opposite reasons."

Dystar smiled; his face a winter landscape suddenly illuminated by a shaft of sunlight. "Surfeit is not my enemy. I am troubled, rather, by what I would term an aversion to purchased pleasure."

"I am glad it is for sale," grumbled Finnerack. "I would find little elsewhere."

Etzwane looked ruefully at the expensive flask of wine. "How then do you spend your money?"

"Foolishly," said Dystar. "Last year I bought land in Shkoriy: a high valley with an orchard, a pond, and a cottage, where I thought to pass my senility. . . . Such is the folly of foresight."

Finnerack tasted the wine, put the goblet down, and looked off across the hall.

Etzwane began to feel uncomfortable. A hundred times he had envisioned the meeting between Dystar and himself, always in dramatic terms. Now they sat at the same table and the occasion was suffocated in dullness. What could he say? "Dystar! You are my father; in my face you see your own!" Bathos. In desperation Etzwane said, "At Brassei your mood was better than tonight; I recall that you played with zest."

Dystar gave him a quick glance. "Is the situation so evident? Tonight I am stale; I have been distracted by events."

"The trouble in Shkoriy?"

Dystar was silent for a moment, then nodded. "The savages have taken my valley, where I often went, where nothing ever changed." He smiled. "A mood of melancholy induces music; on occasions of real tragedy I become merely insipid. . . . By repute I am a man who plays only by caprice. Still, here are two hundred people come to listen, and I would not wish to disappoint them."

Finnerack, now drunk, his mouth sagging in a crooked smile, said, "My friend Etzwane professes musicianship; you should press him into service."

" 'Etzwane'? The master musician of old Azume," said Dystar. "Do you know this?"

Etzwane nodded. "My mother lived on Rhododendron Way. I was born nameless and took the name 'Gastel Etzwane' for my own."

Dystar reflected a moment, perhaps occupied with his own recollections of Rhododendron Way. Too long ago, thought Etzwane; he would remember nothing.

"I must perform." Dystar moved back to his bench. He took up the darabence to play a somewhat trivial set of melodies, as might be heard in the Morningshore dancehalls. Just as Etzwane began to lose interest, Dystar altered the set of his blare valve to construct a sudden new environment: the same melodies, the same rhythm, but now they told a disturbed tale of callous departures and mocking laughter, of roof demons and storm birds. Dystar muted the whines, throttled the valves, and slowed his tempo. The music asserted the fragility of everything pleasant and bright, the triumph of darkness, and ended in a dismal twanging chord. . . . A pause, then a sudden coda remarking that, on the other hand, matters might easily be quite the reverse.

Dystar rested a moment. He struck a few chords, then

played a complicated antiphony: glissandos swooping above a placid melody. His expression was abstracted, his hands moved without effort. Etzwane thought that the music came from calculation rather than emotion. Finnerack's eyelids were drooping; he had taken too much food and wine. Etzwane called the steward and paid the score; then he and Finnerack departed the Silver Samarsanda and returned to the River Island Inn.

Etzwane went out into the garden and stood in the quiet, looking up at the Schiafarilla, behind which, according to legend, lay old Earth. . . . When he returned to the drawing room, Finnerack had gone to his couch. Etzwane took a stylus and on a card wrote a careful message, upon which he impressed the sigil of the Anome.

He summoned a boy. "Take this message to the Silver Samarsanda, deliver it into the hands of Dystar the druithine, none other. Do not respond to any questions: give over the message and depart. Do you understand?"

"I do." The boy took the message and went off, and presently Etzwane went to his own couch. . . . As for the Repast of Forty-Five Dishes, he doubted if ever again he would dine so lavishly.

CHAPTER SIX

Prompted by doubt and uneasiness, Etzwane decided to pass by the cantons of the far west and return at once to Garwiy. He had been gone longer than he intended; in Garwiy events moved faster than elsewhere in Shant.

There was no balloon-way link between Maschein and Brassei, by reason of adverse winds and poor terrain, but the Jardeen River served almost as well. Rather than await the scheduled riverboat, Etzwane chartered a swift pinnace, with two lateen sails and a crew of ten to man sweeps or haul on the towrope in case of necessity.

East on a great loop through the sylvan foothills of Lor Ault they sailed, then north down Methel Vale, with mountains rising on both sides. At Griave in Fairlea they met the Great Ridge Route of the balloon-way, only to learn that all north-bound balloons had been delayed by gales driving in from the Sualle. Continuing to Brassei Junction, they boarded the balloon *Aramaad*. The Sualle gales had waned; the Shellflower winds provided a splendid reach; the *Aramaad* spun north along the slot at a steady sixty miles an hour. Late in the afternoon they slid down the Vale of Silence, through the Jardeen Gap, and five minutes later descended to Garwiy Station.

At sunset Garwiy was at its most entrancing, with the

low light from three suns drenching the glass of the tall spires, generating colour in prodigal quantities. From all directions, high and low, on and through the pure glass slabs, the domes, bulbs, bosses, and carved ornaments, among and around the balustrades of high balconies, the ranked arches and buttresses, the crystal scrolls and prismatic columns flowed the tides of saturated colour: pure purples to charm the mind; limpid greens, dark and rich, watergreen, leaf-green, emerald; dark and light blues, with ultramarine, smalt, and the range of middle blues; reflections and after-images of scarlet, inner shadows of light which could not be named; or near surfaces the lustre of time: acrid metallic films. As Etzwane and Finnerack moved slowly east, the suns departed; the colours became clouded with pearl and quickly died. Etzwane thought: of all this ancient grandeur I am master. I can gratify each whim; I can take, I can give, I can build or lay waste. . . . He smiled, unable to accept the ideas; they were artificial and unreal.

Finnerack could never before have seen Garwiy; Etzwane wondered as to his reactions. Finnerack was at least overtly unimpressed. He had given the city a single all-encompassing glance, and thereafter appeared more interested in the urbane folk who walked Kavalesko Avenue.

At a kiosk Etzwane bought a journal. The colours black, ochre, and brown immediately struck his eyes. He read:

> From Marestiy arresting news! The militia and a band of Roguskhoi have been engaged in a battle. The savage intruders, having worked awful damage in Canton Shkoriy, which must now be reckoned to-

tally under Roguskhoi control, sent a foraging party north. At the border a Marest troop staunchly denied the intruders passage, and a battle ensued. Though greatly outnumbered, the insensate red brutes advanced. The Marest men discharged arrows, killing or at least incommoding certain of the enemy; the others pressed forward without qualm. The Marest militia, adopting flexible tactics, fell back into the forest, where their arrows and fire-wad flings denied the Roguskhoi entry. The treacherous savages returned the fire-wads to set the forest ablaze, and the militia was forced back into the open. Here they were set upon by another band of savages, assembled for just such a bloodthirsty purpose. The militia suffered many casualties, but the survivors have resolved to extract a great revenge when the Anome provides them potency. All feel certain that the detestable creatures will be defeated and driven away.

Etzwane showed the report to Finnerack, who read with half-contemptuous disinterest. Etzwane's attention meanwhile had been drawn to a box outlined in the pale blue and purple of sagacious statement:

Here are presented the remarks
of Mialambre: Octagon, the
respected High Arbiter of Wale:

The years during and immediately after the Fourth Palasedran War were decisive; during these times was forged the soul of the hero Viana Paizifiume. He has rightly been called the progenitor of modern Shant. The Hundred Years War undeniably derived from his policies; still, for all its horror, this century now seems but a shadow on the water. Paizifiume created the awful authority of the Anome and, as a logical corollary, the employment of the coded torc. It is a system beautiful in its simplicity – unequivocal rigour balanced against responsibility, economy, effectiveness – which in the main has been kind to Shant. The Anomes have been largely competent; they have honoured all their commitments – to the cantons, allowing each its traditional style; to the patricians, imposing no arbitrary restraints; to the generality, making no exorbitant demands. The previous cantonal wars and depredations have receded to the edge of memory and are currently unthinkable.

Critical minds will discover flaws in the system. Justice, a human invention, is as protean as the race itself, and varies from canton to canton. The traveller must be wary lest he contravene some unfamiliar local ordinance. I cite those unfortunate wayfarers through Canton Haviosq who, when passing a shrine, have neglected the sign of sky, stomach, and soil, to their dismay; likewise the virgins careless enough to enter Canton Shalloran without certificates. The indenture system has shortcomings; the notorious vices of Canton Glirris are inherently wrong. Still, when all is weighed, we have enjoyed many placid centuries.

If the study of human interactions could become a science, I suspect that an inviolate axiom might be discovered to this effect: *Every social disposition creates a disparity of advantages.* Further: *Every innovation designed to correct the disparities, no mat-*

ter how altruistic in concept, works only to create a new and different set of disparities.

I make this remark because the great effort which must now wrench Shant will beyond all question change our lives, in modes still unimaginable.

Etzwane looked once more to see who had formulated the piece. Mialambre: Octagon of Wale ... Finnerack demanded somewhat peevishly: "How long do you propose to stand reading in the street?"

Etzwane signalled a passing diligence. "To Sershan Palace."

Finnerack presently spoke: "We are being followed."

Etzwane looked at him in surprise. "Are you sure?"

"When you stopped to buy the journal a man in a blue cape stepped off to the side. While you read he stood with his back turned. When we walked forward he did likewise. Now a diligence follows behind."

"Interesting," said Etzwane.

The diligence turned left from Kavalesko Avenue out upon the Parade of the Chama Reyans. A diligence coming at no great distance behind turned also.

"Interesting," said Etzwane once again.

For a space they rolled along the Parade, then swung up the Metempe, a marble avenue connecting central Garwiy with the three Ushkadel terraces. Similax trees stood against the sky to cast plum-coloured gloom over the pale stone. Behind, inconspicuously, came the second diligence.

A road glanced off to the side, under tape trees' and similax. Etzwane called up to the driver: "Turn here!"

The driver tapped the neck of the long-legged pacer; smartly the diligence swung to the left, under tape trees so full and supple that the foliage stroked the top of the diligence. "Stop," said Etzwane. He jumped out. "Drive forward slowly."

The diligence continued, the pacers walking. Etzwane ran back to the intersection.

Silence, except for the rustle of the tapes, then the jingle of an approaching diligence. The sound grew louder; the diligence reached the intersection, halted. A keen-featured face peered up the side road.... Etzwane stepped forward; the man turned him a startled look, then spoke a quick word to his driver. The diligence spun away up the Metempe.

Etzwane rejoined Finnerack, who turned him a crooked side-glance, expressing a variety of emotions: dislike, vindication, saturnine amusement, and together, in an unlikely combination, curiosity with indifference. Etzwane, at first inclined to keeping his own counsel, decided that if his plans were to have application Finnerack had best be informed as fully as possible. "The Chief Discriminator of Garwiy is disposed to intrigue. This is my supposition, at least. If I am killed he is the first to suspect."

Finnerack gave a noncommittal grunt. Etzwane looked back down the Metempe; no one seemed to be following.

The diligence turned into the Middle Way as green-spark street lamps came to life. Far around the arc of the Ushkadel they drove, past the ranked palaces of the Aesthetes, and at last came to the portal of the Sershans. A bulb of massive glass flickered pale blue and violet.* Etz-

*In Shant no colour could be used arbitrarily. A green gate bulb implied festivity, and in conjunction with purple or dark scarlet lustres gave hospitable welcome to all comers. Greyed golds told of mourning;

wane and Finnerack alighted; the diligence jingled off into the gloom.

Etzwane crossed the wide loggia, followed, at a casual stroll, by Finnerack. Etzwane stopped to listen; from within came that almost imperceptible stir which told of routine and unexcited occupation. Was that not the rasp of new fibres in a wood-horn? Etzwane grimaced; he had no real bent for intrigue, coercion, large designs. What an improbable condition that he, Gastel Etzwane, should be master of Shant! Still, better he than Finnerack – or so came a message from the under part of his mind.

Etzwane put his misgivings aside. He took Finnerack to the entrance, where in response to his signal a footman drew aside the door.

Etzwane and Finnerack stepped into the reception hall, into a magic environment of opposing vitran panels, where nymphs disported in Arcadian landscapes. Aganthe came slowly forward. He looked drawn, even a trifle unkempt, as if events had eroded his morale; he saw Etzwane with a gleam of hope. Etzwane asked, "Have affairs gone well?"

"Not well!" declared Aganthe, with a ring in his voice. "The ancient Sershan Palace has never before been so misused. The musicians play jigs and ballintrys in the Pearlweb Salon; the children swim in the garden fountain; the men have ranged their caravans along the Ancestral Parade. They tie clotheslines between the Named Trees; they strew refuse without remorse. Lord Sajarano –" Aganthe controlled his flow of words.

---

violet indicated formality and receptiveness only to intimate intrusion; blue, or blue with violet, signified withdrawal and privacy. The word *kial'etse*, the mingling of violet and blue, might be used as an epithet, for example, *ls Xhiallinen kial'etse*: the snobbish and hyperaesthetic Xhiallinens. White glow attended ritual occasions.

"Well?" Etzwane prompted. "What of Lord Sajarano?"

"Again I use candour, since this is what you require. I have often speculated that Lord Sajarano might suffer a nervous disease, and I have wondered at his odd activities. I have not recently seen Lord Sajarano and I fear a tragedy."

"Take me to the musician Frolitz," said Etzwane.

"He will be found in the Grand Parlour."

Etzwane found Frolitz drinking Wild Rose wine from a ceremonial silver mug and gloomily watching three children of the troupe, who disputed posession of a hand-illuminated geography of West Caraz. At the sight of Etzwane and Finnerack he wiped his mouth and rose to his feet. "Where have you stayed so long?"

"I have travelled a wide circuit of the south," replied Etzwane, with the diffidence of long habit. "Naturally in all haste. I hope that you have profited by your rest?"

"Such profits are brummagem," snapped Frolitz. "The troupe rusticates."

"What of Sajarano?" Etzwane asked. "Has he given you difficulty?"

"No difficulty whatever; in fact he has vanished. We have been distracted with bewilderment."

Etzwane sank into a chair. "How and when did he disappear?"

"Five days ago, from his tower. The stairs were closed off; he acted no more distrait than usual. When he was served his evening meal, the window was open; he was gone like an *eirmelrath*."*

The three went up to Sajarano's private rooms. Etzwane looked from the window. Far below spread patterns

Eirmelrath: a malicious ghost of Canton Green Stone.

104

of moss. "Never a mark!" declared Frolitz. "Not a bird has disturbed the lay of the growth!"

A single narrow stairs connected the tower to the lower floors. "And here sat Mielke, on these selfsame stairs, discussing affairs with an under-maid. Agreed; they were not alert to the possibility of Sajarano stepping upon them on his way to freedom; still the occasion seems remote."

"Was there a rope in the room? Could he have torn up the draperies or bed linen?"

"Even with a rope he must have disturbed the moss. The linens were intact." Frolitz jumped to his feet. Holding his arms wide, fingers clenched and quivering, he asked: "How then did he leave? I have known many strange mysteries, but none so strange as this."

Etzwane wordlessly brought forth his pulse-emitter. He encoded the colours of Sajarano's torc and touched the red "Seek" button; the instrument immediately returned the thin whine of contact. He swung the mechanism in an arc; the whine waxed, then waned. "However Sajarano escaped, he fled no great distance," said Etzwane. "He seems to be up on the Ushkadel."

With Finnerack and Frolitz, Etzwane set forth into the night. They crossed the formal garden and climbed a flight of alabaster steps, the Schiafarilla casting a pale white light to show them the way. They crossed a pavilion of smooth white glass, where the secret Sershan pageants were performed, then pushed through a dense grove of similax, giant cypress, contorted ivorywoods, which ended only when they stepped out upon High Way. The pulse-emitter took them neither right nor left, but up into the dark forest above High Way.

Frolitz began to grumble. "By training and by inclination I am a musician, not a prowler of forests, nor a searcher for creatures who chose to flit off alone, or in company."

"I am no musician," said Finnerack, staring up into the forest. "Still I think it sensible to proceed only with lanterns and weapons."

Frolitz reacted sharply to the implications latent in Finnerack's remark. "A musician knows no fear! Sometimes he takes heed of reality; is this fear? You speak like a man with his head above the clouds."

"Finnerack is no musician," said Etzwane. "This is stipulated. Still, let us go for lights and weapons."

Half an hour later they returned to High Way, with glass lanterns and antique swords of forged iron-web. Etzwane also carried the energy pistol given him by Ifness.

Sajarano of Sershan had not moved from his previous position. Three hundred yards up the Ushkadel they found his corpse, laid out on a growth of white and grey lovelace.

The three swung their lanterns; the rays jerked nervously through the shades and nooks. One at a time they turned back to the shape at their feet. Sajarano, never large nor imposing, seemed a gnomish child, with his thin legs straight, his back arched as if in pain, his fine poet's forehead thrust back into the lovelace. The jacket of violet velvet was disarranged; the bony chest was bare, displaying a ghastly, gaping wound.

Etzwane had seen such a wound before, in the body of the Benevolence Garstang, on the day following his death.

106

"This is not a good sight," said Frolitz.

Finnerack grunted as if to say that he had seen worse, far worse.

"The ahulphs perhaps have been here," muttered Etzwane. "They might return." He played his lantern once more through the shadows. "Best that we bury him."

With swordblades and hands they scratched a shallow grave into the mould, presently Sajarano of Sershan, erstwhile Anome of Shant, was covered away from sight.

The three trudged back down to High Way, where by common impulse they turned a final glance up the hill. They then proceeded down to Sershan Palace.

Frolitz would not pass through the great glass doors. "Gastel Etzwane," he stated, "I want no more of Sershan Palace. We have enjoyed the best of foods and liquors; we own the finest instruments in Shant. Still, let us not deceive ourselves: we are musicians, not Aesthetes, and it is time that we depart."

"Your work is done," Etzwane agreed. "Best that you return to the old ways."

"What of you?" demanded Frolitz. "Do you desert the troupe? Where will I find a replacement? Must I play your parts and my own as well?"

"I am involved against the Roguskhoi," said Etzwane, "a situation even more urgent than good balance in the troupe."

"Can't other folk kill Roguskhoi?" growled Frolitz. "Why must the musicians of Shant leap to the forefront?"

"When the Roguskhoi are gone I will rejoin the troupe, and we will play to draw the ahulphs down from the hills. Until then –"

"I will not hear this," said Frolitz. "Kill Roguskhoi during the day, if this is to your taste, but at night your place is with the troupe!"

Etzwane laughed weakly, half convinced that Frolitz' suggestion was sound. "You're off to Fontenay's?"

"At this very instant. What keeps you here?"

Etzwane looked up at the palace where Sajarano's personality pervaded every room. "Go your way to Fontenay's," said Etzwane. "Finnerack and I will be along as well."

"Spoken like a rational man!" declared Frolitz with approval. "It's not too late for a few tunes yet!" In spite of his previous declaration, he marched into the palace to rally the troupe.

Finnerack spoke in a wry voice: "A man flits from a high tower to be found with a hole in his chest, as if an ahulph had tested him with an auger. Is this how life goes in Garwiy?"

"The events are beyond my comprehension," said Etzwane, "although I have seen something similar before."

"This may be.... So now you are Anome, without challenge or qualification."

Etzwane stared coldly at Finnerack. "Why do you say that? I am not Anome."

Finnerack gave a coarse laugh. "Then why did not the Anome discover Sajarano's death five days ago? It is a grave matter. Why have you not communicated with the Anome? If he existed, you would think of nothing else; instead you argue with Frolitz and make plans to play your tunes. That Gastel Etzwane should be Anome is strange enough; that he should not be is too much to believe."

"I am not Anome," said Etzwane. "I am a desperate makeshift, a man struggling against his own deficiencies. The Anome is dead; a void exists. I must create the illusion that all is well. For a period I can do this; the cantons control themselves. But the Anome's work accumulates: petitions go unanswered, heads are not taken, crimes go unpunished; sooner or later some clever man like Aun Sharah will learn the truth. Meanwhile I am impelled to mobilize Shant against the Roguskhoi as best I can."

Finnerack gave a cynical grunt. "And who then will be Anome? The Earthman Ifness?"

"He has returned to Earth. I have two men in mind: Dystar the druithine and Mialambre: Octagon. Either might qualify."

"Hmmf . . . And how do I fit into your schemes?"

"You must guard my back. I don't want to die like Sajarano."

"Who killed him?"

Etzwane looked off into the darkness. "I don't know. Many strange events happen in Shant."

Finnerack showed his teeth in a tight grin. "I don't want to die either. You are asking me to share your risks, which obviously are large."

"True. But are we not both motivated? We equally want peace and justice for Shant."

Finnerack again gave his dour grunt; Etzwane had no more to say. They went into the palace. Aganthe came to their summons. "Master Frolitz and his troupe are leaving the palace," said Etzwane. "They will not be returning and you can put matters to rights."

Aganthe's mournful face lit up. "Good news indeed! But what of Lord Sajarano? He is nowhere in the palace. I find here a cause for concern."

"Lord Sajarano had gone forth on his travels," said Etzwane. "Lock the palace securely; make sure that no one intrudes. In a day or so I will make further arrangements."

"I live by your commands."

When they stepped forth, Frolitz and the troupe were already departing, with a rumble of wheels and jocular calls.

Etzwane and Finnerack slowly descended the Koronakhe Steps. The Schiafarilla had dropped below the Ushkadel; up had come Gorcula the Dragonfish, with the twin orange eyes, Alasen and Diandas, blazing down at Durdane. Finnerack began to look back over his shoulder. Etzwane became infected by his restiveness. "Do you see someone?"

"No."

Etzwane quickened his pace; they reached the pale expanses of Marmione Plaza; here they paused in the shadows beside the fountain. No one came behind. With somewhat more assurance they continued down Galias Avenue and presently arrived at Fontenay's Inn, on the banks of the Jardeen River.

At the side of the common room Etzwane and Finnerack consumed a supper of stewed clams, bread, and ale. Looking across the well-remembered room Etzwane was moved to reminiscence. He told of his adventures after fleeing Angwin Junction. He described the Roguskhoi raid on Bashon and the events subsequent; he spoke of his association with Ifness, the cold and competent Fellow of the Historical Institute. In this very room Etzwane had encountered the bewitching Jurjin, now, like Sajarano and Garstang, dead. "These events run black and yellow

110

with mystery. I am fascinated and bewildered; I also fear a dreadful enlightenment."

Finnerack pulled at his chin. "I share only little of your fascination, still I risk the full scope of this enlightenment."

Etzwane felt a throb of frustration. "You now know the circumstances; what is your decision?"

Finnerack drank his ale and set the mug down with a thud: the most emphatic gesture Etzwane had yet seen him make. "I will join you and for this reason: the better to further my own ends."

"Before we go further, what are these ends?"

"You already must know. In Garwiy and elsewhere through Shant rich men live in palaces. They gained their wealth by robbing me, and others like me, of our lives. They must make restitution. It will cost them dear, but pay they shall, before I die."

Etzwane said in a voice without accent: "Your goals are understandable. For the present they must be put aside, lest they interfere with larger matters."

"The Roguskhoi are the imminent enemies," said Finnerack. "We shall drive them back to Palasedra, and then wreak an equal justice upon the magnates."

"I promise nothing so wide as this," said Etzwane. "Fair restitution, yes. Cessation of abuses, yes. Revenge — no."

"The past cannot be erased," said Finnerack woodenly.

Etzwane pressed the matter no further. For better or worse, he must make do with Finnerack, at least for the present. The future? . . . If necessary, he would be merciless. He reached into his pocket. "I now give you the instrument I took from the Benevolence Garstang. This is how to encode a torc." Etzwane demonstrated. "Mind!

111

here is the critical operation! First you must press 'Grey' to disarm the self-destruction cell. 'Red' is 'Seek'; 'Yellow' is 'Kill.' "

Finnerack examined the box. "I am to keep this?"

"Until I require its return."

Finnerack turned his twisted grin upon Etzwane. "What if I craved power? I need only set the code to your colour and press 'Yellow.' Then Jerd Finnerack would be Anome."

Etzwane shrugged. "I trust in your loyalty." He saw no point in explaining that his torc carried, in the place of dexax, a warning vibrator.

Finnerack scowled down at the pulse-emitter. "By accepting this, I bind myself to your schemes."

"This is the case."

"For the moment," said Finnerack, "our lives go in the same direction."

Etzwane realized that he could expect nothing better. "The man I most distrust," he said, "is the Chief Discriminator; he alone knew of my interest in Camp Three."

"What of the balloon-way officials? They would also know, and perhaps they would act."

"Unlikely," said Etzwane. "The Discriminators must often make such inquiries in the course of routine. Why should the balloon-way distinguish Jerd Finnerack from any other? Only Aun Sharah could connect me with you. Tomorrow I will reduce his scope. . . . Finally, here is Frolitz."

Frolitz saw them at once and came swaggering over to the table. "You have had a change of heart; my words are wisdom after all."

"I want no more of Sershan Palace," said Etzwane. "We think alike in this regard."

"Wise! And here comes the troupe, straggling in like dock coolies. Etzwane, to the stand."

Etzwane automatically rose to the familiar command, then sank back into his chair. "My hands are stiff as sticks. I cannot play."

"Come, come," blustered Frolitz. "I know better. Oil your joints with the guizol; Cune will use tringolet; I will play khitan."

"For a fact I have no heart for music," said Etzwane. "Not tonight."

Frolitz turned away in disgust. "Listen then! During this last month I have altered several passages; pay heed."

Etzwane sat back. From the stand came the beloved sounds of instruments being tuned, then Frolitz' instructions, one or two muttered replies. Frolitz gave a nod, a jerk of the elbow, and once again the familiar miracle: from chaos, music.

CHAPTER SEVEN

Etzwane and Finnerack took breakfast at a cafe to the side of Corporation Plaza. Finnerack had accepted funds from Etzwane and immediately purchased new garments: black boots, a smart black cape with a stiff round collar in the ancient fashion. Etzwane wondered if Finnerack's new appearance signified a change in his attitudes, or whether the appearance merely certified a previous condition.

Etzwane brought his mind back to the problems of the present. "Today we have much to do. First: we visit Aun Sharah, whose office overlooks the square. He will be deep in thought; he will have evolved many plans and discarded them all, or so I hope. He will know of our presence in Garwiy; he probably knows that we sit here now at breakfast. He might even put a bold face on the matter and come forth to meet us."

They scanned the square but saw no sign of Aun Sharah.

Etzwane said, "Set your emitter to this code." He recited the colours of Aun Sharah's torc. "Touch 'Grey' first, never forget. . . . Good. Now we are armed."

They crossed the square, entered the Jurisdictionary, mounted the steps to the Offices of the Discriminators.

As before, Aun Sharah came forth to greet Etzwane.

Today he wore a trim suit of dark ultramarine, with cloth shoes of the same colour, and a star sapphire dangled from his left ear by a short silver chain. He spoke with easy cordiality. "I have been expecting you. This I would expect to be Jerd Finnerack."

They entered Aun Sharah's office. Etzwane asked, "How long have you been back?"

"Five days." Aun Sharah reported the events of his journey; he had encountered every condition between sullen apathy and earnest effort.

"My experiences were much the same," said Etzwane. "All is about as we expected. One episode in Canton Glaiy, however, puzzles me. When I arrived at Camp Three the Chief Custodian, a certain Shirge Hillen, had anticipated my arrival and displayed considerable hostility. What could explain such behaviour?"

Aun Sharah gazed reflectively across the square. "The inquiries I made at the balloon-way offices conceivably sent alarms all the way to Camp Three. They are defensive in regard to their labour policies."

"There seems no other explanation," said Etzwane, glancing at Finnerack, who maintained a stony silence. Etzwane leaned back in his seat. "The Anome feels that he must now undertake drastic changes. He can govern a peaceful Shant; the energies of a Shant at war exceed his control; some of his authority must be delegated. He feels that a man of your competence is wasted in a position as limited as this."

Aunt Sharah made a smiling gesture. "I am a limited man in a limited position; this is my niche; I have no soaring ambitions."

Etzwane shook his head. "Never underestimate yourself; be certain that the Anome does not."

Rather curtly Aun Sharah asked, "What precisely do you plan?"

Etzwane reflected a moment. "I want you to administer the material resources of Shant: the metals, fibres, glass, wood. This is obviously a complicated business; and I would like you to take time – three or four days, even a week – to learn something about your new job."

Aun Sharah raised his eyebrows into quizzical arches. "You want me to leave here?"

"Exactly correct. As of now you are no longer Chief Discriminator, but rather Director of Material Procurement. Go home, think about your new job. Study the cantons of Shant and their products, learn what substances are in short supply and which are not. Meanwhile, I'll occupy your office; I have none of my own."

Aun Sharah asked in delicate disbelief: "You want me to leave – now?"

"Yes. Why not?"

"But – my private files . . ."

" 'Private'? Affairs which do not pertain to the office of the Chief Discriminator?"

Aun Sharah's smile became a trifle wild. "Personal effects, memoranda . . . All this seems so abrupt."

"By necessity. Events are occurring abruptly; I have no time for formalities. Where is the roster of Discriminator personnel?"

"In yonder cupboard."

"It includes your unofficial operatives?"

"Not all of them."

"You have a subsidiary list?"

Aun Sharah hesitated, then reached into his pocket and brought forth a notebook. He looked into it, frowned, carefully tore out a page, and placed it on the desk. Etzwane saw a list of a dozen names, each followed by a code symbol. "These persons do what?"

"They are informal specialists, so to speak. This man informs me on poisons, this on illicit indentures; this one and this one on affairs of the Aesthetes, where, surprisingly, hidden crimes sometimes occur. These three are receivers of stolen goods."

"What of this person, for instance?"

"He is an ahulph owner; a tracker."

"And this?"

"The same. All the others as well."

"All own ahulphs?"

"My information is not so exact. Perhaps some obtain ahulphs by other means."

"But all are trackers?"

"So I believe."

"There are no other spies or trackers available for duty?"

"You have the entire roster," said Aun Sharah shortly. "I'll take a few personal adjuncts now." He jerked open a cabinet in his desk and brought forth a grey ledger, a dart gun, a decorative iron chain with an iron medallion, a few other oddments. Etzwane and Finnerack stood to the side watching. Finnerack spoke for the first time. "The ledger is a personal adjunct?"

"Yes. Confidential information."

"Confidential from the Anome?"

"Unless he is interested in exploring my private life."

Finnerack said no more.

Aun Sharah went to the door, where he paused. "The changes you are making: are they the Anome's concepts or your own?"

"They stem from the new Anome. Sajarano of Sershan is dead."

Aun Sharah gave a short laugh. "I hardly expected him to survive."

"He died by means mysterious to me and to the new Anome as well," said Etzwane evenly. "The Shant of today is a strange place."

Aun Sharah became thoughtful. He opened his mouth to speak, then closed it again. With a sudden jerk he turned away and departed the office.

Etzwane and Finnerack immediately set about exploring the cupboards and shelves. They examined the roster and puzzled over the cryptic marks which Aun Sharah had posted beside many of the names. They found large-scale maps for each canton of Shant and for the citites of Garwiy, Maschein, Brassei, Ilwiy, Carbado, Whearn, Ferghez, and Oswiy. A set of indexes listed important men of each canton, with references to a master file and more of Aun Sharah's symbols; there were likewise detailed studies of the Aesthetes of Garwiy, again with a variety of cryptic references.

"No great matter," said Etzwane. "Aun Sharah's notes will be obsolete in a year. They relate to Old Shant; we have no interest in secrets and scandals. In any event I want to reorganize the Discriminators."

"How so?"

"They are now civil and cantonal police; they also gather information elsewhere in Shant. I want to detach this last function and establish a new Shant-wide agency to provide the Anome detailed intelligence regarding all of Shant."

"It is an interesting idea. I would be glad to control such an agency."

118

Etzwane laughed to himself with a straight face. Finnerack was sometimes wonderfully transparent. "Our first problem is the identity of the men who followed us yesterday evening. I would like you to organize this matter, at least. Acquaint yourself with the Discriminators; call a meeting of the personnel. Stress that Aun Sharah is no longer Chief Discriminator; that all orders must now derive from me. As soon as possible I want to look over all the operatives, all the trackers official and unofficial. If I see the man, I will recognize him."

Finnerack hesitated. "All very well, but how should I proceed?"

Etzwane considered a moment. To the side of Aun Sharah's desk was a bank of buttons. Etzwane pressed the top button. At once a clerk entered the room, a man plump and anxious, no older than Etzwane himself.

Etzwane said: "The former Chief Discriminator is no longer in authority, by order of the Anome. Henceforth you will take orders only from me and from Jerd Finnerack, here beside me; do you understand?"

"I do."

"What is your name?"

"I am Thiruble Archenway, with the status of Clerk Lieutenant."

"This top button summons yourself. What of these other buttons?"

Archenway explained the function of each button, while Etzwane took notes. "I have several tasks to be accomplished at once," said Etzwane. "First, I want you to introduce Jerd Finnerack throughout the office. He will be making certain arrangements. I want you then to summon three men to me here, by authority of the Anome, as quickly as is convenient. First: Ferulfio the Master Elec-

119

trician. Second: the technist Doneis. Third: Mialambre: Octagon, Arbiter of Wale."

"As quickly as possible." Thiruble Archenway bowed to Finnerack. "Sir, please step this way. . . ."

"One moment," said Etzwane.

Archenway swung about. "Yes?"

"What are your ordinary duties?"

"Errands much like those you have just put to me. I customarily adjust the Chief Discriminator's calendar, arrange appointments, screen mail, deliver messages."

"I remind you that Aun Sharah is no longer associated with the Discriminators. I want absolutely no leakage of information, gossip, hints, or implications from this office, through you or anyone else. Perhaps you had better circulate a bulletin to this effect."

"I will do as you require."

Ferulfio the Master Electrician was a man thin and pale, with quicksilver eyes. "Ferulfio," said Etzwane, "by repute you are a man as silent as a fanshank and twice as discreet."

"That I am."

"You and I will now go to Sershan Palace; I will admit you to a room housing the former Anome's radio system. You will transfer the equipment to this office and arrange it along yonder wall."

"As you say."

Etzwane, disliking Aun Sharah's desk, ordered it removed. He brought in two green leather divans, two chairs of purple-stained woadwood, upholstered in plum-coloured leather, and a long table, upon which a pert and pretty girl file clerk, watching Etzwane sidelong, placed a bouquet of irutiane and amaryls.

Archenway came into the room. He looked this way and that. "Very pleasant; a nice change. You also need a new rug. Let me think...." He paced back and forth. "A floral, perhaps the Fourth Legend, in violet and coral? Somewhat too definite, too limiting; after all, you wish to establish your own moods. Better one of the Aubry Concentrics; which are frequently delightful. The connoisseurs think them ill-proportioned, but I find this very distortion quaint and amusing. ... Perhaps after all a Burazhesq would be best, in dark grey, thracide,* umber."

"I am agreeable," said Etzwane. "Order in such a rug. We all should work in pleasant surroundings."

"My precise philosophy!" declared Archenway, "I am sorry to say that my own office leaves something to be desired. I could work more efficiently in a situation on the front elevation, somewhat larger and lighter than my present cubbyhole."

"Are any such offices vacant?"

"Not at the moment," admitted Archenway, "I can readily recommend changes. In fact, if you will allow me, I will at this instant prepare a schedule of long overdue adjustments."

"In due course," said Etzwane. "We can't do everything at once."

"I trust that you will keep the matter in mind," said Archenway. "I am now half-stifled in gloom; the door strikes my leg every time someone opens it, and the colours, in spite of my best efforts, are stupid and depressing.... Meanwhile, the technist Doneis awaits your convenience."

*Thracide: a sour, intense carmine.

121

Etzwane swung around in astonishment. "You keep Doneis waiting while you chatter of rugs and your inclinations in offices? You'll be lucky to end up tonight with any office whatever."

In consternation Archenway hurried from the room, to return with the tall, bone-thin Doneis. Etzwane ushered the technist to a divan and seated himself opposite. "You have submitted no report," said Etzwane. "I am anxious to learn what has been accomplished."

Doneis refused to relax; he sat bolt upright on the divan. "I have submitted no report because we have achieved no reportable results. You need not remind me of the need for haste; I understand this from high to low. We do the best we can."

"Do you have nothing whatever to tell me?" demanded Etzwane. "What are your problems? Do you need money? Additional personnel? Are their problems of morale? Do you lack authority?"

Doneis raised his sparse eyebrows. "We need neither money nor further personnel, unless you can supply five dozen intensively trained persons of superlative intelligence. Problems of discipline arose at first; we are not accustomed to working together. Matters are now somewhat better. We pursue what may be a promising line of inquiry. Are you interested in the details?"

"Of course!"

"There is a long-known class of materials," said Doneis, "which emerges from the retort as an extremely dense white material of waxy and somewhat fibrous texture. We call these materials the halcoids. They show a most curious propensity. When a surge of electricity passes through them, they alter to a translucent crystalline solid, with an appreciable increment in size. In the case of Halcoid

122

Four, this increment is almost one-sixth. Not a great deal, one might think, but the change occurs instantly, and with irresistible force; indeed, if Halcoid Four is not altered under pressure, it accelerates its surface to such an extent that in effect it explodes. One of our number has recently produced Halcoid Four with its fibres parallel, and this we call Halcoid Four-One. Upon an electrical impulse Four-One expands longitudinally only, the terminal surfaces moving at remarkable speed, which at midpoint we reckon to be about one-quarter the velocity of light. It has been proposed that projectiles be formed of Halcoid Four-One. We are now performing tests, but I cannot announce even presumptive results."

Etzwane was impressed by the exposition. "What other lines do you pursue?"

"We produce arrows with dexax heads, exploded by contact; these are complicated and uncertain. We are striving to perfect this weapon, as it would prove effective at middle ranges. I can give you little more news; we have essentially only settled ourselves to our work. The ancients projected light strong enough to burn away vision, but these skills are lost; our power-pods, while durable, provide only small surges."

Etzwane displayed the energy pistol which he had obtained from Ifness. "Here is a weapon from Earth. Can you learn anything useful from it?"

Doneis scrutinized the weapon. "The workmanship is beyond our capabilities. I doubt if we could learn more than the fact of our own deterioration. Of course, we have no metals of rare and various kinds, though we do fine work with our glasses and crystals." He somewhat reluctantly returned the pistol to Etzwane. "As to another matter: military communication. Here there is no lack of capability; we are skilled in the controlled pulsing of electrical currents; we manufacture coded torcs by the thousands. But the problems are still critical. To manufacture military equipment we must commandeer the facilities and skilled workmen currently manufacturing torcs. If we simply skim the torc factories of their best, then we risk producing faulty torcs, with possibly tragic consequence."

"Is there sufficiency of torcs on storage?"

"Never; this is impractical. We use the codes of recent fatalities in the new torcs to minimize the complexity of the code. If we did not do this, the codes might extend to nine, ten, or even eleven colours: a great and obvious nuisance."

Etzwane puzzled over the problem. "Is there no other less urgent industry from which workers might be diverted?"

"None whatever."

"We have a single recourse," said Etzwane. "Torcs are of no value to dead people. Produce the radios. The young people must wait for their torcs until the Roguskhoi are destroyed."

"This is my own reading of the matter," agreed Doneis.

"One last matter," said Etzwane. "Aun Sharah has become Director of Material Procurement for all Shant. Whatever your needs, you must now consult him."

Doneis had departed. Etzwane leaned back on the divan to think. Suppose the war lasted ten years; suppose for ten years pubescent children were denied their torcs. They would then be almost his own age before they encountered adult responsibilities. Would they willingly give over their unbridled freedom? Or would a whole generation of hooligans be loosed upon the complicated structure of Shant? ... Etzwane pressed the button to summon Thiruble Archenway.... He pressed again. Into the room came the girl who had prepared the bouquet. "Where is Archenway?"

"He has stepped out for his afternoon wine. He will shortly return. Incidentally," she added in a demure voice, "a distinguished gentleman sits in the hall, and it might be that he has come to speak to the Chief Discriminator. Archenway left no instructions."

"Be good enough to show him in. Your name is what?"

"I am Dashan of the house of Szandales, a clerk in Archenway's office."

"How long have you worked in this capacity?"

"Only three months."

"Hereafter when I press the bell, you will answer. Thiruble Archenway is insufficiently alert."

"I will do my best to help your Lordship in every possible way."

As she left the room she turned a quick backward glance over her shoulder, from which much or little might be assumed, depending upon the mood of the person who looked.

Dasham of Szandales tapped at the door, then looked demurely through. "The gentleman Mialambre: Octagon, High Arbiter of Wale."

Etzwane jumped to his feet; into the room came Mialambre: a man short and sturdy, if somewhat narrow-chested, in an austere gown of grey and white. His lordly head supported a stiff brush of white hair; his gaze was intense and somewhat minatory; he did not seem a man of easy congeniality.

Dashan of Szandales waited expectantly in the doorway. Etzwane said, "Bring us refreshments, if you please." To Mialambre: Octagon he said, "Please sit down; I did not expect you so soon; I am sorry to have kept you waiting."

"You are the Chief Discriminator?" Mialambre's voice was low and harsh; his gaze probed every aspect of Etzwane's appearance.

"At the moment there is no Chief Discriminator. I am Gastel Etzwane, executive assistant to the Anome. When you talk to me, you are, in effect, face to face with the Anome."

Mialambre's gaze, if anything, became more intense. Perhaps from juridical habit, he made no effort to ease the conversation, but silently awaited Etzwane's remarks.

"Yesterday the Anome read your observations in the *Spectrum*," said Eztwane. "He was much impressed by the scope and clarity of your viewpoints."

The door opened; Dashan wheeled in a table with a pot of tea, crisp cakes, candied sea fruit, a pale green flower in a blue vase. She spoke over her shoulder to Etzwane in a confiding voice: "Archenway is pale with rage."

"I'll speak to him later. Serve our distinguished visitor his needs, if you will."

Dashan poured tea and quickly left the office.

"I will be candid," said Etzwane. "A new Anome has assumed control of Shant."

Mialambre gave a grim nod, as if certain speculations of his own had been validated. "How was the event brought about?"

"To be candid once again, coercion was used. A group

126

of persons became alarmed by the passive policy of the old Anome. A change was made; we now undertake to defend the land."

"Not an instant too soon. What do you want of me?"

"Advice, counsel, and cooperation."

Mialambre: Octagon compressed his lips. "I would wish to learn your doctrines before committing myself to such an association."

"We have no particular point of view," said Etzwane. "The war must bring changes and we want them to occur in the right direction. Conditions in Shker, Burazhesq, Dithibel, Cape might well be altered for the better."

"There you tread on uncertain ground," declared Mialambre. "The traditional basis of Shant is looseness of association. To enforce a central doctrine must alter this situation, and not necessarily for the better."

"I understand this," said Etzwane. "Problems are sure to arise; we need capable men to solve them."

"Hmmf, how many such men have you recruited?"

Etzwane sipped his tea. "They do not yet outnumber the problems."

Mialambre gave a grudging nod. "I can render a conditional acceptance. The work is challenging."

"I am pleased to hear this," said Etzwane. "My temporary headquarters is Fontenay's Inn. I would like you to join me there, and we will confer at greater length."

"Fontenay's Inn?" Mialambre's voice was more puzzled than disapproving. "Is that not a tavern by the riverbank?"

"It is."

"As you wish." Mialambre frowned. "I must now bring up a practical matter. In Wale my family, consisting

127

of seven persons, subsists upon a jurist's income, which is not high. To lay the subject bare, I need money to pay my debts, lest the sheriff put me into a state of indenture."

"Your salary will be adequate," said Etzwane. "We will discuss this tonight as well."

Etzwane found Finnerack seated at a table in the central document chamber, listening to two Discriminators of high rank. Each vied for his ear; each indicated a separate array of documents. Finnerack listened with grim patience, and upon seeing Etzwane dismissed the two with a jerk of his hand; they departed with what dignity they could muster. Finnerack said, "Aun Sharah seems to have been flexible and undemanding. These two were his second and third in command. I will use them in the Department of Urban Discrimination."

Etzwane raised his eyebrows in surprise. Finnerack apparently had taken to himself the task of reorganizing the department, an activity which would seem to exceed his instructions. Finnerack went on to detail other of his evaluations. Etzwane listened with more interest for the working of Finnerack's judgements than for the subject matter itself. Finnerack's methods were direct to the point of naïveté and, as such, must work awe upon the subtle folk of Garwiy, who could only interpret simplicity as majesty, silence as craft. Etzwane became amused. The Discriminators were a typical Garwiy institution: complicated, devious, arbitrary, a situation which Finnerack appeared to regard as a personal affront. Etzwane, a musician, almost envied Finnerack his brutal power.

Finnerack concluded his exposition. "Next you wanted to look over the roster."

"Yes," said Etzwane. "If I recognize someone, Aun Sharah's candour becomes suspect."

"It becomes worse than that," said Finnerack. He picked up one of his lists. "If you like we can start now."

None of the Discriminators presently at hand resembled the hawk-faced man Etzwane had glimpsed through the window of the diligence.

The suns had rolled low down the sky. Etzwane and Finnerack wandered across Corporation Plaza to a cafe, where they drank verbena tea and watched the folk of Garwiy idle past; and none who saw these two young men – one slight, saturnine, and dark, the other gaunt, with sun-scorched blond hair and eyes like polished turquoise – could know that the destiny of Shant lay between them. Etzwane picked up the *Spectrum* from a nearby chair. An ochre-bordered panel caught his eye. He read with a heavy sensation:

> From Marestiy by radio comes a report of an engagement between the newly organized militia and a band of Roguskhoi. The savage intruders, having wreaked an awful damage upon Canton Shkority, sent a foraging party north. At Gasmal Town on the border a troop of men denied them passage and ordered their retreat. The red brutes ignored the lawful injunction and a battle ensued. The Marestiy defenders discharged arrows and slung stones, many of which caused discomfort to the enemy, and infuriated them into what one observer described as "a stampede of furious red beasts." Such intemperate conduct will never prevail against the mighty weapons being forged by the Anome; sensible of this the

Marestiy militia adopted a flexible tactic. Final events and outcome are not yet known.

"The creatures are moving," said Etzwane. "Even those who have fled towards the sea are not safe."

CHAPTER EIGHT

In the plum-coloured Garwiy evening Etzwane and Finnerack made their way under coloured lights to Fontenay's Inn. At the back table Frolitz and the troupe ate a supper of broad beans and cheese, which Etzwane and Finnerack joined.

Frolitz was in a sour mood. "Gastel Etzwane's hands are tired and worn. Since his outside activities are more important than the welfare of the troupe, I will not require him to play an instrument. If he wishes, he may rattle the histels, or snap his fingers from time to time."

Etzwane held his tongue. After the meal, when the troupe brought forth their instruments, Etzwane joined them on the stand. Frolitz struck a pose of astonishment. "What is this? The grand Gastel Etzwane favours us with his presence? We are profoundly grateful. Would you be so kind as to take up your woodhorn? Tonight I work the khitan."

Etzwane blew in the familiar old mouthcup, fingered the silver buttons of which he had once been so proud. . . . Strange how differently he felt! The hands were his own; his fingers moved of their own accord up and down the buttons, but the vantage was higher, the perspectives were longer; and he played with an almost imperceptible elongation of tension at the beat.

At the intermission Frolitz came back to the troupe in a state of excitement. "Notice the man in the far corner – can you guess who sits there in silence, without his instrument? It is the druithine Dystar!" The troupe peered at the austere silhouette, each man wondering how his music had sounded in the mind of the great druithine. Frolitz said, "I asked what he did here; he said he had come at the will of the Anome. I asked, would he play music with the troupe? He said, yes, it would be his pleasure, that our work had brought the mood upon him. So now he joins us. Etzwane, to play the gastaing; I play woodhorn."

Fordyce, standing next to Etzwane, muttered, "At last you play beside your father. And still he does not know?"

"He does not know." Etzwane took up the gastaing: an instrument of deeper tone than the khitan, with a plangent resonance which must remain under the control of the damping sleeve if the harmony were not to be overwhelmed. Unlike many musicians, Etzwane enjoyed the gastaing and the subtleties to be achieved by expert tilting and sliding of the sleeve.

The troupe took up their instruments and stood waiting on the bandstand: the conventional respect due a musician of Dystar's quality. Frolitz left the stand, went to speak to Dystar; the two returned. Dystar bowed to the musicians, and his gaze rested a thoughtful instant on Etzwane. He took Frolitz' khitan, struck a chord, bent the neck, tested the scratch-box. In accordance with his prerogatives, he started a tune, a pleasant melody, deceptively simple.

132

Frolitz and Mielke, on the clarion, played ground notes, careful to stay harmonically aside, with the guizol and gastaing striking unobtrusive accents.... The music proceeded; the first tune came to an end: an exercise in which each participant explored the musical surroundings. ... Dystar relaxed his position and sipped from the beaker of wine which had been placed beside him. He nodded to Frolitz, who now in his turn blew a theme into the mouthcup of his woodhorn – a gasping, rasping, sardonic statement, foreign to the fluid clarity of the instrument, which Dystar emphasized with harsh, slow strokes of the scratch-box, and the music was off and away: a polyphony melancholy and deliberate, in which every instrument of the troupe could clearly be heard. Dystar played calmly, his invention every instant opening new perspectives into the music.... The melody broke and faltered, in a manner anticipated by all; Dystar struck out an astounding exercise, starting in the upper register, working down through a perplexing combination of chords, with only an occasional resonance of the gastaing for support; down through upper-middle and lower-middle registers, backwards and forwards, like a falling leaf; this way and that, into the lower tones, to finish with a guttural elbow at the scratch-box. On the woodhorn Frolitz blew a quaver a minor interval below, which dwindled and died into the resonance of the gastaing.

As convention demanded, Dystar now gave up his instrument and went to a table at the side of the room. The troupe sat quietly for a moment or two. Frolitz considered. With a malicious twitch of the lips he handed the khitan to Etzwane. "We now play something slow and quiet – what is that night piece of Old Morningshore? *Zitrinilla* ... Third mode. Careful, all, with the breakoff from the second strain. Etzwane: the time and the statement..."

Etzwane crooked the khitan, adjusted the scratch-box. The mischievous Frolitz, he well knew, had thrust him into a position from which any sensible man must recoil: the playing of khitan after one of Dystar's most brilliant improvisations. Etzwane paused a moment to think his way through the tune. He struck a chord and played the statement at a somewhat slower tempo than usual.

The tune proceeded, wistful and melancholy, and came to its end. Frolitz blew a phrase to signal a variation at a different rhythm. Etzwane found himself playing alone, the condition he had been hoping to avoid: he must now set himself up for measure against Dystar.... He played slow chords quickly damped, creating a pattern of sound and silence which became interesting to him, and which he restated in an inversion. Resisting the temptation to embellish, he played a spare, stately music. The troupe supplied ground notes, which presently became a broad theme, swelling up like a wave over the khitan, then subsiding. Etzwane played a set of clanging disharmonic chords and a soft resolution; the music ended. Dystar rose to his feet and signalled all to his table. "Beyond question," said Dystar, "here is the first troupe of Shant. All are strong, all use the sensitivity of strength. Gastel Etzwane plays as I at his age could only have hoped to play; he has known much experience of life."

"He is an obstinate man," said Frolitz. "With an important future as a Pink-Black-Azure-Deep Greener, he meddles instead with Aesthetes and *eirmelraths* and other matters which do not concern him. My counsel goes for nought."

Etzwane said in a mild voice: "Frolitz refers to the

134

war against the Roguskhoi, which occupies someting of my attention."

Frolitz threw wide his arms in a gesture of vindication. "From his own mouth you have heard the words."

Dystar nodded gravely. "You have cause for concern." He turned to Etzwane. "In Maschein I spoke to you and your friend who sits yonder. Immediately thereafter I received the Anome's command to journey here to Fontenay's Inn. Are these events related?"

Frolitz looked accusingly at Etzwane. "Dystar too? Must every musician in Shant go forth against the savages before you are appeased? We strike them with our tringolets, pelt them with guizols. . . . The scheme is inept!" Signalling his troupe he stalked back to the stand.

"Frolitz' remarks are irrelevant," said Etzwane. "I am indeed involved against the Roguskhoi, but on this basis –" He explained his situation in the same terms he had used with Finnerack. "I need support from the wisest persons of Shant, and for this reason I requested that you come here."

Dystar seemed mildly amused rather than startled or awed. "So then: I am here."

A figure loomed over the table. Etzwane looked up into the bleak visage of Mialambre:Octagon. "I am puzzled by your policies," stated Mialambre. "You ask that I meet you at a tavern to discuss matters of policy; I find you drinking liquors and consorting with the tavern musicians. Is the whole affair a hoax?"

"By no means," said Etzwane. "This is Dystar, an eminent druithine, and like yourself a man of wisdom. Dystar, before you stands Mialambre: Octagon, no musician, but a jurist and a philosopher, whose assistance I have also solicited."

135

Mialambre seated himself somewhat stiffly. Etzwane glanced from one to the other: Dystar detached and self-contained, an observer rather than a participant; Mialambre astute, exacting, a person relating each fact of existence to every other fact by a system based on the ethos of Wale. The two, thought Etzwane, had nothing in common but integrity; each would find the other incomprehensible; yet if one became Anome he would rule the other. Which? Either? ... Etzwane, looking over his shoulder, beckoned to Finnerack, who had been standing somewhat aloofly by the wall.

Finnerack had changed to a sombre garment of black twill, tight at wrists and ankles. Without change of expression he came to the table. "Here," said Etzwane, "for all his gloom is a man of probity and competence. His name is Jerd Finnerack; he tends to energetic action. We are a disparate group, but our problems run on several levels and require disparate talents."

"This is all very well, or so I suppose," said Mialambre. "Still, I find the situation irregular and our surroundings incongruous. You deal with all of Shant rather more informally than the elders control the business of our village."

"Why not?" asked Etzwane. "The government of Shant has been and is a single man, the Anome; what could be less formal than this? The government travels with the Anome; if he sat here tonight, here would be the government."

"The system is flexible," Mialambre agreed. "How it functions in times of stress remains to be seen."

"The system depends upon the men who direct it," said Etzwane, "which is to say ourselves. Much work lies be-

136

fore us. I will tell you what so far has been done: we have mobilized militias in sixty-two cantons."

"Those not now overrun," remarked Finnerack.

"The technists of Garwiy contrive weapons; the folk of Shant at last realize that the Roguskhoi must and will be defeated. On the other side of the coin, the organization to coordinate so much effort simply does not exist. Shant is a sprawling beast with sixty-two arms and no head. The beast is helpless; it struggles and thrashes in sixty-two directions but is no match for the ahulph which gnaws at its belly."

On the stand Frolitz had taken the troupe into a muted nocturne, which he played only when he felt out of sorts.

Mialambre said: "Our deficiencies are real. Two thousand years has brought many changes. Viana Paizifiume fought the Palasedrans with a brave, even ferocious army. They wore no torcs; discipline must have been a severe problem. Even so, they dealt the Palasedrans terrible blows."

"They were men in those days," said Finnerack. "They lived like men, they fought like men, and if necessary died like men. They pursued no 'flexible tactics.' "

Mialambre nodded in dour agreement. "We shall not find their like in the Shant of today."

"Yet," mused Etzwane, "they were only men, no more and no less than ourselves."

"Not true," insisted Mialambre. "The men of old were harsh and wilful, responsible to no one but themselves. They were therefore self-reliant, and here is the 'more.' The folk today are allowed no such exercises; they trust the justice of the Anome rather than the effect of their own force. They are obedient and lawful: here the

137

olden folk were 'less.' So we have lost and so we have gained."

"The gains have no meaning," said Finnerack, "if the Roguskhoi destroy Shant."

"This will not come to pass," Etzwane declared. "Our militias must and will strike them back!"

Finnerack uttered his harsh laugh. "How can the militia do this? Can children fight ogres? A single man inhabits Shant: the Anome. He cannot do the fighting; he must order his children forth to battle. The children are fearful; they rely on the single man and the result is preordained. Defeat! disaster! death!"

There was silence except for the slow, sad music of the nocturne.

"I suspect that you overstate your case," said Mialambre in a cautious voice. "Surely Shant cannot be totally bereft of warriors; somewhere live brave men to protect their homes, to assault and conquer."

"I met a few," said Finnerack. "Like me they worked at Camp Three. They had no fear of pain, death, or the Faceless Man; what could he do worse than what they knew? Here were warriors! Men without fear of the torc! These men were free; can you believe this? Give me a militia of such brave free man and I will conquer the Roguskhoi!"

"Unfortunately," said Etzwane, "Camp Three is no more. We can hardly torment men until they lose their fear of death."

"Is there no better way to set a man free?" cried Finnerack in a rough voice. "This instant I can tell you a better way!"

Mialambre was puzzled; Dystar wondered; only Etzwane knew Finnerack's meaning. Beyond question he referred to his torc, which he must regard the instrument of his suffering.

The group sat quietly, brooding over Finnerack's words. Presently, in a voice of idle reflection, Etzwane asked: "Suppose the torcs were taken from all your necks: what then?"

Finnerack's face was stoney; he deigned no reply.

Dystar said: "Without my torc I would be mad with joy."

Mialambre seemed astounded both by the concept and by Dystar's response. "How can this be? The torc is your representation, the signal of your responsibility to society."

"I recognize no such responsibility," said Dystar. "Responsibility is the debt of people who take. I do not take, I give. Thereafter my responsibility is gone."

"Not so," exclaimed Mialambre. "This is an egotistical fallacy! Every man alive owes a vast debt to millions – to the folk around him who provide a human ambience, to the dead heroes who gave him his thoughts, his language, his music; to the technists who built the spaceships which brought him to Durdane. The past is a precious tapestry; each man is a new thread in the continuing weave; a thread by itself is without meaning or worth."

Dystar gave generous acquiescence. "What you say is truth. I am at fault. Nonetheless, my torc is unwelcome; it coerces me to the life I would prefer to live by my own free will."

"Suppose you were Anome," asked Etzwane. "What would be your policy in this regard?"

"There would be no more torcs. People would live without fear, in freedom."

" 'Freedom'?" cried Mialambre in unaccustomed fervour. "I am as free as is possible! I act as I please, within the lawful scope. Thieves and murderers lack freedom; they may not rob and kill. The honest man's torc is his protection against such 'freedom.' "

Dystar again conceded the jurist his argument. "Still, I was born without a torc. When the Sanhredin guild-master clamped my neck, a weight came upon my spirit which has never departed."

"The weight is real," said Mialambre. "What is the alternative? Illegality and defiance. How would our laws be enforced? Through a coercive corps? Spies? Prisons? Tortures? Hypnotism? Drugs? Men without restraint are ahulphs. I declare that the flaw is not the torc; it resides in the human disposition which makes the torc necessary."

Finnerack said, "The correctness of your remarks rests upon an assumption."

"Which is?"

"You assume the altruism and good judgment of the Anome."

"True!" declared Mialambre. "For two thousand years we have had this general condition."

"The magnates will agree to this. At Camp Three we thought the reverse; and we are correct, not you. What man of justice could allow a Camp Three to exist?"

Mialambre was not daunted. "Camp Three was a carbuncle upon the private parts; filth under the rug. No system lacks its flaw. The Anome enforces only canton law; he makes no law of his own. The customs of Canton Glaiy are insensitive; perhaps this is why Camp Three was located in Glaiy. Were I Anome, would I enforce new laws upon Glaiy? A dilemma for every thoughtful man."

Etzwane said, "The argument is beside the point; at

least temporarily. The Roguskhoi are about to destroy us. There will be no more torcs, no more Anome, no more men, unless we fight with effectiveness. Our performance to date has not been good."

"The Anome is the single free man of Shant," said Finnerack. "As a free man I too would fight; an army of free men could defeat the Roguskhoi."

Mialambre said, "The idea is unrealistic, in more ways than one. In the first place, the unclamped children are years from manhood."

"Why wait?" demanded Finnerack. "We need only unclamp our warriors."

Mialambre laughed quietly. "It is not possible. Fortunately so. We would have suffered the Hundred Years War for nothing. The torcs have kept the peace. The compulsion of the torc is best; I cite you the chaos of Caraz."

"Even though manhood is lost?" demanded Finnerack. "Do you envision an infinite future of halcyon peace? The pendulum must swing. The torcs must be unclamped."

Dystar asked, "How is this to be done?"

Finnerack jerked his thumb towards Etzwane. "An Earthman taught him the sleight. He is a free man; he can do as he likes."

"Gastel Etzwane," said Dystar, "take then this torc from my neck."

The decision came to Etzwane's mind by an indirect and emotional process. "I will remove your torcs. You shall be free men like myself. Finnerack will control an army of brave free men. No further children will be clamped by torcs – if only for this reason: the torc makers now supply radios to the new militia."

Mialambre said despondently: "For better or worse, Shant enters a new time of convulsion."

"For better or worse," said Etzwane, "the convulsion is upon us. The force of the Anome is waning; he can no longer control the spasms. Mialambre and Dystar, you must work together. Mialambre, with such staff as you elect, you shall range Shant and correct the worst flaws: the Camp Threes, the Temple Bashons, the indenture brokers, the indenture system itself. You cannot avoid conflict and controversy; these are unavoidable. Dystar, only a great musician could do what I now require of you. Alone, or with such folk as you select, you must range Shant, to tell folk by word and by the force of music of the common heritage, the unity which must come to us, unless the Roguskhoi drive us all out into the Beljamar. The details of these operations – to correct and to unify, to bring justice and common purpose – must be yours to calculate. Now, let us go up to my chambers, where you shall all become free men like myself."

CHAPTER NINE

Days passed. Etzwane engaged a suite on the fourth level of the Roseale Hrindiana, on the east side of Corporation Plaza, three minutes walk from the Jurisdictionary. Finnerack moved in with him, but two days later took a somewhat less luxurious suite in the Pagane Towers across the plaza. The pleasures of wealth held no fascination for Finnerack; his meals were spare and simple; he drank no wines or spirits; his wardrobe consisted of four relatively plain garments, each unrelieved black. Frolitz had unceremoniously taken his troupe up into Purple Fan; Mialambre: Octagon had assembled a staff of consultants, though he had not yet overcome all his misgivings in regard to the changes he would be working upon Shant.

Etzwane argued: "Our goal is not uniformity; we quell only those institutions which victimize the helpless: grotesque theologies, indenture, the old-age houses of Cape. Where once the Anome enforced law, in the new times he becomes a source of recourse."

"If torcs are no longer used, the Anome's function changes of necessity," Mialambre noted in a dry voice. "The future is unreadable."

Dystar had gone off by himself, with words to no one.

143

Mialambre: Octagon or Dystar the druithine? Either could fulfill the office of Anome; each was deficient in the other's strength. ... Etzwane wished that he could make a quick decision and unburden himself; he had no taste for authority.

Meanwhile Finnerack reorganized the Discriminators with brutal zest. The comfortable old routines were shattered; out went the timeservers, including Thiruble Archenway; departments and bureaus were consolidated. The new Intelligence Agency was Finnerack's special interest, a situation which sometimes caused Etzwane misgivings. Consulting with Finnerack in his office, Etzwane studied the spare form, the corded face, the drooping mouth, the bright blue eyes, and wondered as to the future. Finnerack now wore no torc; Etzwane's authority extended only so far as Finnerack chose to acknowledge it.

Dashan of Szandales came into the office with a tray of refreshments. Finnerack, suddenly remembering one of his arrangements, put a question to her: "The men I required – they are here?"

"They are here." Dashan's voice was terse. She disliked Finnerack and considered herself under Etzwane's authority alone.

Finnerack, unconcerned with inconsequentialities, gave her a brisk order. "Have them marshalled into the back office; we'll be there in five minutes."

Dashan flounced from the room. Etzwane watched her go with a sad half-smile. Finnerack would be a hard man to control. To urge him to greater delicacy was time wasted. Etzwane asked: "What men are these?"

"They are the last of the men on the roster. You have seen all the rest."

Etzwane had almost forgotten Aun Sharah, who in his

present post was reassuringly far from the sources of power.

The two went to the back office. Here waited fourteen men: the trackers and spies on Aun Sharah's informal roster. Etzwane walked from man to man, trying to remember the exact contours of the face he had glimpsed through the window of the diligence: a hard straight nose, a square chin, wide flinty eyes.

In front of him stood such a man. Etzwane said, "Your name, if you please?"

"I am Ian Carle."

To the others Etzwane said, "Thank you; I require nothing more." To Carle he said, "Come, if you please, to my office."

He led the way, with Carle and Finnerack walking behind. Finnerack slid shut the door. Etzwane motioned Carle to a divan; Carle silently obeyed.

Etzwane asked, "Have you ever been in this office before?"

Carle stared Etzwane eye to eye for five seconds. He said, "I have."

Etzwane said, "I want to learn something of your previous work. My authority to ask questions comes directly from the Anome; I can show you the warrant, should you require assurance. Your own conduct is not in question."

Ian Carle gave an unemotional sign of assent.

"A short time ago," said Etzwane, "you were instructed to meet the balloon *Aramaad* at Garwiy Depot, there identify a certain man – myself as a matter of fact – and follow him to his destination. Is this true?"

Carle paused only two seconds. "This is true."

"Who gave you these instructions?"

Carle spoke in an even voice, "The then Chief Discriminator, Aun Sharah."

"Did he provide background or reason for your assignment?"

"None. This was not his habit."

"What were your exact instructions?"

"I was to follow the designated man, observe whomever he met; were I to see the tall, white-haired man of uncertain age I was to abandon Gastel Etzwane and follow the white-haired man. I was naturally to gather all supplementry information of interest."

"What was your report?"

"I informed him that the subject, obviously suspicious, had no difficulty picking me out, and attempted to make physical contact with me, which I avoided."

"What other instructions did Aun Sharah then give you?"

"He told me to station myself near Sershan Palace, to be at all times discreet, to ignore the previous subject, but to watch for the tall, white-haired man."

Etzwane sat down on the divan and glanced at Finnerack, who stood with arms clasped behind his back, eyes boring into the face of Ian Carle. Etzwane felt puzzlement. The information had been supplied; Aun Sharah's activities had been illuminated. What did Finnerack see or sense that he, Etzwane, had missed?

Etzwane asked, "What other report did you make to Aun Sharah?"

"I made no other reports. When I came with my information, Aun Sharah was no longer Chief Discriminator."

"Information?" Etzwane frowned. "What information did you bring on this occasion?"

"It was general in nature. I witnessed a grey-haired man of middle size leave Sershan Palace, whom I conceived might be the person in question. I followed him to Fontenay's Inn, where I identified him as Frolitz, a musician. I returned up Galias Avenue, passing you and this gentleman near the fountain. As I turned into Middle Way I encountered a tall, white-haired man walking eastward. He hailed a diligence and asked to be taken to the Splendour of Gebractya. I followed as rapidly as possible, but I did not find him."

"Since, have you seen either the white-haired man or Aun Sharah?"

"Neither have I seen."

From somewhere, thought Etzwane, Aun Sharah had secured a description of Ifness, in whom he had taken considerable interest. Ifness had returned to Earth; the white-haired man Ian Carle had followed presumably had been an Aesthete from one of the palaces along Middle Way.

Etzwane asked, "What garments did the tall, white-haired man wear?"

"A grey cloak, a loose grey cap."

These were Ifness' preferred garments. Etzwane asked, "Was he an Aesthete?"

"I think not; he carried himself like a man from an outer canton."

Etzwane tried to remember some particular characteristic by which Ifness could be identified. "Can you describe his face?"

"Not in detail."

"If you see him again, communicate with me at once."

"As you desire." Ian Carle departed.

147

Finnerack spoke caustically, "There you have Aun Sharah, Director of Material Procurement. I say, drown him tonight in the Sualle."

One of Finnerack's worst faults, reflected Etzwane, was intemperance and excessive reaction, which made dealing with him a constant struggle for moderation. "He did only what you and I would have done in his place," said Etzwane shortly. "He gathered information."

"Oh? What of the message to Shirge Hillen at Camp Three?"

"That has not been proved upon him."

"Bah. When I was a boy I worked in my father's currant patch. When I found a weed I pulled it up. I did not look at it or hope that it might become a currant plant. I dealt with the weed at once."

"First you made sure it was a weed," said Etzwane.

Finnerack shrugged and stalked from the room. Dashan of Szandales came into the room, looking back towards Finnerack's departing shape with a shudder. "That man frightens me. Does he always wear black?"

"He is a man for whom the persistence and fatefulness of black were invented." Etzwane pulled the girl down upon his lap. She set an arch moment or so, then jumped to her feet. "You are a terrible philanderer. What would my mother say if she knew how things went?"

"I am interested only in what the daughter says."

"The daughter says that a man from the Wildlands has brought you a crate of wild animals, and his beasts await you on the freight ramp."

The superintendent of the station gang at Conceil Siding had brought his Roguskhoi imps to Garwiy. He said, "It's been a month since you came through the Wildlands.

148

You fancied my little pets then; what of them now?"

The imps Etzwane had seen at Conceil Siding had grown a foot. They stood glaring from behind the hardwood bars of the cage. "They were never angels of delights," declared the superintendent. "Now they're well on their way to becoming true fiends. On the right stands Musel; on the left Erxter."

The two creatures stared back at Etzwane with unblinking antagonism. "Put your finger through the bars and they'll twist it off for you," said the superintendent with relish. "They're as mean as sin and no two ways about it. First I thought to treat them well and win them over. I fed them tidbits; I gave them a fine pen; I said 'chirrup,' and I whistled little tunes. I tried to teach them speech and I thought to reward good behaviour with beer. To no avail. Each attacked me tooth and nail when I gave him the option. So then I thought I'd learn the truth of the matter. I separated them, and Erxter I continued to gratify and appease. The other, poor Musel, I set about to cow. When he'd strike out at me I'd deal him a buffet. When he'd gnash at my hand I'd prod him with a stick; many the beatings he's earned and collected. Meanwhile Erxter dined on the best and slept in the shade. At the end of the experiment was there any difference in their savagery? Not a twitch; they were as before."

"Hmmf." Etzwane backed away as both came to the bars. "Do they speak; do they have words?"

"None. If they understand me they give no signal. They won't cooperate or perform the smallest task, for love or hunger. They raven up every crust I throw to them, but they'd starve rather than pull a lever to get themselves meat. Now then, fiends!" He rapped on the bars of the cage. "Wouldn't you like my ankle to chew?"

149

He turned back to Etzwane. "Already the rascals know the difference between the male and female! You should see them bestir themselves when a woman walks past and still so young in years. I consider it a disgrace."

Etzwane asked, "How do they recognize a woman?"

The superintendent was puzzled. "How does anyone recognize a woman?"

"For instance, if a man walked by in woman's garments, or a woman dressed as a man: what then?"

The superintendent shook his head in wonder for Etzwane's subtleties. "All this is beyond my knowledge."

"It is something which we will learn," said Etzwane.

All across Shant the placards appeared, in dark blue, scarlet, and white:

> To fight the Roguskhoi a special corps has been formed:
> THE BRAVE FREE MEN.
> They wear no torcs.
> If you are brave:
> If you would lose your torc:
> If you would fight for Shant:
> You are invited to join the Brave Free Men.
> The corps is elite.
> Present yourself to the agency at Garwiy City.

CHAPTER TEN

Down from the Hwan came the Roguskhoi, for the first
time marching under clear and obvious leadership, to the
wonder of all. Who had instructed the red savages? Even
more of a mystery: from where had they derived their
massive scimitars, alloyed from a dozen rare metals?
Whatever the answers, the Roguskhoi thrust north at a
tireless lunging lope: four companies of about two hundred warriors each. They drove into Ferriy, to send the
ironmongers fleeing in a panic. Ignoring the iron-vats and
tanks of precious new cultures, the Roguskhoi swept wide
into Cansume. At the border the Cansume militia, one of
the strongest of Shant, waited with their dexax-tipped
pikes. The Roguskhoi advanced with sinister care, scimitars at the ready. On the open plain the men of Cansume
had no choice but to retreat; scimitars hurled at close range
would cut them apart. They moved back into the nearby
village Brandvade.

To lure the Roguskhoi the militia thrust forth a crowd
of frightened women, and the Roguskhoi, ignoring the
bellows of their chieftains, were stimulated into an attack.
They stormed the village, where, among the stone huts,
their scimitars could not be hurled. Pikeheads penetrated
horny red hide; dexax exploded, and within minutes fifty
Roguskhoi were dead.

The Roguskhoi officers reasserted themselves; the columns drew back and continued towards Waxone, Cansume's principal city. Along the way irregular units of the militia set up ambushes, from which they fired cane arrows with negligible effect. The Roguskhoi jogged out into the melon fields before Waxone, and here they stopped short, confronted by the most imposing array the men of Shant had yet put forward. An entire regiment of militia faced them, reinforced by four hundred Brave Free Men mounted on pacers. The Brave Free Men wore uniforms after the style of the Pandamon Palace Guards: pale blue trousers with purple braid down the sides, a dark blue blouse with purple frogging, helmets of cemented glass fibres. They carried dexax-tipped pikes, a brace of hand grenades, short, heavy glaywood swords, edged with forged ironweb. The militia carried hand axes, grenades, and rectangular shields of leather and wood; they had been instructed to advance towards the Roguskhoi, protecting themselves and the cavalry from the Roguskhoi scimitars. At a range of fifty feet they would hurl their grenades, then open ranks for the charge of the Brave Free Men.

The Roguskhoi stood at one end of the melon field, glowering towards the shields of the militia. The four Roguskhoi chieftains stood to the side, distinguished from the ordinary warriors by black leather neckbands supporting bibs of chain mail. They seemed older than the troopers; their skin showed duller and darker; flaps of skin or muscle, like wattles, grew under their chins. They watched the advancing militia in mild perplexity, then uttered a set of harsh sounds; the four companies moved forward at a passionless trot. From the militia came a thin sound, and the shields quivered. The Brave Free Men behind gave hoarse shouts and the militia steadied. At a distance of a hundred yards the Roguskhoi halted and brought their scimitars down, around, and back; their muscular processes knotted and tensed. In this position the Roguskhoi were a fearsome sight. The line of the militia sagged; some reflexively hurled their grenades, which exploded halfway between the lines.

From the rear the Cansume officers, somewhat insulated, blew *Advance* on their bugles; the line of shields moved forward, step by step. The Roguskhoi likewise lunged ahead and more futile grenades were thrown. Shields on the left wing sagged, leaving the Brave Free Men without protection. For half a second they hesitated, then charged, plunging against the instant hail of scimitars, which cut down man and pacer before they had moved twenty feet. Nonetheless grenades were thrown by dying arms; Roguskhoi disappeared in dust and flame.

The rest of the line sagged but cohered. A bugle blared *Charge;* the militia, now demoralized, faltered and broke too soon; again the shields fell aside, leaving the Brave Free Men exposed to the whirling scimitars. The survivors charged; pikes struck into copper chests. Explosion! dust, fumes, stench; a melee. Bludgeons pounded; gargoyle faces scowled and bellowed; grenades lofted over the line of battle, generating explosions, fountains of dust, whirls of detached arms and legs. A hideous din rose and fell: furious bugles, Roguskhoi grunts and bellows, the wild braying of wounded pacers, the despair of dying men.... The dust settled. Dead were half the Roguskhoi and all the Brave Free Men. The Cansume militia fled back into Waxone. The Roguskhoi moved slowly forward; then, altering direction, turned aside into Ferriy.

Finnerack made an anguished report of the battle. "There lay the best of Shant, in a mire of black blood! When they might have drawn back, they refused; from pride they charged to their deaths. Freedom they had earned so well: to what avail?"

Etzwane was surprised by the intensity of Finnerack's grief. "We know now that our men are as brave as the men of old," said Etzwane. "All of Shant will know this as well."

Finnerack seemed not to have heard. He paced back and forth, clenching and unclenching his hands. "The militia failed. They were traitors; they would go to cut withe, had I their judgment."

Etzwane said nothing, preferring not to divert Finnerack's emotion towards himself. Finnerack never would be allowed judgment of anyone.

"We can't fight the creatures at close range," said Finnerack. "What of our technists? Where are their weapons?"

"Sit down; control your distress," said Etzwane. "I will tell you of our weapons. The technists are impeded by great forces which must be regulated. A sliver of material hurls itself at enormous speed, and thereby produces a very large recoil. For use as handweapons the slivers must be made almost invisibly thin, and to absorb the recoil a ballast is ejected to the rear. The projectiles reach the ultimate limit of cold in expanding, otherwise they would instantly destroy themselves; rather, they drive a gust of hot air ahead which augments the impact. I have seen tests of fixed cannon; up to a range of a mile the guns will be most deadly. Beyond this distance the projectile erodes to nothing.

"The guns I have seen are by no means light or compact, owing to the necessary ballast. Possibly smaller weapons can be contrived; this is not yet certain. The large weapons are possible, but these must be braced against a tree, or a great stone, or thrust-poles, and hence are not so convenient. Still progress has been made.

"In addition, we are producing most ingenious glass arrows. The heads contain an electret, which upon impact produces an electric charge, which in turn detonates a disabling or even lethal charge of dexax. The problem here, I am told, is quality control.

"Finally, we are producing rocket guns: very simple, very cheap devices. The tube is cemented glass fibre, the projectile is ballasted either with a stone cylinder or an impact-detonated charge of dexax. This is a short-range weapon; accuracy is not good.

"All in all, there is cause for optimism."

Finnerack sat stock-still. He had become a man as different from the shaggy brown creature of Camp Three as that man was from the Jerd Finnerack of Angwin Junction. His frame had filled out; he stood erect. His hair, no longer a sun-crisped mat, clung to his head in golden-bronze ringlets; his features jutted forth without compromise; the mad glare of his eyes had become a blue glitter. Finnerack was a man without warmth, humour, forgiveness, and very few social graces; he wore only the black of implacability and doom, an idiosyncrasy which had earned him the soubriquet "Black Finnerack."

Finnerack's energy was boundless. He had reorganized the Discriminators with savage disregard for old procedures, previous status, or tenure, arousing not so much resentment as astonishment and awe. The Intelligence Agency became his own; in every city of Shant he established sub-agencies, linked by radio to Garwiy. The Brave

Free Men he took even more completely to himself, and wore a Brave Free Man uniform (black rather than pale and dark blue) to the exclusion of all his other clothes.

The Brave Free Men had instantly excited the imagination of all Shant. To Garwiy came men by the hundreds, of all ages and sorts, in numbers far beyond Etzwane's capacity to de-torc. He took Ifness' machine to Doneis, who called in a team of electronic technists. Gingerly they disassembled the case to peer down at the unfamiliar components, the exact engineering, the inexhaustible power cells. Such a machine, they decided, detected electron movement and generated magnetic pulses to cancel the flow.

After numerous experiments the technists were able to duplicate the function of Ifness' mechanism, though in no such compact package. Five of the devices were installed in the basement of the Jurisdictionary; teams of functionaries worked day and night removing torcs from persons accepted into the corps of Brave Free Men. Finnerack himself screened the applicants; those whom he rejected often made a furious protest, for which Finnerack had a stock reply: "Bring me the head of a Roguskhoi and his scimitar; I'll make you a Brave Free Man." Perhaps once a week one of the rejected applicants returned contemptuously to hurl head and scimitar at his feet, whereupon Finnerack, without comment, kicked head and scimitar into a chute and took the man into the corps. Of those who attempted a Roguskhoi head and failed, no one knew the number.

Finnerack's energy was so furious that Etzwane sometimes felt himself an onlooker rather than a participant in the great events. The situation reflected the efficiency of his own leadership, he told himself. So long as affairs proceeded in a correct direction, he could make no complaint. When Etzwane put questions, Finnerack responded clearly, if tersely, seeming neither to welcome nor to resent Etzwane's interest: a fact which, if anything, increased Etzwane's uneasiness; did Finnerack consider him futile, a man whom events had overtaken and passed by?

Mialambre: Octagon had taken his Justice of Shant teams out into the cantons; Etzwane received reports of his activities from incoming intelligence despatches.

The news of Dystar was less circumstantial. Occasionally word came from some far place, always to the same effect: Dystar had come, he had played music of unimaginable grandeur, exalting all who heard, and then he had gone his way.

Finnerack had disappeared. At his rooms in the Pagane Tower, at the Jurisdictionary, at the Brave Free Men camps, Finnerack was nowhere to be found.

Three days passed before he returned. To Etzwane's questions Finnerack at first made evasive remarks, then declared that he had been "looking over the countryside, taking a rest."

Etzwane put no further questions, but he was far from satisfied. Was there a woman in Finnerack's life? Etzwane thought not. His actions were uncharacteristic. Finnerack returned to work with his old verve, but Etzwane thought him a trifle less certain, as if he had learned something to perplex or unsettle him.

Etzwane wanted to know about Finnerack's activities, but would have been forced to call on the Intelligence Agency for help, which seemed not only inappropriate but foolish. . . . Must he then organize a second, competing intelligence system to bring him his information? Ridiculous!

The day after Finnerack's return Etzwane visited the technist workshops along the Jardeen estuary. Doneis took him along a set of benches where the new guns were in production. "Projectiles of pure Halcoid Four-One have not proved practical," said Doneis. "They expand almost instantaneously, producing unacceptable recoil. We have tried three thousand variations, and now use a stuff which expands at about one-tenth the speed of Four-One. In consequence the weapon requires only a thirty-pound ballast. Halcoid-Prax additionally is harder and less susceptible to atmospheric friction. The new splint is still no larger than a needle. . . . Here the trigger is fitted into the stock. . . . These are the elastic bands which prevent the ballast from flying to the rear. . . . The electret is inserted; the ballast is installed. . . . The mechanism is tested. . . . Here is the firing range, where the sights are mounted. We find that the weapon has an essentially flat trajectory across its entire range which is slightly in excess of a mile. Do you care to test this gun?"

Etzwane picked up the weapon, rested it upon his shoulder. A yellow dot in the optical sights, directly in front of his eye, indicated the impact area.

"Drop the magazine into this socket, throw this clamp. When you press the trigger the ballast will strike the electret, producing an impulse which stimulates the splint. Be prepared for the recoil; brace yourself."

Etzwane peered through the lens and placed the yellow dot on the glass target. He pressed the yellow button, to feel an instant shock which thrust him backward. Down the range appeared a streak of white fire, impinging upon the now shattered target.

Etzwane put down the weapon. "How many can you produce?"

"Today we will finish only twenty, but we should soon triple this number. The principal problem is ballast. We have requisitioned metal from all Shant, but it is slow in arriving. The Director of Material Procurement informs me that he has the metal but transportation is not available. The Director of Transportation tells me to the contrary. I don't know which to believe. I any event we are not getting our metal."

"I'll take care of the matter," said Etzwane. "You'll get your metal in a hurry. Meanwhile, I have a somewhat different problem for your attention: a pair of Roguskhoi imps, probably six months to a year old, already vicious, already alert to the presence of women. I think we should learn how and why they are so stimulated, what processes are involved. In short, are they affected visually, by odour, telepathically, or how?"

"I understand precisely. The problem is one of obvious importance; I will put our biologists to work at once."

Etzwane conferred first with the Aesthete Brise, the Director of Transportation, then with Aun Sharah. As Doneis had averred, each blamed the other for the lack of massive amounts of metal in Garwiy. Etzwane went into explicit detail and concluded that the problem was one of priority. Aun Sharah had preempted the available ships to transport food to the refugee-swollen maritime cantons.

"The health of the people is important," Etzwane told Aun Sharah, "but our first concern is killing Roguskhoi, which means metal to Garwiy."

"I understand all this," Aun Sharah replied shortly.

159

His complacent ease had gone, his complexion had lost its smooth tone. "I do the best that I can; remember, this is not my chosen occupation."

"Is this not true of all of us? I am a musician; Mialambre is a jurist; Brise is an Aesthete; Finnerack is a withe cutter. We are all fortunate in our versatility."

"Possibly true," said Aun Sharah. "I hear you have greatly changed my old Discriminators."

"We have indeed. All Shant is changing: I hope not for the worse."

The Roguskhoi swept on through north-central and northeast Shant, roaming at will through Cansume, most of Marestiy, and large parts of Faible and Purple Stone. Three times they attempted to swim the River Maure into Green Stone; on each occasion the regional militia put forth in fishing boats to pelt the invaders with dexax grenades. In the water the Roguskhoi were helpless; men knew the exhilaration of slaughtering their previously invincible opponents. The successes, however, were not real; the Roguskhoi were insensitive both to their own losses and to the human exultation; they marched thirty miles upstream to Opalsand, where the Maure flowed only three feet deep, and crossed in force. Their intent clearly was to sweep through Green Stone, Cape, Galwand, and Glirris and grind the survivors against the Roguskhoi forces already in Azume. They would thereby destroy millions of men, capture millions of women, and control all northeast Shant – a disaster of unthinkable proportions.

Etzwane conferred with Finnerack, Brise, and SanSein, this last the nominal commander of the Brave Free Men. Approximately two thousand Brave Free Men had now been armed with halcoid guns: a corps which Finnerack had intended to dispatch through Fairlea into the Hwan foothills of Sable, to hold Seamus and Bastern and to ambush and harass the Roguskhoi as they came down from the Hwan. The northeast, so he declared, must be written off; he saw no profit in desperate half-measures doomed to failure. For the first time Etzwane took issue with Finnerack on a major decision; to Etzwane a lack of reaction in the north-east meant the betrayal of millions; he found the idea unacceptable. Finnerack was unmoved. "Millions must die; the war is bitter. If we are to win we must steel ourselves to death and think in terms of grand strategy rather than a series of hysterical, small-scale operations.

"The principle is correct," said Etzwane. "On the other hand, we can't let preconceived doctrine tie us in knots. Brise, what ships now lie in Shellflower Bay?"

"Small vessels, the Stonebreaker packet, a few merchantmen, fishing craft: all these mostly in Seacastle harbour."

Etzwane spread out his maps. "The Roguskhoi march north up Maure Valley. The militia will impede them with grenades and land-mines. If we land our troops by night, here at this village Thran, they can occupy this ridge above Maurmouth. Then when the Roguskhoi appear, we will deal with them."

San-Sein examined the maps. "The plan is feasible."

Finnerack grunted and turned half about in his seat.

Etzwane said to San-Sein: "March your men to Seacastle, embark upon the vessels that Brise will provide; set forth at once to the east."

"We will do our utmost; but will there be time?"

"The militia must hold three days, by any ruse and tactic. Three days of fair winds should fetch you to Thran harbour."

Forty-two pinnacles, smacks, and trawlers, each carrying thirty Brave Free Men, set forth to the relief of the northeast. San-Sein himself commanded the operation. Three days the wind held fair; on the third night the winds died, to the disgust of San-Sein, who had wished to enter the harbour by night. Dawn found the fleet still a half-mile offshore, with any conceivable advantage of stealth or surprise gone by the boards. Cursing the calm weather, San-Sein scrutinized the shore through a telescope and went suddenly rigid with consternation. The lens of the telescope showed a sinister stir invisible to the naked eye. Roguskhoi crowded the harbour-front houses of Thran village. The militia had not held. The Roguskhoi had won through to the sea, to set up an ambush of their own.

A dawn wind had come to send ripples dancing over the water. San-Sein signalled his vessels together and issued new orders.

On the freshening breeze the flotilla drove into Thran harbour; instead of tying up at the jetty or anchoring, they grounded upon the shingle. The Brave Free Men, debarking, formed a skirmish line; they slowly advanced towards the harbour-side houses, from which the Roguskhoi demon masks now peered openly.

The Roguskhoi burst forth like ants from a broken ant hill to charge the beach. They were met by a thousand streaks of incandescent air and destroyed.

By Intelligence Agency radio San-Sein reported the operation to Etzwane and Finnerack. "We lost not a man; we killed six hundred. As many more retreated to Maurmouth and up the course of the Maure. There now is no question; with the guns we can hunt down the creatures as if they were crippled ahulphs. But this is not all the story. We succeeded, but only by luck. Had we put into Thran by night, as planned, I would not be here now to report the disaster. The Roguskhoi knew of our approach; they were apprised. Who betrayed us?"

Etzwane asked, "Who knew the plans?"

"Four only: those who formed them."

Etzwane sat in cogitation; Finnerack scowled towards the diaphragm.

"I will look into the matter," said Etzwane. "Meanwhile we have saved the northeast: a cause for rejoicing. Pursue the creatures; hunt them down, but use caution; beware ambushes and narrow places. The future at last looks good."

Finnerack snorted. "You, Gastel Etzwane, are an optimist who sees only a foot in front of his nose. The Roguskhoi were sent here to destroy us; do you believe that their sponsors, and I refer to the Palasedrans, will submit so easily? The future holds only trouble."

"We shall see," said Etzwane. "I must say that never before have I been called an optimist."

While reporting the foray to Brise, Etzwane inquired as to a possible leakage of information. Brise was perplexed and indignant. "Are you asking if I informed anyone of the raid? Do you take me for a fool? The answer is an unqualified no."

"The question was a formality," said Etzwane. "To close off the matter completely, there was no arrangement or understanding between you and the Office of Material Procurement?"

Brise hesitated, then chose his words carefully. "There was absolutely no mention of a raid."

Etzwane's senses were alert to the slightest subtlety of intonation. "I see. What precisely was your discussion?"

"A trivial affair. The Director wanted ships sent to Oswiy, coincidentally on the exact date of the raid. I told him no, and in jocular fashion suggested that he schedule his shipment from Maurmouth instead." Brise hesitated. "Perhaps in some remote sense this might be considered an indiscretion, were I speaking with a person other than the Director of Material Procurement."

"Precisely so," said Etzwane. "In the future, please joke with no one."

Finnerack approached Etzwane the next day. "What of Brise?"

Etzwane had already considered his response. To evade or dissemble was too compromise his integrity. "Brise claims to have maintained absolute discretion. However, he made a jocular request that Aun Sharah have freight shipments ready at Maurmouth."

Finnerack made a guttural sound. "Ah! So now we know!"

"It seems so. I must consider what to do."

Finnerack raised his blond eyebrows incredulously. "What to do? Is there any question?"

"There is indeed. Assuming that, like Sajarano, Aun Sharah favours a victory of the Roguskhoi, the matter of interest to us is 'Why?' Both Sajarano and Aun Sharah are men of Shant, born and bred. What sets them apart? Lust for power or wealth? Impossible in Sajarano's case; what more could he want? Have the Palasedrans seduced them with a drug? Have they devised a telepathic method of instilling obedience? We must get to the bottom of these matters, before the same techniques are practiced on you and me. After all, why should we be immune?"

Finnerack smiled his crooked, angry smile. "The same question has often crossed my mind, especially when you are lenient with our enemies."

"I am not lenient; be assured of this," said Etzwane. "But I must be subtle."

"What of punishment?" Finnerack demanded. "Aun Sharah contrived the deaths of twelve hundred Brave Free Men! Should he escape because of subtlety?"

"His guilt is not proved. To kill Aun Sharah on suspicion, or because of rage, could do absolutely no good. We must learn his motives?"

"What then of the Brave Free Men?" stormed Finnerack. "Must they risk their lives willy-nilly? I am responsible to them, and I must protect them."

"Finnerack, you are responsible not to the Brave Free Men, but to the central authority of Shant, which is to say: me. You must not let energy and emotion overpower your reason. Let us be clear on this. If you feel that you cannot work to a long-range plan, you had best detach yourself from the government and fix upon some other occupation." Etzwane met Finnerack's flaming blue stare. "I do not claim infallibility," he continued. "In regard to Aun Sharah, I agree that he is probably guilty. It is absolutely essential that we learn the reason behind his actions."

Finnerack said, "The knowledge is not worth the life of a single man."

"How do you know this?" demanded Etzwane. "We don't know what the reason is; how can you assess it?"

165

"I have no time for these matters just now," grumbled Finnerack. "The Brave Free Men occupy my time."

Here was the opportunity for which Etzwane had been hoping. "I agree that you have far too much work. I'll put someone else in charge of the Intelligence System and give you help with the Brave Free Men."

Finnerack's grin became wolfish. "I don't need any help with the Brave Free Men."

Etzwane ignored him. "Meanwhile we'll watch Aun Sharah carefully and give him no scope to harm us."

Finnerack had departed. Etzwane sat thinking. Events seemed to be going favourably. The new weapons were successful; Mialambre and Dystar, each in his way, contributed to the new nation which Shant must now become. Finnerack with his passion and obstinacy posed the most immediate problem; he was not a man to be easily controlled, or even influenced.... Etzwane gave a bark of sardonic laughter. When, alone and fearful, he had yearned for a loyal and trustworthy henchman, the image of the placid blond boy at Angwin Junction had come to his mind. The Finnerack Etzwane had finally recruited was a man totally unsuited to Etzwane's needs; he was stubborn, wayward, cantankerous, headstrong, secretive, moody, inflexible, vengeful, narrow-minded, pessimistic, uncooperative, perhaps neither trustworthy nor loyal. Finnerack admittedly had done excellent work with the Brave Free Men and the Intelligence Agency, all of which was beside the point. Etzwane's original fear had now dissipated. No matter what his own fate, the war against the Roguskhoi had created its own momentum. New Shant was an irrevocable reality. In twenty years, for better or worse, torcs would be museum pieces and the Anome would wield a different sort of power. (Who would then be Anome? Mialambre: Octagon? Dystar? San-Sein?)

Etzwane went to look down into Corporation Plaza. Dusk was coming on. Tonight he must consider tactics in regard to Aun Sharah.

He departed his office and descended to the plaza. The folk of Garwiy had now learned of the great victory at Maurmouth; as he walked Etzwane could hear fragments of excited conversation. He was reminded of Finnerack's gloomy prognostication; conceivably Finnerack was right. The worst might be yet to come.

Etzwane went to his suite in the Roseale Hrindiana, where he planned to bathe, dine, read intelligence reports, perhaps dally a bit with Dashan of Szandales.... He opened the door. The suite was dim, almost dark. Unusual! Who had turned down the lights? He stepped within and touched the light-wand. Illumination failed to come. Etzwane became dizzy. The air held an odd, acid tang. He staggered to a divan, then, thinking better of relaxing, started to the door. His senses failed him. He tried to reach and grope; he felt the door latch.... A hand took his arm and led him sagging back into the room.

All was not as it should be, thought Etzwane. He felt peculiarly uneasy, yet fatigued and torpid, as if his sleep had been interrupted by dreams. He sat up from his couch, unaccountably weak; perhaps he had dreamt indeed: the dark, the numbness, the hand on his arm, then – voices.

Etzwane rose to his feet and went to look out across the Hrindiana gardens. The time was early morning: about the time he usually arose. He went into the bathroom, and stared in wonder at the haggard face in the

167

mirror. His beard was a dark stubble; his pupils were large and dark. He bathed, shaved himself, dressed, and descended to the garden, where he took breakfast. He found himself to be ravenously hungry and thirsty as well.... Strange. With his breakfast came a copy of the morning journal. He chanced to notice the date – Shristday? Yesterday had been Zaelday; today was Ettaday.... Shristday? Something was wrong.

He walked slowly to the Jurisdictionary. Dashan greeted him with excitement and wonder. "Where have you been? We have all been helpless with anxiety!"

"I've been away," said Etzwane. "Somewhere."

"For three days? You should have let me know," scolded Dashan.

Finnerack likewise had been gone three days, reflected Etzwane. Strange.

CHAPTER ELEVEN

In Garwiy a new feeling pervaded the air: hope and elation, mingled with melancholy for the passing of a long and placid era. Children no longer took the torc, and it was understood that after the war all deserving persons might have their torcs removed. What then of law and discipline? Who would keep the peace when the Anome lost the last of his coercive powers? For all the elation a degree of uncertainty could be felt everywhere. Etzwane brooded long hours over the situation. He was, so he feared, bequeathing to the new Anome a vexing array of problems.

Dystar came to Garwiy and presented himself to Etzwane. "To the best of my ability I have done your bidding. My task is at an end. The folk of Shant are one; events have made them one."

Etzwane realized suddenly that his indecision had been artificial. The Anome of Shant must be a man of the broadest possible scope, the most profound imagination. "Dystar," said Etzwane, "your task is done, but another awaits, which only you can fulfil."

"This I doubt," said Dystar. "What is the task?"

"You are now Anome of Shant."

"What? . . . Nonsense. I am Dystar."

Etzwane was taken aback by Dystar's displeasure. He said stiffly, "My hopes are only for Shant. Someone must be Anome; I thought to choose the best."

Dystar, now half-amused, spoke in a milder voice: "I have neither taste nor facility for such affairs. Who am I to judge the theft of a bullock or calculate the tax on candles? If I had power, my deeds would be wild and ruinous: towers among the clouds, pleasure barges a mile long to waft musicians through the isles of the Beljamar, expeditions to the Lost Kingdom of Caraz. No, Gastel Etzwane; your vision exceeds your practicality: often the case with a musician. Employ the wise Mialambre for your Anome, or better, use none at all; what advantage in an Anome when there are no torcs to explode?"

"All very well," said Etzwane in a huff, "but – reverting to the practicality which I so miserably lack – who would govern in this case? who would order? who would punish?"

Dystar had lost interest in the matter. "These are tasks for specialists, folk who have interest in such affairs. . . . As for myself, I must take myself away, perhaps to Shkoriy. I can play no more music; I am done."

Etzwane leaned forward in wonder. "You cannot expect me to believe this! What can be your reason?"

Dystar smiled and shrugged. "I escaped the torc; I knew the exaltation of freedom, to my great melancholy."

"Hmmf . . . But do not go to Shkoriy to brood; what could be more futile? Seek out Frolitz, attach yourself to his troupe; here is cure for melancholy, I can assure you of this."

"You are right," said Dystar. "It is what I will do. I thank you for your wise advice."

For two moments the secret trembled on Etzwane's tongue, but he said only: "I wish I could join you." Certainly, on some merry night in a far tavern, while the troupe drank wine and talked at large, Fordyce or Mielke or Cune or even Frolitz would confide to Dystar his connection with Etzwane.

Dystar had gone his way. As an idle exercise Etzwane tried to contrive a theoretical government which might serve Shant as well as a wise and decisive Anome. He became interested in his construction; he refined and modified, and presently evolved what seemed a feasible disposition.

He specified two interacting organs of government. The first, a Council of Patricians, would include the directors of transportation, trade and economics, communication, law and justice, military forces, an Aesthete of Garwiy, a musician, a scientist, a historian, two persons of eminence, and two persons selected by the second council. The Council of Patricians would be self-perpetuating, selecting its own members, discharging them by a consensus of two-thirds. One of the group would be chosen First of Shant, to serve a term of three years or until voted from office by a consensus of two-thirds.

The second body, the Council of Cantons, would comprise representatives from each of the sixty-two cantons and additional delegates from the cities Garwiy, Brassei, Maschein, Oswiy, Ilwiy, and Whearn.

The Council of Cantons might propose acts and measures to the Council of Patricians and further might expel a member of the Council of Patricians by a two-thirds vote. A separate College of Justice would guarantee equity to each person of Shant. The Director of Law and Justice, sitting on the Council of Patricians, would be selected from the fellows of the College of Laws.

Etzwane called together Mialambre: Octagon, Doneis, San-Sein, Brise, and Finnerack and set forth his proposals. All agreed that the system merited at least a trial, and only Finnerack put forth serious objections. "You overlook one matter: at large and living in Shant are the magnates who won their ease through the pain of others. Should not the concept of indemnification be codified into the new system?"

"This is more properly a matter of adjudication," said Etzwane.

Finnerack warmed to his subject. "Further, why should some toil for a mouthful of bread while long-fingered sybarites partake of Forty-Five Dishes? The good things should be divided; we should start the new system on a basis of equality."

Mialambre responded: "Your sentiments are generous and do you credit. All I can say it that such drastic redistributions have previously been attempted, always to result in chaos and cruel tyranny of one sort or another. This is the lesson of history, which we must now heed."

Finnerack offered no further opinions.

Seven companies of Brave Free Men, augmented by the now enthusiastic militia, attacked the Roguskhoi on four broad fronts. The Roguskhoi, adapting to their new vulnerability, moved by night, sheltered in forests and wildernesses, attacked by surprise, seeking always women, sometimes at vast risk to themselves. Grudgingly they retreated from the coast, back through cantons Marestiy and Faible.

Etzwane received a report from Doneis, the Director of Technical Achievement. "The Roguskhoi imps have been studied at length. They prove to be creatures of the most peculiar sort, and it is hard to understand their human semblance; nevertheless they require a human woman as hostess for their spawn. In what conceivable environment could they have so evolved?"

"In Palasedra, so it has been suggested."

"This is possible; Palasedrans have long been evolving a warrior sort. Certain Caraz mariners claim to have seen the creatures. It is a great puzzle."

"Have you learned how the Roguskhoi identify women?"

"There was no problem here. One of the female essences lures them. They are drawn as sure as an ahulph strikes carrion; they will detect the most evanescent whiff and strive through any obstacle to sate themselves."

The Brave Free Men now numbered over five thousand. Finnerack had become more remote and single-minded than ever; rancour seemed to burn inside him like fire in a stove. Etzwane's uneasiness grew in proportion. To reduce the scope of Finnerack's authority, Etzwane fragmented the leadership into five phases. Black Finnerack became Captain of Strategy; San-Sein was Captain of Field Operations; additionally there were Captains of Logistics, Recruitment and Training, and Weaponry.

Finnerack protested the new situation in a cold fury. "Always you make things more cumbersome! In the place of one Anome you give us a hundred politicians; for one responsible and efficient commander you substitute a committee of five. Is this sensible? I wonder at your motives!"

"They are simple," said Etzwane. "An Anome can no longer control Shant; a hundred men are needed. The war, the armies of Shant, their strategy, tactics, and goals are likewise too large for the control of a single man."

Finnerack removed his black hat and threw it into a corner. "You underestimate me."

"This, I assure you, is not the case," said Etzwane.

The two examined each other for a moment without friendliness. Etzwane said, "Sit down a moment; I want to ask you something."

Finnerack went to a divan, leaned back, thrust his black boots out across the Burazhesq rug. "What is your question?"

"A short time ago you disappeared for three days. When you returned you gave no account of your whereabouts. What happened to you during this time?"

Finnerack gave a sour grunt. "It is unimportant."

"I think not," said Etzwane. "A short time ago I went to my suite and was drugged by some sort of gas, or so I suppose. I awoke three days later, without any knowledge of what had transpired. Is this what happened to you?"

"More or less," Finnerack brought the words forth reluctantly.

"Have you noticed any consequences of this event? Do you feel yourself different in any way?"

Finnerack again paused before replying. "Of course there are no differences. Do you feel differences?"

"No. None whatever."

Finnerack had departed; Etzwane still lacked insight into the workings of Finnerack's mind. Finnerack had no obvious weaknesses: no yearning for ease, wealth, drink, fair women, soft living. Etzwane could not say as much for himself, though recognizing the dangers of self-indulgence he tried to live in relative austerity. Dashan of Szandales, either by her initiative or his own – Etzwane had never felt certain of the matter – had become his mistress. The situation pleased Etzwane because of its convenience. In due course, when once again he became a musician, the situation no doubt would alter.

San-Sein, the Captain of Field Operations, one morning came into Etzwane's office with a roll of charts. "We are presented an opportunity of great promise," he stated. "The Roguskhoi have broken; they retreat towards the Hwan. One horde moves south through Ascalon and Seamus, another in Ferriy has pulled back into Bastern, and this column from Cansume has entered South Marestiy and marches towards Bundoran. Do you see where they tend?"

"If they plan to return into the Wildlands, they more than likely will pass up Mirk Valley."

"Exactly. Now here is my plan, which I have already discussed and cleared with Finnerack. Suppose that we harry the column close on the rear, enough to keep them curious, but that here at Mirk Defile we prepare an ambush."

"All very well," said Etzwane, "but how do you bring troops to Mirk Defile?"

"Notice the balloon-way and the prevailing winds. If we loaded forty balloons at Oswiy and let them fly free they would reach Mirk Defile in six hours. The winch-tender need only put down to discharge troops, then continue south to the Great Ridge Route."

Etzwane considered. "The idea sounds appealing. But

175

what of the winds? I was born in Bashon and as I recall they blow up the Mirk as often as down. Have you spoken to the meteorologists?"

"Not yet. Here are the wind arrows on the chart."

"The project is far too chancy. Suppose we run into a calm? They often occur about this time. We'd have forty balloonloads of men lost deep in the Wildlands. Rather than balloons we need gliders." Etzwane suddenly remembered the builders of Canton Whearn. He reflected a moment, then bent over the map. "Mirk Defile is the obvious route. Suppose the Roguskhoi learned of the ambush? They might very well turn aside at Bashon and head west, past Kozan, before turning south into the Wildlands. We can put troops into Kozan without difficulty; the balloon-way passes only twenty miles west. Here on Kozan Bluffs is where we must set up our ambush."

"But how do we apprise the Roguskhoi of the Mirk ambush, so that they will turn aside?"

"Leave that to me. I know a subtle method. If it succeeds, well and good. If it fails, we are no worse off than before. Your instructions are these: confide to no one that the Mirk Valley ambush is non-operative. The secret must lie between you and me alone. Ready your troops at Oswiy; load the balloons but, rather than allowing them to drift free, send them south along the balloon-way into Seamus. Disembark, march to Kozan Bluffs, and establish your ambush."

San-Sein was gone. The plot had been set into motion. Once again Brise would be the instrument of news leakage to Aun Sharah.

Etzwane went to his telephone and called the Intelligence Agency radio operator. "Make contact with Pelmonte in Canton Whearn. Request that the Superintendent be brought to the microphone, and thereupon notify me."

An hour later Etzwane heard the voice of the Superintendent of Whearn. Etzwane said, "Do you remember when Gastel Etzwane, the Anome's assistant, passed through Whearn several months ago?"

"I do indeed."

"At such time I recommended that you build gliders. What progress have you made in this direction?"

"We have done your bidding. We have built gliders to the best design. With a dozen complete, and with no word from you, we have somewhat slowed the pace of our construction."

"Proceed once again at full haste. I will send men to Whearn to take delivery."

"Do you plan to send flyers?"

"We have none to send."

"Then they must be trained. Select a contingent of your best, send them to Pelmonte. In due course they will fly the gliders wherever you wish."

"This is what shall be done. Thanks to men like yourself the Roguskhoi are in retreat. We have come a long way these last few months."

CHAPTER TWELVE

Brise spoke to Etzwane. "I have followed your instructions. Aun Sharah knows of the Mirk ambush. It is a job for which I do not consider myself fitted."

"Nor more do I. But the job must be done. Now we will wait for eventualities."

Reports came hourly to Etzwane. A Roguskhoi column formed of four raiding parties, representing the total force which had subdued northeast Shant, marched south down the Mirk Valley, accompanied by an unknown number of captive women. Brave Free Men mounted on pacers harried the Roguskhoi flanks and rearguard, and themselves suffered casualties as a result of Roguskhoi counter manoeuvres; the route of the column was marked by a line of corpses.

The horde approached Bashon, where the temple, deserted and forlorn, had already entered the first stages of decay.

At Rhododendron Way the column paused. Six chieftains, conspicuous for bibs and chain mail hanging over their chests, conferred and peered down Mirk Valley towards the Hwan. There was, however, no indecision; they swung west along Rhododendron Way, passing under the great, dark trees. Hearing the news, Etzwane remembered an urchin named Mur playing in the white dust under these same trees. At the end of Rhododendron Way, with open country before them, the chieftains paused once again to confer. An order was passed down the column; a score of warriors stepped off into the foliage beside the Way. The threat of their scimitars effectually prevented any close pursuit by the cavalry, which must now retreat and circle either north or south of the Way.

The Roguskhoi left the main road and slanted south into the Hwan foothills. Above them bulked Kozan Bluffs, a knob of grey limestone pocked by ancient caves and tunnels.

The Roguskhoi approached the bluff. In the west appeared a company of Brave Free Men; from the east came the cavalry which had harried the rear. The Roguskhoi jogged down towards the Hwan, passing close under Kozan Bluff. From the holes and crannies came sudden white streaks of gunfire. From the east the Brave Free Men cavalry approached; and likewise from the west.

Placards of purple, green, pale blue, and white announced the new government of Shant:

The Brave Free Men have liberated out country. For this we rejoice and celebrate the unity of Shant. The Anome has graciously given way to an open and responsive government, consisting of a Purple House of Patricians and a Green House of the Cantons. Already three manifestos have been issued:

There are to be no more torcs.
The indenture programme is to be highly modified.
Religious systems may commit no further crimes.

The Purple Patricians include the following:

Listed were the directors and their functions. Gastel Etzwane, a director-at-large, was declared Executive Director. The second director-at-large was Jerd Finnerack. San-Sein was Director of Military Affairs.

Aun Sharah occupied the top floor of an ancient blue and white glass structure behind Corporation Plaza, almost under the Ushkadel. His office was very large, almost eccentrically bare of furnishing. The high north wall consisted entirely of clear glass panes. The worktable was at the centre of the room; Aun Sharah sat looking north through the great expanse of glass. When Etzwane and Finnerack entered the room, he nodded courteously and rose to his feet. For five seconds a silence held; the three stood each in his attitude in the great bare room, fateful as players on a stage.

Etzwane spoke formally, "Aun Sharah, we are forced to the conviction that you are working adversely to the interests of Shant."

Aun Sharah smiled as if Etzwane had paid him a compliment. "It is hard to please everybody."

Finnerack took a slow step forward, then drew back and said nothing.

Etzwane, somewhat nonplussed by Aun Sharah's agreeable demeanour, spoke on. "The fact of your actions is established. Still, we are puzzled as to your motives. In fostering the cause of the Roguskhoi, how do you gain, how do you serve yourself?"

Aun Sharah, still smiling – peculiarly, so Etzwane thought – asked: "Has the fact been demonstrated?"

"Abundantly. Your conduct has been under scrutiny for several months. You prompted Shirge Hillen of Camp Three to kill me; you put spies on my movements. As Director of Material Procurement you have in several instances substantially lessened the war effort by diverting labour into non-essential projects. At Thran in Green Stone your ambush of Brave Free Men failed, by luck alone. In the engagement at Kozan Bluff we have achieved decisive proof. You were informed that Mirk Defile was to be guarded, whereupon the Roguskhoi veered aside and were destroyed. The reality of your guilt is established. Your motives are a cause for perplexity."

The three again stood silently in the centre of the vast, bleak room.

"Please sit down," said Aun Sharah gently. "You have pelted me with such a barrage of nonsense that my mind is confused and my knees are weak." Etzwane and Finnerack remained standing; Aun Sharah sat down and took up stylus and paper. "Please repeat your bill of charges, if you will."

Etzwane did so, and Aun Sharah made a list. "Five items: all wind and no susbstance. Many men have been destroyed for as little."

Etzwane began to feel perplexed. "You deny the charges then?"

Aun Sharah smiled his curious smile. "Let me ask rather, can you prove any of the charges?"

"We can," said Finnerack.

"Very well," said Aun Sharah. "We will consider the items one at a time – but let us call in the jurist Mialambre: Octagon to weigh the evidence, and Director of Transportation Brise as well."

"I see no objection to this," said Etzwane. "Let us go to my office."

Back in his old office Aun Sharah waved the others to seats, as if they were underlings he had summoned to conference. He addressed Mialambre: "Not half an hour ago Gastel Etzwane and Black Finnerack entered my office to deliver a set of five charges, so preposterous that I suspect their sanity. The charges are these:" Aun Sharah read off his list.

"The first accusation, that I notified Shirge Hillen of Etzwane's coming is no more than an unfounded suspicion, the more vicious in that Etzwane has made no attempt to find an alternative solution. I suggested that he investigate the balloon-way offices; this he neglected to do. I made a few quiet inquiries; in twenty minutes I learned that a certain Parway Harth had in fact sent out an intemperate and somewhat ambiguous message which Shirge Hillen might well have understood as an order to kill Gastel Etzwane. I can prove this three different ways; through Parway Harth, through a subordinate who took the message to the balloon-way radio, and through the files in the balloon-way radio office.

"Item Two: the charge that I put spies upon Gastel Etzwane. The reference is to a surveillance performed by one of my trackers: an act of casual interest. I do not deny this charge; I claim that it is too trivial to be significant of anything whatever.

"Item Three: as Director of Material Procurement I have in several instances diminished the war effort. In hundreds of instances I have augmented the war effort. I complained to Gastel Etzwane that my abilities did not lie in this direction; he stubbornly ignored my statement.

182

If the war effort suffered, the fault is his alone. I did my best.

"Items Four and Five: I arranged a Roguskhoi ambush at Thran and I attempted to betray an ambush of our own in Mirk Valley. A few days ago I stepped into the office of Director Brise. In a most peculiar and embarrassed manner he contrived an elephantine hint as to an ambush in Mirk Valley. I am a suspicious man, skilled at intrigue. I detected a plot. I declared as much to Brise; I further insisted that he leave me alone not for an instant, day or night; he must absolutely assure himself that I had transmitted no information. I convinced him that such was his duty to Shant, that if any ambush were in fact betrayed we must learn the true culprit. To do this we must be able to demonstrate my innocence beyond argument. He is a reasonable and honourable man; he agreed to my analysis of the situation. I ask you now, Brise: did I, during the applicable period, inform anyone at any time of anything whatsoever?"

"You did not," said Brise shortly. "You sat in my office, in my company and that of my trusted associates, for two days. You communicated with no one, you betrayed no ambush."

"We received news of the battle at Kozan," Aun Sharah went on. "Brise now confessed to me that he considered himself to blame for the fact that suspicion had fallen upon me. He reported his conversation with Gastel Etzwane.

"I understand now that I am linked to the ambush at Thran by one question and one answer. I required that Brise send bottoms to Oswiy; he said no, I must send my goods to Maurmouth. On this basis my guilt in regard to the Thran ambush is assumed. The concept is far fetched but remotely possible, except for a secondary fact which once again Gastel Etzwane has not noticed. This question and this answer, in a thousand variations, has become a joke between Brise and myself: repartee as we coordinate our functions. I ask him for transport at one place, he says impossible, find freight at another. Brise, is this correct?"

"It is correct," said Brise in an uncomfortable voice. "The question and the answer might be repeated five times a day. Aun Sharah could have understood nothing of significance in the remarks regarding Oswiy and Thran. I reported them to Gastel Etzwane because he required my every word; I neglected to put them into context."

Aun Sharah asked Etzwane: "Do you have any other charges?"

Etzwane gave a sick laugh. "None. I am clearly unfit to make a rational judgment on anyone or anything. I apologize to you and will make amends as best I can. I must seriously consider resigning from the Purple House."

Mialambre: Octagon spoke in a gruff voice: "Come now, the matter need go no farther; this is no time for extravagant acts."

"Except in this single regard," said Aun Sharah. "You spoke of amends. If you are serious, return me to my own work; give me back my Discriminators."

"So far as I am concerned," said Etzwane, "they are yours, any that are left. Finnerack has turned the place inside out."

The Roguskhoi had been driven back into the Wildlands, and for a period the war dwindled to a halt. Finnerack presented his estimate of the situation to Etzwane. "They are as if in an impregnable fortress. Our radius of

184

penetration is twenty miles; beyond this line the Roguskhoi breed, re-arm, re-group, and presumably re-cast their strategies."

Etzwane mused. "We have captured thousands of scimitars; they are made of an alloy unknown in Shant. What is the source of supply? Do they operate foundries deep in the Hwan? A great mystery."

Finnerack gave an indifferent nod. "Our strategy now is self-evident. We must organize our total manpower and gradually occupy the Hwan. It is a toilsome and complicated task, but is there any other method?"

"Probably not," said Etzwane.

"Then back to Palasedra with the brutes! And let the Palasedrans interfere at their peril!"

"Presuming that the Palasedrans are responsible, which is not yet proved."

Finnerack stared in astonishment. "Who else but the Palasedrans?"

"Who else but Aun Sharah? I have learned my lesson."

CHAPTER THIRTEEN

Summer brought a lull to the war, which extended into the long mild autumn. Shant repaired its damage, mourned its dead men and kidnapped women, augmented its armed might. The Brave Free Men, expanding in numbers and organization, separated into regional divisions, with the cantonal militia serving functions of support and supply. Weapons poured from the Shranke assemblies; the Roguskhoi scimitars, melted and moulded, became ballast.

Gliders flew forth from Whearn: double-winged craft, light as moths. A special corps of the Brave Free Men became the Flyers of Shant. Their training at first was makeshift and merciless; those who survived instructed the others. By sheer necessity the Flyers became a skilled and cohesive force, and as natural consequence began to make prideful demonstration of reckless daring and élan.

To arm the gliders, the technists produced a ferocious new weapon, a simplified, non-ballasted version of the halcoid gun. The projectile was composite: halcoid joined to a metal, the firing tube was open at each end. When fired, the halcoid struck forward, the metal was ejected aft; in effect the weapon acted in both directions, eliminating recoil and the need for ballast. When fired from a glider, the ejected missile usually spent itself harmlessly in the air; on the ground the guns were intolerably dangerous.

Before sending gliders out against the Roguskhoi, Finnerack drilled the Flyers in battle tactics, the dropping of bombs with accuracy, and safety techniques with respect to the halcoid gun.

From the first Finnerack had been fascinated with the gliders; he learned to fly, and presently, not altogether to Etzwane's surprise, he relinquished his command over the Brave Free Men in order to assume control of the Flyers.

In the middle of autumn the ground armies began to move up into the Hwan, pushing west from Cansume, Haghead, and Lor-Asphen, retaking cantons Surrume and Shkoriy. A second force moved south through Bastern, Seamus, and Bundoran, into the Wildlands itself. Other companies worked east and south, from Shade and Sable, penetrating the Mount Misk region, and here the Roguskhoi put up fierce resistance. Theirs was now a lost cause. Trained ahulphs spied out their concentrations, which then were bombed or subjected to halcoid fire from guns mounted in clusters of six.

On other occasions the Roguskhoi were baited into ambush by lures of "female essence," to which they were intensely responsive. Another time, gliders sprayed a Roguskhoi camp with a solution of "female essence" with horrid effect. The Roguskhoi, confused by the contradictory stimuli of nose and eye, seemed to become insanely cantankerous; in short order they were cuffing each other and then exchanging bludgeon blows, until almost all were dead; at once gliders set out across all the Wildlands laden not with dexax but with canisters of "female essence."

Ahulphs, somewhat belatedly set out to spy, reported the course of the Roguskhoi supply route. It led from the Great Salt Bog into the swamps of Canton Shker, then proceeded north under a dense forest of raintree and parasol daraba, up through the Moaning Mountains and into the Hwan.

The military command dispatched a force to cut the line at the forest edge. Finnerack wanted to react more vehemently. "Is this not evidence? The Palasedrans are responsible. The Salt Bog is no barrier; why should they be spared a taste of their own medicine?"

The command captains frowned down at their charts, lacking argument against convictions so emphatic. Finnerack, somewhat chastened after the Aun Sharah fiasco, had been reanimated by his new role as Flyer. He now wore a Flyer uniform of fine black cloth, cut to something more than ordinary flair. Here, thought Etzwane, with the Flyers of Shant, was Finnerack's natural function: he had never before seemed so zestful and energetic. The power and freedom of flight had exalted him; he walked the world like a man apart, superior in basic fibre to the groundlings, who would never know the terrible joys of sweeping silently across the hills, rising and falling, circling, veering, then swooping like a hawk to blast apart a marching column. . . . Etzwane had long lost all fear of Finnerack's turning the Brave Free Men against the government. Too many safeguards had been set up; in retrospect Etzwane saw that he might have been over-cautious. Finnerack showed no interest in the sources of power;

he seemed satisfied to crush his enemies. For Finnerack, Etzwane thought, a world without enemies would be a very dull place. He now answered Finnerack in his most reasonable voice: "We don't want to punish the Palasedrans for at least three reasons. First, we're not yet finished with the Roguskhoi. Second, Palasedran responsibility is not certain. Third, it would be a poor policy to embroil ourselves needlessly in a war with the Palasedrans. They are a fierce people who give back twice as good as they take, as Shant has learned to its sorrow. Suppose the Roguskhoi are an oversight, a mistake? Or the work of a dissident group? We can't plunge Shant into a war so recklessly. After all, what do we know of Palasedra? Nothing. The place is a closed book to us."

"We know enough," said Finnerack. "They have bred an array of weird soldier-beasts, this we learn from Caraz mariners. We find the Roguskhoi trail leading into the Salt Bog towards Palasedra. These are facts."

"True. But they are not all the facts. We need more knowledge. I will send an envoy to Chemaoue."

Finnerack gave a bitter laugh and swung half about in his chair, the helmet of the Flyers askew on his blond curls.

Etzwane said: "We need be neither weak nor truculent; we are not forced to make such a choice. We will drive the Roguskhoi from our lands, and meanwhile we must try to learn the Palasedran intentions. Only a fool acts before thinking, as I have learned."

Finnerack turned to look at Etzwane; the blue eyes showed a narrow glitter, like sunlight reflecting from a far ledge of ice. Then he shrugged and sat back in his seat, a man at peace with himself.

The Roguskhoi were in retreat. The Brave Free Men thrusting into the Hwan from Shade, Sable, Seamus, and Bastern suddenly encountered no resistance whatever. Glider patrols and free balloon reconnaissance told the same story: the Roguskhoi were streaming south in dozens of columns. For the most part they moved by night, taking what shelter they could during the day. Gliders harassed them from overhead, spitting halcoid, dropping bombs of dexax. "Female essence" had lost its initial effect; the Roguskhoi, while perturbed and agitated, no longer indulged in suicidal paroxysms.

The Flyers were at the pinnacle of their glory. The blue and white uniforms aroused a delirium of adulation; nothing was too good for a Flyer of Shant.

Finnerack likewise had reached his zenith. Watching him as he dealt with business of the Flyers, Etzwane found it hard to recall the pleasant-faced boy he had known at Angwin Junction. For all practical purposes, the boy had died at Camp Three. . . . What of the small, dark, pinch-faced boy who had escaped Angwin Junction? Looking in the carbon-fume mirror, Etzwane saw a face hollow-cheeked and sallow, with a mouth straight and still. . . . He had known a rich life indeed, thought Etzwane. If Finnerack were now at the crest of his career, Etzwane considered his work done. He longed to detach himself – to become what? A wandering musician once more? Shant seemed suddenly too small, too limited. Palasedra was a hostile land; Caraz a vast mystery. The name Ifness came into Etzwane's mind. He thought of the planet Earth.

The Roguskhoi, commanded by their roaring chieftains, loped down from the Wildlands, through Canton Shker,

190

and into the Great Salt Bog. The Brave Free Men, attacking on the flanks, took a terrible toll, as did the Flyers, veering, swooping, projecting streaks of incandescent air.

The columns dwindled to a trickle, then ended. The Brave Free Men roamed the length and breadth of the Hwan, finding an occasional sickly imp or bands of starving women, but no more Roguskhoi.

Shant was free of its invaders. The Roguskhoi had retired into the Great Salt Bog, a place of black ooze, rust-coloured ponds, occasional islands overgrown with coral trees, other islands of sand rising stark and bare, pale green reeds, snakegrass, black limberleaf.

In the Salt Bog the Roguskhoi seemed secure and easy and wallowed effortlessly through the ooze. The Brave Free Men pursued until the ground grew soft, then reluctantly drew back. The Flyers knew no such limits. The black morasses, the knolls of bright white sand, the coral-tree forests, the winds thrusting in from both the Blue and Purple Oceans created draughts and shafts of rising and falling air; sunlight shimmered down between tall thunderheads; the gliders soared and swooped at will, no longer pursuing, now wreaking vengeance.

Deeper and deeper into the Great Salt Bog moved the Roguskhoi, harried by the merciless gliders. Etzwane felt impelled to caution Finnerack: "Whatever else, do not enter alien territory! Hector the Roguskhoi as you like, back and forth across the Great Salt Bog, but under no circumstances provoke the Palasedrans!"

Finnerack showed his small, hard grin. "The boundaries are where? In the centre of the Bog? Show me where the exact line lies."

"So far as I know there is no precise boundary. The

Salt Bog is like a sea. If you verged too close against the southern shore of the Bog, the Palasedrans would claim encroachment."

"Bog is bog," said Finnerack. "I understand the Palasedran's distress, but I give them no compassion."

"This is beside the point," said Etzwane patiently. "Your orders are: do not operate your gliders within sight of Palasedra."

Finnerack stood bristling in front of Etzwane, who for the first time felt the uncloaked thrust of Finnerack's hatred. Etzwane was affected by a sensation of physical disgust. Finnerack was a good hater. When Etzwane had first identified himself, Finnerack had admitted hate for the boy who had caused him woe, but had not the balance been righted? Etzwane drew a slow, deep breath. Conditions were as they were.

Finnerack had spoken, in a low, dangerous voice: "Do you still give me orders, Gastel Etzwane?"

"I do, by authority of the Purple House. Do you serve Shant, or the gratification of your personal passions?"

Finnerack stared at Etzwane ten seconds, then swung away and departed.

The envoy returned from his mission to Chemaoue, with no satisfactory news. "I could make no direct contact with the Eagle-Dukes. They are proud and remote. I cannot fathom their purposes. I received a message to the effect that they could not deal with slaves; if we wanted transactions, we must send down the Anome. I replied that Shant no longer was under the Anome's rule, that I was an emissary of the Purple and Green, but they seemed not to heed."

Etzwane conferred in private with Aun Sharah, who once more occupied his old office overlooking Corporation Plaza.

"I have assiduously studied both sets of circumstances," said Aun Sharah. "In regard to the two ambushes the essential facts are clear. Four persons were informed as to the Thran operation: yourself, San-Sein, Finnerack, and Brise. You and San-Sein knew of the Kozan Bluff ambush, which succeeded; you two are eliminated. Brise most certainly have deduced that the Mirk Valey ambush was bogus; he might easily have presumed the Kozan Bluff ambush. He too can be eliminated in the Mirk Valey ambush. Accordingly we must regard Finnerack as the traitor."

Etzwane was silent a moment. Then he said, "I have thought along these same lines. The logic is sound; the conclusion is absurd. How can the most zealous warrior of Shant be a traitor?"

"I don't know," said Aun Sharah. "I returned to this office, I altered arrangements to suit myself, as you see. In the process I discovered a whole array of eavesdrop devices. I took the liberty of inspecting your suite at the Hrindiana, where I found another such set. Finnerack of course had easy opportunity to arrange these devices."

"Incredible," muttered Etzwane. "Have you located the terminus of the system?"

"They feed into a radio transmitter, which broadcasts continuously at a low level."

"The devices, the radio — they are Shant manufacture?"

"They are standard Discriminator adjuncts."

"Hmmf . . For the present we'll wait and watch. I don't care to make any more premature accusations."

193

Aun Sharah smiled thoughtfully. "Now as to the second investigation: I learned very little. Finnerack simply dropped from sight for three days. Two men of Canton Parthe occupied the suite next to Finnerack. They departed a day or so after Finnerack's 'return.' I took detailed descriptions and I feel that they were not Parthans, whatever the colour of their torcs: they hung up no door fetish and frequently wore blue.

"I naturally made inquiry at the Roseale Hrindiana. Two similar men occupied the suite directly above yours prior to your experience. They then departed without notifying the Hrindiana officials."

"I am baffled," said Etzwane. "I also am greatly afraid. ... I asked Finnerack if he felt differently; he said no. I feel no differently either."

Aun Sharah regarded Etzwane curiously, then made one of his delicate gestures. "I can tell you no more. Naturally I am searching for the Parthans, and Finnerack is being kept under unobtrusive observation. Something suggestive may turn up."

The Flyers of Shant pressed the Roguskhoi ever deeper into the bog, giving no respite; the air above the great morass stunk of carrion. The Roguskhoi moved always southward – towards a destination? to put all distance between themselves and the Flyers of Shant? No one could say, but presently the northern half of the Salt Bog was as empty of Roguskhoi as Shant itself.

In the gallant colours of victory, the journals of Garwiy published a proclamation of the Purple and Green:

The war must now be considered at an end, although the Flyers continue to wreak retribution for the countless Roguskhoi atrocities. It is impossible to feel pity for the brutes.

However, we must now terminate our campaign. The glorious feats of the Brave Free Men and the Flyers of Shant will live forever in the history of the race. These noble men must now devote their energies to the regeneration of Shant.

THE WAR IS AT AN END

Finnerack was late to the meeting of the Purple House. Entering the chamber, he marched with slow steps to his place at the marble table.

Etzwane was speaking. "Our great struggle is done, and I feel that my responsibility is ended. This being the case –"

Finnerack interrupted him. "One moment, so that you may not be resigning under a misapprehension. I have just now received news from Shker. The Flyers of Shant, operating in the southern area of the Great Salt Bog, this morning encountered a dense column of Roguskhoi making at speed for the Palasedran shore. We attacked and approached Palasedra. Our manoeuvres were under careful surveillance, and it may be that the Roguskhoi movements were intended to draw us into a condition of technical incursion." Finnerack paused. "This was the event. Our gliders were intercepted by black Palasedran gliders, flown with great skill. In the first engagement they destroyed four gliders of Shant, losing none. In the second engagement we altered our tactics and shot down two enemy gliders, while losing two more of our own. I have received no further reports."

Mialambre broke the silence. "But you were instructed to avoid a close approach to Palasedra."

195

"Our basic purpose," said Finnerack, "is to destroy the enemy. His whereabouts is immaterial."

"You may think so. I do not. Must we fight a new Palasedran war because of your intractability?"

"We have already been fighting a Palasedran war," said Finnerack. "The Roguskhoi were not generated out of nothingness."

"This is your opinion! Who gave you the right to act for all Shant?"

"A person does what his inner soul directs." Finnerack jerked his head towards Etzwane. "Who gave him the right to take to himself the authority of the Anome? He had no more right than I."

"The difference is real," retorted Mialambre. "A man sees a house on fire. He rouses the inhabitants and extinguishes the blaze. Another, in order to punish the arsonist, fires a village. One man is a hero, the other is a maniac."

San-Sein said: "Black Finnerack, your courage is beyond all question. Unfortunately, your zeal is excessive. Recklessness destroys our freedom of action. Convey these orders instantly to the Flyers of Shant: return to the home territory! Do not again fare forth into the Great Salt Bog until so commanded!"

Finnerack moved his helmet, tossed it upon the marble. "I cannot give these orders. They are not realistic. When the Flyers of Shant are attacked, they fight back with unyielding ferocity."

"Must we send Brave Free Men to control our own Flyers?" roared San-Sein, suddenly in a fury. "If they fly forth again, we will take their gliders and rip off their uniforms! We, the Purple and Green of Shant, are in authority!"

Into the chamber burst a steward! "From the city Chemaoue in Palasedra comes a strong radio message: the Chancellor demands the voice and ear of the Anome."

The entire Council of Patricians listened to the words of the Palasedran Chancellor, spoken in a language of odd accents and altered sound quality. "I am Chancellor to the Hundred Sovereigns. I will speak to the Anome of Shant."

Etzwane spoke. "The rule of the Anome is ended. You now address the Council of Patricians; say what you will."

"I ask you then: why do you attack us after two thousand years of peace? Have not four wars and four defeats taught you to beware?"

"The attacks were directed against the Roguskhoi. We drive them back whence they came."

The atmosphere crackled softly while the Chancellor collected his thoughts. He said, "They are nothing of ours. You have driven them from the Bog into Palasedra; is this not an offensive act? You have sent your gliders into our lands; is this not an intrusion?"

"Not if, as we are convinced, you sent the Roguskhoi against us in the first place."

"We worked no such acts. Do you believe this? Send your envoys to Palasedra; you shall see for yourself. This is our generous offer. You have acted with irresponsibility. If you choose not to learn the truth, we will consider you spitefully stupid and men will die."

"We are neither spiteful nor stupid," Etzwane returned. "It is only sensible that we discuss and adjust our differences; we welcome the opportunity to do so, especially if you can demonstrate your non-involvement in our troubles."

"Send your envoys," said the Chancellor. "Fly them by a single glider to the port Kaoime; they will come to no harm, and there our escort will meet them, with proper demeanour."

CHAPTER FOURTEEN

Palasedra hung below Shant like a gnarled, three-fingered
hand, with the Great Salt Bog for a wrist. The mountains
of Palasedra formed the bones of the Palasedran hand.
They rose in naked juts, and many held aloft the lonely
castles of the Eagle-Dukes. The forests of Palasedra
tumbled down the seaward valleys. Giant loutranos with
straight black trunks supported disproportionately small
parasols of dough-coloured pulp. Around their shanks
surged a dark green froth of similax and wax-pod, which
in turn towered above arbours of gohovany, argove, jajuy.
The towns of Palasedra guarded the valley sea mouths.
Tall stone houses with high-pitched roofs stood cramped
together, one growing from the next like crystals in a rock
Palasedra! a strange, grim land, where every man reckoned himself noble and acknowledged only the authority
of an "honour" which everyone recognized but no one
enforced; where no door was locked, where no window
was shuttered; where each man's brain was a citadel as
quiet as the castle of an Eagle-Duke.

At Kaoime the glider from Shant slid to a landing on
the narrow beach. Four men climbed down from the sad-
dles within the truss. The first was the flyer, the remain-

199

ing three were Etzwane, Mialambre, and Finnerack, who had agreed to visit Palasedra only after his courage, judgment, and quality of intelligence had been mocked and challenged – whereupon Finnerack declared his willingness to explore the far side of Caraz if need be.

The stern houses of Kaoime looked down from the back of the beach. Three tall men wearing fitted black gowns and high-crowned black hats came forward. Their movements were stately and mannered.

These were the first Palasedras Etzwane had seen and he examined them with interest. They exemplified a race somewhat different from his own. Their skin, pallid as parchment, showed a faint arsenical tarnish to glancing light. Their faces were long, thin, and convex, the forehead and chin receding, the nose a prow. One spoke in a muffled guttural voice, forming his words somewhere behind his palate. For this reason, and because he used a strange, oddly accented dialect, his speech was almost incomprehensible. "You are the envoys from Shant?"

"We are."

"You wear no torcs; you have for a fact thrown off the yoke of your tyrant?"

Mialambre started to make a didactic qualification; Etzwane said, "We have altered our style of government; this is a fact."

"In that case, I greet you in my official capacity. We fly at once to Chemaoue. With me then, to the sky-lift."

They mounted to a platform of woven withe. With a surge and a sway an endless cable took them aloft: up under the argoves, through a hole in the dark green mat and into the airy aisles between the loutranos, up past the dough-coloured parasols into the lavender light of the three suns. A platform stood on spider-leg stilts at the lip of a cliff; here they disembarked. A glider awaited them: an intricate device of struts, cords, vanes, with a cabin of withe and film hanging under bat-wing sails.

The one Palasedran and the three men of Shant entered the cabin. Far across the plateau a group of enormous men, indistinctly seen, thrust a wicker basket full of stones over the precipice. A cable accelerated the glider; smoothly it climbed into the sky and was launched out into the empty spaces.

The Palasedran showed no disposition for conversation. Etzwane presently asked, "You know why we are here?"

The Palasedran said, "I read no exact knowledge. Your ideas find no correspondence with mine."

"Ah," said Mialambre, "you were sent to read our minds."

"I was sent to convey you politely to Chemaoue."

"Who is Chancellor? One of the Eagle-Dukes?"

"No, we are now five castes rather than four. The Eagle-Dukes concern themselves with honour."

"We are ignorant of Palasedra and its customs," said Etzwane. "If the Chancellor is not an Eagle-Duke, how does he rule them?"

"The Chancellor rules no one. He acts only for himself."

"But he speaks for Palasedra?"

"Why not? Someone must do so."

"What if he commits you to an unpopular course of action?"

"He knows what is expected of him. It is the way we conduct ourselves, doing what is expected of us. If we fail, our sponsors bear the brunt. Is this not right?" He touched the band of his hat, which bore a dozen heraldic badges. "These folk have sponsored me. They gave me their trust. Two are Eagle-Dukes. . . . Behold yonder, the castle of Duke Ain Palaeio."

The castle occupied a saddle between two crags: a mouldering structure almost invisible against the surrounding stone. To either side stood a handful of black cypresses. Grey-green stoneflower grew in festoons down the foundation walls. . . . The castle fell behind and was lost to view.

Up columns of wind, down slopes of air floated the black glider, sliding ever southward. The mountains became lower; the loutranos disappeared; the similax and argove gave way to hangman tree, dark oak, occasional groves of cypress.

The afternoon waned; the winds and draughts became less definite. As the sun rolled behind the western mountains, the glider slid softly down towards a distant leaden shine of water, and presently landed in the dusk beside the town of Chemaoue.

A vehicle of pale varnished wood on four tall wheels stood waiting. The draught animals were naked men, bulky of leg and chest, seven feet tall, with skins of a peculiar ruddy ochre. The small neat heads lacked hair; the blunt features showed no expression. Finnerack, who had spoken little during the journey – if anything he seemed uneasy and looked frequently, almost with longing, back the way they had come – now turned Etzwane a sardonic glance, as if claiming vindication for his theories.

Mialambre demanded of the Palasedran: "These creatures are the work of your man-makers?"

'They are, though the process is not quite as you assume it to be."

"I make no assumptions; I am a jurist."

"Are never jurists irrational? Especially the jurists of Shant?"

"Why the jurists of Shant, specifically?"

"Your land is rich; you can afford irrationality."

"Not so!" declared Mialambre. "By saying this, you make all your words suspect."

"A matter of no consequence."

The carriage trundled through the dusk. Watching the heaving orange backs, Etzwane asked: "The man-makers continue to do their work in Palasedra?"

'We are imperfect.'

"What of these toiling creatures? Do they become perfect?"

"They are good enough as they are. Their stock was cretinous; should we then waste cooperative flesh? Should we kill the cretins and condemn sensitive men to such toil?" The Palasedran's lips curved in a sour smile. "It would be as if we put all our cretins into the upper castes."

"Before we sit down to a ceremonial banquet," said Mialambre, "let me ask this: do you use these creatures for food?"

"There will be no ceremonial banquet."

The carriage rattled along the esplanade, then halted at an inn. The Palasedran made a gesture. "Here you may rest for a period."

Etzwane stared haughtily at the Palasedran. "You bring the envoys of Shant to a waterfront tavern?"

"Where else should we take you? Do you care to pace up and down the esplanade? Should we loft you to the castle of Duke Shaian?"

"We are not sticklers for formality," explained Mialambre. "Still, if you sent envoys to Shant, they would be housed in a splendid palace."

"You accurately represent the distinction between our nations."

Etzwane alighted from the carriage. "Come," he said shortly. "We are not here for pomp and ceremony."

The three marched to the inn. A door of timber planks opened into a narrow room panelled with varnished wood. High along one wall yellow lamps flickered; below were tables and chairs.

An old man with a white shawl over his head stepped forward. "Your wants?"

"A meal and lodging for the night. We are envoys from Shant."

"I will prepare a room. Sit then, and food will be served to you."

The single other occupant of the room, a spare man in a grey clock, sat at a table with a platter of fish before him. Etzwane stopped short, puzzled by the familiar poise of head. The man looked around, nodded, returned to work fastidiously at his fish.

Etzwane stood indecisively, then went to stand by the man's table. "I thought you had returned to Earth."

"Such were the orders of the Institute," said Ifness. "However I made an urgent protest and I am now on Durdane in a somewhat altered capacity. I am happy to say, moreover, that I have not been expelled from the Institute."

"Good news indeed," said Etzwane. "May we join you?"

"Certainly."

The three took seats. Etzwane performed introductions. "These persons are Patricians of Shant: Mialambre: Octagon and Jerd Finnerack. This gentlemen" — he indicated Ifness — "is an Earthman and Fellow of the Historical Institute. His name is Ifness."

"Precisely true," said Ifness. "I have had an interesting sojourn upon Durdane."

"Why did you not make your presence known?" demanded Etzwane. "You owed a large responsibility to the situation."

Ifness made a gesture of indifference. "Your management of the crisis was not only competent but local. Is it not better that the enemies of Shant fear Shant rather than Earth?"

"The question is many-sided," said Etzwane. "What do you do here in Palasedra?"

"I study the society, which is of great interest. The Palasedrans dare anthromorphological experiments which have few counterparts elsewhere. A frugal people, they adapt human waste material to a set of useful functions. The indefatigable resource of the human spirit is a continuing wonder. In an austere land the Palasedrans have evolved a philosophical system by which they take pleasure in austerity."

Etzwane recognized Ifness' old tendency towards evasive prolixity. "In Garwiy I noticed no tendency of your own towards austerity, nor did you espouse a philosophy glorifying want."

"You observed accurately," said Ifness. "As a scholar I am able to transcend my personal inclinations."

205

For a brief period Etzwane tried to puzzle out the sense of Ifness' words, then said: "You do not seem to wonder at our presence here in Palasedra."

"A person who conceals his curiosity has knowledge thrust upon him, so I have learned."

"Did you know that the Roguskhoi have sought refuge on Palasedran soil? That our Flyers and the Black Dragons of Palasedra have engaged in combat?"

"This is interesting information," declared Ifness, neglecting a direct answer to the question. "I wonder how the Palasedrans will deal with the Roguskhoi."

Finnerack snorted in disgust. "Do you doubt that the Palasedrans sponsor the Roguskhoi?"

"I do indeed, if only for socio-psychological reasons. Consider the Eagle-Dukes who live in grandeur: are these men to gnaw quietly at the vitals of an enemy? I could not be so convinced."

Finnerack said curtly, "Theorize as you will. What my instincts assert, I believe."

Food was brought to the table: salt fish stewed in vinegar, coarse bread, a pickle of sea fruits. "The Palasedrans have no concept of gastronomy," Ifness noted. "They eat from hunger. Pleasure as defined by a Palasedran is victory over hardship, the assertion of self over environment. The Palasedrans swim at dawn towards the sunrise. When a storm rages they climb a crag. As a secret accomplishment a man may know five phases of mathematics. The Eagle-Dukes build their own towers with stone they quarry with their own hands; some gather their own food. The Palasedrans know no music; one food is as good as another; they adorn themselves only with the emblems of their guarantors. They are neither cordial nor generous, but they are too proud to be suspicious."

Ifness paused to study first Mialambre, then Etzwane, and finally Finnerack. "The Chancellor will presently arrive. I doubt if he will show much sympathy for your problems. If you have no objection I will join your group in the role, let us say, of observer. I have already represented myself as a traveller from Shant."

"As you wish," said Etzwane, despite Finnerack's grunt.

Mialambre: said, "Tell us of the planet Earth, the home of our perverse ancestors."

Ifness pursed his lips. "Earth is not a world briefly to be described. We are perhaps over civilized; our ambitions are no longer large. Our schismatics go forth to the outer worlds; by some miracle we continue to generate adventurers. The human universe constantly expands, and here, if anywhere, is the basic essence of Earth. It is the home world, the source from which all derives."

"Our ancestors left Earth nine thousand years ago," said Mialambre. "They fared through space a vast distance to Durdane, where they thought to be isolated forever. Perhaps now we are no longer remote from other Earth-worlds."

"This is the case," said Ifness. "Durdane still lies beyond the human perimeter, but to no great degree. . . . The Chancellor has arrived. He comes to transact the business of state in this waterfront tavern, and perhaps it is as good a system as any."

The Chancellor stood in the doorway, talking to someone in the street, then he turned and surveyed the room: a man tall and gaunt, with a stubble of grey hair, an enormous crescent of a nose. He wore the usual black gown, but rather than a hat he wore a workman's white shawl about his head.

Etzwane, Finnerack, Mialambre rose to their feet; Ifness sat looking down at the floor as if in sudden reverie.

The Chancellor approached the table. "Please sit down. Our business is simple. Your flyers entered Palasedra; the Black Dragons drove them back. You state that you invaded us to punish the Roguskhoi; these, you further claim, are agents of Palasedra. I say: the Roguskhoi are now on Palasedran soil and Palasedrans shall deal with them. I say: the Roguskhoi are not agents of Palasedra. I say: to send your flyers into Palasedra was a rash and foolish act – indeed, so rash and so foolish that we have held back our hands from sheer astonishment."

Ifness made an approving sign and uttered a somewhat sententious remark, apparently addressed to no one: "Another aspect of human behaviour to confuse and deter our enemies: which is to say, unpredictable forebearance."

The Chancellor frowned aside, not finding in Ifness' approval the exact degree of meek and happy gratitude he might have expected. He spoke more sharply. "I say: we shall disregard your acts, insofar as official and purposeful malice seem to be lacking. In the future you must control your flyers. This, in sum, is my statement. I will now hear your response."

Mialambre cleared his throat. "Our presence here speaks for itself. We hope to foster calm and easy relations between our countries, to our mutual benefit. Ignorance induces suspicion; it is not surprising that some of us saw in the Roguskhoi a renewed threat from Palasedra."

Finnerack spoke in a cold voice: "The Brave Free Men and the Flyers of Shant have defeated the Roguskhoi, who thereupon took purposeful refuge in Palasedra. You

208

assert that the Roguskhoi are not your agents. You do not, however, disclaim responsibility for their existence, you who shamelessly breed men to special uses as if they were cattle; if this is the case, the Roguskhoi remain a Palasedran responsibility. They have done vast damage to Shant, and we demand indemnification."

The Chancellor drew back; he had not expected remarks so energetic, nor, for that matter, had Etzwane and Mialambre. Ifness nodded approvingly. "Finnerack's demands are by all accounts justified, if in fact Palasedran responsibility for the Roguskhoi is real. We have heard no official Palasedran statement either admitting or denying such responsibility."

The Chancellor's grizzled eyebrows became a bar across the bridge of his enormous nose. He spoke to Ifness. "I am puzzled by your exact status in this colloquy."

"I am an independent counsellor," said Ifness. "Gastel Etzwane will endorse my presence, though officially I represent neither Shant nor Palasedra."

The Chancellor said, "It is all the same to me. To make our position absolutely clear, the Palasedrans deny responsibility of any sort whatever for the Roguskhoi."

Finnerack challenged the remark: "Why then do they take refuge in Palasedra? Where did they come from if not Palasedra?"

The Chancellor spoke in a measured voice: "Our most recent intelligence is this: they are creatures sent here from the planet Earth. A spaceship discharged them into the Engh, a remote valley not far from the Salt Bog." Etzwane turned to stare at Ifness, who looked blandly at the far wall. Finnerack uttered a harsh bark of laughter. The Chancellor went on: "So much we have learned from ahulphs of the neighbourhood. The Roguskhoi now

209

return to the Engh. They will not arrive; a force of Palasedran warriors goes now to destroy them. Tomorrow I go
to witness the battle and collect further information; accompany me, if you wish."

CHAPTER FIFTEEN

The Chancellor laid a map upon the table and gestured out into the predawn murk. "There is the Engh. From here it appears no more than a defile or a gully. The mountains in fact enclose a large, barren meadow, as is evident from the map." The Chancellor tapped a horny finger-nail down upon the parchment. "The glider discharged us here; we now stand at this point, overlooking the valley of the River Zek. Troops deploy in yonder forest; they will presently move forward."

"And what of the Roguskhoi?" asked Etzwane.

"The main force has left the Great Salt Bog and now approaches. The prodromes have already entered the Engh, which we have not disturbed." He peered into the dawn sky. "There is no wind to support the Black Dragons; our reconnaissance is incomplete. As yet I have not been informed of battle plans."

The three suns rolled up into the sky; violet light flooded the valley; the river Zek showed a series of col-oured glints. Finnerack pointed to the north. "Here come the advance parties. Why do you not harass them on the flank?"

"I am not battle-chief," said the Chancellor. "I can

supply no opinion. . . . Stand back so that we cannot be observed."

Scout parties jogged up the valley; in the distance a dark mass advanced like a tidal bore.

An instrument at the Chancellor's belt tinkled. He held it to his ear and presently scanned the sky. He returned the instrument to his belt.

The Roguskhoi approached in hulking, long strides, features fixed and blank. To the side jogged the chieftains, distinguished by their pectoral bibs of chain mail.

The Chancellor's belt radio jingled; he listened with stern attention, then said, "No alteration of plan."

He returned the radio to his belt and stood a moment looking silently towards the Engh. He said, "Last night the spaceship returned to the Engh. It waits there now, for purposes open to conjecture."

Mialambre spoke sardonically to Ifness. "Can you suggest an explanation for this?"

"Yes," said the Ifness. "I can indeed." He asked the Chancellor: "What is the semblance of the spaceship? Have men disembarked? What is its insignia, if any?"

"I learn that the ship is a great round disc. The ports lay open, making ramps to the ground. No one has left the ship. Skirmishers now attack the rear of the column."

An irregular rattle of explosions reached their ears. The Roguskhoi chieftains swung about, then uttered sharp orders; groaning and rumbling, the Roguskhoi broke apart to form battle squads. The length of the column was now visible. Full-grown warriors marched at front and rear; in the centre were imps, bantlings, and perhaps a hundred dazed and haggard women.

From the forest came the blast of a horn; the Palasedran troops moved deliberately forth.

Etzwane was perplexed. He had expected gigantic warriors to match the Roguskhoi bulk for bulk; the Palasedran troops were not as tall as himself, but immensely broad of shoulder and deep of chest, with arms dangling almost to the ground. The heads hunched low, the eyes peered from under black helmets, seeming to look in two directions. They wore ochre trousers, fibre epaulettes, and greaves; for weapons they carried sabres, short-handled axes, small shields, and dart guns.

The Palesedrans bounded forward at a trot. The Roguskhoi halted, taken aback. The chieftains bawled commands, the squads reformed. The Palasedrans halted; the two armies faced each other, a hundred yards apart.

"A curious confrontation, to be sure," mused Ifness. "Each solution to the problem offers advantages.... Hmmm. Ogres versus trolls. The weapons I judge equivalent. Tactics and agility, of course, must decide the issue."

The Roguskhoi chieftains called sudden, harsh orders; abandoning women and imps the Roguskhoi warriors ran at a lumbering trot for the Engh. The Palasedrans ran on a converging course, and the armies came together, not face to face, but side to side, the Roguskhoi hacking and slicing, the Palasedrans bounding in and out, chopping, occasionally shooting darts at Roguskhoi eyes, and when occasion offered, tackling the legs of a vulnerable Roguskhoi, to bring the maroon bulk toppling. The scimitars took a corresponding toll; the way became littered with arms, legs, heads, and torsos; red blood mingled with black.

The battle reached the mouth of the Engh; and here a second Palasedran army bounded down from the rocks. The Roguskhoi thrust forward, striving to enter the Engh by dint of sheer strength. Behind in the valley remained the women and imps. The women became prey to hysteria. They picked up discarded weapons and slashed at the hopping imps, screaming in maniac delight.

The Roguskhoi warriors had gained the floor of the Engh. Here, with room for their agility, the Palasedrans became more effective.

Finnerack first, with Ifness and Etzwane close behind, then Mialambre and the Chancellor, came over a low, wooded ridge and looked down into the Engh, an irregular flat area about a half-mile in diameter, carpeted with scrub and blue rockweed. At the centre rested the spaceship: a flattened hemisphere of brown metal two hundred feet in diameter.

Etzwane asked Ifness, "What sort is the spaceship?"

"I don't know." Ifness brought forth his camera and made a series of photographs.

On three sides segments of the hull hung open. Standing in the apertures were creatures Etzwane thought to be either andromorphs or men; in the shadows he could not be certain.

In the Engh the battle raged, the Roguskhoi step by step thrusting towards the spaceship, the bibbed chieftains in the van, the rank and file arranged in such a fashion as to protect them from the bounding Palasedrans.

Finnerack gave a grunt of anguish and started down the hill. "Finnerack!" cried Etzwane. "Where are you going?"

Finnerack paid no heed. He broke into a trot. Etzwane set off after him. "Finnerack! Come back here; are you mad?"

Finnerack ran, waving his arms towards the spaceship. His eyes bulged wide-open, but he did not appear to see;

214

he stumbled, and Etzwane was on him. Etzwane clutched Finnerack's waist, pulled back. "What are you doing? Have you gone insane?"

Finnerack groaned, kicked, fought; he drove his elbows into Etzwane's face.

Ifness stepped forward and struck two smart blows; Finnerack fell numbly back.

"Quick, or they'll kill us from the ship," said Ifness.

Mialambre and Ifness took Finnerack's arms, Etzwane his legs; they carried him back into the shelter of the trees. Using Finnerack's garments, Ifness tied his ankles and wrists.

In the Engh the Palasedrans, wary of the spaceship, drew back. Up the ramps marched the surviving Roguskhoi chieftains and a hundred warriors. The ports snapped shut. Like a glow-beetle, the ship took on a silver luminescence. Emitting a rasping squeal it rose into the sky and presently was gone.

The Roguskhoi remaining in the valley moved slowly to the spot where the spaceship had rested; here they formed a rough circle, to stand at bay. The chieftains had departed; of the copper horde which had almost overwhelmed Shant less than a thousand survived.

The Palasedrans, drawing back, formed a pair of lines to the right and left of the Roguskhoi; they stood quietly, awaiting orders. For ten minutes the armies surveyed each other soberly, without signal of hostility; then the Palasedrans withdrew to the edge of the Engh and retired up the slope. The Roguskhoi remained at the centre of the valley.

The Chancellor made a signal to the men of Shant. "We now adopt our original strategy. The Roguskhoi are sealed into the Engh and they will never escape. Even your blue-eyed madman must concede the Roguskhoi to be off-world creatures."

Ifness said, "As to this there was never any doubt. The purpose for the incursion remains a mystery. If a conventional conquest were the plan, why were the Roguskhoi armed only with scimitars? Can folk who fly space contrive no better weapons? It seems unreasonable on the face of the matter."

"Evidently they took us lightly," said the Chancellor. "Or perhaps they thought to test us. If so, we have dealt them harsh instruction."

"These conjectures are reasonable," Ifness said. "There is still much to be learned. Certain of the Roguskhoi chieftains were killed. I suggest that you convey these corpses to one of your medical laboratories and there perform investigations, in which I would wish to participate."

The Chancellor made a curt gesture. "The effort is unnecessary."

Ifness drew the Chancellor aside and spoke a few calm sentences, and now the Chancellor gave grudging agreement to Ifness' proposals.

CHAPTER SIXTEEN

In a state of sullen apathy Finnerack marched back down the valley. Several times Etzwane started to speak to him; each time, eery and sick at heart, he held his tongue. Mialambre, less imaginative, asked Finnerack: "Do you realize that your act, sane or the reverse, imperilled us all?"

Finnerack made no response; Etzwane wondered if he even heard.

Ifness said in a grave voice, "The best of us at times act upon odd impulses."

Finnerack said nothing.

Etzwane had expected to be flown back across the Great Salt Bog; the black glider, however, took them south to Chemaoue, where the man-powered carriage conveyed them once again to the dour inn at the harbour. The chambers were as cheerless as the refectory, with couches of stone cushioned only by thin, sour-smelling pads. Through the open window came a draught of cool salt air and the sound of harbour water.

Etzwane passed a cheerless night, during which he was not aware of having slept. Grey-violet light finally entered the high window. Etzwane arose, rinsed his face with cold water, and went down to the common room, where he was presently joined by Mialambre. Ifness and Finnerack failed to appear. When Etzwane went to investigate, he found their chambers vacant.

At noon Ifness returned to the inn. Etzwane anxiously inquired in regard to Finnerack. Ifness replied with care and deliberation. "Finnerack, if you remember, displayed a peculiar irresponsibility. Last night he departed the inn and set off along the shore. I had anticipated something of the sort and asked that he be kept under surveillance. Last night, therefore, he was taken into custody. I have been with the Palasedran authorities all morning and they have, I believe, discovered the source of Finnerack's odd conduct."

The rancour which Etzwane had once felt in connection with the secretive Ifness began to return. "What did they find out – and how?"

"Best perhaps that you come with me and see for yourself."

Ifness spoke in a casual voice: "The Palasedrans are now convinced that the spaceship is not a product of Earth. I naturally could have told them as much, in the process betraying my own background."

Mialambre asked irritably. "Where then did the spaceship originate?"

"I am as anxious to learn this as yourself – in fact I work on Durdane to this end. Since the Earth-worlds lie beyond the Schiafarilla, the spaceship presumably comes from the general direction opposite, towards the centre of the galaxy It is a sort I have never seen before."

"You informed the Palasedrans of all this?"

"By no means. Their opinions were altered by this morning's events. The Roguskhoi chieftains, if you recall, wore a protective bib; this aroused my curiosity. . . . Here are the laboratories."

Etzwane felt a thrill of horror. "This is where they brought Finnerack?"

"It seemed a sensible procedure."

They entered a building of black stone smelling strongly of chemical reeks. Ifness led the way with assurance along a side corridor into a large chamber illuminated by an array of skylights. Tanks and vats stood to right and left; tables ran down the middle. At the far end four Palasedrans in grey smocks considered the bulk of a dead Roguskhoi. Ifness gave a nod of approval. "They commence a new investigation. . . . It may be profitable for you to watch."

Etzwane and Mialambre approached and stood by the wall. The Palasedrans worked without haste, arranging the hulk to best advantge. . . . Etzwane looked about the room. A pair of large brown insects or crustaceans moved inside two glass jars. Glass tanks displayed floating organs, moulds and fungus, a swarm of small white worms, a dozen unnameable objects. . . . The Palasedrans, using an air-driven circular saw, sliced into the great chest. . . . They worked five minutes with great dexterity. Etzwane began to feel an almost unbearable tension; he turned away. Ifness however was intent. "Now watch."

With deftness and delicacy the Palasedrans extracted a white sac the size of two clenched fists. A pair of heavy, trailing tendons or nerves appeared to lead up into the neck. The Palasedrans carefully cut channels into the dark flesh, through bone and cartilage, to draw forth the cords intact. The entire organ now lay on the table. Suddenly it evinced a squirming life of its own. The white sac broke away; out crawled a glossy brown creature, something between a spider and a crab. The Palasedrans at once clapped it into a bottle and placed it on the shelf beside its two fellows.

"There you see your true enemy," said Ifness. "Sajarano of Sershan, during our conversations, used the word 'asutra.' Its intelligence appears to be of the highest order."

In horrified fascination Etzwane went to stare into the bottle. The creature was gnarled and convoluted like a small brown brain; eight jointed legs left the underside of the body, each terminating in three strong little palps. The long fibres or nerves extended from one end through a cluster of sensory organs.

"From my brief acquaintance with the asutra," said Ifness, "I deduce it to be a parasite; or better perhaps, the directive half of a symbiosis, though I am certain that in its native environment it uses neither creatures like the Roguskhoi nor yet men for its hosts."

Etzwane spoke in a voice he found hard to control. "You have seen these before?"

"A single specimen only: that which I took from Sajarano."

A dozen questions pushed into Etzwane's mind: grisly suspicions he did not know how to voice and perhaps did not wish verified. He put Sajarano of Sershan and his pathetic, mangled corpse out of his mind. He looked from one bottle to the other, and though he could not identify eyes or visual organs he had the disturbing sense of scrutiny.

"They are highly evolved and specialized," stated Ifness. "Still, like man they exhibit a surprising hardihood and no doubt can survive even in the absence of their hosts."

Etzwane asked: "What then of Finnerack?" — although he knew the answer to the question even before he asked.

"This," said Ifness, tapping one of the bottles, "was the asutra which occupied the body of Jerd Finnerack."

"He is dead?"

"He is dead. How could he be alive?"

"Once again," said Ifness in a nasal voice of intense boredom, "you insist that I render you information regarding matters either not essentially your concern, or which you might ascertain independently. Still, I will in this case make a concession and perhaps ease your agonies of bewilderment.

"As you know, I was ordered off the plant Durdane by representatives of the Historical Institute, who felt that I had acted irresponsibly. I forcefully asserted my opinions; I won others to my point of view and was sent back to Durdane in a new capacity.

"I returned at once to Garwiy, where I satisfied myself that you had acted with energy and decision. In short, the men of Shant, given leadership, reacted to the threat with ordinary human resource."

"But why the Roguskhoi in the first place? Why should they attack the folk of Shant? Is it not extraordinary?"

"By no means. Durdane is an isolated world of men, where experiments with human populations can be discreetly performed. The asutra appear to be anticipating an eventual contact between their realm and the Earth-worlds; perhaps they have had unhappy experiences in the past.

"Remember, they are parasites; they will try to effect their aims through proxies. First, then, they attempt an

221

anti-human simulacrum which impregnates human females and in the process renders them sterile: a biological weapon, in fact, which man has often used against insect pests.

"Their remarkable creation is the Roguskhoi. Certainly hundreds, perhaps thousands of men and women have known the asutra laboratories: a thought to haunt your dark nights. The asutra must consider their creatures acceptable human replicas, which of course they are not; the more subtle human gaze recognizes them for monsters at once; still, biologically they fulfil their function.

"To insure a meaningful experiment, the Roguskhoi must be accorded a period of non-interference; hence the Anome has a monitor implanted in his body, and his Benevolences fare no better. By a system not at all clear the asutra control the activities of their hosts. Sajarano complained of his 'secret soul,' 'the voice of his soul'; I recall Finnerack mentioning his conscience. No doubt the asutra learned to admonish men in their laboratories.

"The Roguskhoi, as weapons, were faulty; the essential concept was a fallacy. Once the artificial passivity of the Anome had ended, the men of Shant reacted with ordinary human energy. No doubt the asutra could have supplied weapons and subjugated Shant, but this was not their purpose; they wished to test and perfect indirect techniques.

"Suppose the men could be induced to destroy each other? This concept, or so I suspect – here I am on uncertain ground – led to the planting of a control in Finnerack. His pugnacity was reinforced; he was compelled to challenge the Palasedrans – an act not at all contrary to his own instincts.

"This second experiment likewise led to failure, although in principle it seems a more reasonable tactic. There was insufficient preparation; I suspect the scheme to be a hasty improvisation."

"All very well," said Mialambre with a scowl, "but why should Finnerack be used rather than, say, Gastel Etzwane, who has always wielded more real influence?"

"At one time Finnerack looked to be a man of irresistible power," said Ifness. "He controlled the Intelligence Agency and also commanded the Brave Free Men. His star was on the rise, and so he certified his doom."

"This is the case," admitted Mialambre. "In fact, I can fix upon the precise time of his alteration. He disappeared for three days. . . ." His voice dwindled; his eyes shifted towards Etzwane.

A heavy silence came over the chamber.

Etzwane brought his clenched fists slowly down on the table. "So it must be. The asutra have altered me as well."

"Interesting!" remarked Ifness. "You are conscious of strange voices, agonizing pangs, a constant sense of discontent and unease? These were the symptoms which eventually drove Sajarano to suicide."

"I know none of these. Nevertheless I was drugged precisely as was Finnerack. The same Parthans were on hand. I am doomed, but I die with my goals achieved. Let us go to the laboratory and have an end to the business."

Ifness made a reassuring sign. "Conditions are not so bad as you fear. I suspected that such an effort might be made upon you, and was on hand to thwart the attempt. In fact, I occupied a suite in the Hrindiana precisely beside your own. The attempt failed; the Parthans died; the asutra went to Earth in a jar and you awoke three days later tired and bewildered, but none the worse for all that."

223

Etzwane sank back into his seat.

Ifness continued, "In Shant the asutra have suffered a small but significant defeat. Their experiments have gained them precisely that attention they sought to avoid, thanks to the alertness of the Historical Institute. What have we learned? That the asutra either expect or prepare for antagonistic relations with the human race. Perhaps a collision between a pair of expanding world-systems is at last imminent.... Here comes the Chancellor, no doubt to announce that your glider is ready. As for me, I have eaten salt fish once too often, and if you permit, I will accompany you to Shant...."

The Asutra

Chapter 1

The Roguskhoi and their dominant asutra had been expelled from Shant. Belabored on the ground by the Brave Free Men, tormented from above by the Flyers of Shant, the Roguskhoi had retreated south, across the Great Salt Bog into Palasedra. In a dismal valley the horde had been destroyed, with only a handful of chieftains escaping in a remarkable red-bronze spaceship – and so the strange invasion of Shant had come to an end.

For Gastel Etzwane the victory brought a temporary joy after which he fell into a dour and introspective mood. He became aware of a vast aversion to responsibility, to public activity in general; he marveled that he had functioned as well and as long as he had. Returning to Garwiy he took himself from the Council of Purple Men with almost offensive abruptness; he became Gastel Etzwane the musician: so much, no more. At once his spirits soared; he felt free and whole. Two days the mood persisted, then waned as the question *What now?* found no natural or easy response.

On a hazy autumn morning, with the three suns lazing behind self-generated disks of milk-white, pink, and blue nimbus, Etzwane walked along Galias Avenue. Tape trees trailed purple and gray ribbons about his head; beside him moved the Jardeen River on its way to the Sualle. Other folk strolled along Galias Avenue, but none took notice of the man who so recently had ruled their lives. As Anome, Etzwane of necessity had avoided notoriety; he was not a conspicuous man in any event. He moved with economy, spoke in a flat voice, used no gesticulations, all of which made for a somber force disproportionate to his years. When Etzwane looked in a mirror he often felt a discord between his image, which was saturnine, even a trifle grim, and what he felt to be his true self: a being beset by doubts, shivered by passions, jerked here and there by irrational exhilarations; a person oversusceptible to charm and beauty, wistful with longing for the un- attainable. So Etzwane half-seriously regarded himself. Only when he played music did he feel a convergence of his incongruous parts.

What now?

He had long taken the answer for granted: he would rejoin Frolitz and the Pink-Black-Azure-Deep Greeners. Now he was not so sure, and he halted to watch broken strands from the tape trees drifting along the river. The old music sounded in his mind far away, a wind blowing out of his youth.

He turned away from the river and continued along the avenue, and presently came upon a three-storied structure of black and gray-green glass with heavy mul- berry lenses bulging over the street: Fontenay's Inn, which put Etzwane in mind of Ifness, Earthman and Research Fellow of the Historical Institute. After the destruction of the Roguskhoi he and Ifness had flown by balloon across Shant to Garwiy. Ifness carried a bottle containing an asutra taken from the corpse of a Rogusk- hoi chieftain. The creature resembled a large insect, eight inches long and four inches in thickness: a hybrid of ant and tarantula, mingled with something unimaginable. Six arms, each terminating in three clever palps, depended from the torso. At one end ridges of purple-brown chitin

6

protected the optical process: three oil-black balls in shallow cavities tufted with hair. Below trembled feeder mechanisms and a cluster of mandibles. During the journey Ifness occasionally tapped on the glass, to which the asutra returned only a flicker of the optical organs. Etzwane found the scrutiny unnerving; somewhere within the glossy torso subtle processes were occurring: ratiocination, or an equivalent operation; hate, or a sensation analogous.

Ifness refused to speculate upon the nature of the asutra. 'Guesses are of no value. The facts, as we know them, are ambiguous.'

'The asutra tried to destroy the folk of Shant,' declared Etzwane. 'Is this not significant?'

Ifness only shrugged and looked out across the purple distances of Canton Shade. They now sailed close-hauled into a north wind, bucking and sliding as the winch-tender coaxed the best from the *Conseil*, a notoriously cranky balloon.

Etzwane attempted another question. 'You examined the asutra you took from Sajarano: what did you learn?'

Ifness spoke in a measured voice. 'The asutra metabolism is unusual and beyond the scope of my analysis. They seem a congenitally parasitical form of life, to judge from the feeding apparatus. I have discovered no disposition to communicate, or perhaps the creatures use a method too subtle for my comprehension. They enjoy the use of paper and pencil and make neat geometrical patterns, sometimes of considerable complication but no obvious meaning. They show ingenuity in solving problems and appear to be both patient and methodical.'

'How did you learn all this?' demanded Etzwane.

'I devised tests. It is all a matter of presenting inducements.'

'Such as?'

7

'The possibility of freedom. The avoidance of discomfort.'

Etzwane, faintly disgusted, mulled the matter over for a period. Presently he asked, 'What do you intend to do now? Will you return to Earth?'

Ifness looked up into the lavender sky, as if taking note of some far destination. 'I hope to continue my inquiries; I have much to gain and little to lose. With equal certainty I will encounter official discouragement. My nominal superior, Dasconetta, has nothing to gain and much to lose.'

Curious, thought Etzwane; was this the way things went on Earth? The Historical Institute imposed a rigorous discipline upon its Fellows, enjoying absolute detachment from the affairs of the world under examination. So much he knew of Ifness, his background, and his work. Little enough, everything considered.

The journey proceeded. Ifness read from *The Kingdoms of Old Caraz*; Etzwane maintained a half-resentful silence. The *Conseil* spun up the slot; cantons Erevan, Maiy, Conduce, Jardeen, Wild Rose passed below and disappeared into the autumn murk. The Jardeen Gap opened ahead; the Ushkadel rose to either side; the *Conseil* blew along the Vale of Silence, through the gap, and so to South Station under the astounding towers of Garwiy.

The station gang hauled the *Conseil* down to the platform; Ifness alighted, and with a polite nod for Etzwane set off across the plaza.

In a sardonic fury Etzwane watched the spare figure disappear into the crowd. Ifness clearly meant to avoid even the most casual of relationships. Now, two days later, looking across Galias Avenue, Etzwane was once again reminded of Ifness. He crossed the avenue and entered Fontenay's Inn.

8

The day-room was quiet; a few figures sat here and there in the shadows musing over their mugs. Etzwane went to the counter, where he was attended by Fontenay himself. 'Well then: it's Etzwane the musician! If you and your khitan are seeking a place, it can't be done. Master Hesselrode and his Scarlet-Mauve-Whiters work the stand. No offense intended; you scratch with the best of them. Accept a mug of Wild Rose ale, at no charge.'

Etzwane raised the mug. 'My best regards.' He drank. The old life had not been so bad after all. He looked around the chamber. There: the low platform where so often he had played music; the table where he had met lovely Jurjin of Xhiallinen; the nook where Ifness had waited for the Faceless Man. In every quarter hung memories which now seemed unreal; the world had become sane and ordinary . . . Etzwane peered across the room. In the far corner a tall, white-haired man of uncertain age sat making entries into a notebook. Mulberry light from a high bull's-eye played around him; as Etzwane watched, the man raised a goblet to his lips and sipped. Etzwane turned to Fontenay. 'The man in the far alcove – what of him?'

Fontenay glanced across the room. 'Isn't that the gentleman Ifness? He uses my front suite. An odd type, stern and solitary, but his money is as downright as sweat. He's from Canton Cape, or so I gather.'

'I believe I know the gentleman.' Etzwane took his mug and walked across the chamber. Ifness noted his approach sidewise, from the corner of his eye. Deliberately he closed his notebook and sipped from his goblet of ice water. Etzwane gave a polite salute and seated himself; had he waited for an invitation, Ifness might well have kept him standing. 'On impulse I stepped in, to recall our adventures together,' said Etzwane, 'and I find you engaged at the same occupation.'

9

Ifness' lips twitched. 'Sentimentality has misled you. I am here because convenient lodging is available and because I can work, usually without interruption. What of you? Have you no official duties to occupy you?'

'None whatever,' said Etzwane. 'I have resigned my connection with the Purple Men.'

'You have earned your liberty,' said Ifness in a nasal monotone. 'I wish you the pleasure of it. And now' – With meaningful exactitude he arranged his notebook.

'I am not reconciled to idleness,' said Etzwane. 'It occurs to me that I might be able to work with you.'

Ifness arched his eyebrows. 'I am not sure that I understand your proposal.'

'It is simple enough,' said Etzwane. 'You are a Fellow of the Historical Institute; you perform research on Durdane and elsewhere; you could use my assistance. We have worked together before; why should we not continue to do so?'

Ifness spoke in a crisp voice. 'The concept is impractical. My work for the most part is solitary, and occasionally takes me off-planet, which of course –'

Etzwane held up his hand. 'This is precisely my goal,' he declared, though the idea had never formed itself in terms quite so concrete. 'I know Shant well; I have traveled Palasedra; Caraz is a wilderness; I am anxious to visit other worlds.'

'These are natural and normal yearnings,' said Ifness. 'Nevertheless, you must make other arrangements.'

Etzwane pensively drank ale. Ifness watched stonily sidewise. Etzwane asked, 'You still study the asutra?'

'I do.'

'You feel that they have not yet done with Shant?'

'I am convinced of nothing.' Ifness spoke in his didactic monotone. 'The asutra tested a biological weapon against the men of Shant. The weapon – which is to say, the

10

Roguskhoi – failed because of crudities in execution, but no doubt served its purpose; the asutra are now better informed. Their options are still numerous. They can continue their experiments, using different weapons. On the other hand they may decide to expunge the human presence on Durdane altogether.'

Etzwane had no comment to make. He drained his mug and in spite of Ifness' disapprobation signaled Fontenay for replenishment. 'You are still trying to communicate with the asutra?'

'They are all dead.'

'And you made no progress?'

'Essentially none.'

'Do you plan to capture others?'

Ifness gave him a cool smile. 'My goals are more modest than you suspect. I am concerned principally for my status in the Institute, that I may enjoy my accustomed perquisites. Your interests and mine engage at very few points.'

Etzwane scowled and drummed his fingers on the table. 'You prefer that the asutra do not destroy Durdane?'

'As an abstract ideal I will embrace this proposition.'

'The situation itself is not abstract,' Etzwane pointed out. 'The Roguskhoi have killed thousands! If they won here they might go on to attack the Earth worlds.'

'The thesis is somewhat broad,' said Ifness. 'I have put it forward as a possibility. My associates, however, incline to other views.'

'How can there be doubt?' Etzwane demanded. 'The Roguskhoi are or were an aggressive force.'

'So it would seem, but against whom? The Earth worlds? Ridiculous; how could they avail against civilised weaponry?' Ifness made an abrupt gesture. 'Now please excuse me; a certain Dasconetta asserts his status at my

11

expense, and I must consider the matter. It was pleasant to have seen you ...'

Etzwane leaned forward. 'Have you identified the asutra home-world?'

Ifness gave his head an impatient shake. 'It might be one of twenty thousand, probably off towards the center of the galaxy.'

'Should we not seek out this world, to study it at close hand?'

'Yes, yes; of course.' Ifness opened his journal.

Etzwane rose to his feet. 'I wish you success in your struggle for status.'

'Thank you.'

Etzwane returned across the room. He drank another mug of ale, glowering back towards Ifness, who serenely sipped ice water and made notes in his journal.

Etzwane left Fontenay's Inn and continued north beside the Jardeen, pondering a possibility which Ifness himself might not have considered ... He turned aside into the Avenue of Purple Gorgons, where he caught a diligence to the Corporation Plaza. He alighted at the Jurisdictionary and climbed to the offices of the Intelligence Agency on the second floor. The director was Aun Sharah, a handsome man, subtle and soft-spoken, with an Aesthete's penchant for casual elegance. Today he wore a suave robe of gray over a midnight blue body-suit; a star sapphire dangled from his left ear by a silver chain. He greeted Etzwane affably but with a wary deference that reflected their previous differences. 'I understand that you are once again an ordinary citizen,' said Aun Sharah. 'The metamorphosis was swift. Has it been complete?'

'Absolutely; I am a different person,' said Etzwane. 'When I think over the past year I wonder at myself.'

'You have surprised many folk,' said Aun Sharah in a dry voice. 'Including myself.' He leaned back in his chair.

12

'What now? Is it to be music once more?'

'Not just yet. I am unsettled and restless, and I am now interested in Caraz.'

'The subject is large,' said Aun Sharah in his easy, half-facetious manner. 'However, your lifetime lies before you.'

'My interest is not all-embracing,' said Etzwane. 'I merely wonder if Roguskhoi have ever been seen in Caraz.'

Aun Sharah gazed reflectively at Etzwane. 'Your term as private citizen has quickly run its course.'

Etzwane ignored the remark. 'Here are my thoughts. The Roguskhoi were tested in Shant and defeated. So much we know. But what of Caraz? Perhaps they were originally deployed in Caraz; perhaps a new horde is in formation. A dozen possibilities suggest themselves, including the chance that nothing whatever has happened.'

'True,' said Aun Sharah. 'Our intelligence is essentially local. Still, on the other hand, what can we do? We strain to encompass the work already required of us.'

'In Caraz news drifts down the rivers. At the seaports mariners learn of events occurring far inland. What if you circulated your men along the docks and through the waterfront taverns, to find what might be the news from Caraz?'

'The idea has value,' said Aun Sharah. 'I will issue such an order. Three days should suffice, at least for a preliminary survey.'

Chapter 2

The thin, dark, solitary boy who had taken to himself the name of Gastel Etzwane* had become a hollow-cheeked young man with an intense and luminous gaze. When Etzwane played music the corners of his mouth rose to bring a poetic melancholy to his otherwise saturnine features; otherwise his demeanor was quiet and controlled beyond the ordinary. Etzwane had no intimates save perhaps old Frolitz the musician, who thought him mad . . .

On the day following his visit to the Jurisdictionary he received a message from Aun Sharah. 'The investigation has yielded immediate information, in which I am sure you will be interested. Please call at your convenience.'

Etzwane went at once to the Jurisdictionary.

Aun Sharah took him to a chamber high in one of the sixth-level cupolas. Four-foot-thick sky lenses of water-green glass softened the lavender sunlight and intensified the colors of the Canton Glirris rug. The room contained a single table twenty feet in diameter, supporting a massive contour map. Approaching, Etzwane saw a surprisingly detailed representation of Caraz. Mountains were carved from pale Canton Faible amber, with inlaid quartz

---

* Among the Chilites of Temple Bashon, each Pure Boy selected for himself a name exemplifying his hopes for the future. Gastel was an heroic flyer of ancient times, Etzwane a legendary musician. The name had caused Etzwane's soul-father, Osso, shock and dissatisfaction.

to indicate the presence of snow and ice. Silver threads and ribbons indicated the rivers; the plains were gray-purple slate; cloth in various textures and colors represented forests and swamps. Shant and Palasedra appeared as incidental islands off the eastern flank.

Aun Sharah walked slowly along the northern edge of the table. 'Last night,' he said, 'a local Discriminator* brought in a seaman from the Gyrmont docks. He told a strange tale indeed, which he had heard from a bargeman at Erbol, here at the mouth of the Keba River.' Aun Sharah put his finger down on the map. 'The bargeman had floated a load of sulfur down from this area up here' – Aun Sharah touched a spot two thousand miles inland – 'which is known as Burnoun. About here is a settlement, Shillinsk; it is not shown . . . At Shillinsk the bargeman spoke to nomad traders from the west, beyond these mountains, the Kuzi Kaza . . . '

Etzwane returned to Fontenay's Inn in a diligence, to meet Ifness on his way out the door. Ifness gave him a distant nod and would have gone his way had not Etzwane stepped in front of him. 'A single moment of your time.'

Ifness paused, frowning. 'What do you require?'

'You mentioned a certain Dasconetta. He would be a person of authority?'

Ifness looked at Etzwane sidelong. 'He occupies a responsible post, yes.'

'How can I get in touch with Dasconetta?'

Ifness reflected. 'In theory, several methods exist. Practically, you would be forced to work through me.'

'Very well; be so good as to put me into contact with

* Discriminator: in the language of Shant, *avistioi* – literally, 'nice discriminator'. The *avistioi* originally were inspectors hired by the Garwiy Aesthetes, and only gradually assumed the function of the cantonal police. Etzwane and Aun Sharah had expanded their scope.

Dasconetta.'

Ifness gave a wintry chuckle. 'Matters are not all that simple. I suggest that you prepare a brief exposition of your business. You will submit this to me. In due course I will be in contact with Dasconetta, at which time I may be able to transmit your message, assuming, naturally, that I find it neither tendentious nor trivial.'

'All very well,' said Etzwane, 'but the matter is urgent. He will be sure to complain at any delay.'

Ifness spoke in a measured voice. 'I doubt if you are capable of predicting Dasconetta's reactions. The man makes a fad of unpredictability.'

'Nevertheless, I believe that he will give serious regard to my business,' said Etzwane, 'especially if he is concerned for his prestige. Is there no way to communicate with him directly?'

Ifness made a gesture of weary resignation. 'Well then, briefly, what is your proposal? If the matter is important, I can at least advise you.'

'I realise this,' said Etzwane. 'But you are preoccupied with research; you stated that you could not cooperate with me, that you lacked authority, and you implied that all must be referred to Dasconetta. Hence, the rational course is to discuss my business with Dasconetta at once.'

'You have misinterpreted my remarks,' said Ifness, his voice rising a trifle. 'I stated that I had no place for you in my entourage, that I could not escort you on a tour of the Earth worlds. I did not indicate that my authority was insufficient or that I deferred to Dasconetta in any respect, save that imposed by an administrative technicality. I must listen to your business, since this is my function. So then, what is the matter which has so excited you?'

Etzwane spoke tonelessly. 'A report out of Caraz has come to my attention. It may be no more than a rumor, but I feel that it must be investigated. To this end I need

16

a swift vehicle, which I am sure Dasconetta can supply.'

'Aha! Well, well, indeed. And what is the nature of this rumor?'

Etzwane went on in a flat voice. 'Roguskhoi have appeared in Caraz: a considerable horde.'

Ifness gave a curt nod. 'Go on.'

'The horde fought an army of men, who reputedly used energy weapons. The Roguskhoi were apparently defeated, but here the rumor is uncertain.'

'What is the source of this information?'

'A mariner who heard the tale from a Caraz bargeman.'

'Where did the occurrence take place?'

'Is not this irrelevant?' asked Etzwane. 'I am requesting only a suitable vehicle in which to investigate the business.'

Ifness spoke gently, as if to an irrational child. 'The situation is more complex than you suppose. If you communicated this request to Dasconetta, or anyone else of the Coordination, they would merely refer the matter back to me, with a sharp comment as to my competence. Further, you know the proscriptions which control Fellows of the Institute: we never interfere with the flow of local events. I have violated this precept, of course, but so far I have been able to justify my acts. If I allowed you to place this remarkable request before Dasconetta, they would think me not only irresponsible but foolish. There is no help for it. I agree that the rumor is significant, and whatever my personal inclinations I may not ignore it. Let us return into the tavern; I now require from you all factual information.'

For an hour the discussion continued, Etzwane politely persistent, Ifness formal, rational, and impervious as a block of glass. Under no circumstances would he attempt to procure for Etzwane a vehicle of the type he had in mind.

'In that case,' said Etzwane, 'I will proceed with less efficient transportation.'

The statement surprised Ifness. 'You seriously intend to venture into Caraz? Such a journey might occupy two or three years – assuming day-to-day survival.'

'I have taken all this into account,' said Etzwane. 'Naturally I will not trudge afoot through Caraz. I intend to fly.'

'By balloon? By glider?' Ifness raised his eyebrows. 'Across the wilds of Caraz?'

'Long ago the folk of Shant built a combination craft, the so-called "Farway". The fuselage and wing roots were gas-inflated; the wings were long and flexible. Such a craft is heavy enough to glide, but light enough to stay aloft on a breath.'

Ifness toyed with a silver trinket. 'And once you touch ground?'

'I am vulnerable, but not helpless. A man, single-handed, can kite himself up in an ordinary glider; still, he must wait for wind. The Farway rises against an easy breeze. The voyage will be a risk, I agree.'

'A risk? Suicide.'

Etzwane nodded somberly. 'I would prefer the use of a power vehicle such as Dasconetta might supply.'

Ifness gave the silver trinket a petulant jerk. 'Return here tomorrow. I will arrange for air transportation. You will be under my orders.'

For the folk of Shant the affairs of the next canton were of small concern; Caraz was as far as the Schiafarilla*

---

* Schiafarilla: a cluster of two thousand magnificent stars which illuminated the summer nights of Shant. The Earth worlds lay on the far side of the Schiafarilla.

and not nearly so visible. Etzwane, a musician, had traveled every region of Shant and was somewhat wider in his viewpoints; nevertheless Caraz was to him no more than a far region of windy wastes, mountains, and chasms of incomprehensible scale. The rivers of Caraz straddled vast plains, brimming too wide to be seen from bank to bank. Durdane, nine thousand years before, had been settled by fugitives, recalcitrants, and dissidents; the wildest and most irredeemable had fled to Caraz to lose themselves forever, wandering from one hazy distance into the next. Their descendants still roamed the solitudes.

At noon Etzwane returned to Fontenay's Inn, but found no sign of Ifness. An hour passed, and another. Etzwane went outside and paced up and down the avenue. His mood was placid, if somewhat heavy. Irritation towards Ifness, so he had concluded, was self-defeating. As well feel anger towards the three suns.

Ifness at last appeared, striding up Galias Avenue from the direction of the Sualle. His face was set in long, pensive lines; for a moment it seemed as if he would walk past Etzwane without acknowledgment, but at the last moment he stopped short. 'You wanted to meet Dasconetta,' said Ifness. 'So you shall. Wait here; I will be no more than a moment.'

He stepped into the tavern. Etzwane looked up into the sky as a bank of clouds passed before the suns; gloom pervaded the city. Etzwane frowned and shivered.

Ifness returned, wearing a black cloak which flapped dramatically as he walked. 'Come,' said Ifness, and turned up the avenue.

Etzwane, thinking to assert his dignity, made no move to follow. 'Where?'

Ifness swung about, eyes glittering. He spoke in an even voice. 'In a joint enterprise each party must learn what to expect from the other. From me you may count on information adequate to the needs of the moment; I will not burden you with over-elaboration. From you I will expect alertness, discretion, and responsiveness. We will now proceed, to Canton Wild Rose.'

Etzwane felt he had won at least a minor concession, and went silently with Ifness to the balloon-way station.

The balloon *Karmoune* tugged at the guys; immediately upon Ifness and Etzwane's stepping into the gondola, the ground crew loosed the judas-dolly; the balloon swung aloft. The winch-tender canted to the beam wind; the *Karmoune* fled south, dolly singing in the slot.

Through Jardeen Gap they flew, with the Ushkadel bulking to either side. Etzwane glimpsed the palace of the Sershans glittering through the forest of similax and cypress. The pleasant vales of Canton Wild Rose spread before them and presently they came to the town Jamilo. The *Karmoune* showed an orange semaphore; the ground crew shackled the running-dolly and walked the judas-dolly to the depot, bringing the *Karmoune* down to the landing ramp. Ifness and Etzwane alighted; Ifness signaled a diligence. He gave the driver a terse order; the two climbed aboard and the pacer* sprang off down the road.

For half an hour they drove up the Jardeen Valley, past the country places of the Garwiy Aesthetes,† then through an orchard of strawberry trees to an ancient manor house. Ifness spoke to Etzwane in a measured voice. 'You may be asked questions. I cannot suggest your responses, but be succinct and volunteer no information.'

---

* Pacer: a draft beast evolved from bullocks brought to Durdane by the first settlers. Horses similarly imported died of gland fever or were killed by ahulphs.

† The construction of the glass city Garwiy was controlled by the Aesthetic Society, which eventually became a caste of hereditary nobility, the Aesthetes.

20

'I have nothing to hide,' said Etzwane, somewhat curtly. 'If I am questioned, I will answer as my best judgment advises.'

Ifness made no reply.

The diligence halted in the shadow of an old-style observation tower. The two men alighted; Ifness led the way through a rank garden, across a courtyard paved with pale-green marble, into the front hall of the manor. He halted and signaled Etzwane to do likewise. No sound was to be heard; the house seemed deserted. The air smelled of dust, dry wood, old varnish. A shaft of lavender afternoon light slanted down through a high window to play on a faded portrait of a child in the quaint costume of olden times . . . At the end of the hall a man appeared. For a moment he stood watching, then came a step forward. Ignoring Etzwane, he spoke to Ifness in a suave, rhythmical language, to which Ifness made a brief reply. The two moved away and passed through a doorway; Etzwane unobtrusively followed, into a tall, twelve-sided room paneled in snuff-brown madera and illuminated by six high bull's-eyes of dusty purple glass. Etzwane examined the man with candid interest. Could he be Dasconetta, living like a ghost in this ancient house? Strange, if not incredible. He was a strongly built man of middle size, abrupt but tightly controlled of movement. A pelt of glossy black hair formed a prow halfway down his high and prominent forehead, then coved back from the temples, and again around the ears. His nose and chin were pallid; his mouth showed almost no lip whatever. After a single flash of his black eyes, he paid Etzwane no further attention.

Ifness and Dasconetta (if this were his identity) spoke in measured sentences, Ifness stating, Dasconetta acknowledging. Etzwane settled upon a camphorwood bench and watched the conversation. There was clearly no friendship between the two men. Ifness was not so much on the defensive as wary; Dasconetta listened attentively, as if matching each word against a previous statement or point of view. On one occasion Ifness half-turned towards Etzwane, as if to command corroboration or to draw forth some special fact; Dasconetta halted him with a wry word.

Ifness set forth a demand, which Dasconetta rejected. Ifness persisted and now Dasconetta performed a strange act: he reached behind him and by some unknown method brought into view a square four-foot panel composed of a thousand blinking white and gray shapes. Ifness made a set of remarks, to which Dasconetta gave a reply. Both examined the square panel, which blinked and flickered black, gray, and white. Dasconetta turned back to face Ifness with a quiet smile.

The conversation continued another five minutes. Dasconetta spoke the final sentence; Ifness turned away, walked from the room. Etzwane followed.

Ifness marched silently back to the diligence. Etzwane, controlling his exasperation, asked, 'What have you learned?'

'Nothing new. The policy group will not approve my plans.'

Etzwane looked back at the old manor, wondering why Dasconetta would choose to make his headquarters here. He asked, 'What then is to be done?'

'About what?'

'About a vehicle to take us to Caraz.'

Ifness said in an offhand voice, 'That is not my primary concern. Transportation can be contrived if and when needful.'

Etzwane struggled to maintain an even voice. 'What then was your "primary concern"?'

'I suggested an investigation by agencies other than the

22

Historical Institute. Dasconetta and his clique are unwilling to risk an adulteration of the environment. As you saw, Dasconetta was able to manipulate a consensus.'

'What of Dasconetta? Does he reside permanently here in Wild Rose?'

Ifness allowed a small twitch of a smile to his lips. 'Dasconetta is far away, beyond the Schiafarilla. You saw his simula; he spoke to mine. The business is accomplished by a scientific method.'

Etzwane looked back towards the old house. 'And who is there?'

'No one. It is joined to a similar structure on the world Glantzen Five.'

They climbed into the diligence, which set off towards Jamilo.

Etzwane said, 'Your conduct is incomprehensible. Why did you assert that you could not take us to Caraz?'

'I made no such assertion,' said Ifness. 'You drew a faulty inference, for which I cannot accept responsibility. In any event the situation is more complicated than you suppose, and you must be prepared for subtlety.'

'Subtlety or deception?' demanded Etzwane. 'The effect is much the same.'

Ifness held up his hand. 'I will explain the situation, if only to reduce the flow of your reproaches . . . I conferred with Dasconetta neither to persuade him nor to requisition transportation, but, rather, to provoke his adoption of an incorrect policy. He has now made this error, and furthermore obtained a consensus through the use of incomplete and subjective information. The way is open for a demonstration to cut the ground out from under his feet. When I make an investigation I will be acting outside Standard Procedures, which will embarrass Dasconetta and catch him in a dilemma. He must commit himself even more completely to an obviously incorrect

23

position or perform a humiliating reversal.'

Etzwane gave a skeptical grunt. 'Has not Dasconetta taken all this into consideration?'

'I think not. He would hardly have called for a consensus and argued from so rigid a position. He is sure of his case, which is based on Institute Regulation; he imagines me fretting and constrained. The opposite is true; he has opened the door upon a set of rewarding prospects.'

Etzwane was unable to share Ifness' enthusiasm. 'Only if the investigation yields significant results.'

Ifness shrugged. 'If the rumors are incorrect, I am no worse off than before, except for the stigma of the consensus, which Dasconetta planned in any event.'

'I see . . . Why did you take me to this encounter?'

'I hoped that Dasconetta might question you, in order to embarrass me further. He cautiously decided against this procedure.'

'Hmmf.' Etzwane was not flattered by the role which Ifness had laid out for him. 'So now what do you plan?'

'I intend to study the events which purportedly have occurred in Caraz. The affair puzzles me: why should the asutra test the Roguskhoi again? They are a faulty concept; why deploy them a second time? Who are the men who used energy weapons in the rumored battle? Certainly not Palasedrans, certainly not men of Shant. There is mystery here; I confess that I am tantalised. So now, tell me: exactly where did this rumored engagement occur? It is agreed that we will join forces for this particular investigation.'

'Near the settlement Shillinsk, on the Keba River.'

'I will check my references tonight. Tomorrow we will depart. There is no room for delay.'

Etzwane became silent. The reality of the situation now faced him; he felt a mood of awe and presentiment. In a thoughtful voice he said, 'I will be ready.'

Late in the evening Etzwane once more called upon Aun Sharah, who showed no surprise to learn of Etzwane's plans. 'I can supply another trifle – no, two trifles – of information. The first is negative, in that we have spoken to mariners from other shores of Caraz. None mention Roguskhoi. The second item is a rather vague report of spaceships, which might or might not have been sighted in the Orgai region, west of the Kuzi Kaza. The report goes no further than this. I wish you good luck and will anxiously await your return. I understand your motives but I doubt if they would persuade me to venture into central Caraz.'

Etzwane gave a hollow chuckle. 'I have nothing better to do at the moment.'

Chapter 3

Etzwane arrived early at Fontenay's Inn. He wore a suit of gray hard-cloth, a jacket of water-repellent bast against the mists and rains of Caraz, ankle boots of chumpa* leather. In his pouch he carried the energy gun Ifness had given him long ago.

Ifness was nowhere upon the premises. Once again Etzwane walked fretfully up and down the avenue. An hour passed; then a diligence drew up beside him. The driver signaled. 'You are Gastel Etzwane? Please come with me.'

Etzwane scrutinised the man with suspicion. 'Where?'

'To a place north of the city; such are my instructions.'

'Who instructed you?'

'A certain Ifness.'

Etzwane entered the diligence. They drove north beside the Jardeen estuary, which presently spread wide to become the Sualle. The city fell behind; they followed a waterfront road through a dreary wasteland of rubble, nettles, sheds and warehouses, and a few dilapidated cabins. At an ancient house built of slag bricks the diligence halted. The driver made a sign; Etzwane alighted. The diligence drove back the way it had come.

---

* Chumpa: a large, indigenous animal similar to the quasi-biped ahulphs but less intelligent and characterised by a ferocious disposition.

Etzwane knocked on the door of the house, evoking no response. He went around to the back, where at the foot of a rocky slope a boathouse extended over the water. Etzwane followed a path down the slope and looked into the boathouse, to find Ifness loading parcels into a sail boat.

Etzwane stood wondering if Ifness had lost his faculties. To sail such a boat across the Green Ocean, around the north coast of Caraz to Erbol, thence up the Keba River to Burnoun was, to say the least, impractical, if for no other reason than the length of the journey.

Ifness seemed to read his mind. In a dry voice he said, 'By the very nature of our research, we cannot fly grandly about Caraz in an air-yacht. Are you ready to depart? If so, step into the boat.'

'I am ready.' Etzwane took himself aboard the boat. Ifness cast off the mooring lines and pushed the boat out upon the face of the Sualle. 'Be so good as to raise the sail.'

Etzwane heaved upon the halyard; the sail billowed; the boat moved out upon the water. Etzwane seated himself gingerly upon a thwart and considered the receding shore. He glanced into the cabin at the parcels Ifness had brought aboard and wondered what they contained. Food and drink? Enough for three days, at the most a week. Etzwane shrugged and looked out over the Sualle. Suns' light glinted from ten million cat's-paws in thirty million pink, blue, and white sparks. Astern rose the wonderful glass shapes of Garwiy, colors muted by distance. He might never see the glass towers of Garwiy again.

For an hour the boat sailed out upon the Sualle until the shores were indistinct and no other boats could be seen. Ifness said curtly, 'You may lower the sail and then unship the mast.'

Etzwane obeyed. Ifness meanwhile brought forth sections of transparent stuff, which he fitted into a wind-

27

screen around the cockpit. Etzwane watched silently. Ifness made a last survey around the horizon, then raised the cover from a cuddy at the stern. Etzwane noticed a black panel, a set of white, red, and blue knobs. Ifness made an adjustment. The boat lifted into the air, dripping water, then slanted into the sky. Ifness touched the knobs; the boat curved west, to fly high over the mud flats of Fenesq. Ifness said in a casual voice, 'A boat is the least conspicuous vehicle in which to travel; it arouses attention nowhere, not even in Caraz.'

'An ingenious artifice,' said Etzwane.

Ifness nodded indifferently. 'I lack accurate charts and we must navigate by rule of thumb. Shant maps are only guesses. We will follow the Caraz coast to the mouth of the Keba River, something over two thousand miles, so I should reckon. We can then follow the Keba south without risk of losing our way.'

Etzwane recalled the great map in the Jurdisdictionary. In the general area of Shillinsk he had noticed several rivers; the Panjorek, the Blue Zura, the Black Zura, the Usak, the Bobol. To attempt an overland short cut was to risk coming down upon the wrong river. He turned his attention down upon the flatlands of Canton Fenesq, tracing the canals and waterways which radiated from the four Fen towns. The cantonal border appeared in the distance: a line of black alyptus trees; beyond the bogs and moors of Canton Gitanesq extended into purple murk.

Ifness, crouching in the cabin, brewed a pot of tea. Sitting up under the forward screen, with wind hissing overhead, the two drank tea and ate nut cakes from one of the parcels Ifness had brought aboard. Etzwane thought that Ifness seemed relaxed and almost genial. To attempt a conversation was to risk rebuff, but now Ifness himself vouchsafed a remark. 'Well, we are off in good style and without interference from any source.'

28

'Did you expect any?'

'Not seriously. I doubt if the asutra maintain agents in Shant; the area can be of little real interest to them. Dasconetta might have placed an information with the Institute monitors, but I believe we were too quick for them.'

'Your relationship with Dasconetta seems awkward indeed.'

Ifness gave a nod of acquiescence. 'In an organisation such as the Institute, a Fellow achieves status by demonstrating judgment superior to that of his colleagues, particularly those who are reckoned astute. I have outmaneuvered Dasconetta so decisively that I begin to be worried: what is he up to? How can he thwart me without endorsing my viewpoint? It is a dangerous and complicated business.'

Etzwane frowned sidewise at Ifness, whose motivations and attitudes, as usual, he found incomprehensible. 'Dasconetta concerns me less than our work in Caraz, which perhaps is not so complicated but equally dangerous. Dasconetta, after all, is neither a ritual murderer nor a cannibal.'

'Such acts have not been proved against him, certainly,' said Ifness with a faint smile. 'Well well, perhaps you are right. I must turn my attention to Caraz. According to Kreposkin* the region of the middle Keba is relatively placid, especially north of the Urt Unna foothills. Shillinsk would seem to lie within this area. He mentions river pirates and a local tribe, the Sorukh. On the river islands live the degenerate Gorioni, whom even the slavers ignore.'

Below rose the Hurra Hills, and where the Cliffs of Day hurled back the swells of the Green Ocean, Shant came to an end. For an hour they flew over blank, empty water, then at the horizon appeared a vague dark mark: Caraz. Etzwane stirred himself. Ifness sat with his back to the

* Kreposkin, *The Kingdoms of Old Caraz.*

29

wind, cogitating over his notebook. Etzwane asked, 'How do you propose to conduct the investigation?'

Ifness closed his notebook, looked over the side and around the sky before replying. 'I have no specific plans. We are setting out to solve a mystery. First we must gather facts, then draw our conclusions. At the moment we know very little. The Roguskhoi seem to have been artificially developed as an antihuman weapon. The asutra who control them are a parasitical race, or, more sympathetically, might be said to live in symbiosis with their hosts. The Roguskhoi failed in Shant. Why do we find them in Caraz? To conquer territory? To guard a colony? Develop a resource? At the moment we can only wonder.

Caraz dominated the western horizon. Ifness swung the boat a point or two north and slanted gradually against the shoreline. Late in the afternoon mud flats appeared below, marked by tremulous wisps of surf. Ifness adjusted course and all night the boat drifted at half-speed along the coast, following trails of phosphorescent foam. Predawn murk discovered the hulk of Cape Comranus ahead, and Ifness pronounced Kreposkin's maps worthless. 'Essentially he informs us only that a Cape Comranus exists, that it is to be found somewhere along the Caraz shore. We must use these maps with skepticism.'

All morning the boat followed the coast, which after Cape Comranus had veered eastward, past a succession of crouching headlands separated by mud flats. At noon they flew over a peninsula of barren stone extending fifty miles north, unidentified on Kreposkin's maps; then the sea returned. Ifness allowed the boat to descend until they drifted only a thousand feet above the beach.

Halfway through the afternoon they crossed the mouth of a vast river: the Gever, draining the Geverman Basin, into which the whole of Shant might have been fitted. A

30

village of a hundred stone cabins occupied the lee of a hill; a dozen boats swung at anchor. This was the first habitation they had seen on Caraz.

Persuaded by Kreposkin's map, Ifness turned the boat westward and inland, across a densely forested wilderness extending north past the reach of vision: the Mirv Peninsula. A hundred miles fell astern. From an almost invisible clearing a wisp of smoke lazed up into the air. Etzwane glimpsed three timber cabins, and for ten minutes he looked astern, wondering what sort of men and women lived lost in this northern forest of Caraz ... Another hundred miles passed, and they came to the far shore of the Mirv Peninsula, in this case to validate Kreposkin's map. Once again they flew over water. Ahead the estuary of the Hietze River opened into the land: a cleft twenty miles wide studded with steep-sided islands, each a miniature fairyland of delightful trees and mossy meadows. One of the islands supported a gray stone castle; beside another a cargo vessel lay moored.

During the late afternoon, clouds rolled down from the north; plum-colored gloom fell across the landscape. Ifness slowed the boat and upon consideration descended to a sheltered crescent of beach. As lightning began to lash the sky, Etzwane and Ifness rigged a tarpaulin over the cockpit, then, with rain drumming on the fabric, they drank tea and ate a meal of bread and meat. Etzwane asked, 'Suppose the asutra attacked Durdane with spaceships and powerful weapons: what would the people of the Earth worlds do? Would they send warships to protect us?'

Ifness leaned back against the thwart. 'These are unpredictable matters. The Coordinating Board is a conservative group; the worlds are absorbed in their own affairs. The Pan-Humanic League is no longer influential, if ever it was. Durdane is far away and forgotten; the

31

Shciafarilla intervenes. The Coordination might make a representation, depending upon a report from the Historical Institute, which enjoys prestige. Dasconetta, for purposes to which I have alluded, seeks to minimise the situation. He will not acknowledge that the asutra are the first technologically competent nonhuman creatures we have encountered, a highly important occasion.'

'Curious! The facts speak for themselves.'

'True. But there is more to it, as you might guess. Dasconetta and his clique advocate caution and further research; in due course they propose to issue the announcement under their own aegis; I will never be mentioned. This scheme must be thwarted.'

Etzwane, engaged in rueful reflections regarding the quality of Ifness' concern, went to look out into the night. The rain had dwindled to a few dark drops; the lightning flickered far to the east, back over the Mirv. Etzwane listened, but could hear no sound whatever. Ifness also stepped out to look at the night.

'We might proceed, but I am uncertain in regard to the Keba and the intervening rivers. Kreposkin is exasperating in that he can neither be totally scorned nor totally trusted. Best that we wait for the light.' He stood peering through the dark. 'According to Kreposkin, yonder along the beach is the site of Suserane, a town built by the Shelm Fyrids some six thousand years ago . . . Caraz, then as now, was savage and vast. No matter how many enemies fell in battle, more always came. One or another warrior tribe laid Suserane waste; now there is nothing left: only the influences Kreposkin calls *esmeric*.'

'I do not know that word.'

'It derives from a dialect of old Caraz and means the association or atmosphere clinging to a place: the unseen ghosts, the dissipated sounds, the suffused glory, music,

32

tragedy, exultation, grief, and terror, which according to Kreposkin never dissipates.'

Etzwane looked through the dark towards the site of the old city; if *esmeric* were present, it worked but weakly through the dark. Etzwane returned to the boat and tried to sleep on the narrow starboard berth.

The morning sky was clear. The blue sun, Etta, swung up near the horizon, producing a false blue dawn, then pink Sasetta slanted sidewise into the sky, then white Zael, and again blue Etta. After a breakfast of tea and dried fruit, and a cursory glance at the site of old Suserane, Ifness took the boat into the air. Ahead, dull as lead in the light from the east, a great river mouth gaped into the mass of Caraz. Ifness named the river the Usak. At noon they passed the Bobol, and at midafternoon reached the mouth of the Keba, which Ifness identified by the chalk cliffs along the western shore and the trading post Erbol, five miles inland.

Ifness swung south over the watercourse, here forty miles wide with three sun trails across the brimming surface. The river seemed to curve somewhat to the right, then at the horizon's verge it swept majestically back to the left. Three barges, miniscule from the height, floated on the face of the river, two inching upstream to the force of billowing square sails, another drifting downstream with the current.

'The charts are of small benefit henceforth,' said Ifness. 'Kreposkin mentions no settlements along the middle Keba, although he refers to the Sorukh race, a warlike folk who never turn their backs in battle.'

Etzwane studied Kreposkin's rude maps. 'Two thousand miles south along the river, into the Burnoun district: that would take us about here, to the Plain of Blue Flowers.'

Ifness was not interested in Etzwane's opinions. 'The maps are only approximations,' he said crisply. 'We will fly a certain distance, then undertake a local investigation.' He closed the book and turning away became absorbed in his own thoughts.

Etzwane smiled a trifle grimly. He had become accustomed to Ifness' mannerisms and no longer allowed himself to become wrathful. He went forward and looked out over the tremendous purple forests, the pale-blue distances, the bogs and swamps of mottled green, and, dominating the landscape, the flood of the river Keba. Here was where he had come, to wild Caraz, because he feared staleness and insipidity. What of Ifness? What had urged the fastidious Ifness to such vicissitudes? Etzwane started to ask the question, then he held his tongue; Ifness would give a mordant answer, with Etzwane none the better informed.

Etzwane turned and looked south, into Caraz, where so many mysteries awaited illumination.

The boat flew all night, holding its course by the reflection of the blazing Schiafarilla upon the river. At noon Ifness lowered the boat towards the river, which here ran irregularly about ten miles wide, swelling, narrowing, and encompassing a myriad of wooded islands.

'Be on the lookout for habitation, or even better, a riverboat,' Ifness told Etzwane. 'We now require local information.'

'How will you understand? The folk of Caraz speak an outlandish yammer.'

'Nonetheless, we will manage, or so I believe,' said Ifness in his most didactic drawl. 'The Burnoun and the Keba Basin are linguistically uniform. The folk use a dialect derived from the language of Shant.'

34

Etzwane looked sidewise in disbelief. 'How can this be? Shant is far distant.'

'The circumstance derives from the Third Palasedran War. Cantons Maseach, Gorgach, and Parthe collaborated with the Eagle Dukes, and many folk, dreading Pandamon vengeance, fled Shant. They made their way up the Keba and imposed their language on the Sorukhs, who ultimately enslaved them. The history of Caraz is far from cheerful.' Ifness leaned over the gunwales and pointed to a straggle of huts on the riverbank, hardly to be seen behind a covert of tall reeds. 'A village, where we can gain information, even if only negative.' He reflected. 'We will employ a harmless hoax to facilitate the matter. These people are indomitably superstitious and will enjoy a demonstration of their beliefs.' He adjusted a dial; the boat slowed and hung motionless in mid-air. 'Let us now ship the mast and raise the sail, then make a change or two in our costume.'

Down from the sky floated the boat, sail billowing, with Etzwane at the tiller ostensibly steering. Both he and Ifness wore white turbans and carried themselves in a portentous manner. The boat settled upon the flat before the huts, still puddled from the rainstorm of two days before. A half-dozen men stood stock-still; as many slatternly women peered from the doorways; naked children crawling in the mud froze in place or backed whimpering away to shelter. Stepping from the boat, Ifness sprinkled a handful of blue and green glass gems upon the ground. He pointed to a portly elder who stood dumbfounded at hand. 'Approach, if you please,' spoke Ifness in a coarse dialect barely intelligible to Etzwane. 'We are benevolent wizards and intend you no harm; we want information in regard to our enemies.'

The old man's chin trembled, agitating his dirty whiskers; he clutched his ragged homespun tunic about his belly and essayed a few steps forward. 'What information do you require? We are only clamdiggers, no more; we know nothing beyond the flow of the river.'

'Just so,' intoned Ifness. 'Still, you are witness to comings and goings, and I notice a shed yonder for the storage of trade goods.'

'Yes, we have modest dealings in clam cake, clam wine, and crushed clamshell of good quality. But for knowledge of loot or precious things you must ask elsewhere. Even the slavers pass us by.'

'We seek news of a tribe of invading warriors: large, red-skinned demons who slaughter men and copulate with the women to notorious degree. These are the Roguskhoi. Have you had news regarding these folk?'

'They have not troubled us, the Sacred Eel be thanked. The traders tell us of fighting and an epic battle, but in all my life I have heard nothing else, and no one has used the name "Roguskhoi".'

'Where then was the fighting?'

The clamdigger pointed south. 'The Sorukh regions are still far: it is ten days' sail to the Plain of Blue Flowers, though your magic boat will speed you there in half the time . . . Are you permitted to teach the lore which propels your craft? It would be a great convenience for me.'

'Such a question best had not be asked,' said Ifness. 'We now proceed to the Plain of Blue Flowers.'

'May the Eel expedite your passage.'

Ifness stepped back into the boat, gave Etzwane a formal signal. Etzwane worked the rudder and adjusted the sheets, while Ifness touched his controls. The boat rose, the sails caught the wind; the boat sailed off across the river. The men ran down to the water's edge to stare after them, followed by the children and women from the huts. Ifness chuckled. 'We have made memorable at least one

36

day of their lives, and fractured a dozen rules of the Institute.'

'Ten days' journey,' mused Etzwane. 'The barges move two or three miles an hour: fifty miles a day, more or less. Ten days' journey would be five hundred miles.'

'By just such a degree are Kreposkin's charts inaccurate.' Standing up in the cockpit Ifness raised his arm in a final flourish of benign farewell to the gaping folk of the village. A grove of waterwood trees hid them from sight. Ifness spoke over his shoulder to Etzwane: 'Lower the sail; unship the mast.'

Etzwane silently obeyed the command, reflecting that Ifness seemed to enjoy the role of wandering magician. The boat moved south up the river. Silver-trunked almacks lined the bank, their silver-purple fronds glinting green to the motion of the breeze. To right and left flatlands disappeared into the dove-gray haze of distance, and always the great Keba reached out ahead.

Afternoon waned; and the banks remained desolate of life, to Ifness' muttered disgust. The sun sank; twilight fell across the landscape. Ifness stood precariously on the foredeck, peering down into the dark. At last an array of flickering red sparks appeared on the riverbank. Ifness swung the boat around and down; the sparks became a dozen leaping campfires, arrayed in a rough circle, twenty or thirty yards in diameter.

'Ship the mast,' said Ifness. 'Hoist the sail.'

Etzwane thoughtfully appraised the fires and the folk who worked within the circle of light. Beyond he glimpsed large carts with crooked eight-foot wheels and leather hoods; they had come upon a band of nomads, of a temperament presumably more edgy and truculent than the placid clamdiggers. Etzwane looked dubiously towards Ifness, who stood like a statue. Very well, thought Etzwane, he would indulge Ifness in his mad jokes, even

37

at the risk of flowing blood. He set up the mast, lifted the great square sail, then adjusting his turban, went back to the tiller.

The boat settled into the circle of firelight. Ifness called down, 'Beware below; move aside.'

The tribesmen looked up; jumping and cursing they sprang back. An old man tripped and spilled a tub of water upon a group of women, who screamed in fury.

The boat landed; Ifness with a stern mien held up his hand. 'Quiet! We are only two wizards of the night. Have you never seen magic before? Where is the chief of the clan?'

No one spoke. The men, in loose white shirts, baggy black breeches and black boots, stood back, uncertain whether to flee or attack. The women, in loose patterned gowns, wailed and showed the whites of their eyes.

'Who is the chief?' bawled Ifness. 'Can he not hear? Can he not walk forward?'

A hulking, black-browed man with black mustaches came slowly forward. 'I am Rastipol, chief of the Ripchiks. What do you want of me?'

'Why are you here and not fighting the Roguskhoi?'

' "Roguskhoi"?' Rastipol blinked. 'Who are they? We fight no one at this moment.'

'The Roguskhoi are red demon-warriors. They are only half human, though they show enthusiasm for human women.'

'I have heard of them. They fight the Sorukh; it is none of our affair. We are not Sorukh; we are out of the Melch race.'

'And if they destroy the Sorukh, what next?'

Rastipol scratched his chin. 'I have not considered the matter.'

'Exactly where has the fighting occurred?'

38

'Somewhere to the south, out on the Plain of Blue Flowers, or so I suppose.'

'How far is this?'

'Four days to the south is Shillinsk Town, at the edge of the Plain. Can you not learn this by magic?'

Ifness raised a finger towards Etzwane. 'Transform Rastipol into a sick ahulph.'

'No, no,' cried Rastipol. 'You have misjudged me. I meant no harm.'

Ifness gave a distant nod. 'Guard your tongue; you allow it a dangerous freedom.' He signaled Etzwane. 'Sail on.'

Etzwane worked the tiller and waved his hand towards the sail, while Ifness moved his dials. The boat lifted into the night sky, showing its keel to the firelight. The Rip-chiks watched silently from below.

During the night the boat drifted slowly south. Etzwane slept on one of the narrow berths; he was not aware whether or not Ifness did the same. In the morning, cold and cramped, he went out into the cockpit to find Ifness looking out over the gunwale. A mist concealed the land below, the boat floated alone between gray mist and lavender sky.

For an hour the two sat in dour silence, drinking tea. At last the three suns rolled high and the mist began to dissipate, swirling and drifting, revealing irregular districts of land and river. Below them, the Keba made a mighty swing to the west, where it was joined from the east by a tributary, the Shill. On the west bank three docks thrust out into the Keba, marking a settlement of fifty or sixty huts and a half-dozen larger structures. If-ness exclaimed in satisfaction. 'Shillinsk at last! It exists in spite of Kreposkin!' He lowered the boat to the face of the water. Etzwane stepped the mast and hoisted the sail;

the boat proceeded across the water to the docks. Ifness
brought the boat up the water-steps; Etzwane jumped
ashore with a line; Ifness followed more deliberately. Etzwane payed out the line; the boat drifted downstream
and took a place among a dozen fishing smacks, not
notably different from itself. Ifness and Etzwane turned
towards Shillinsk Town.

Chapter 4

The cabins and sheds of Shillinsk were built from gray
stone quarried from a near-by ledge and rough-laid between balks of driftwood. Directly behind the docks stood
the Shillinsk Inn, a relatively imposing structure of three
stories. Lavender suns' light glared on gray stone and
black timber; the shadows, by some ocular accommodation, appeared green, the color of old water in a barrel.

Shillinsk Town seemed quiet, only half alive. No sound
could be heard except the lap of waves along the shore.
Two women walked slowly along the riverside trail; they
wore baggy black breeches, blouses of dark purple, head-
kerchiefs of rich rust-orange. Three barges lay alongside
the docks, one empty and two partially laden. Several
barge-tenders were bound for the tavern; Ifness and Etzwane followed a few paces to the rear.

The barge-tenders pushed through the driftwood doors,
with Ifness and Etzwane behind them, into a common
room considerably more comfortable than the rude exterior suggested. A fire of sea-coal blazed in a huge fire-
place; the walls had been plastered, whitewashed, and
decorated with festoons and rosettes of carved wood. A
group of barge-tenders sat before the fire eating a stew of
fish and reed root. To the side, half in the shadows, two
men of the district sat hunched over their wooden mugs.
Firelight molded their slab-sided faces; they spoke little

41

and peered distrustfully sidewise, watching the barge-tenders. One displayed a black mustache bushy as a dust brush, the other wore both a chin beard and a two-inch copper nose ring. With fascination Etzwane saw him knock up the ring with the rim of his mug and drink. They wore the Sorukh costume: black breeches, loose shirts embroidered with fetish signs, and from their waists hung scimitars of the white metal *ghisim*, an alloy of silver, platinum, tin, and copper, forged and hardened by a secret process.

Ifness and Etzwane settled at a table near the fire. The innkeeper, a man bald and flat-faced, with a deformed leg and a hard stare, hobbled over to learn their wants. Ifness spoke for lodging and the best meal available. The innkeeper announced that he could serve clam soup, herbs, and sweet beetles; grilled meat with water-greens, bread, blue-flower marmalade, and vervain tea: a meal which Ifness had not expected and which he pronounced satisfactory.

'I must discuss my recompense,' said the innkeeper. 'What do you have to trade?'

Ifness brought forth one of his glass jewels. 'This.'

The innkeeper drew back and showed the palm of his hand in disdain. 'What do you take me for? This is no more than coarse glass, a bauble for children.'

'Indeed then,' said Ifness. 'What is its color?'

'It is the color of old grass, verging towards river water.'

'Look.' Ifness closed the gem in his hand, then opened it. 'What color now?'

'A clear crimson!'

'And now?' Ifness exposed the gem to the warmth of the fire and it glinted green as an emerald. 'Now – take it into the dark and tell me what you see.'

The innkeeper went off to a closet, and presently returned. 'It shines blue and sends off rays of several colors.'

'The object is a starstone,' said Ifness. 'Such are occasionally taken from the center of meteorites. It is in fact too valuable to exchange for mere food and lodging, but we have nothing else.'

'It will suffice, or so I suppose,' stated the landlord in a pompous voice. 'How long does your barge remain at Shillinsk?'

'Several days, until we conclude our business. We deal in exotic goods, and at this moment we required the neck bones of dead Roguskhoi, which have a medicinal efficacy.'

' "Roguskhoi"? What are they?'

'You call them differently. I refer to the red, half-human warriors which have pillaged the Plain of Blue Flowers.'

'Ah! We call them the "Red Devils". They are of value after all?'

'I make no such assertions; I merely traffic in bones. Who would be the local dealer in such merchandise?'

The innkeeper uttered a coarse bark of laughter, which he quickly stifled, and turned a look towards the two Sorukh, who had been attending the conversation.

'In these parts,' said the inkeeper, 'bones are so common as to be worthless, and a man's life is at little greater price. Observe this leg, which my mother maimed to protect me from the slave-takers. They were then the Esche from the Murd Mountains across the Shill. Now the Esche are gone and Hulkas have come, and all is as before, or worse. Never turn your back to a Hulka, or you'll find a chain around your neck. Four from Shillinsk have been taken during this last year. Hulka or Red Devil – which is worse? Take your choice.'

The mustached Sorukh suddenly joined the talk. 'The Red Devils are extinct, except for their bones, which as you know belong to us.'

43

'Precisely the case,' declared the second Sorukh, the ring swinging against his lip as he spoke. 'We know the therapeutic effect of Red Devil bones, and we intend to realise a fair profit.'

'All very well,' said Ifness, 'but why do you assert their extinction?'

'The matter is common knowledge across the Plain.'

'And who accomplished this act?'

The Sorukh tugged at his beard. 'The Hulkas perhaps, or a band from over the Kuzi Kaza. It seems that magic was worked on both sides.'

'The Hulkas lack magic,' remarked the innkeeper. 'They are ordinary slavers. The tribes beyond the Kuzi Kaza are ferocious, but I have never heard magic ascribed to them.'

The ring-nosed Sorukh made a sudden harsh gesture. 'This is not germane.' He turned to Ifness. 'Do you intend to buy our bones, or shall we take them elsewhere?'

'I naturally want to inspect them,' said Ifness. 'Let us go look, then we can talk more to the point.'

The Sorukhs sat back in shock. 'Here is absurdity taken to the point of offense. Do you think we carry merchandise on our backs like Tchark women? We are proud folk and resent an affront!'

'I intended no offense,' said Ifness. 'I merely expressed a desire to see the merchandise. Where is it stored?'

'Let us make a short matter of the situation,' said the Sorukh with the mustache. 'The bones remain at the battlefield, or so I suppose. We will sell our interest for a modest trade, and then you can do what you wish with the bones.'

Ifness thought a moment. 'This procedure is scarcely to my advantage. What if the bones are of poor quality? Or impossible to transport? Either bring the bones here or conduct us to the bones, so that I may judge their value.'

44

The Sorukhs became glum. Turning aside they muttered together. Ifness and Etzwane set upon the food served by the innkeeper. Etzwane, glancing towards the Sorukhs, said, 'They are only planning how best to murder us and take our wealth.'

Ifness nodded. 'They are also puzzled why we are not more concerned; they fear an unexpected trick. Still, they will never reject the bait.'

The Sorukhs reached a decision and watched through heavy-lidded eyes until Etzwane and Ifness had finished their meal, whereupon the Sorukhs moved to the adjoining table, bringing with them an organic waft. Ifness shifted position and regarded the two with his head thrown back. The Sorukh with the mustache essayed a friendly smile. 'Matters can be arranged to our mutual benefit. You are prepared to inspect the bones and pay for them on the spot?'

'Definitely not,' said Ifness. 'I will examine the bones and inform you if they are worth the transport here to Shillinsk.'

The Sorukh's smile lingered a second or two, then vanished. Ifness went on. 'Can you provide transportation? A comfortable cart drawn by pacers?'

The Sorukh with the ring in his nose gave a snort of disdain. 'That is not possible,' said the Sorukh with the mustache. 'The Kuzi Kaza would break up the cart.'

'Very well then; we will require riding pacers.'

The Sorukhs drew back. They muttered together, the ring-nosed man surly and unwilling, the man with the mustache first urgent, then persuasive, then compelling – and finally he had his way. They returned to Ifness and Etzwane. 'When will you be ready to depart?' asked the mustached man.

'Tomorrow morning, as early as feasible.'

'At sunrise we will be ready. But a further important

45

matter: you must pay a rent for the pacers.'

'Ridiculous on the face of it!' scoffed Ifness. 'I am not even sure that the bones exist! And you expect me to pay out rent on what might be a wild-goose chase? By no means; I was not born yesterday.'

The ring-nosed Sorukh started to make an angry argument, but the mustached man held up his hand. 'You will see the bones, and the pacer rent will be absorbed in the ultimate transaction.'

'That is more to the point,' said Ifness. 'Upon our return to Shillinsk we will arrange an inclusive price.'

'At sunrise we depart; be ready.' The two Sorukhs left the inn; Ifness sipped hot infusion from a wooden bowl.

Etzwane demanded: 'You plan to ride the plain on a pacer? Why not fly the boat?'

Ifness raised his eyebrows. 'Is the matter not self-evident? A boat in the middle of a dry plain is a conspicuous object. We would have no freedom of action; we could never leave the boat.'

'If we leave the boat at Shillinsk, we will never see it again,' grumbled Etzwane. 'These people are thieves, one and all.'

'I will make certain arrangements.' Ifness considered a moment, then crossed the room and spoke with the innkeeper. He returned and resumed his seat at the table. 'The innkeeper declares that we might leave ten treasure chests aboard our boat without fear of molestation. He accepts full responsibility, and the risk is thereby reduced.' Ifness mused a moment or two upon the flames of the fire. 'Nevertheless, I will arrange a warning device to discourage those pilferers who might escape his vigilance.'

Etzwane, who had no taste for an arduous ride across the Plain of Blue Flowers in company with the Sorukhs, said sourly, 'Instead of a flying boat, you should have contrived a flying cart, or a pair of flying pacers.'

'Your concepts have merit,' said Ifness benignly.

For the repose of its patrons the inn provided boxes filled with straw in a row of small chambers on the second floor. Etzwane's cubicle commanded a view of the harbor. The straw, however, was not fresh; during the night it rustled with obscure activity, and the previous occupant had urinated in a corner of the room. At midnight Etzwane, aroused by a sound, went to look out the window. He observed furtive motion along the dock, near the area where the boat was moored. The starlight was too dim for precise vision, but Etzwane noticed a hobbling irregularity in the gait of the skulker. The man stepped into a dinghy and rowed quietly out to the boat. He shipped his oars, made fast the dinghy, and clambered aboard the boat, to be instantly surrounded by tongues of blue flame, while sparks jumped from his hair to the rigging. The man danced across the deck and more by accident than design plunged overboard. A few moments later he feebly hauled himself into his dinghy and rowed back to the dock.

At sunrise Etzwane arose from his straw and went to the first-floor washroom, where he found Ifness. Etzwane reported the events of the night, regarding which Ifness showed no great surprise. 'I will see to the matter.'

For breakfast the innkeeper served only tea and bread. His limp was more pronounced than ever and he glowered spitefully towards Ifness as he banged the food down upon the table.

Ifness said sternly, 'This is spartan fare; are you so exhausted from your foray that you cannot provide a suitable breakfast?'

The innkeeper attempted a blustering retort, but Ifness cut him short. 'Do you know why you are here now, instead of dancing to the music of blue sparks? Because I

47

require a satisfactory breakfast. Need I say more?'

'I have heard enough,' muttered the innkeeper. He hobbled back into the kitchen, and presently brought forth a cauldron of stewed fish, a tray of oatcake and eel-jelly. 'Will this appease your appetite? If not, I can furnish some good boiled ermink and a sack of cheese.'

'We have enough,' said Ifness. 'Remember, if on my return I find so much as a splinter of the boat disarranged, you shall dance again to the blue music.'

'You misinterpret my zeal,' declared the innkeeper. 'I rowed out to the boat because I thought I heard a suspicious noise.'

'The matter is at an end,' said Ifness indifferently, 'so long as now we understand each other.'

The two Sorukhs looked into the inn. 'Are you ready to depart? The pacers are waiting.'

Etzwane and Ifness went out into the cool morning. Four pacers pulled nervously at their curbs, hooking and slashing with back-curved horns. Etzwane considered them of good stock, long-limbed and deep-chested. They were equipped with nomad steppe-saddles of chumpa leather, with pouches for food and a rack on which a tent, blanket, and night boots might be lashed. The Sorukhs refused to provide these articles for Ifness and Etzwane. Threats and persuasion had no effect, and Ifness was forced to part with another of his multicolored jewels before the requisite food and equipment were supplied.

Before departure Ifness required the identities of the two Sorukhs. Both were of the Bellbird fetish in the Varsk clan; the mustached man was Gulshe; he of the ringed nose was Srenka. Ifness wrote the names in blue ink upon a strip of parchment. He added a set of marks in crimson and yellow, while the Sorukhs looked on uneasily. 'Why do you do this?' challenged Srenka.

'I take ordinary precautions,' said Ifness. 'I have left

48

my jewels in a secret place and now carry no valuables; search me if you care to do so. I have worked a curse upon your names, which I will lift in good time. Your plans to murder and rob us are unwise and had best be dismissed.'

Gulshe and Srenka scowled at what was obviously an unpleasant turn of events. 'Shall we be on our way?' suggested Ifness.

The four mounted and set off across the Plain of Blue Flowers.

The Keba, with its fringe of almacks, receded and at last was lost to sight. To all sides the plain rolled in great sweeps and swells out into the sunny lavender haze. Purple moss padded the soil; shrubs held aloft flowers which colored the plain a soft sea-blue in all directions. To the south appeared an almost imperceptible shadow of mountains.

All day the four men rode, and at nightfall made camp in a shallow swale beside a trickle of dank water. They sat around the fire in an atmosphere of guarded cordiality. It developed that Gulshe himself had skirmished with a band of the Roguskhoi only two months previously. 'They came down out of the Orgai Mountains, not far from Shagfe, where the Hulka maintain a slave depot. The Red Devils had raided the slave depot twice before, killing men and carrying off the women, and Hozman Sorethroat, the agent, sought to protect his property. He offered a half-pound of iron for each Red Devil hand we brought back. I and two dozen others went forth to gain wealth, but we achieved nothing. The Devils ignore arrows, and each is worth ten men in a close fight, and so we returned to Shagfe without trophies. I rode east to Shillinsk for the Varsk conclave, and saw nothing of the great battle in which the Red Devils were destroyed.'

Ifness asked in a voice of mild interest: 'Am I to understand that the Hulka defeated the Red Devils? How is this possible, if each Devil is worth ten men?'

Gulsh spat into the flames but made no reply. Srenka leaned forward to push a stick into the coals, the ring in his nose flickering with orange reflections. 'It is said that magic weapons were used.'

'By the Hulka? Where would they get magic weapons?'

'The warriors who destroyed the Red Devils were not Hulka.'

'Indeed. Who were they then?'

'I know nothing of the matter; I was at Shillinsk.'

Ifness pursued the subject no further. Etzwane rose to his feet, and climbing to the top of the rise, looked around the horizon. He saw only darkness. He listened, but could hear no sound. The night was fine; there seemed no threat from chumpa or bad ahulphs. The two Sorukhs were another matter. The same thought had occurred to Ifness, who now went to kneel before the fire. He blew up a blaze, then holding his hands to either side, made the flames jump back and forth while the Sorukhs stared in amazement. 'What are you doing?' asked Gulshe in awe.

'A trifle of magic, for my protection. I laid a command upon the fire spirit to enter the liver of all who wish me harm and there abide.'

Srenka pulled at his nose ring. 'Are you a true magician?'

Ifness laughed. 'Do you doubt it? Hold out your hand.'

Srenka cautiously extended his arm. Ifness pointed his finger and a crackling blue spark leapt to Srenka's hand. Srenka emitted a ridiculous falsetto squawk of astonishment and jerked back speechless. Gulshe sprang erect and hurriedly retreated from the fire.

'That is nothing,' said Ifness. 'Only a trifle. You are still alive, are you not? So then, we will sleep securely, all of us, knowing that magic guards us from harm.'

Etzwane spread his blanket and bedded himself down.

50

After a mutter or two Gulshe and Srenka arranged their own gear somewhat off to the side, near the tethered pacers. Ifness was more deliberate and sat for half an hour staring into the dying fire. At last he took himself to his own bed. For half an hour Etzwane watched the glitter of Gulshe's and Srenka's eyes from the shadow of their hoods; then he dozed and slept.

The second day was like the first. In the middle afternoon of the third day the foothills of the Kuzi Kaza came down to meet the plain. Gulshe and Srenka took counsel and established landmarks for themselves. By nightfall they had reached a desolate upland region of limestone cliffs and pinnacles. Camp was made beside a great sinkhole of dark mirror-smooth water. 'We are now in the Hulka land,' Gulshe told Ifness. 'If we are set upon, our best safety is flight, in four different directions – unless by magic you are able to insure our defense.'

'We will act as circumstances direct,' said Ifness. 'Where are the Red Devil bones?'

'Not far distant: beyond the ridge. Can you not sense the presence of so much death?'

Ifness responded in a measured voice: 'An intellect in full control of itself unfortunately must sacrifice that receptivity which distinguishes the primitive mentality. This is an evolutionary step I have, on the whole, been happy to make.'

Srenka tugged at his nose ring, uncertain whether or not Ifness had spoken in disparagement. He looked at Gulshe; they gave each other shrugs of perplexity, then went to their beds, where they muttered together for half an hour. Srenka seemed to be urging some action which Gulshe resisted; Srenka grumbled raucously; Gulshe made an ameliorative statement and both fell silent.

Etzwane sought his own blankets, where he lay wakeful, uneasy for reasons beyond his understanding. 'Perhaps,' he told himself, 'my mentality is primitive and credulous.'

During the night he awoke often to lie listening, and once heard the bickering of distant ahulphs. Another time a far mellifluous hooting reverberated through the stone defiles, to send eerie shudders along Etzwane's skin; it was a sound he could not identify. He had no awareness of returning to sleep, but when he awoke next, the sky glowed lavender to the approach of the three suns.

After a glum breakfast of dried fruit and tea, the four set forth again, passing through a series of limestone defiles, then out upon a high meadow. They rode through a forest of gallows trees, then up a barren valley. A five hundred foot crag loomed above them, with the parapets of a ruined castle at the crest. Gulshe and Srenka halted to consider the trail ahead. 'Is the castle inhabited?'

'Who knows?' growled Gulshe. 'Enough such places exist, with rogues and murderers waiting to roll down a rock, that the traveler must take care.'

Srenka pointed a crooked finger. 'Lyre birds fly above the stones; the way may be considered safe.'

'How far now to the battlefield?' asked Ifness.

'An hour's ride, around the root of yonder mountain . . . Come now; at a fast pace. Lyre birds or not, I mistrust these old bandit dens.'

The four rode forward at a smart gait, but the ruined castle offered no menace and the lyre birds soared as before.

They rode down from the pass. Gulshe pointed towards the great mountain, hunching like a sullen beast over the plain below. 'Thence the Red Devils came, on their way to Shagfe – there, to the north, you can barely see the Shagfe stockade. Early in the morning the men attacked, from positions they had taken during the night, and the

Red Devils were encircled. The battle lasted two hours, and all the Red Devils, with their captive women and imps, were dead; and the band which had destroyed them marched south and was seen no more: a great mystery . . . There! The place where the Red Devils camped. The battle raged in this vicinity. Ah! Smell the carrion!'

'What of the bones?' enquired Srenka with a sly grin. 'Do they meet your expectations?'

Ifness rode forward, across the scene of carnage. Roguskhoi corpses lay everywhere, in a clutter of twisted limbs and contorted postures. Decomposition was far advanced; ahulphs had toyed with the idea of devouring the black flesh and some had died from the experiment; these lay curled in furry balls down the slope.

Ifness rode in a great circle, gazing intently down at the corpses, sometimes halting to study one or another of the stinking red shapes at length. Etzwane halted his pacer somewhat to the side, where he could watch the Sorukhs. Ifness rode up and halted beside Etzwane. 'What do you make of the situation?'

'Like yourself, I am puzzled,' said Etzwane.

Ifness looked sidewise, eyebrows disapprovingly high. 'Why then am I puzzled?'

'Because of the wounds, which are not those of swords or cudgels.'

'Hmmf. What else have you noticed?'

Etzwane pointed. 'He with chain bib yonder appears to be a chieftain. He has suffered damage to his chest. The asutra he carried was destroyed. I noticed another dead chieftain across the field with a similar wound. The men who killed the Roguskhoi, like ourselves, knew of the asutra.'

Ifness gave a curt nod of the head. 'So it would seem.'

The Sorukh approached, wearing artificial smiles. 'The

'bones then,' Srenka put forward, 'what of all these fine bones?'

'They are obviously not in saleable condition,' said Ifness. 'I can make no firm offer until you clean and dry them, make up standard bales, and convey them to the Shillinsk dock.'

Gulshe gave his flowing mustache a sad tug; Srenka was less controlled. 'I feared such duplicity!' he cried. 'We have no guarantee of profit; we have invested time and property to no avail, and I for one will not let the matter rest on these terms.'

Ifness said coldly, 'Upon our return to Shillinsk I will compensate you and your comrade generously; as you point out, you have done your best. However, I cannot undertake to buy a field full of corpses in order to gratify your avarice. You must find another customer.'

Srenka twisted his face into a ferocious grimace, his lower canine tusks gripping his nose ring. Gulshe warned him with a gesture. 'The protests are reasonable. Our friend understandably cannot burden himself with merchandise in its present condition. I am certain that a mutually profitable arrangement is possible. In a year the bones will be well weathered and in prime condition, or we might rent slaves to boil and strip the carcasses. In the meantime let us leave this foul place; I feel a presentiment.'

'To Shagfe then,' growled Srenka. 'At Shagfe I plan to drink a crock of Baba's cellar brew.'

'A moment,' said Ifness, scrutinising the hillside. 'I am interested in the band which destroyed the Red Devils. Where did they go after the victory?'

'Back the way they had come,' sneered Srenka. 'Where else?'

'They did not visit Shagfe?'

'At Shagfe you can make your own enquiries.'

54

Etzwane said, 'Ahulphs might track them.'

'They are a month gone and far away,' said Ifness. 'The effort might well be tedious.'

'In Shagfe we will undoubtedly hear news,' suggested Gulshe.

'To Shagfe then,' said Srenka. 'I thirst for old Baba's cellar brew.'

Ifness turned a reflective glance towards Shagfe. Gulshe and Srenka already were riding down the long slope. They halted and looked back. 'Come along then; the day will not last forever; yonder is Shagfe!'

'Very well,' said Ifness. 'We will visit Shagfe.'

Shagfe, a dreary and unprepossessing settlement, baked in the lavender sunlight. Rude mud huts straggled along a wind-scoured street; behind was a scatter of leather tents. A rambling flat-roofed structure of mud and wattle dominated the town: the inn and grog shop. A clattering windmill near by drew water into a tank, which overflowed into a trough; here sat a band of ahulphs who had come to drink. They had brought rock crystals and already had bartered for rags of yellow cloth, which they wore rakishly tied to their hearing knobs.

Riding into Shagfe the four passed the slave pens: a complex of three sheds and three fenced yards in which a score of men, as many women, and several dozen blankeyed children were confined.

Ifness, drawing his pacer to a halt, turned to Gulshe. 'Who are these captives, local persons?'

Gulshe examined the group without interest. 'They appear to be strangers, probably excess folk sold by the hetman of their clan. They might be persons taken in raids beyond the mountains. Or they might be persons seized and sold by private enterprises.' Gulshe gave a curious choked chuckle. 'In short, they are anyone unable to prevent otherwise. Here there is no one to say us nay, and each man must see to his own welfare.'

'Such an existence is unpleasant,' said Etzwane in disgust.

Gulshe looked at him without comprehension and turned to Ifness as if questioning Etzwane's sanity; Ifness smiled grimly. 'Who buys the slaves?'

Gulshe shrugged. 'Hozman Sore-throat takes them all, and pays a good weight of metal in the bargain.'

'You are very knowledgeable in this regard,' said Etzwane in a dour voice.

Srenka said, 'And what of that? Do you begrudge us a livelihood? Perhaps the time has come for an understanding.'

'Yes,' said Gulshe, 'the time has come.' He brought forth a heavy-bladed knife of polished black glass. 'Magic is not proof against my knife, and I can split either of you as if you were melons. Dismount from the pacers and stand facing the pens.'

Ifness asked in a mild voice, 'Am I to understand that you intend us an inconvenience?'

'We are men of trade,' Srenka declared in a boisterous voice. 'We live for profit. If we cannot sell bones, we will sell slaves, and for this reason we have brought you to Shagfe. I likewise am adept with the throwing-knife. Dismount!'

'It is humiliating to be captured directly in front of the slave pens,' said Ifness. 'You show no regard for our sensibilities, and if for this reason alone, we refuse to gratify your wishes.'

Srenka guffawed. Gulshe allowed a yellow line of teeth to show below his mustache. 'Dismount; to the ground, and promptly!'

Etzwane spoke softly, 'Have you forgotten the curse imposed at Shillinsk?'

56

'Hundreds of curses already ride our backs; what harm is another?' Gulshe jerked his knife. 'Dismount.'

Ifness shrugged. 'Well, then, if we must, we must . . . Destiny plays strange tricks.' Alighting wearily, he placed his hand on the pacer's haunch. The pacer roared in pain and sprang forward, into Gulshe's pacer, toppling the beast to the ground. Srenka flung his knife at Etzwane, who had dropped to the ground; the knife cut the air a foot over his shoulder. Ifness reached up, grasped Srenka's nose-ring. Srenka emitted a quivering hiss, which would have been a scream had he been able to articulate. 'Hold him by the ring,' Ifness instructed Etzwane. 'Keep him in a state of compliance.' Ifness went to where Gulshe, scrambling, cursing, clawing at the ground, attempted to gain his feet. Ifness laid a comradely hand on Gulshe's shoulder; Gulshe gave a spasmodic jerk and fell once more to the ground. 'I fear I must take your knife,' said Ifness. 'You will not need it again.'

Etzwane and Ifness continued towards the mud-and-wattle inn, leading the riderless beasts. Ifness said, 'Six ounces of silver for two able individuals; it seems no great sum. Perhaps we were gulled. But no matter, in any event. Gulshe and Srenka will profit greatly by learning another facet of the slavery trade . . . I could almost wish that . . . but no! It is uncharitable to think of my colleague Dasconetta in this connection. Almost I regret the parting of ways with Gulshe and Srenka. They were picturesque companions.'

Etzwane looked back over his shoulder to the slave pens. Except for Ifness' energy pack, he would now be peering forth from between the withes. Still – these were the risks he had weighed in Garwiy; he had elected to face them rather than pursue a life of security, music and ease . . . Ifness was speaking, as much to himself as to Etzwane:

'I regret only that we failed to learn more from Gulshe and Srenka . . . Well, here we are at the hostelry. In retrospect the inn at Shillinsk seems a haven of palatial luxury. We will represent ourselves not as wizards nor research students, nor even bone merchants. The most prestigious occupation at Shagfe is slavery, and slavery is our trade.'

At the inn they paused to survey the settlement. The afternoon was warm and placid: infants crawled in the dirt; older children played at slave-taking among the tents, leaping forth with ropes to drag away their captives. At the trough under the windmill three squat dark-haired women in leather pants and straw capes bickered with the ahulphs. The women carried sticks and struck at the ahulphs' long sensitive feet whenever they attempted to drink: the ahulphs in turn kicked dirt at the women and screamed abuse. Beside the road a dozen crones in shapeless straw cloaks huddled beside offerings of goods to be traded: mounds of dark-red meal, thongs of dried meat, blue-black finger grubs in boxes of wet moss, fat greenbeetles tethered to stakes, sugar pods, boiled birds, cardamoms, salt crusts. Above, the vast bright sky; to all sides, the hot flat plain; far in the east a band of riders, visible only as a vibration of black specks, with a thin plume of lavender dust above . . . Ifness and Etzwane approached the inn, and entered by a hole in the mud wall. The common room was dim and dank-smelling. A rack behind the counter supported three barrels; elsewhere were benches and stools where half a dozen men sat with earthenware bowls of sour seed wine or mugs of the famous Shagfe cellar brew. Conversation halted; the men stared at Ifness and Etzwane with a still intensity. The sole illumination was the purple glare of outdoors seeping through the door-hole. Ifness and Etzwane peered around the room while their eyes adjusted to the dimness.

A short, bare-chested man with long white hair ambled

forward. He wore a leather apron and knee boots, and was apparently Baba the proprietor. He inquired their needs in a rough dialect which Etzwane understood more through divination than comprehension.

Ifness responded in a fair simulation of the dialect. 'What sort of lodging are you able to provide us?'

'The best to be had in Shagfe,' declared Baba the inn-keeper. 'Anyone will tell you as much. Is your question motivated by sheer curiosity?'

'No,' replied Ifness. 'You may show us the best you have to offer.'

'That is simple enough,' said Baba. 'This way, if you please.' He led them down an ill-smelling corridor, past a rudimentary kitchen where a great kettle of porridge simmered over a fire, and into a bare courtyard, sheltered around the periphery by an overhanging roof. 'Select whatever area you wish. The rain generally sweeps in from the south and the south bay is the driest.'

Ifness nodded gravely. 'The lodging is adequate. What of our pacers?'

'I will take them to my stable and feed them hay, pro-vided that you make suitable recompense. How long is your stay?'

'A day or two, or even longer, depending upon the transaction of our business. We are slave traders with a commission to buy a dozen stout Red Devils to row the galley of an east coast potentate. We understand, how-ever, that the Red Devils have all been killed, which is sad news to hear.'

'Your misfortune is my great luck, for they were on the march towards Shagfe and might well have destroyed my hostelry.'

'Perhaps the conquerors took captives?'

'I believe not, but in the common room sits Fabrache the Lucky Little Survivor. He claims to have witnessed

59

the battle, and who is to doubt his word? If you were to provide a mug or two of cellar brew, his tongue would wag freely, I vouch for this.'

'A happy thought. Now, as to the fee for shelter and food, for us and our pacers ...'

The haggling proceeded, Ifness driving a hard bargain in order to avoid a reputation for openhandedness. After five minutes a value defined as two ounces of silver was placed upon high-quality food and lodging for a period of five days.

'Very good then,' said Ifness, 'though as usual I have allowed a skillful rhetorician to persuade me into foolish extravagance. Let us now confer with Fabrache the Lucky Little Survivor. How did he gain this unusual cognomen?'

'It is no more than a child's pet name. Three times as an infant his mother attempted to drown him, and each time he pushed up through the mud. She gave up her task in disgust, and even bestowed the diminutive upon him. He became a man without fear; he reasonably argues that if Gaspard the God desired his death, he would not have overlooked this early opportunity ...'

Baba led the way back to the common room. He called, 'I introduce to the company the noble Ifness and Etzwane, who have come to Shagfe to buy slaves.'

A man to the side gave a dispirited moan. 'So now they compete with Hozman Sore-throat to drive prices still higher?'

'Hozman Sore-throat has bid for no Red Devils, which these traders require.' Baba the innkeeper turned to a tall, thin man with a long, dismal face and a beard hanging below his chin like an icicle of black hair. 'Fabrache, what are the facts? How many Red Devils still survive?'

Fabrache responded with the deliberation of an obstinate man. 'The Red Devils are extinct in the Mirkil district, which is to say, in the neighborhood of Shagfe. I spoke with men of the Tchark race from south of the Kuzi Kaza; they reported that the Red Devil bands had joined into a single horde, which then had marched north. Two days later I watched an army of magicians destroy this horde. Each Red Devil was killed and then rekilled: an astounding sight which I will never forget.'

'The magic army took no captives?' asked Ifness.

'None. They destroyed the Red Devils and marched away into the east. I descended to the battlefield to salvage metal, but ahulphs had preceded me and every ounce was preempted. But this is not all my tale. As I turned towards Shagfe I saw a great ship lift into the air, light as fluff, and disappear behind the clouds.'

'A miraculous vision!' declared Ifness. 'Innkeeper, supply this man a mug of cellar brew.'

Etzwane asked, 'Was the ship round as a disk and the color of copper-bronze?'

Fabrache the Lucky Little Survivor made a negative sign. 'This was an impressive black globe. The copper disks you mention were seen at the great battle of spaceships; the disks and the black globes fought together.'

Ifness nodded gravely and darted a warning glance towards Etzwane. 'We have heard something of this battle. Eight copper ships engaged six black globes at a place whose name I forget.'

The others in the room hastened to contradict him. 'Your information is inaccurate. Four of the black globes attacked two of the copper disks, and the copper ships were broken into fragments.'

'I wonder if we refer to the same battle,' Ifness mused. 'When did your affair occur?'

'Only two days ago; we have spoken of little else since. Such events have never before occurred in the Mirkil district.'

61

'Where did this battle take place?' asked Ifness.

'Over yonder in the Orgai Mountains,' said Fabrache. 'Behind Thrie Orgai, or so it is said; I have not been there myself.'

'Think of it, so close to Shagfe!' exclaimed Baba the innkeeper. 'Hardly two days' ride on a sound pacer!'

'We are traveling in that direction,' said Ifness. 'I would like to inspect the locality.' He addressed the Lucky Little Survivor. 'Would you care to act as our guide?'

Fabrache tugged at his beard. He glanced aside at one of his fellows. 'What is the news of the Gogursk clan? Have they made their west-faring?'

'No fear for the Gogursks,' said his friend. 'This year they drive south to Lake Urman for crabs. The Orgai is empty of threat, except naturally for the predations of Hozman Sore-throat.'

From outside the inn sounded a thud of hooves, the creaking of leather, hoarse voices. The landlord looked out through the doorway and spoke over his shoulder, 'Kash Blue-worms.'

At this two of the men present rose quickly and departed by the back corridor. Another called out, 'Fabrache, what of you? Did you not take four Blue-worm girls to Hozman?'

'I am not one to discuss my business in public,' said the Lucky Little Survivor. 'In any case, the incident occurred last year.'

The tribesmen entered the room. After glaring through the dimness they strode to tables and rapped on the planks for drink. They were nine in number, burly, moon-faced men with fringe beards, wearing limp leather trousers, black boots studded with flint cabochons, blouses of faded green jute, headgear of dry seed pods sewed into the shape of a pointed casque; these rattled with each motion of the head. Etzwane thought them the most ruffianly band of his experience, and leaned back from the unpleasant odors that had accompanied them into the room.

The oldest of the Kash gave his head-rattles a shake, and called out in a roaring voice, 'Where is the man who buys slaves at high prices?'

Fabrache responded in a subdued voice, 'He is not present.'

Baba the innkeeper asked cautiously, 'You have slaves to sell?'

'We do indeed, consisting of those persons now present, save only the innkeeper. Please consider yourselves our captives.'

Fabrache uttered a cry of indignation. 'This is not customary procedure! A man is entitled to drink beer at Shagfe in security!'

'Additionally,' Baba declared, 'I will tolerate no such conduct. What would happen to my custom? You must retract your threat.'

The old Kash grinned and rattled his seed pods. 'Very well; in view of the general protest we will put our best interests to the side. Still, we must have a word with Hozman Sore-throat. He has treated the Kash clan with severity; where does he sell so many of our folk?'

'Others have put similar questions, but received no answer,' said Baba. 'Hozman Sore-throat is not now in Shagfe, and I know nothing of his plans.'

The old Blue-worm made a gesture of resignation. 'In that case we will drink your cellar brew and make a meal of your cooked food, the odor of which I detect.'

'All very well, and how will you pay?'

'We carry with us sacks of safad oil, to settle our score.'

Baba said, 'Bring in the oil, while I work the scum off a new cask of cellar brew.'

The evening passed without bloodshed. Ifness and Etz-

63

wane sat to the side watching the burly figures lurch back and forth across the firelight. Etzwane tried to define the way in which these roaring celebrants differed from the general population of Shant: intensity, gusto, a focus of every faculty upon the immediate instant – such qualities characterised the folk of Caraz. Trivial acts induced exaggerated reactions. Laughter racked the ribs; rage came fierce and sudden; woe was so intense as to be intolerable. Upon every aspect of existence the clansmen fixed a keen and minute perception, allowing nothing to go unnoticed. Such raptures and transports of emotion left little time for meditation, Etzwane mused. How could a Blue-worm Hulka become a musician when he suffered a congenital lack of patience? Wild dancing around the campfire, mêlées, and murders – this was more the barbarian style . . . Etzwane and Ifness presently departed the company. They unrolled their blankets under the overhang of the courtyard and lay down to rest. For a period Etzwane lay listening to the muffled revels from the common room. He wanted to ask Ifness his theories regarding the battle between spaceships which had occurred behind Thrie Orgai, but had no stomach for a caustic or ambiguous reply . . . If the asutra and their hosts had manned the copper disks, what race had built black space-globes? For that matter, what race of men with magic weapons had destroyed the Roguskhoi? Why had men, Roguskhoi, copper and black spaceships all come to Caraz to do battle? . . . Etzwane put a cautious question to Ifness, 'Do any of the Earth worlds build space-vessels in the shape of black globes?'

The question was succinct and precise; Ifness could find no fault with it. He answered in an even voice, 'To my knowledge, no.' And he added, 'I am as puzzled as yourself. It would appear that the asutra have enemies somewhere among the stars. Perhaps human enemies.'

'This possibility alone justifies your defiance of Das-conetta,' declared Etzwane.

'So it might seem.'

The Kash Blue-worms chose to sleep in the open beside their pacers; Etzwane and Ifness passed a tranquil night.

In the cool mauve morning Baba brought them mugs of hot cellar brew with floating dollops of the sour local cheese. 'If you fare towards Thrie Orgai, depart early. You will cross the Wild Waste by midafternoon, and can spend the night in a tree along the Vurush.'

'Good advice,' said Ifness. 'Prepare us a breakfast of fried meat and bread, and send a boy to arouse Fabrache. Additionally, we will drink herbal tea with our meal, rather than this excellent but overnutritious brew.'

'Fabrache is on hand,' said the innkeeper. 'He wants to leave while the Blue-worms are still torpid. Your breakfast is already prepared. It consists of porridge and locust paste, like everyone else's. As for the tea, I can boil up a broth of pepperweed, if this suits your taste.'

Ifness gave a resigned acquiescence. 'Bring our pacers around to the front; we depart as soon as possible.'

Chapter 5

The Kash Blue-worms were stirring when Ifness, Etzwane, and Fabrache rode forth. One man growled a
malediction; another half rose to look after them; but
they were in no mood for exertion.

From Shagfe the three rode west across the Wild Waste,
an alkali flat stretching out to the limits of vision. The
surface was a hard bone-white crust, powdered with a
soft, acrid dust. Across the waste marched a dozen wind-
devils, back and forth like dancers of a pavane, out to the
horizon and back again, some tall and stately against the
brilliant sky, others low to the ground, scurrying without
dignity, presently collapsing into purposeless puffs and
wisps. For a period Fabrache kept a watch to the rear, but
when the huddle of huts disappeared into the dusty
lavender distance and no bounding black shapes came in
pursuit, he showed a somewhat more confident disposition. Looking sidewise towards Ifness, he spoke in a
cautious voice, 'Last night we struck no formal contract,
but I assume that we travel in confederacy and that
neither party will attempt subjugation of the other.'

Ifness endorsed this point of view. 'We have no particular interest in slavery,' said Ifness. 'We sold a pair of prime
Sorukhs on our way into Shagfe, but to speak frankly, the
life of a slaver is too precarious and unrewarding, at least
in the Mirkil district.'

66

'The region is over exploited,' said Fabrache. 'Since Hozman Sore-throat became active the population has diminished by a half. At Shagfe Inn we would see many strange faces, many different costumes and styles. Each Hulka clan maintained from three to seven fetish groups; then there would be Sorukhs from Shillinsk district, Shovel-heads and Alulas from Lake Nior, folk from over the Kuzi Kaza. A small slaver such as myself could earn a modest livelihood and keep a girl or two for his own use. Hozman Sore-throat has put an end to all this. Now we must scour the countryside for sheer sustenance.'

'Where does Hozman Sore-throat market his merchandise?'

'Hozman keeps good secrets,' said Fabrache with a spiteful sniff. 'Someday he will go too far. The world is going sour; it was not thus when I was a boy. Think of it! Spaceships in battle; Red Devils looting and killing; Hozman Sore-throat and his illusory boon of inflationary prices. Then when he destroys us and depopulates Mirkil district, he will move on and work the same outrage elsewhere.'

'I look forward to meeting Hozman,' said Ifness. 'He must have interesting tales to tell.'

'To the contrary; he is as terse as a costive chumpa.'

'We shall see, we shall see.'

As the day progressed, the air quieted and the wind-devils disappeared; the three crossed the flat with no discomfort other than the baking heat. By midafternoon the first slopes of the Orgai bulked ahead and the Wild Waste lay behind. As the three suns dropped behind the mountains, they rode over a hill and saw before them the broad Vurush, flowing from behind the Thrie Orgai and north into the haze. A grove of gnarled yews grew down to the water's edge, and here Fabrache chose to camp for the night, though chumpa traces were evident along the shore.

'They cannot be avoided, no matter where we camp,' said Fabrache. 'Three men with firebrands can keep them at a distance, if such a need arises.'

'Then we must keep watch during the night?'

'Not at all,' replied Fabrache. 'The pacers will watch, and I will keep the fire ablaze.'

He tethered the pacers to a tree and built a fire on the shore. Then, while Ifness and Etzwane collected a stack of resinous yew branches, Fabrache snared a dozen mud crabs, which he cracked, cleaned, and toasted, and meanwhile cooked meal cakes on hot, flat stones. 'You are highly efficient,' said Ifness. 'It is a pleasure to watch you at work.'

Fabrache gave his head a dour shake. 'I know nothing else but this; a skill acquired across a lifetime of hardship. I take no great pleasure from your compliment.'

'Surely you have other skills?'

'Yes. I am reckoned a good barber. Occasionally in jest I imitate the mating antics of the ahulphs. But these are modest accomplishments; ten years after my death I will be forgotten, and one with the soil of Caraz. Still, I consider myself a fortunate man, more so than most. I have often wondered why it was given to me to live the life of Kyril Fabrache.'

'These reflections, at one time or another, have occurred to all of us,' said Ifness, 'but unless we are agreed upon a religion of gradated reincarnation, the question is ingenuous.' He rose to his feet and surveyed the landscape. 'I assume that the Red Devils never ranged this far west?'

Piqued by Ifness' indifference to his quest for personal truth, Fabrache gave only a short reply. 'They never even reached Shagfe.' He went off to tend the pacers.

68

Ifness considered the mass of the Orgai to the north, where the crag Thrie Orgai flared purple in the last rays of the setting suns. 'In this case, the spaceship battle would seem isolated from the slaughter of the Roguskhoi,' he mused. 'The events are of course related; there can be no doubt of this much ... Tomorrow will be an interesting day.' He made one of his rare gesticulations. 'If I can produce a spaceship, even a hulk, I am vindicated. Dasconetta will be gray with rage; even now he gnaws his knuckles by the hour . . . We can only hope that these spaceships exist in fact, that they are something more than mare's nests.'

Etzwane, vaguely irked by the nature of Ifness' aspirations, said, 'I can see no value to a wrecked spaceship; they have been known for thousands of years, and must be common throughout the system of Earth worlds.'

'True,' declared Ifness, still elevated by his visions of triumph, 'but these are the product of human knowledge, and many knowledges exist.'

'Bah,' growled Etzwane. 'Iron is iron, glass is glass, and this is the same here or at the end of the universe.'

'True once more. The gross elementals are known to all. But there is no finite limit to knowledge. Each set of apparent ultimates is susceptible to examination and must be analysed in new terms. These succeeding layers of knowledge are numberless. Those familiar to us are each derived from the level above, or below. Conceivably entire disassociated phases of knowledge exist; the field of parapsychology comes to mind. The basic law of the cosmos is this: in a situation of infinity, whatever is possible exists in fact. To particularise, the technology which propels an alien spaceship may be different from that of Earth, and such a technology must be a matter of intense interest, if only philosophically.' Ifness considered the fire. 'I must remark that augmented knowledge is not necessarily a boon, and might easily be dangerous.'

'In that case,' Etzwane asked, 'why are you so anxious to broadcast this knowledge?'

Ifness chuckled. 'First, it is my normal human inclination to do so. Second, the group of which I am part – from which Dasconetta would naturally be expelled – is competent to control the most dangerous secrets. Thirdly, I cannot overlook my personal advantage. If I deliver an alien spaceship to the Historical Institute, even a wrecked hulk, I will gain great prestige.'

Etzwane turned away to make up his bed, reflecting that of Ifness' three reasons, the last was probably the most cogent.

The night passed without incident. Three times Etzwane awoke. Once he heard from far off the rumbling challenge of a chumpa and from an even greater distance the answering calls of an ahulph tribe, but none came to disturb the camp by the river.

Fabrache awoke before dawn. Blowing up the fire, he prepared a breakfast of porridge boiled with pepper meat and tea.

Not long after dawn the three mounted their pacers and set off to the south along the banks of the Vurush. Gradually they rose into the Orgai.

Shortly before noon Fabrache jerked his pacer to a halt. He cocked his head as if listening, and looked slowly to all sides.

'What is the matter?' asked Ifness.

Fabrache said nothing. He pointed ahead towards the gap into a stony valley. 'Here is where the black globes discovered the disk ships; here is where the battle took place.' Rising to stand in his stirrups he searched the hillsides and reexamined the sky.

'You have a presentiment,' said Etzwane softly.

Fabrache pulled nervously at his beard. 'The valley has

70

known a wonderful event; the air still tingles . . . Is there not something more?' Fretfully he swung his gaunt body around in the saddle, rolling his eyes from side to side. 'There is pressure upon me.'

Etzwane scanned the valley. To right and left, harsh gullies cut into sandstone, the high areas baking white-violet in the sunlight, the deep shadows a black bottle-green. A flicker of motion caught his eye; not a hundred feet distant crouched a large ahulph, considering whether or not to hurl a stone. Etzwane said, 'Perhaps you feel the gaze of yonder ahulph.'

Fabrache swung about, annoyed that Etzwane had seen the creature first. The ahulph, a blue-black buck of a variety unknown to Etzwane, shook its ear fibers uneasily and started to move away. Fabrache called out in de-da pidgin. The ahulph paused. Fabrache spoke again, and with the swaggering waggishness typical of the higher ahulphs, it bounded down from the jut. Politely it released a waft of 'gregariousness'* and sidled forward. Fabrache dismounted from his pacer and signaled Etzwane and Ifness to do likewise. Tossing a chunk of cold grain cake to the ahulph, he spoke again in de-da. The ahulph made a fervent and elaborate response.

Fabrache turned to Ifness and Etzwane. 'The ahulph watched the battle. He has explained to me the sequence of events. Two copper disk-ships landed at the end of the valley and remained there almost a week. Persons came out to walk around. They stood on two feet, but exuded a

* The higher ahulphs control four odors, signifying gregariousness, hostility, and two varieties of excitement unknown to the human race. The innumerable races of lower ahulphs vent only hostility and an attractive scent. The ahulph mentality at times seems to resemble human intelligence, but the similarity is misleading, and attempts to deal with ahulphs on a basis of human rationality end in frustration. The ahulph, for instance, cannot understand working for hire, no matter how carefully the matter is explained.

nonhuman odor. The ahulph paid no attention to their appearance. They did nothing during their stay and came outside only at dawn and dusk. Three days ago, at noon, four black globes appeared a mile overhead. The disk-ships were taken by surprise. The black globes sent down lightning bolts and exploded both disk-ships, then departed as abruptly as they had come. The ahulphs watched the wrecks, but felt diffident about approaching. Yesterday a large disk-ship dropped from the sky. After hovering an hour, it lifted the hulk which had suffered the least damage and carried it away. Fragments of the second hulk remain.'

'Interesting news,' murmured Ifness. 'Toss the creature another morsel of grain cake. I am anxious to inspect the shattered hulk.'

Fabrache scratched his chin where the first hairs of his beard had their roots. 'I must admit to a diffidence not unlike that of the ahulph. The valley holds an uncanny presence which I do not care to test.'

'Do not apologise,' said Ifness. 'You are not known as the Lucky Little Survivor for nothing. Will you await us here, in company with the ahulph?'

'This I will do,' said Fabrache.

Ifness and Etzwane set off up the valley. They rode a mile, the sandstone rising to either side in crags and juts. The valley floor widened to become a sandy flat, and here they found the hulk of the second ship. The outer skin had been rent and torn in a dozen places; one entire section had disappeared. From the gaps spewed tangled metal and viscous oozes. The top surface had been exploded into tatters, which lay scattered across the plain; the ground below showed rings of white, green, and yellow powder.

Ifness gave a hiss of vexation. He snatched out his camera and photographed the hulk. 'I had expected nothing better than this; still I had hoped. What a trophy had the ship been susceptible to study! A new cosmology, in effect, to compare with our own! A tragedy to find it thus!'

Etzwane felt mildly surprised at Ifness' vehemence: such a display was unusual. They moved closer and the wrecked spaceship exerted an eerie fascination, a strange, sad majesty. Ifness alighted from his pacer. He picked up a fragment of metal, hefted it, cast it aside. He went up to the hulk, peered into the interior, shook his head in disgust. 'Everything of interest is either vaporised, crushed, or melted; we have nothing to learn here.'

Etzwane spoke. 'You notice that a segment of the ship is missing? Look yonder in that gulch: there it has lodged.'

Ifness looked where Etzwane had directed. 'The ship was attacked first, perhaps, by a burst of explosive force, and then struck again, with energy sufficient to cause the melting.' He set off towards the gulch, about fifty yards distant, into which a pie-shaped section of the ship had wedged itself. The outer skin, dented and distorted but by some miracle untorn, had plastered itself across the narrow opening like a great bronze seal.

The two scrambled up the stones until they could step over to the crumpled metal. Ifness tugged at the edge of a fractured section. Etzwane joined him; by dint of straining the two bent aside the sheet to provide an opening into the hull. A vile odor issued forth: a stench of decay, different from any Etzwane had known before . . . He became rigid, held up his hand. 'Listen.'

From below came a faint scraping sound, persisting two or three seconds.

'Something seems to be alive,' Etzwane peered down into the dark. The prospect of entering the broken ship had no appeal for him.

Ifness had no such qualms. From his pouch he brought an object which Etzwane had never seen before: a transparent cube half an inch on a side. Suddenly it emitted a flood of light, which Ifness turned into the dim interior. Four feet below a broken bench slanted across what seemed to be a storage chamber; a clutter of objects flung from racks lay mounded against the far wall. Ifness stepped down upon the bench and jumped to the floor. Etzwane took a last wistful look around the valley and followed. Ifness stood surveying the heaped articles against the wall. He pointed. 'A corpse.' Etzwane moved to where he could see. The dead creature lay on its back, pressed against the wall. 'An anthropomorphic biped,' said Ifness. 'Distinctly not a man; not even manlike, except for two legs, two arms, and a head. It even smells different from human carrion.'

'Worse,' muttered Etzwane. He bent forward, studying the dead thing, which wore no garments save various straps for the support of three pouches, one at either hip, one at the back of the head. The skin, a purplish-black parchment, seemed as hard as old leather. The head displayed a number of parallel bony ridges, originating at the top of a protective ring around the single eye and running back across the scalp. A mouth-like orifice appeared at the base of the neck. Pads of matted bristle conceivably served as auditory organs.

Ifness saw something which had escaped Etzwane. He reached for a tubular rod, then lunged forward and thrust. In the shadows at the back of the dead creature's neck was a stir of sudden movement, but Ifness was too quick; the rod struck into a small dark object. Ifness pried the body away from the wall, struck again at the small six-legged creature who had ridden in the pouch at the back of the dead neck.

'Asutra?' asked Etzwane.

Ifness gave his head a jerk of assent. 'Asutra and host.'

Etzwane inspected the two-legged creature once more.

'It is something like the Roguskhoi in the hard skin, the shape of the head, the hands and feet.'

'I noted the similarity,' said Ifness. 'It might be a collateral form, or the stock from which the Roguskhoi derived.' He spoke tonelessly; his eyes darted this way and that. Etzwane had never seen him so keen. 'Quietly now,' said Ifness.

On long, soft steps he went to the bulkhead and turned his light through an aperture.

They looked along a hall twenty feet long, the bulkheads twisted and distorted. Into the far end seeped a wan daylight, filtering through overhead fractures.

Ifness strode quietly down the hall into the terminating room, holding the light-cube in one hand, an energy gun in the other.

The room was vacant. Etzwane could not imagine its function or purpose. A bench flanked three walls, with cabinets above containing objects of glass and metal to which Etzwane could put no name. The outside skin and one wall pressed on to the fractured rock, which comprised the fourth wall. Ifness glared in all directions like a gaunt gray hawk. He cocked his head to listen; Etzwane did the same. The air was thick and quiet. Etzwane asked in a low voice, 'What is this room?'

Ifness gave his head a curt shake. 'They contrive things differently on Earth-world ships . . . I can understand nothing of this.'

'Look there.' Etzwane pointed. 'More asutra.' A glass tray at the end of the bench contained a murky fluid in which floated three dozen dark ellipsoids, like so many black olives. Below, indistinct in the matrix, hung still arms.

Ifness went to examine the tank. A tube entered one of the sides; from this tube filaments led up to the asutra. 'They seem cataleptic,' said Ifness. 'Perhaps they take energy, or information, or entertainment.' He stood thinking a moment, then spoke. 'We can do no more. The matter is now too large for our sole discretion, and in fact is overwhelming.' He paused to look around the chamber. 'There is material here to occupy ten thousand analysts, to astound the Institute. We will return at once to Shillinsk. From the boat I can signal Dasconetta, and through him order out a salvage ship.'

'Something aboard is yet alive,' said Etzwane. 'We cannot leave it to die.' As if to reinforce his remark, a scraping sound issued from behind the crumpled wall opposite the hall.

'A ticklish business,' muttered Ifness. 'What if twenty Roguskhoi burst out upon us? . . . On the other hand, something might be learned from a host not under asutra control. Well then, let us look. But careful and easy! We must be on guard.'

He went to the area where the wall met the rock. At the center and bottom, contact was not complete, leaving irregular openings, the diameter of a man's head, through which air could pass. Etzwane peered through the center gap. For a moment he saw nothing, then abruptly a round object the size of a large coin came into view, reflecting a nacreous pink and green shimmer. Etzwane drew back, oppressed by a thrilling of the nerves. He collected himself and spoke in a low voice. 'It is one of the host-things. I looked into its eye.'

Ifness made a curt sound. 'If it is alive, it is mortal, and there is no need for panic.'

Etzwane choked back a retort, and taking up a metal bar, began to attack the rock. Ifness stood back, an enigmatic expression on his face.

The rock, shattered by the impact of the ship, broke away in chunks. Etzwane worked with a furious energy, as if to distract himself. The center gap grew wide. Etzwane

76

paid no heed and drove the bar furiously into the rock . . . Ifness held up his hand. 'Sufficient.' He stepped forward, flashed his light into the hole, to reveal a dark, waiting shape. 'Come forth,' said Ifness, and gestured, his hand in the illumination.

There was first silence. Then slowly, but without hesitation, the creature pulled itself through the hole. Like the corpse it stood naked but for a harness and three pouches, one of which held an asutra. Ifness spoke to Etzwane. 'Lead the way to the outside. I will direct the creature to follow you.'

Etzwane turned away. Ifness stepped forward, touched the creature's arm, pointed.

The creature stalked after Etzwane — down the hall, into the chamber which was open to the sky.

Etzwane climbed up on the bench, pushed his head up into the daylight. Never had air seemed so clear and sweet. And in the sky a mile overhead hovered a great disk-ship, slowly rotating on its vertical axis, the three suns laying three-colored reflections on the copper-bronze skin. Another mile above hung four smaller ships.

Etzwane stared up in consternation. The large disk-ship descended slowly. He called the news back down to Ifness.

'Hurry,' said Ifness. 'Help the creature up and hold fast to his harness.'

Etzwane scrambled out and stood waiting. From below rose the purple-black head, ridges of bone running across the scalp. The head protruded, and the shoulders, with the pouch containing the asutra. On sudden impulse Etzwane seized the pouch and pulled it away from the black body. A nerve cord stretched; the creature uttered a guttural gasp and released its grip on the edge of the hole, and would have fallen backward had Etzwane not clamped his arm around the corded neck. With his other hand he drew the dagger from his belt and slashed the

77

nerve; the asutra, squirming and clutching, pulled free. Etzwane threw it to the surface of the ship, then heaved the dark creature up after it. Ifness quickly followed. 'What is the commotion?'

'I pulled the asutra loose. There it goes yonder. Hold the host; I will kill it.'

Ifness, frowning in displeasure, obeyed. The black host-creature lunged after Etzwane; Ifness clung to its harness. Etzwane ran after the scuttling black object. He picked up a stone, held it high, smashed it down upon the black bulb.

Ifness meanwhile had propelled the suddenly listless creature behind a wall of rock, screening the descending spaceship from its sight. Etzwane, leading the pacers, joined them.

Ifness asked in a frosty voice, 'Why did you kill the asutra? You have left us an empty shell, hardly worth the effort of removing.'

Etzwane said drily, 'I recognise this. I also notice the descending ship, and I have been told that the asutra communicate telepathically with their fellows. I thought to afford us a better chance of escape.'

Ifness grunted. 'The telepathic capability of the asutra has never been established.' He looked up the gulch. 'The way appears to be feasible. We must hurry, however . . . It is possible that Fabrache may think better of waiting overlong.'

Chapter 6

The gulch, narrow, tortuous, and strewn with boulders, afforded no scope for riding. Etzwane scrambled ahead, leading the pacers. Behind came the dark creature, its unearthly tendons twitching and pulling in unfamiliar sequences. At the rear strolled Ifness, cool and detached.

Once behind the ridge they veered to the south and so returned to where they had left Fabrache. They found him lolling at his ease against a rock overlooking the valley, where now no spaceships could be seen, wrecked or otherwise. Fabrache leapt to his feet with an ejaculation of shock, for they had come up on him quietly from the side. Ifness held up his hand, admonishing Fabrache to placidity and composure. 'As you see,' said Ifness, 'we have succored a survivor of the battle. Have you seen its like before?'

'Never!' declared Fabrache. 'I am not pleased to see it now. Where will you sell it? Who would care to buy such a thing?'

Ifness gave one of his rare chuckles. 'It commands value as a curiosity, if nothing else. A collector's item, so to speak. I have no doubt as to our eventual profit. But what occurred yonder in the valley?'

Fabrache stared in wonder. 'What? Did you not witness the happening at first hand?'

'We took refuge behind the hill,' Ifness explained. 'Had

we remained to watch, we ourselves might have been observed, with no telling as to the consequences.'

'Of course, of course; this is clear enough. Well, the rest of the affair surpasses my comprehension. A great ship descended and seized upon the wreck and took it up as if it were a biscuit –'

'Did they hoist one section?' Ifness demanded, 'Or two?'

'Two. The ship swooped a second time, and I thought, alas! what a sad end for my slaving companions! Then, as I sat there reflecting upon the remarkable life which it has been my good fortune to live, you crept up and found me musing. Aha!' Fabrache shook his head in mournful self-reproach. 'Had you been Hozman Sore-throat, my time as a free man would now be done. What now is our program?'

'We will proceed back to Shagfe with all speed. First, pour out a cup of water. This creature was pent for several days.'

Fabrache poured with a rueful smirk, as if reflecting upon the odd quirks of fate to which he was continually subjected. The creature without hesitation turned the contents of the cup into its throat, and did the same for three more cupfuls. Ifness then proffered a cake of jellied meat, which the creature cautiously refused, then dried fruit, which it dropped into its throat. Ifness offered it pounded seeds from which Fabrache made his bread, salt, and lump-fat, all of which the creature rejected.

The supplies were redistributed, and the dark creature was mounted on the pack animal, which jerked and shuddered at the alien scent, and walked with stiff legs and rounded nostrils.

The four set off down the Vurush Valley, along the route they had come, and the miles fell back into the afternoon. The alien rode stolidly, showing no interest in the landscape, hardly moving in the saddle. Etzwane asked Ifness, 'Do you think it is in a state of shock, or grief or terror? Or is it only semi-intelligent?'

'As yet, we have no basis for assessment. In due course I would hope to learn a great deal.'

'Perhaps it could act as interpreter between men and asutra,' said Etzwane.

Ifness frowned, a signal that the idea had not yet occurred to him. 'This is of course a possibility.' He looked towards Fabrache, who had drawn up his pacer. 'What is the matter?'

Fabrache pointed to the east, where the slopes of the Orgai eased down upon the plain. 'A party of riders – six or eight.'

Ifness rose in his saddle, gazed across the distance. 'They are riding in our direction at a good rate of speed.'

'We had best do likewise,' said Fabrache. 'In this land one cannot take the friendship of strangers for granted.' He jerked his pacer into a full lope and the others followed suit, Etzwane applying the quirt to the pacer ridden by the alien.

Down the valley they coursed, Ifness frowning in distaste. The alien rode stiffly erect, clutching the back-curving horns of his beast. Etzwane judged that for the first two miles they gained ground, then for another two miles held their own, then the pursuing band seemed to gain. Fabrache, with long frame crouched grotesquely low and beard flapping over his shoulder, urged his pacer to its utmost efforts. He yelled over his shoulder, 'It is Hozman Sore-throat and his slaving band! Ride for freedom! Ride for your life!'

The pacers were tiring. Time after time they stumbled into a lurching jog, which aroused Fabrache to frantic measures. The pursuing pacers had also become winded, and they too slackened speed. The suns were low in the west, laying three trails upon the surface of the Vurush, Fabrache appraised the distance to the pursuing band and measured it against the height of the suns. He gave a call of despair. 'We will be slaves before dark, and then we will learn Hozman's secret.'

Ifness pointed ahead. 'There, on the shore, a camp of wagons.'

Fabrache peered and gave a croak of hope. 'We shall arrive in time and claim protection . . . Unless they are cannibals, we are in luck.'

A few moments later he called back, 'They are the Alula; I now recognise their wains. They are a hospitable folk and we are safe.'

On a level area near the river, fifty wains with crooked eight-foot wheels had been drawn up to form a hollow square, the wheels and dropped sideboards creating a staunch fence. A single opening faced the river. The slavers, trailing by three hundred yards, their pacers coughing and stumbling, gave up the chase and swerved aside towards the river.

Fabrache led the way around the wall of wains and halted before the opening. Four men jumped forward in a crouching, splay-legged posture of threat. They wore jerkins of black chumpa-hide strips, helmets of black leather, and carried crossbows three feet wide. 'If you be riders with the group yonder, go your way. We want no business with you.'

Fabrache leapt from his pacer and stepped forward. 'Put aside your weapons! We are travelers of the Orgai and fugitives from Hozman Sore-throat! We request protection for the night.'

'All very well, but what of that one-eyed demoniac creature? We have heard tales; it is a Red Devil!'

'Nothing of the sort! The Red Devils are all dead,

killed in a recent battle. This is the sole survivor of a wrecked spaceship.'

'In that case, kill it as well. Why should we nurture off-world enemies?'

Ifness spoke in a measured and aristocratic voice, 'The matter is more complicated than this. I intend to learn the language of this creature, if it is able to talk. This knowledge will help us defeat our enemies.'

'It is a matter for Karazan. Stand in your tracks; we are a suspicious people.'

A moment later an enormous man strode forward, taller by a head than Fabrache. His face was no less impressive than his bulk; keen eyes glittered under a broad brow, a short beard clothed his cheeks and chin. He required a single second to appraise the situation, then turned a glance of contemptuous derogation towards the guards. 'What is the difficulty? When have Alula feared three men and a monster? Let them in.' He scowled down at the riverbank where Hozman Sore-throat and his band rested their pacers, then sauntered back the way he had come. The warriors put aside their crossbows and stood back. 'Enter as you will. Take your pacers to the pen. Bed yourselves where you like, except in company with our wives.'

'You have our gratitude,' Fabrache declared. 'Mind, that is Hozman Sore-throat, the expert slaver, yonder; let no one stray outside the camp, or he will never to be seen again.'

Etzwane was intrigued by the camp, and by certain elements of barbaric splendor which in the popular imagination of Shant characterised all the tribes of Caraz. The green, pink, and magenta tents had been embroidered in marvelous starbursts and radiants. The carved tent stakes stood eight feet tall, displaying fetishes of four sorts: winged scorpions, wisk-weasels, Lake Nior kingfish, Lake Nior pelicans. The men of the camp wore trousers of pounded ahulph leather, glossy black boots, embroidered vests over loose white blouses. Married women wound their heads with purple and green scarves, their full gowns were of various colors; girls, however, swaggered about in breeches and boots like the men. Before each tent a cauldron bubbled over a fire, and the odors of spices and stewing meat permeated the camp. In front of the ceremonial wain sat the elders, passing a leather flask of aquavita back and forth. Near by four other men, each wearing a string of golden beads, made desultory music upon stringed instruments.

No one gave the newcomers more than cursory attention; they went to the area indicated to them, unloaded their pacers, and laid out their beds. The alien watched without apparent interest. Fabrache dared not go to the river for clams or crayfish and cooked an austere meal of porridge and dried meat; the alien drank water and thrust a quantity of porridge into its maw without enthusiasm. Children of the camp began to gather and watched in wide-eyed wonder. They were joined by others, progressively older, and presently one put a timid question, 'Is the creature tame?'

'It seems to be,' said Etzwane. 'It came to Durdane in a spaceship, so it is certainly civilised.'

'Is it your slave?' asked another.

'Not exactly. We rescued it from a wrecked spaceship, and now we want to learn how to talk to it.'

'Can it do wonderful magic?'

'Not to my knowledge.'

'Does it dance?' asked one of the girls. 'Bring it to where the music is played and we will watch its fanciful acts.'

'It neither dances nor plays music,' said Etzwane.

84

'What a tiresome beast.'

A woman came to scold the children and sent them about their business, and the group was left in peace.

Fabrache spoke to Ifness. 'How do you intend to keep the creature for the night? Must we stand a guard?'

'I think not,' said Ifness. 'It might then consider itself a prisoner and seek to escape. It knows that we are its source of food and security, and I believe that it will stay with us of its own volition. Still we will maintain an unobtrusive watch.' Ifness now addressed himself to the creature and attempted the rudiments of communication: placing down first one pebble, then two, then three, while saying 'One . . . two . . . three . . . ' and signaling the alien to do likewise, but to no avail. Ifness next directed the creature's attention to the sky, where the stars blazed bright and clear. Ifness pointed here and there in a questioning fashion, and even took the creature's hard finger and pointed it about the sky. 'It is either extremely intelligent or extremely stupid,' grumbled Ifness. 'Still, were the asutra in command we would derive no more information. There is no cause for complaint.'

From the central fire came the sound of energetic music, and Etzwane went to watch the dancing. The youths and maidens, forming into lines, swayed, kicked, capered, swung each other in circles, all in the most exuberant fashion. The music seemed uncomplicated to Etzwane, even somewhat naive, but as vigorous and forthright as the dancing. Some of the girls were extremely handsome, he thought, and showed little diffidence . . . He toyed with the idea of playing music and went so far as to examine a spare instrument of bizarre and exaggerated construction. He sounded the strings, but the frets were oddly spaced and tuning was to a strange mode. Etzwane doubted his ability to use the instrument. He struck a few chords, using his usual fingering. The results were strange

85

but not displeasing. A girl stood over him, smiling. 'Do you play music?'

'Yes, but this instrument is unfamiliar to me.'

'What is your race and fetish?'

'I am a man of Shant; I was born a Chilite in Canton Bastern.'

The girl shook her head in bewilderment. 'They must be far lands; I have never heard of them. Are you a slave-taker?'

'No. My friend and I came to look at the strange space-ships.'

'Such things are interesting.'

The girl was pretty, vivacious, and beautifully formed, and Etzwane thought that she seemed pleasantly disposed. He suddenly felt an inclination to play music, and bent his head over the instrument to learn its system of harmonics . . . He returned the strings, and found that by thinking in the unusual Kudarian mode the instrument fell under his control. He cautiously played a few phrases, and tried to follow the music, with a degree of success.

'Come,' said the girl. She took him to the other musicians and brought him the leather flask from which all had been drinking. Etzwane allowed himself a cautious swallow; the sting of the spirit caused him to laugh and blow out his breath. 'Laugh again!' the girl commanded. 'Musicians should never be somber, even when their mood is tragic; their eyes should show colored lights.'

One of the musicians glowered first at the girl then at Etzwane, who decided to be discreet. He played tentative chords, and with increasing confidence joined the music. The theme was simple and played insistently again and again, but each time with a small alteration: the prolongation of a beat, a twanged note, a trifle of emphasis here or there. The musicians seemed to vie in producing the most subtle changes in the succession; and meanwhile

86

the music became even more intense and compelling, and the dancers swirled, jerked arms, kicked, and stamped in the firelight . . . Etzwane began to wonder when the music would stop, and how. The others would know the signal; they would try to catch him napping, so that when he played on alone he would seem ridiculous: an ancient prank to work upon the stranger. All would know when the tune should end; there would be a side-glance, a raised elbow, a hiss, a shift of position . . . The signal came; Etzwane felt its presence. As he had expected, the music stopped short; he instantly broke into a variation in a different mode, a pulsing statement even more compelling than the first theme, and presently the musicians, some grinning, some with wry winces, again joined the music . . . Etzwane laughed and bent over the instrument, which now had become familiar, and began to produce runs and trills . . . The music at last halted. The girl came to sit beside Etzwane and proffered the flask of spirit. Etzwane drank and, putting down the flask, asked, 'What is your name?'

'I am Rune the Willow Wand, of the Pelican fetish. Who are you?'

'My name is Gastel Etzwane. In Shant we do not reckon our clans or fetishes, only our canton. And, as it used to be, the colors of our torc, which now we wear no more.'

'In different lands are different customs,' agreed the girl. 'Sometimes it is puzzling. Over the Orgai and along the Botgarsk River live the Shada, who cut off a girl's ears if she so much as speaks to a man. Is this the custom of Shant?'

'Not at all,' said Etzwane. 'Among the Alula are you allowed to speak to strangers?'

'Yes, indeed; we obey our own inclinations in such matters; and why should we not?' She tilted her head and gave Etzwane a candid inspection. 'You are of a race thinner and keener than ours. You have what we call the *aersk** look.'

Etzwane was not displeased by the flattery. The girl apparently was somewhat wayward and wanted to enlarge her horizons by flirting with a strange young man. Etzwane, though of a wary disposition, was not unwilling to oblige her. He asked, 'The musician yonder: he is not your betrothed?'

'Galgar the Wisk-weasel? Do I seem the sort who would consort with a man like Galgar?'

'Of course not. I notice also that he keeps poor time in his music, which indicates a deficient personality.'

'You are amazingly perceptive,' said Rune the Willow Wand. She moved closer; Etzwane smelled the tree-balsam she used as a scent. She spoke in a soft voice, 'Do you like my cap?'

'Yes, of course,' said Etzwane, puzzled by the lack of sequence in the girl's remarks. 'Although it seems about to fall off your head.'

Ifness had come to sit by the fire. He now raised an admonitory finger, and Etzwane went to learn his requirements. 'A word of caution,' said Ifness.

'Unnecessary. I am more than cautious; I look in all directions at once.'

'Just so, just so. Remember that in the Alul camp we are subject to their laws. Fabrache tells me that the Alul women can assert a marital connection with some simplicity. Do you notice how certain of the maidens wear their caps askew? If a man removes the cap or so much as sets it straight, he is held to have disarranged her intimate apparel, and if she raises an outcry, the two must marry.'

Etzwane looked through the dying firelight towards

* *Aersk:* untranslatable. Loosely, a fearless nobleman of the high crags, whose first needs are space, sunlight, and storms.

Rune the Willow Wand. 'The caps are precariously placed . . . An interesting custom.' He slowly went to rejoin the girl. She asked, 'What has that peculiar person been telling you?'

Etzwane cast about for a reply. 'He noticed my interest in you; he warned me not to compromise myself or offend you by touching your garments.'

Rune the Willow Wand smiled and cast a contemptuous glance towards Ifness. 'What an old prig! But he need not fear! My three best friends have arranged to meet their lovers near the river and I agreed to walk with them, although I have no lover and will be wistful and lonely.'

'I advise you to walk some other night,' said Etzwane. 'Hozman Sore-throat prowls the vicinity; he is the arch-slaver of Caraz.'

'Pff. Do you refer to the rogues who chased you hither? They rode north; they are gone. They would never dare molest the Alula.'

Etzwane gave his head a skeptical shake. 'If you are lonely, come talk to me yonder behind the wain where I have spread my blankets.'

Rune the Willow Wand stood back, eyebrows arched in disdain. 'I am not interested in such a graceless proceeding. To think that I considered you *aersk*.' She twitched her cap securely down on her head and sauntered away. Etzwane gave a rueful shrug and presently went to his blankets. For a period he watched the alien, who sat motionless in the shadows, showing only its outline and the soft glow of its single eye.

Etzwane felt somewhat reluctant to sleep with the alien so near at hand; after all, they knew nothing of its proclivities. But presently he drowsed . . . After a time he awoke uneasily, but the creature sat immobile, and Etzwane went back to sleep once more.

An hour before dawn a bellow of enormous rage jerked Etzwane from his slumber. He jumped to his feet to see a number of Alul warriors rushing forth from their wains. They spoke back and forth, then all dashed for their pacers, and presently Etzwane heard the thud of retreating hooves.

Fabrache had gone forth for information; he returned, dolefully wagging his head. 'It's just as I warned them and they would not believe. Last night four maidens went to walk down by the river and never returned. Hozman Sore-throat is to blame. The Alula ride in vain, for once Hozman makes his pluck his victims are never seen again.'

The riders returned disconsolate; they had cast about for tracks without success, and they had no ahulphs to follow the slave-taker's trail. The leader of the search party was the massive Karazan. He flung himself from the saddle and marched across the compound to confront Ifness. 'Tell me where the slave-taker may be found, that we may either win back our flesh and blood or pull him apart with our bare hands.'

Ifness indicated Fabrache. 'My friend here, also a slaver, can provide information far more detailed and intimate than I.'

Fabrache gave his beard a judicious tug. 'I know nothing of Hozman Sore-throat, neither his race, nor his clan, nor his fetish. I can assure you of two facts only. First, he often visits Shagfe, to buy at the collecting station; and second, whoever Hozman takes is gone forever.'

'That remains to be seen,' said Karazan. 'Where is Shagfe?'

'A day's journey to the east.'

'We ride at once for Shagfe! Bring forth the pacers!'

'Our own destination is Shagfe,' said Ifness. 'We will ride in your company.'

90

'Make haste,' said the Alula. 'Our mission will not be conducive to leisure or reverie.'

Eighteen pacers loped across the Wild Waste, the riders slouched low, capes flapping over their shoulders. Shagfe appeared in the distance: a gray and black smudge upon the violet-gray background of hills and haze.

At sunset the riders pounded into Shagfe, to halt in a swirl of dust before the inn.

Baba looked through the door-hole, pale eyebrows in astounded arcs at the sight of the alien creature. The Alula descended and entered, with Ifness, Fabrache, Etzwane, and the silent black creature coming behind.

At the benches hunched the Kash Blue-worms, drunk and surly. At the sight of their tribal enemies, the Alula, they drew themselves up and muttered together. Fabrache spoke to Baba, 'My friends here have a bit of business with Hozman Sore-throat. Has he been seen today?'

Baba said peevishly, 'I make a rule against discussing the affairs of my customers. I am not –'

Karazan strode forward, to loom above Baba. 'Answer the question.'

'I have not seen Hozman since early this morning,' growled Baba.

'Aha, what's this? Early morning?'

'True! With these two hands I served his gruel while the suns clambered over the horizon.'

'How can this be?' Karazan demanded in a menacing voice. 'He was seen at sundown where the Vurush comes down from the Orgai. At midnight he made his presence felt. How could he have eaten breakfast here at dawn?'

The innkeeper reflected. 'It might be possible, on a good Angos pacer.'

'Well then, what was his pacer this morning?'

'An ordinary Jerzy.'

'Perhaps he changed his mount,' Ifness suggested.

The Alula snorted. He turned back to Fabrache. 'You can certify that Hozman chased you down the Orgai Mountains?'

'I am sure. Have I not seen Hozman Sore-throat many a time, riding with his band and alone?'

A voice spoke to their backs. 'I hear my name mentioned, I trust in a kindly reference.'

All swung about. Hozman Sore-throat stood in the door-hole. He came forward, a pale, stern-faced man of ordinary stature. A black cloak concealed his garments, except for the maroon scarf which muffled his neck.

The Alula said, 'Last night on the river Vurush you took four of our people. We want them restored to us. The Alula are not for the slave pens; this we will make clear to every slave-taker of Caraz.'

Hozman Sore-throat laughed, putting aside the threat with the ease of long practice. 'Are you not over hasty? You accost me without basis.'

Karazan took a slow step forward. 'Hozman, your time is upon you.'

The landlord bustled close. 'Not in the inn! This is the first law of Shagfe!'

The Alula thrust him aside with a sweep of his massive arm. 'Where are our people?'

'Come now,' said Hozman briskly. 'I can't be blamed for every disappearance in the Mirkil district. At Vurush River under the Orgais? Last night? A far distance for a man who breakfasted at Shagfe.'

'A not impossible distance.'

Hozman smilingly shook his head. 'If I owned pacers that staunch and swift, would I deal in slaves? I would breed pacers and make my fortune. As for your people, the Orgai is chumpa country; here may be the tragic truth.'

Karazan, pale with rage and frustration, stood speechless, unable to find a crevice in Hozman's defense. Hozman glimpsed the black creature in the shadow of the doorway. He jerked forward, intent and startled. 'What does the Ka do here? Is it now your ally?'

Ifness said evenly, 'I captured it under Thrie Orgai, near where you met us yesterday afternoon.'

Hozman turned away from the creature he had called a 'Ka'; nevertheless his eyes strayed back towards where it stood. He spoke in easy, jocular tones, 'Another voice, another accusation! If words were blades, poor Hozman would writhe on the ground in a hundred pieces.'

'As he will, in any event,' said Karazan menacingly, 'unless he returns the four Alul girls he stole.'

Hozman calculated, looking back and forth between Ifness and the Ka. He turned to Karazan. 'Certain of the chumpas are my agents,' he said in a voice like cream. 'Perhaps they hold your Alul girls. If such is the case, will you trade four for two?'

'How do you mean, "four for two"?' growled Karazan.

'For your four, I'll take this white-haired man and the Ka.'

'I veto the proposal,' said Ifness promptly. 'You must put forward a better offer.'

'Well, the Ka alone then. Think! A savage alien for four handsome girls.'

'A remarkable offer!' declared Ifness. 'Why do you want the creature?'

'I can always find customers for such a curiosity.' Hozman moved politely aside to allow newcomers into the common room: two Kash Blue-worms, drunk and ugly, the hair matted on their foreheads. The foremost jostled Hozman. 'Stand back, reptile. You have brought us all to poverty and degradation; must you now block my path as well?'

93

Hozman moved away, his lips curling in a smile of contempt. The Kash Blue-worm stopped short and thrust forward his face. 'Do you dare to mock me? Am I ludicrous?'

Baba sprang forward. 'No combat in here, never in the common room!'

The Kash swung his arm in a backhanded blow, knocking Hozman to the floor, at which Baba brought forth a cudgel and with amazing dexterity drove the Kash cursing and lumbering from the inn. Ifness solicitously reached to help Hozman to his feet. He glanced at Etzwane. 'Your knife, to cut off a growth.'

Etzwane jumped forward. Ifness held aside Hozman's maroon scarf; Etzwane slashed the straps of the little harness, while Hozman lay thrashing and kicking. The innkeeper gaped in amazement, unable to wield his cudgel. With his nose wrinkled in distaste Ifness lifted the asutra, a flattened creature marked with faint brown and maroon stripes. Etzwane slashed the nerve and Hozman emitted the most appalling scream yet heard in the inn at Shagfe.

A hard, strong shape struck between Ifness and Etzwane: the Ka. Etzwane raised his knife, ready to stab, but the Ka was already gone with the asutra and out into the yard. Ifness ran in pursuit, with Etzwane close behind. They came upon a macabre scene, indistinct in swirls of boiling dust. The Ka, talons protruding from its feet, stamped upon the asutra and tore it to shreds.

Ifness, putting away his energy gun, stood grimly watching. Etzwane said in astonishment, 'It hates the asutra more than we do.'

'A curious exhibition,' Ifness agreed.

From within the inn came a new outcry and the thud of blows. Clutching his head, Hozman ran frantically out into the yard, with the Alula in pursuit. Ifness, moving with unusual haste, intervened and waved off the Alula.

94

'Are you totally without foresight? If you kill this man we will learn nothing.'

'What is there to learn?' roared Karazan. 'He has sold our daughters into slavery; he says we will never see them again.'

'Why not learn the details?' Ifness turned to where Etzwane prevented Hozman from flight. 'You have much to tell us.'

'What can I tell you?' said Hozman. 'Why should I trouble myself? They will tear me apart like the cannibals they are.'

'I am nevertheless curious. You may tell your story.'

'It is a dream,' mumbled Hozman. 'I rode through the air like a gray ghost, I spoke with monsters; I am a creature alive and dead.'

'First of all,' said Ifness, 'where are the people you stole last night?'

Hozman threw his arm up in an unrestrained gesture which suggested imprecision in his thinking processes. 'Beyond the sky! They are gone forever. No one returns after the car drops down.'

'Ah, I see. They have been taken into an aircraft.'

'Better to say that they are gone from the world Durdane.'

'And when does the car drop down?'

Hozman looked furtively aside, with his mouth pinched into a crafty knot. Ifness spoke sharply, 'No temporising! The Alula are waiting to torture you and we must not inconvenience them.'

Hozman gave a hoarse laugh. 'What do I care for torture? I know I must die by pain; so I was told by my witch-uncle. Kill me any way you like; I have no preference.'

'How long have you carried the asutra?'

'It has been so long I have forgotten my old life . . .

When? Ten years ago, twenty years. They looked into my tent, two men in black garments; they were no men of Caraz, nor men of Durdane. I rose to meet them in fear, and they put the mentor upon me.' Hozman felt his neck with trembling fingers. He looked sidelong towards the Alula, who stood attentive, hands at the hilts of their scimitars.

'Where are the four you stole from us?' asked Karazan.

'They are gone to a far world. You are curious as to what is to be their lot? I cannot say. The mentor told me nothing.'

Ifness made a sign to Karazan and spoke in an easy voice, 'The mentor was able to communicate with you?'

Hozman's eyes became unfocused, words began to gush from his mouth. 'It is a condition impossible to describe. When I first discovered the creature I went crazy with revulsion – but only for a moment! It performed what I call a pleasure-trick, and I became flooded with joy. The dreary Balch swamp seemed to swim with delightful odors, and I was a man transformed. There was at that moment nothing which I could not have accomplished!' Hozman threw his arms to the sky. 'The mood lasted several minutes, and then the men in black returned and made me aware of my duties. I obeyed, for I quickly learned the penalty of disobedience; the mentor could bless with joy or punish with pain. It knew the language of men but could not speak except in a hiss and a whistle, which I never learned. But I could talk aloud and ask if such a course fulfilled its wishes. The mentor became my soul, closer to me than hands and feet, for its nerves led to my nerves. It was alert to my welfare and never forced me to work in rain or cold. And I never hungered, for my work was rewarded with ingots of good gold and copper and sometimes steel.'

'And what were your duties?' asked Ifness.

Hozman's flow of words was again stimulated, as if they had long been pent inside of him, building a pressure to be released. 'They were simple. I bought prime slaves, as many as could be had. I worked as a slave-taker, and I have scoured the face of Caraz, from the Azur River in the east to the vast Duglov in the west, and as far south as Mount Thruska. Thousands of slaves have I sent into space!'

'How did you so send them?'

'At night, when no one was near and the mentor could warn me of danger, I called down the little car and loaded aboard my slaves, which first I had drugged into a happy stupor: sometimes only one or two, again as many as a dozen or even more. If I chose, the car would take me where I wished to go, quickly through the night, as from the Orgai to Shagfe village.'

'And where did the car take the slaves?'

Hozman pointed into the sky. 'Above hangs a depot hull, where the slaves lie quiet. When the hull is full it flies away to the mentor's world, which lies somewhere in the coils of Histhorbo the Snake. So much I learned to my idle amusement one starry night when I asked my mentor many questions, which it answered by a yes or a no. Why did it need so many slaves? Because its previous creatures were inadequate and insubordinate, and because it feared a terrible enemy, somewhere off among the stars.' Hozman fell silent. The Alula had drawn close to surround him; they now regarded him less with hate than with awe for the weird travail he had undergone.

Ifness asked in his most casual voice, 'And how do you call down the little car?'

Hozman licked his lips and looked off over the plain. Ifness said gently, 'Never again will you carry the asutra which brought such bliss to your brain. You are now one with the rest of us, and we consider the asutra our enemies.'

Hozman said sullenly, 'In my pouch I carry a box with a little button within. When I require the car, I go out into the dark night and push on the button and hold it so until the car comes down.'

'Who drives the car?'

'The device works by a mysterious will of its own.'

'Give me the box with the button.'

Hozman slowly drew forth the box, which Ifness took into his own possession. Etzwane, at a glance and a nod from Ifness, searched Hozman's pouch and person, but found only three small ingots of copper and a magnificent steel dagger with a handle of carved white glass.

Hozman watched with a quizzical expression. 'Now what will you do with me?'

Ifness looked towards Karazan, who shook his head. 'This is not a man upon whom we can take vengeance. He is a puppet, a toy on a string.'

'You have made a just decision,' said Ifness. 'In this slave-taking land his offense is simple overzealousness.'

'Still, what next?' demanded Karazan, 'We have not reclaimed our daughters. This man must call down the car, which we will seize and hold against their release.'

'There is no one aboard the car with whom you can bargain,' said Hozman. Suddenly he added, 'You might go aloft in the car and expostulate in person.'

Karazan uttered a soft sound and looked up into the purple sky of the evening: a colossus in white blouse and black breeches. Etzwane also looked up and thought of Rune the Willow Wand among the crawling asutra . . .

Ifness asked Hozman, 'Have you ever gone aloft to the depot ship?'

'Not I,' said Hozman. 'I had great fear of such an event. On occasion a gray dwarf creature and its mentor came down to the planet. Often have I stood hours through the night while the two mentors hissed one to the other. Then I knew that the depot had reached capacity and that no more slaves were needed for a period.'

'When last did the mentor come down from the depot?'

'A time ago; I cannot recall exactly. I have been allowed small time for reflection.'

Ifness became pensive. Karazan thrust his bulk forward. 'This shall be our course of action: we shall call down the car and ourselves go aloft, to destroy our enemies and liberate our people. We need only wait until night.'

'The tactic leaps to mind,' said Ifness. 'If successful it might yield valuable benefits – not the least being the ship itself. But difficulties present themselves, notably the return descent. You might find yourself in command of the depot ship, but none the less marooned. Such a venture is precarious. I advise against it.'

Karazan made a disconsolate sound and again searched the sky, as if to discover a feasible route to the depot ship. Hozman, seeing an opportunity to slip away unobserved, did so. He walked around the inn to his pacer, to find a Blue-worm rifling the saddlebags. Hozman gave an inarticulate babble of fury and leapt upon the burly back. A second Blue-worm, at the other side of the pacer, drove his fist into Hozman's face, to send Hozman staggering back against the wall of the inn. The Blue-worms continued their ignoble work. The Alula looked on with disgust, half of a mind to intervene, but Karazan called them away. 'Let the jackals do as they will; it is none of our affair.'

'You call us jackals?' demanded one of the Kash. 'That is an insulting epithet!'

'Only for a creature who is not a jackal,' said Karazan in a bored voice. 'You need not take offense.'

The Kash, considerably outnumbered, had no real stomach for a fight and turned back to the saddlebags. Karazan turned away and shook his fist at the sky.

Etzwane, restless and troubled, spoke to Ifness. 'Suppose for a fact that we did capture the ship. Could you not bring it down to the ground?'

'Almost certainly I could not. With definite certainty I do not intend to try.'

Etzwane stared at Ifness with cold hostility. 'We must do something. A hundred, perhaps two hundred people hang up there, waiting for the asutra to take them away to some strange place, and we are the only ones who can help them.'

Ifness laughed. 'You exaggerate my capabilities, at least. I suspect that you have been captivated by certain flirtatious glances and that now you wish to perform a gallant feat, no matter what the difficulties.'

Etzwane contained his first rush of words, especially since the remarks were apt enough to cause him discomfort . . . Why should he suddenly expect altruism from Ifness, after all? From the moment of their first meeting Ifness had consistently refused to divert himself from his own large concerns. Not for the first time, Etzwane regarded Ifness with cold dislike. Their relationship, never close, had shifted into a new and distant phase. But he spoke in an even voice, 'At Shillinsk, could you not call Dasconetta and request an Earth ship for a business of great urgency?'

'I could do this,' said Ifness. 'Furthermore, Dasconetta might well put through the order, and thereby sequester to himself an achievement which rightfully should be credited elsewhere.'

'How long before such a ship could arrive at Shagfe?'

'As to this, I could make no estimate.'

'Within a day? Three days? Two weeks? A month?'

100

'A number of factors are involved. Under favorable conditions a ship might arrive in two weeks.'

Karazan, comprehending nothing of the matter save the time-span involved, declared, 'By that time the depot may be gone, and the people as well, to terrible events on some far, cold world.'

'It is a tragic situation,' agreed Ifness, 'but I can make no recommendations.'

'What of this?' asked Etzwane. 'You ride at best speed to Shillinsk, and there demand assistance from Dasconetta. I will call down the transfer car and go up with the Alula to capture the depot ship. If possible we will return to Durdane; if not we will await your coming.'

Ifness reflected a moment before replying. 'The scheme has a certain mad logic, and conceivably might come to a successful issue. I know a tactic to obviate Dasconetta's interference, which goes to answer one of my previous objections . . . The uncertainties however are numerous; you are dealing with an unknown situation.'

'I understand this,' said Etzwane. 'But the Alula will go aloft in any event and here' – he patted his pouch with the energy gun within – 'is their best hope of success. Knowing this, how could I stand aside?'

Ifness shrugged. 'I personally cannot afford these quixotic extravagances; I would long since have been dead. Still, if you bring down to Durdane an alien spaceship, or even secure it in orbit until my coming, I shall applaud your altruistic bravado. I emphasise, however, that while I will keep your affairs in mind, I can guarantee nothing, and I strongly recommend that you stay below.'

Etzwane gave a bitter chuckle. 'I understand very well. Still, human lives are at stake whether we go up or not. You had best leave for Shillinsk at once. Haste is essential.'

Ifness frowned. 'Tonight? The way is long . . . Still, Baba's inn offers only small solace. I agree; haste is desirable. Well thèn, the Ka and I will ride for Shillinsk with Fabrache to guide us. We leave at once.'

Chapter 7

The suns were three hours gone beyond the far Orgai, and the last purple glow had left the sky. On the plain waited eighteen Alul warriors, with Etzwane and Hozman.

'Here is my usual spot,' said Hozman, 'and now is my ordinary time. The routine is this. I press the button. After twenty minutes I look for a green light overhead. I then release the button and the car lands. My slaves stand in an orderly line. They are drugged and obedient, but not aware, like people in a dream. The door opens and a pale-blue light issues forth. I move forward, marshaling the slaves. If the car contains a mentor it appears on the ledge, and then I must wait while the mentors converse. When the slaves are within and the conversation at an end, I close the door and the car departs. There is no more to be told.'

'Very good. Press the button.'

Hozman did as instructed. 'How often have I done this deed,' he murmured. 'Always I wondered where they went and how they passed their lives. Then, after the car departed, I would look up into the sky and consider the stars . . . But no more, no more. I shall take your pacers to Shagfe and sell them to Baba, and then I shall return to the land where I was born and become a professional seer

. . . Stand in line, close together. You must seem vague and limp.'

The group formed a line and waited. The night was silent. Five miles to the north lay Shagfe, but the fires and oil lamps flickered too dimly to be seen. The minutes passed slowly; Etzwane had never known time so to prolong itself. Each second stretched elastically and departed with reluctance into the past.

Hozman held up his hand. 'The green light . . . The car comes down. I now release the button. Stand ready – but limp and easy; make no moves . . .'

Above sounded a faint sigh and a hum; a dark shape moved across the stars and settled fifty or sixty yards away. An aperture slowly appeared, casting a wan blue glow upon the ground. 'Come,' muttered Hozman. 'In a line, close together . . . There crawls the mentor. You must be quick – but not hasty.'

Etzwane halted at the entrance. A blue glow showed the way within. On a ledge beside a row of colored lights rested an asutra. For an instant Etzwane and asutra looked eye to eye; then the asutra, apprehending its danger, hissed and scuttled backward towards a small passage. Etzwane swung his blade, to chop away the creature's abdomen and block its escape. In revulsion he scraped the jerking parts to the deck, where they were crushed under Alul boots.

Hozman gave a whinny of crazy, high-pitched laughter. 'I am not yet free of the thing's influence; I could feel its emotion. It was furiously angry.'

Karazan pushed into the interior, and the ceiling pressed down upon his head. 'Come, let us do the business while our blood flows hot! Gastel Etzwane, do you understand the use of these swivels and pegs and blinking ghost-lamps?'

'I do not.'

'Come in then; we go to do what we must.'

Etzwane was last to enter. He hesitated, beset by the certain knowledge that their plans were insanely rash. 'On this consideration alone may we expect success,' he told himself hollowly. He looked back into Hozman's face and surprised an expression curiously vital and eager, as if Hozman could hardly keep from shouting aloud in joy.

Here is his revenge, Etzwane gloomily told himself: on us and on the asutra as well. He will go forth now to take vengeance on all Durdane for the horror which has been his life . . . Best that I should kill him now . . . Etzwane paused in the doorway. Outside, Hozman stood expectantly; within, the Alula, incipiently claustrophobic, began to grumble. On a sudden impulse Etzwane jumped back to the ground and jerked at Hozman's arm, which was crooked somewhat behind his back. In his hand he carried a length of white rag Etzwane looked slowly up into Hozman's face. Hozman licked his lips, his brows dropping hangdog low at the outer corners.

'So, then,' said Etzwane, 'you would signal us to our doom, with all the others on the ship.'

'No, no,' stammered Hozman. 'This is my kerchief. It is a habit, no more; I wipe my sweating palms.'

'They sweat understandably,' said Etzwane.

Karazan lurched forth from the car. He apprehended the situation in an instant and turned a terrible stare upon Hozman. 'For this act you can blame no mentor, no evil force which compelled you.' He drew his great scimitar. 'Hozman, on your knees and bend your neck, for your time has come.'

'A moment,' said Etzwane. 'What is the system to closing the door?'

'You must puzzle it out for yourself,' said Hozman. He attempted to spring away, but Karazan lunged to catch the collar of his cape.

Hozman began to plead in a hysterical, tearful voice. 'This is not according to our arrangement! And also, I can supply information to save your lives, but unless you guarantee my freedom, you will never hear it; you may kill me first, and then, while you slave on a far distant world, remember this laugh of mine.' He threw back his head and uttered a wild wail of mockery. 'And you will know I died happy, for I brought ruin to my enemies!'

Etzwane said, 'We don't want your miserable life; we hope to save our own, and your treachery is our worst danger.'

'There will be no more treachery! I trade my life and freedom for your own!'

'Thrust him inside,' said Etzwane. 'If we live, he lives, and upon our return he shall have a flogging.'

'No, no, no!' screamed Hozman. Karazan cuffed him to silence.

'I would prefer to kill the vermin,' said Karazan. 'In with you.' He thrust Hozman into the car. Etzwane studied the door and discovered the inside clamp. He asked Hozman, 'What now? Do I pull the door closed and throw this lever?'

'That is all,' came Hozman's sullen reply. 'The car will leave Durdane of its own volition.'

'Then make ready; we are about to leave.'

Etzwane closed the door. At once the floor thrust into their feet. The Alula gasped, Hozman whimpered. There was a period of acceleration, then ease. The blue illumination made faces unrecognisable and seemed to educe a new dimension of each man's soul. Etzwane, looking on the Alula, felt humble in the face of their bravery; unlike himself, they knew nothing of Ifness' abilities. Then Etzwane asked of Hozman: 'What is this knowledge by which you will save our lives?'

'It is nothing definite,' said Hozman. 'It concerns your

general demeanor and how you must act to avoid instant detection.'

'Well, then, how must we act?'

'You must walk like this, with your arms limp, your eyes blank and mild, your legs loose, as if they barely supported the weight of your bodies.' Hozman stood limp and futile, with long, hopeless creases pinching his face.

Fifteen minutes the speed held, then slackened. Hozman said nervously, 'I know nothing of conditions aboard – but you must strike hard and fast, and make the most of surprise.'

'The asutra ride their hosts?'

'I imagine that they do.'

'For your own sake,' said Etzwane, 'fight and fight well.'

Hozman made no response. A moment passed. The car touched a solid object and slid into a socket, with a small shock of finality. The men tensed themselves. The door opened. They looked into an empty corridor, along which men might walk single file. A voice came from a panel: 'Step forth into the hall; remove all clothing; you will be cleansed by a refreshing spray.'

'Act as if you are too drugged to understand the instruction,' muttered Hozman.

Etzwane moved slowly out into the corridor and languidly walked to the far end, where a door barred the way. The Alula followed, Hozman shambling in their midst. The voice spoke again, 'Remove all clothes; they must be removed.'

Etzwane made tentative motions to obey, then let his arms sag, as if fatigued, and sagged against the wall. From the speaker came a faint hiss and a disgusted mutter. From ceiling orifices jets of an acrid liquid struck down, drenching them to the skin . . . The jets were cut off; the end door opened. Etzwane staggered through into a large

107

circular chamber. Here waited half a dozen biped creatures, gray and lumpy of skin, squat in stature, batrachian in aspect. Five eyes like orbs of milk-glass protruded from the squat heads; the feet were flaps of gray-green muscle. On the nape of each neck rested an asutra. Etzwane had no need to call a signal. Pent energy exploded within the Alula; they lurched forward; in five seconds the gray host-things lay dead in spouts of gray-green blood, with the asutra crushed and hacked. Etzwane glared around the room, nostrils dilated, the energy gun in readiness. But no new gray creatures appeared. He ran on long, stealthy steps to the end of the chamber, where narrow corridors led in two directions. He listened and heard no sound save a low pulsing hum. Half the Alula set off with Karazan to the left; Etzwane led the others to the right. The corridors, narrow and low, had been built to asutra concepts of scale; Etzwane wondered how Karazan fared. He came to a narrow ramp; at the top he saw the gleam of stars. Up he clambered at his best speed and burst out into a control dome. A low bench circled the room; at one area a dozen small tanks displayed quantities of colored liquids. One end of the chamber was given to a low console, with adjuncts which Etzwane assumed to be controls. On the padded bench beside the controls rested three asutra. At Etzwane's entry, they shrank back against the transparent dome, hissing in shock. One produced a small black mechanism which spat lavender fire towards Etzwane. He had already flung himself aside; the fire struck into the Alula at his back. Etzwane could not use his energy gun for fear of rupturing the dome; he lunged, jerking and ducking across the room. One of the asutra scuttled into a small passageway, no more than a foot square; Etzwane smashed the second creature with the flat of his blade. The third sidled, hissing and whistling, to the bank of controls. Etzwane seized it

108

and threw it into the center of the room, where the Alula stamped it to pulp.

The man who had been struck by the bolt lay staring up through the low dome at the stars; he was dying and nothing could be done for him. Etzwane ordered two men to remain on guard; they gave him truculent stares, challenging his authority. Etzwane ignored their recalcitrance. 'Take care; do not stand where an asutra can aim at you from that little passage yonder. Block off the opening if you can. Be alert!' He departed the room and went off after Karazan.

A ramp led down to a central hold, and here lay the captives from Caraz, drugged and torpid, on shelves which radiated from the walls like the spokes of a wheel. Karazan had killed one of the lumpish gray attendants; two more stood submissively to the side. None of the three carried asutras. In all, two hundred men, women, and children lay stacked like billets of timber and among them Karazan stood in the center of the room, scowling uncertainly from the gray host-creatures to the captives, at a loss, perhaps for the first time in his life.

'These people are well enough as they are,' Etzwane told Karazan. 'Let them sleep. Another matter is more urgent. The asutra have small passages where at least one has taken refuge. We must search the ship, taking great precautions, for the creatures carry energy weapons; already they have killed one man. Our best advantage is to block off the passages as we come to them, until we learn the plan of the ship.'

Karazan said, 'It is smaller than I had expected; not a comfortable or easy place to be.'

'The asutra have built as close to their own scale as possible. With luck we shall soon be back down on the surface. Until then we can only wait and hope that the asutra can't call for help.'

109

Karazan blinked. 'How could they do that?'

'The advanced races talk through empty space, using the power of lightning.'

'Preposterous,' muttered Karazan, looking around the chamber. 'Why, in the first place, should they go to such lengths for slaves? They have the toad-things, the black monsters like your captive, the red demons, and who knows how many other servants?'

'Nothing about the asutra is certain,' said Etzwane. 'One guess is as good as another. Perhaps each of their hosts serves a special function. Perhaps they simply enjoy a variety of hosts.'

'No matter,' growled Karazan, 'we must dig them out of their crannies.' He called instructions to his men and sent them off in pairs. Declaring himself too cumbersome to aid in the search, he took the gray creatures to the observation dome and tried to persuade them to take the ship down to Durdane, without success. Etzwane went off to examine the lift car, still in its socket, and could discover no means to control it. He next searched for food and water, which he found in bins and tanks under the slave hold. The atmosphere seemed fresh; somewhere aboard the ship an automatic renewal system was at work, and Etzwane hoped that if asutra were alive and in hiding they would not think to stifle the intruders. What, in a similar position, would he do himself? If a transfer ship were due from the home-world, he would do nothing, but allow the problem to be solved by exterior means . . . Two by two the Alul warriors came to report. They had discovered the drive system, the energy generators, the air-purification system. They had surprised and killed one asutra riding the neck of his gray host, but had encountered no others; in a dozen areas they had blocked off asutra passages. Etzwane, now with nothing better to do, made a slow exploration of the ship, trying to learn the

110

location of the asutra refuge. In this work he was assisted by the Alula, who had gained a measure of confidence.

For hours the group studied the ship, estimating distances and volumes, and finally concluded that the private refuge of the asutra lay directly under the control dome, in a space about ten feet square and four feet high. Etzwane and Karazan examined the outside of this space and wondered if they could break in. The walls showed no seams and were formed of a material unknown to Etzwane: neither glass nor metal. The space, Etzwane theorised, constituted the private quarters of the asutra, and he wondered how long they could survive without nourishment – though of course there might be nutriment within the space.

Dawn approached. Durdane was a great black-purple disk surrounded by stars, with a pulsing magenta flare in the east. Blue Etta swung over the horizon, then came pink Sasetta, and finally white Zael, and the face of Durdane awoke to the light.

The ship hung above Caraz, at a distance which Etzwane estimated to be about two hundred miles. Below would be Shagfe village, too inconsequential to be noticed. From south to north extended the Caraz rivers, enormous silver-purple snakes, languid on crumpled plush. In the far southwest was Lake Nior and a line of smaller lakes. Etzwane speculated as to the force which held the depot ship in place, and how long it might take to fall to the surface if the asutra cut off the power. Etzwane winced, imagining the last few seconds . . . Still, the asutra had nothing to gain by destroying their ship. Etzwane reflected upon the curious similarities among creatures as disparate as man, asutra, Roguskhoi, and Ka. All needed sustenance and shelter, all used light to locate themselves spatially . . . To communicate all used sound, rather than light or touch or odor, for simple and universal reasons. Sound pervaded and filled an area; sound could be produced with minimal energy; sound was infinitely flexible. Telepathy? A faculty unevenly useful to a man but perhaps employed more consistently by other species; indeed, to regard a faculty so basic as restricted to the human race would be irrational. The study and comparison of intelligent life-forms must be a fascinating endeavor, thought Etzwane . . . He scanned the sky in all directions, which was dead black and blazing with stars. Much too early to expect Ifness and an Earth ship. But not too early to fear the coming of an asutra vessel. The depot ship itself was a squat cylinder, studded at twenty-foot intervals with thick cones ending in white-metal radiants. The skin, Etzwane noted, was not the copper of the ships he had previously seen, but a burnished gray-black, on which shone oily lusters of crimson, dark blue, and green. Etzwane went once more to study the controls. No doubt but that these were in principal similar to the controls of an Earth ship, and he suspected that Ifness, had he been allowed the opportunity, might have puzzled out the functions of the odd little fingers and knobs and tanks of gray jelly . . . Karazan appeared from below. Claustrophobia had made him edgy and irritable; only in the observation dome, with unobstructed space surrounding him, did he tend to relax. 'I cannot break the wall. Our knives and clubs are unequal to the task, and I cannot understand the asutra tools.'

'I don't see how they can menace us,' Etzwane reflected, 'provided that all the passages are blocked. If they became desperate they could possibly burn their way out and attack us with their guns . . . If they would lower us to the ground they could go their way, in spite of Ifness' yearning for a spaceship, which he can procure at some other time.'

'I agree in every respect,' said Karazan. 'I dislike this

112

hanging in mid-air like a bird in a cage. If we could make the creatures understand us, no doubt an accommodation could be arranged. Why not try once more with the toad-men? We have nothing better to do.'

They went down to the slave hold, where the toad-men crouched in apathy. Etzwane led one of them to the observation dome, and by dint of gestures towards the controls and down at the surface, indicated that the creature should lower the vessel to the ground – but to no avail; the gray thing stood staring in all directions, the palps rising and falling at its breathing orifices in evidence of some unknowable emotion.

Etzwane went so far as to push the creature towards the controls; it became rigid and exuded a foul-smelling slime from glands down its dorsal ridge. Etzwane desisted from his efforts.

After a half hour of cogitation he went to the blocked-off asutra passage and cautiously removed the sacks of cereal cake stopping the aperture. He hissed and whistled in as conciliatory a manner as he could contrive, then listened. No sound, no response. He tried again, and waited. Again without success. Etzwane closed off the hole once more, irritated and disappointed. The asutra, with intelligence at least equivalent to the human, ought to have recognised that Etzwane was offering a truce.

Etzwane went to look down at Durdane, now fully exposed to the sunlight. Lake Nior had become obscured under a swirl of cirrus; the ground directly below was likewise hidden . . . The asutra's refusal to respond suggested an inability to compromise or cooperate. The creature seemed to expect no quarter and assuredly would give none. Etzwane remembered the Roguskhoi and the horrors they had worked upon the folk of Shant. According to previous assumptions, the Roguskhoi had been an experimental weapon designed for use against the Earth

113

worlds, but now it seemed likely that the asutra had the creatures of the black globe-ships in mind . . . Etzwane scowled down at Durdane. A situation which became ever more mysterious and contradictory. He mustered in his mind those questions which at one time or another had caused him perplexity. Why did the asutra trouble with human slaves when the Ka were equally deft, strong, and agile? Why had the Ka destroyed Hozman's asutra with such passion? How could the asutra hope to match the Roguskhoi against a technically proficient race? And another matter: when the Ka had been trapped in the wrecked spaceship, why had not the asutra escaped, as it easily could have done? Curious matters! Which might or might not at some time be illuminated.

The day dragged past. The men ate rations of the dried meat they had carried with them and cautiously sampled the asutra cereal cake, which proved bland but not unpleasant. The sooner Ifness arrived with a rescue ship the better. Ifness would come, of this Etzwane felt certain. Ifness had never failed in any undertaking; Ifness was too proud a man to tolerate failure . . . Etzwane went down to the slave hold and looked along the pale, still faces. He found Rune the Willow Wand and stood for several minutes examining the even features. He touched her neck, feeling for a pulse, but was confused by the throb of his own heart. It would be pleasant indeed to ride the plains of Caraz alone with Rune. Slowly, reluctantly, he turned away. He wandered around the ship, marveling at the precise workmanship and the expert engineering. What a miracle was a spaceship, which effortlessly could take thinking creatures such vast distances!

Etzwane went back to the dome and gazed in helpless fascination at the controls . . . The suns sank; night concealed the world below.

Night passed; day came, to reveal Hozman Sore-throat

sprawled face down at the back of the slave racks, a cord tight around his neck and his tongue lolling forth. Karazan muttered in disapproval but made no effort to discover the murderers; Hozman's death seemed a matter almost trivial.

The day proceeded. A mood of doubt and uncertainty infected the ship. The zest of victory was gone; the Alula were dispirited ... Once more Etzwane whistled down the passage for the asutra, with no more success than before. He began to wonder if all the asutra were dead. He had seen one enter the passage, but subsequently an asutra riding on the neck of a toad-thing had been killed; it might have been the same asutra.

The day passed; then another and another. Durdane daily showed a different pattern of clouds; otherwise the scene was static. Etzwane assured the Alula that the very lack of event was a good omen, but Karazan retorted, 'I cannot follow your reasoning. Suppose Ifness were killed on his way to Shillinsk? What if he were unable to communicate with his colleagues? Or assume that they refused to listen to him. What then? Our wait here would feel the same as it does now, and would represent no omen whatever.'

Etzwane tried to explain Ifness' peculiar and perverse personality, but Karazan only made an impatient gesture. 'He is a man, and nothing is certain.'

At this moment a cry came from the lookouts, who stood night and day in the observation dome. 'A spacecraft moves through the sky!'

Etzwane jumped up, heart in his mouth. The time was too early, far too early, to expect Ifness. He peered through the dome to where the lookout pointed ... High above, a bronze disk-ship slid lazily across the sky, the suns' light reflecting from its skin.

'It is an asutra ship,' said Etzwane.

Karazan said, somewhat heavily, 'We have only one option, and that is to fight. Surprise is once again our ally, for they cannot expect to find the ship in enemy hands.'

Etzwane glanced at the console. Lights blinked and flickered, signifying what, he did not know. If the disk-ship were attempting to communicate and raised no response, it would approach with caution. Surprise was not so great an ally as Karazan had hoped.

The disk curved north, sank at a slant, and halted, to hang quietly a mile away. Then it flickered suddenly green and disappeared. The sky was empty.

From a dozen throats came the hiss of released breath. 'Now why is that?' Karazan demanded of the company in general. 'I am not the man for this sort of business; I detest puzzlement.'

Etzwane shook his head. 'I can only say that I prefer the ship's absence to its company.'

'It realises our presence and plans to catch us napping,' Karazan grumbled. 'We will be ready.'

For the rest of the day all hands crowded the observation dome, save those sent forth to patrol the ship. The bronze disk did not reappear, and presently the group relaxed and conditions were as before.

Four days dragged past. The Alula lapsed into surly taciturnity and the patrols began to lack crispness. Etzwane complained to Karazan, who gave back an inarticulate mutter.

'If discipline deteriorates, we're in trouble,' Etzwane observed. 'We must maintain morale. After all, everybody understood the circumstances before they left Durdane.'

Karazan made no reply, but a short time later he called his men together and issued a set of instructions. 'We are Alula,' he said. 'We are famed for our fortitude. We must demonstrate this quality now. After all, we are suffering

116

nothing more serious than boredom and cramped quarters. The situation might be worse.'

The Alula listened in somber silence and subsequently went about their routines with greater alertness.

Late in the afternoon an event occurred which drastically altered the situation. Etzwane, looking east over the great mulberry-gray expanse, noticed a black sphere hanging motionless in the sky, at a distance impossible to estimate. Etzwane watched for ten minutes while the black globe hung motionless. On sudden thought he looked down to the control panel, to notice lights blinking and altering color. Karazan entered the compartment; Etzwane pointed out the black globe. Karazan asked in a wistful voice. 'Could it be the Earth ship, to carry us down to the soil?'

'Not yet. Ifness said two weeks at the earliest; the time is too soon.'

'Then what ship flies yonder? Another asutra ship?'

'I told you of the battle at Thrie Orgai,' said Etzwane. 'I would suppose this to be a ship of the asutra's enemies, the people of mystery.'

'As the ship is approaching,' Karazan noted, 'the mystery is about to be elucidated.'

The black ship curved down at a slant, passing a mile south of the depot; it slowed and drifted to a halt. At precisely the point where it had disappeared, the bronze-copper disk-ship materialised with venomous stealth. For an instant it lay quiescent, then spurted forth a pair of projectiles. The black globe, as if by nervous reflex, discharged countermissiles; midway between the ships a soundless dazzle blotted out the sky. Etzwane and Karazan would have been blinded except for the stuff of the dome which resisted the surge of light.

The bronze disk had focused four jets of energy on the black globe, which glowed red and burned open: appar-

117

ently its protective system had failed. In retaliation it projected a gush of purple flame, which for an instant flared over the disk-ship like the blast of a torch; then the flame flickered and died. The black globe rolled over like a dead fish. The disk fired another projectile; it struck into the hole burnt by the converging beams. The globe exploded and Etzwane received an instantaneous image of black fragments flying away from a core of lambent material; among the stuff he thought to glimpse hurtling corpses, grotesquely sprawled and rotating. Fragments struck the depot ship, clanging, jarring, sending vibrations through the hull.

The sky was again clear and open. Of the black globe, not an element remained; the bronze disk had disappeared.

Etzwane said in a hollow voice, 'The disk-ship lies in ambush. The depot is bait. The asutra know we are here; they believe us to be their enemies and they wait for our ships to arrive.'

Etzwane and Karazan searched the sky with a new anxiety. The simple rescue of four girls from Hozman Sore-throat had expanded into a situation far past all their imaginings. Etzwane had not bargained for participation in a space war; Karazan and the Alula had not comprehended the psychological pressures which would be put upon them.

The sky remained clear of traffic; the suns sank at the back of a million magenta cloud-feathers. Night was instant; dusk showed only as a sad, subtle bloom upon the face of Durdane.

During the night the patrols were relaxed, to Etzwane's displeasure. He complained to Karazan, pointing out that conditions remained as before, but Karazan reacted with an irritable sweep of his great arm, consigning Etzwane and his peevish little fears to oblivion. Karazan and the

Alula had become demoralised, Etzwane angrily told himself, to such an extent that they would have welcomed attack, captivity, slavery, anything which might have provided them with a palpable antagonist. Pointless to harangue them, Etzwane brooded; they no longer listened.

Night passed, and the day and other nights and days. The Alula sat huddled in the observation dome; they stared out at the sky, seeing nothing. The time had arrived when Ifness might be expected; but no one any longer believed in Ifness nor the Earth ship; the only reality was the sky cage and the empty panorama.

Etzwane had considered a dozen systems for warning Ifness, should he indeed arrive, and had rejected them all, or, more properly, none was in any degree workable. Presently Etzwane himself lost count of the days. The presence of the other men had long since grown odious, but apathy was a stronger force than hostility, and the men suffered each other in a silent community of mutual detestation.

Then the quality of the waiting changed, and became a sense of imminence. The men muttered uneasily and watched from the observation dome, the whites of their eyes showing. Everyone knew that something was about to occur, and soon, and this was the case. The bronze disk-ship reappeared.

The men aboard the depot gave soft guttural groans of despair; Etzwane made a last wild inspection of the sky, willing the Earth ships into existence. Where was Ifness?

The sky was vacant except for the bronze disk-ship. It eased in a circle around the depot, then halted and slowly approached. It loomed enormous, blotting out the sky. The hulls touched; the depot jerked and quivered. From the location of the entry port came a throbbing sound. Karazan looked at Etzwane. 'They are coming aboard. You have your energy weapon; will you fight?'

Etzwane gave his head a dreary shake. 'Dead we are no use to anyone, least of all ourselves.'

Karazan sneered. 'So it is to be surrender? They will take us away and make us their slaves.'

'This is the prospect,' said Etzwane. 'It is better than death. Our hope is that the Earth worlds at last know the situation and will intervene on our behalf.'

Karazan gave a jeering laugh and clenched his great fists, but still stood indecisive. From below came the sounds of ingress. Karazan told his warriors: 'Make no resistance. Our force falls short of our desires. We must suffer the penalties of weakness.'

Into the dome ran two black Ka, each with an asutra clamped to the nape of its neck. They ignored the men except to shoulder them aside and moved to the controls. One worked the curious little studs with ease and certainty. Deep within the ship an engine whined. The view outside the dome grew dim, then dark; nothing could be seen. Another Ka came to the entrance of the dome. It made gestures, indicating that the Alula and Etzwane were to leave. Suddenly Karazan hunched to the exit, and bending his neck, marched down the ramp towards the slave hold. Etzwane followed, and the others came behind.

Chapter 8

The Alula squatted in the aisles between the slave racks. The Ka ignored them as they moved about their tasks, asutra clamped to their necks like leeches.

The depot ship was in motion. The men felt no vibration, no lunge or surge, but the knowledge was sure, as if the shifting infrasubstance rasped upon a sensitive area of the brain. The men huddled silently, each thinking his own sullen thoughts. The Ka paid them no heed.

Time passed, at a pace impossible to measure. Where uncertainty and taut nerves had previously drawn out the hours, now a dismal melancholy worked to the same effect.

Etzwane's single hope was that Ifness had not been killed on the Plain of Blue Flowers, and that vanity would impel him to their assistance. The Alula knew no hope whatever and were apathetic. Etzwane looked across the chamber to the niche where lay Rune the Willow Wand. He could see the outline of her temple and cheekbone, and felt a sudden warmth. To seem gallant in her sight, he had risked and lost his freedom. Such would be Ifness' insulting opinion. Was it justified? Etzwane heaved a sad sigh. His motives had been complex; he did not know them himself.

Karazan heaved himself to his feet. He stood motionless for ten seconds, then stretched out his great arms, twisted them this way and that, making the muscles writhe. Etzwane became alarmed; Karazan's face was peculiarly calm and intent. The Alula watched, interested but indifferent. Etzwane jumped up, called out sharply. Karazan gave no signal that he had heard. Etzwane shook his shoulder; Karazan slowly turned his head; Etzwane saw no expression in the wide gray eyes.

The other Alula rose to their feet. One muttered to Etzwane, 'Stand back. He is in death-seek.'

Another said, 'It is dangerous to molest folk in this condition; after all, his way may be the best.'

'Not so!' cried Etzwane. 'Dead folk are no good to anyone. Karazan!' He shook the massive shoulders. 'Listen! Do you hear me? If you ever want to see Lake Nior again, listen!'

He thought that a flicker of response appeared in Karazan's eyes. 'We are not without hope! Ifness is alive; he will find us.'

One of the other Alula asked anxiously, 'Do you really believe this?'

'If you knew Ifness you would never doubt it! The man cannot tolerate defeat.'

'This may be,' said the Alula, 'but how does this avail when we are lost upon a far star?'

From Karazan's throat came a hoarse sound and then words. 'How can he find us?'

'I don't know,' Etzwane admitted, 'but I will never lose hope.'

Karazan said in a throbbing voice, 'It is foolish to speak of hope. In vain did you draw me back.'

'If you are a brave man you will hope,' said Etzwane. ' "Death-seek" is the easy way.'

Karazan made no reply. Once more he seated himself, then stretching out full-length he slept. The other Alula muttered together, turning cool glances towards Etzwane, as if his interference with Karazan's 'death-seek' were not to their liking . . . Etzwane went to his accustomed place and presently fell asleep.

The Alula had become unfriendly. Pointedly they ignored Etzwane and pitched their voices so that he could not hear. Karazan did not share the hostility, but sat off by himself, twirling a weighted thong around his finger.

The next time Etzwane slept, he awoke suddenly to find three Alula standing over him: Black Hulanik, Fairo the Handsome, Ganim Thornbranch. Ganim Thornbranch carried a length of cord. Etzwane sat up, energy gun ready at hand. He remembered Hozman Sore-throat and his lolling tongue. The Alula, blank-faced, moved off across the room.

Etzwane reflected a few moments, then went to Karazan. 'Some of your men were about to kill me.'

Karazan nodded ponderously and twirled his thong.

'What is the reason for this?'

It seemed that Karazan might make no response. Then, with something of an effort, he said, 'There is no particular reason. They want to kill someone and have selected you. It is a game of sorts.'

'I don't care to join,' Etzwane declared in a brassy voice. 'They can play with someone from their own group. Order them to let me be.'

Karazan shrugged lethargically. 'It makes little difference.'

'Not to you. To me it makes a great deal of difference.'

Karazan shrugged and twirled his thong.

Etzwane went off to consider the situation. So long as he remained awake, he would live. When he slept, he would die — perhaps not the first, nor even the second time. They would play with him, try to break his nerve. Why? No reason. A game, the malicious sport of a bar-

123

barian tribe. Cruelty? Etzwane was the outsider, a non-Alula with no more status than a chumpa captured for the baiting.

Several recourses suggested themselves. He could shoot his tormentors and abate the nuisance once and for all. A solution not wholly satisfactory. Even if the asutra failed to confiscate the gun, the game would continue in a more vicious form, with everyone waiting until he slept. The best defense was offense, thought Etzwane. He rose to his feet and crossed the chamber, as if on his way to the latrine. His eyes fell on the still form of Rune the Willow Wand; she seemed less appealing than before; she was, after all, an Alul barbarian, no better than her fellows . . . Etzwane turned aside to the room containing the bags of meal cake and the water tanks. In the doorway he halted to inspect the group. They looked back askance. Smiling grimly Etzwane brought forward a case of food and seated himself. The Alula watched with alert but expressionless faces. Etzwane once more rose to his feet. He took a wafer of the meal cake and a mug of water. Reseating himself, he ate and drank. He noticed several of the Alula licking their lips. As if by common impulse, all turned away and somewhat ostentatiously gave themselves to slumber.

Karazan looked on soberly, his noble forehead creased in a frown. Etzwane ignored him. What if Karazan wanted food and drink? Etzwane had come to no firm decision. He would probably provide Karazan his sustenance.

Upon consideration he moved back into the shadows, where he was less vulnerable to a thrown knife: the obvious response of the Alula. Presently, dissatisfied with his arrangements, he stacked several boxes of meal to provide a barricade behind which he could see but not be seen.

He began to feel drowsy. His eyelids sagged . . . He awoke with a start to notice one of the Alula sidling close.

'Two more steps and you're a dead man,' said Etzwane.

The Alula stopped short. 'Why should you deny me water? I took no part in the baiting.'

'You did nothing to control the three who did. Starve and thirst in their company – until they are dead.'

'This is not fair! You do not reckon with our customs.'

'To the contrary. It is now I who do the baiting. When Fairo the Handsome, Ganim Thornbranch, and Black Hulanik are dead, you shall drink.'

The thirsty Alula turned slowly away. Karazan intoned, 'It is an ill thing which has occurred.'

'You might have stopped it,' said Etzwane. 'You chose to do nothing.'

Rising to his feet Karazan glared into the provisions locker; for a moment he seemed the Karazan of old. Then his shoulders slumped. He said, 'This is true. I gave no instructions; why worry about one death when all are doomed?'

'I happen to worry about my death,' said Etzwane. 'And now I am doing the baiting, and the victims are Fairo, Ganim, Hulanik.'

Karazan looked towards the three named men; every eye in the room followed his gaze. The three men made defiant grimaces and glared about them.

Karazan spoke in a conciliatory voice. 'Let us put aside this business; it is unnecessary and unreasonable.'

'Why did you not say this while I was being baited?' demanded Etzwane in a fury. 'When the three are dead you will eat and drink.'

Karazan settled once more to his previous position. Time passed. At first there was an ostentatious show of solidarity with the three, then other groups formed, talking in whispers. The three huddled back between the

125

racks, and their glass knives glittered from the shadows.

Etzwane dozed once more. He awoke, intensely aware of danger. The chamber was still. Etzwane rose to his knees and backed further into the shadows. Across the outer chamber the Alula were watching. Someone had reached the wall and now sidled inch by inch, out of Etzwane's range of vision, towards the provision locker. Who?

Karazan no longer sat by the wall.

A paralysing roar; a vast shape filled the aperture. Etzwane pulled the trigger, more by startlement than design. He saw a star-shaped dazzle as the flame struck into a great face. The lunging man was instantly dead. His body tottered into the wall and fell over backward.

Etzwane came slowly out into the room, which was hushed in horror. He stood looking down at the corpse, wondering what Karazan had intended, for Karazan carried no weapon. He had known Karazan as a large-souled man: simple, direct, and benevolent. Karazan deserved better than his cramped, despairing fate. He looked along the silent white faces. 'The responsibility is yours. You tolerated malice and now you have lost your great leader.'

Among the Alula there was a furtive shifting of position, a secret interchange of glances. Change came so quickly as to numb the mind: from dazed torpor to wild, screaming activity. Etzwane stumbled back against the wall. Alula leapt through the air; there was slashing and hacking and the doing of grisly deeds; and in a moment all was finished. On the deck Fairo, Ganim Thornbranch, Black Hulanik wallowed in their own blood, and two other men as well.

Etzwane said, 'Quick, before the asutra arrive. Drag the bodies into the racks. Find room on the shelves.'

Dead bodies lay beside living. Etzwane broke open a

126

sack of meal and blotted up the blood. In five minutes the slave hold was orderly and calm, if somewhat less crowded than before. A few minutes later three Ka with asutra peering from the napes of their necks passed through the hold, but did not pause.

The Alula, with hunger and thirst sated and with emotions spent, fell into a state of inertness, more stupor than sleep. Etzwane, though distrustful of the unpredictable Alul temperament, decided that vigilance would only foster a new hostility and gave himself up to sleep, first taking the precaution of tying the energy gun to a loop of his pouch.

He slept undisturbed. When at last he awoke, he realized that the ship was at rest.

Chapter 9

The air in the hold seemed stale; the bluish illumination had dimmed and was more depressing than ever. From overhead came the thud of footsteps and fluctuating snatches of nasal Ka warbling. Etzwane rose to his feet and went to the ramp to listen. The Alula also rose and stood looking uncertainly towards the ramp: a far cry from the swaggering warriors Etzwane had met an aeon before at a bend of the Vurush River.

A grinding hiss, a chatter of ratchets: a section of wall drew back; a wash of gray light flooded the .hold, to drown the blue glow.

Etzwane pushed past the Alula, where he could look out the opening. He leaned back in dismay and shock, unable to find meaning in the welter of strange shapes and colors. He looked once more through narrowed eyes, matching the pattern-forming capabilities of his mind against the alien stuff, and aspects of the landscape shifted into mental focus. He saw steep-sided sugarloaf hills overgrown with a lustrous black, dark-green, and brown pelt of vegetation. Beyond and above spread a heavy gray overcast, under which hung pillows of black cloud and a few veils of rain. Along the lower slopes straggled lines of irregular structures, built from rough lumps of an oyster-white material. At ground level the structures formed a denser complex. Most were built of the pallid lumps; a

few seemed monolithic forms of black scoriaceous slag.
Passages wound between and around, slanting and curv-
ing, without apparent purpose. Certain of these were
smooth and wide and carried vehicles: cage-like drays;
wagons, resembling beetles with raised wings; smaller
lizard-like vehicles, darting inches above the surface. At
intervals posts held up enormous black rectangles, lacking
marks or discernible purpose. Etzwane wondered whether
the eyes of Ka and asutra distinguished colors invisible to
himself. The immediate foreground was a flat, paved
area surrounded by a fence of woven bronze. Etzwane,
who by instinct observed and interpreted colors automatically, after the symbology of Shant, noted no purposeful use of color. Somewhere in the confusion of size,
form, and proportion, he thought, symbology must exist;
technical civilisation was impossible without control over
abstractions.

The inhabitants of the place were Ka, at least half of
whom carried asutra on their necks. No gray toad-men
were in evidence, nor were human beings to be seen.

Except one. Into the slave hold climbed a person tall
and spare, in a shapeless, coarse-fibered cloak. Stiff gray
hair lay piled above the seamed gray face like a forkful of
hay; the chin was long and without hair. Etzwane saw
that the person was a woman, though her aspect and
conduct were asexual. She called in a loud, windy voice,
'The persons now awake; follow me to the ground!
Smartly now, quick and easy. This is the first thing to
know; never wait for two commands.' The woman spoke
a dialect barely comprehensible; she seemed bitter and
wild and grim as a winter storm. She set off down the
ramp. Etzwane gingerly followed, glad to win free from
the detested slave hold and its nightmare memories.

The group descended to the paved area under the great
black depot ship. On a walkway above stood four Ka,

looming like dark statues with asutra at their necks. The woman led them into the mouth of a fenced run. 'Wait here; I go to wake the sleepers.'

An hour passed. The men stood hunched against the fence, glum and silent. Etzwane, clinging to his Ifness-inspired shred of faith, was able to take a melancholy interest in the surroundings. The passage of time made the circumstances no less strange. From various directions came the muffled Ka fluting, mingled with the hiss of traffic on the road immediately across the fence. Etzwane watched the eight-wheeled, segmented drays roll past. Who guided them? He could see no cab or compartment other than a small cupola at the front, and within a small dark mass: asutra . . . From the depot ship marched the woman followed by dazed folk who had occupied the shelves. They stumbled and limped and looked here and there in sad amazement. Etzwane noted Srenka and presently Gulshe; the erstwhile bravos hunched along as miserably as the others. Gulshe's gaze passed across Etzwane's face; he gave no signal of recognition. At the end of the procession came Rune the Willow Wand, and she as well looked past Etzwane without interest.

'Halt!' cried the lead woman in her great coarse voice. 'Here we wait for the omnibus. Now let me speak to you. Your old life is gone and irretrievably; this is the world Kahei and you are like fresh-born babes with another life ahead. It is not too bad unless they take you for testing, and then it is death. Still, who lives forever? In the meanwhile, you will never hunger or thirst or lack shelter, and life is tolerable. The men and agile women will be trained to fight in the war, and it is pointless to claim no part in the quarrel or think to avoid battle against men like yourselves; this is the fact and you must do the requirement.

'Waste nothing on grief; it is the easy way and the futile way. Should you wish to breed, make application to

130

one or another intercessor, and a suitable partner will be assigned.

'Insubordination, lagging and loitering, fighting and mischievousness, all are forbidden; penalties are not graduated, but in all cases absolute. The omnibus is here. Climb up the ramp and step to the forward end.'

Crowded on the omnibus, Etzwane could see little of the passing countryside. The road led parallel to the hills for a space, then swung off across a plain. Occasionally a cluster of lumpy gray towers stood against the sky; a velvety growth of moss, dark red, dark green, or violet-black, covered the ground.

The omnibus halted; the slaves filed out upon a concrete compound, surrounded on three sides by structures of oyster-white lumps. To the north rolled low hills, commanded by a landmark crag of rotten basalt. To the east spread a vast black quagmire, disappearing at the horizon into the gloom of the sky. Nearby, at the edge of the compound, rested a bronze disk-ship, all ports open and ramps down upon the concrete. Etzwane thought he recognised the ship as that which had evacuated the Roguskhoi chieftains from the Engh Valley in Palasedra.

The slaves were herded to a barracks. Along the way they passed a set of long, narrow pens exhaling a vile stench. In some of the pens wandered andromorphs of several freakish varieties. Etzwane noticed a dozen Roguskhoi. Another group verged towards the Ka. In one pen huddled half a dozen spindly creatures with Ka torsos and grotesque simulations of the human head. Behind the pens ran a long low shed: the laboratory, so Etzwane realised, where these biological anomalies were created. After years of speculation he had learned the source of the Roguskhoi.

*

131

The captives were separated, men from women, then divided into platoons of eight persons. To each platoon was assigned a corporal drawn from a cadre of the captives already on the scene. To Etzwane's group came an old man, thin, gaunt, seamed as the bark of an old tree, but none the less muscular and incessantly active, all elbows and sharp knees.

'My name is Polovits,' declared the old man. 'The first lesson you must learn, and learn well, is obedience, quick and absolute, because no second chance is offered. The masters are decisive. They do not punish, they destroy. A war is in progress: they fight a strong enemy and have no inclination towards clemency. I remind you once more: to every instruction give smart and scrupulous obedience, or you will not live to receive another order. In the next few days you will see my statements exemplified. There is generally a depletion of one third in the first month; if you value life, obey all orders without hesitation.

'The rules of the cantonment are not complicated. You may not fight. I will adjudicate quarrels, and my judgment is final. You may not sing, shout, or whistle. You may not indulge your sexual desires without prior arrangement. You must be tidy; disorder is not tolerated. There are two principal roads to advancement. First, zeal. A dedicated man will become a corporal. Second, communication. If you learn the Great Song, you will gain valuable privileges, for very few persons can sing with the Ka. It is difficult, as those who try will discover, but fighting in the first rank is worse.'

Etzwane said, 'I have a question. Whom must we fight?'

'Ask no idle questions,' snapped Polovits. 'It is a useless habit and shows instability. Look at me! I have asked never a question and I have survived on Kahei for long years. I was taken from Shauzade district as a child during

132

the second slavings. I saw the Red Warriors created, and it was a hard time. How many of us survive now? I could count their names in a trice. Why did we survive?' Polovits peered from face to face. 'Why did we want to survive?' Polovits' own face showed a haggard triumph. 'Because we were men! Fate has given us the one life to live, and we use it to the best! I make the same recommendation to you: do your best! Nothing else is valid.'

'You cautioned me in regard to idle questions,' said Etzwane. 'I ask a question which is not idle. Are we offered any inducement? Can we hope to see Durdane again as free men?'

Polovits' voice became hoarse. 'Your inducement is persistence of life! And hope – what is hope? On Durdane there is no hope; death comes for all, and it comes here as well. And freedom? It is at your option here and now. Notice the hills; they are empty. The way is open; go now and be free! No one will halt you. But before you go, take heed! The only food is weed and wort; the only water is mist. You will bloat on the herbs; you will call in vain for water. Freedom is yours.'

Etzwane asked nothing more. Polovits pulled the cloak around his thin shoulders. 'We will now eat. Then we will commence our training.'

To eat, the squad stood up to a long trough containing lukewarm mush, stalks of a crisp, cold vegetable, and spiced pellets. After the meal Polovits put the men through calisthenics, then took them to one of the low, lizardlike vehicles.

'We have been assigned the function of "stealthy attack". These are the strike cars. They move on vibrating pads and are capable of high speed. Each man of the squad will be assigned his car, and he must maintain it with care. It is a dangerous and valuable weapon.'

'I wish to ask a question,' said Etzwane, 'but I am not

sure whether you will consider it "idle". I do not want to be struck dead for simple curiosity.'

Polovits put a stony gaze upon him. 'Curiosity is a futile habit.'

Etzwane held his tongue. Polovits nodded curtly and turned to the lizard-car. 'The driver lies flat, with his arms ahead. He looks down into a prism which shows him an adequate field of view. With arms and legs he controls the motion; with his chin he discharges either his torpedoes or his fire-stab.'

Polovits demonstrated the controls, then took the squad to a set of mock-ups. For three hours the group trained at the simulated controls; there was then a rest-break, then a two-hour demonstration of maintenance techniques which each man would be required to use on his vehicle.

The sky darkened; with twilight came a fine rain. In the dismal gray gloom the squad marched to the barracks. For supper the trough held a bland, sweet soup which the men dipped up with mugs. Polovits then said, 'Who among you wishes to learn the Great Song?'

Etzwane asked, 'What is involved?'

Polovits decided that the question was legitimate. 'The Great Song recounts the history of Kahei through symbolic sounds and sequences. The Ka communicate by singing themes of allusion, and you must do the same through the medium of a double-flute. The language is logical, flexible, and expressive, but difficult to learn.'

'I wish to learn the Great Song,' said Etzwane.

Polovits showed him a harsh grin. 'I thought you would decide as much.' And Etzwane decided that he did not like Polovits. The need for dissembling therefore increased; he must truckle and submit; he must throw himself into the program with apparent zeal.

Polovits seemed to perceive the flow of Etzwane's

thoughts and made a cryptic observation, 'In either case I will be satisfied.'

For a period existence went quietly. The sun – or suns – never appeared; the dank gloom oppressed the spirits and made for dreariness and lethargy. The daily routine included calisthenics, periods of training in the lizard-cars, and work sessions, which might consist of food preparation, sorting of ores, shaping and polishing of swamp wood. Neatness was emphasised. Detachments policed the barracks and groomed the landscape. Etzwane wondered whether the insistence upon order reflected the will of the asutra or the Ka. Probably the Ka, he decided; it was unlikely that the asutra altered the personality of the Ka any more than they had affected Sajarano of Sershan, or Jurjin, or Jerd Finnerack, or Hozman Sore-throat. The asutra dictated policy and monitored conduct; otherwise it seemed to remained aloof from the life of its host.

Asutra were everywhere evident. Perhaps half the Ka carried asutra; mechanisms were guided by asutra, and Polovits spoke in awe of asutra-guided aircraft. The latter two functions seemed somewhat plebeian activity for the asutra, Etzwane reflected, and would indicate that asutra, no less than Ka, men, ahulph, and chumpa, were divided into categories and castes.

At the end of the day, an hour was set aside for hygiene, sexual activity, which was permitted on the floor of a shed between the male and female barracks, and general recreation. The evening rain, occurring soon after light left the sky, put a term to the period, and the slaves went to their barracks, where they slept on mounds of dried moss. As Polovits had asserted, no guards or fences restrained the slaves from flight into the hills. Etzwane learned that on rare occasions a slave did so choose to seek freedom. Sometimes the fugitive was never again seen; as often he returned to camp after three or four days of hunger and thirst and thankfully resumed the routine. According to one rumor, Polovits himself had fled into the hills and upon his return had become the most diligent slave of the camp.

Etzwane saw two men killed. The first, a stout man, disliked calisthenics and thought to outwit his corporal. The second man was Srenka, who ran amok. In both cases a Ka destroyed the offender with a spurt of energy.

The Great Song of Kahei was for Etzwane a labor of love. The instructor was Kretzel, a squat old woman with a face concealed among a hundred folds and wrinkles. Her memory was prodigious, her disposition was easy, and she was always willing to entertain Etzwane with rumors and anecdotes. In her teaching she used a mechanism which reproduced the rasps, croaks, and warbles of the Great Song in its classic form. Kretzel then duplicated the tones on a pair of double-pipes and translated the significance into words. She made it clear that the Song was only incidentally music; that essentially it served as the basic semantic reference to Ka communication and conceptual thinking.

The Song consisted of fourteen thousand cantos, each a construction of thirty-nine to forty-seven phrases.

'What you will learn,' said Kretzel, 'is the simple First Style. The Second employs overtones, trills, and echoes; the Third inverts harmony and for emphasis reverses phrases; the Fourth combines the Second with augmentations and variations; the Fifth suggests rather than propounds. I know only the First, and superficially at that. The Ka use abbreviations, idioms, allusions, double and triple themes. The language is subtle.'

Kretzel was far less rigorous than Polovits. She told all she knew without restraint. Did the asutra use or understand the Song? Kretzel rocked her shoulders indifferently back and forth. 'Why concern yourself? You will never address yourself to the things. But they know the Song. They know everything, and have brought many changes to Kahei.'

Encouraged by the woman's loquacity, Etzwane asked other questions. 'How long have they been here? Where did they come from?'

'All this is made clear in the last seven hundred cantos, which report the tragedy which came to Kahei. This very land, the North Waste, has known many terrible battles. But now we must work, or the Ka will presume sloth.'

Etzwane made himself a set of double-pipes, and as soon as he had subdued his aversion for the Ka musical intervals, which he found unnatural and discordant, he played the first canto of the Great Song with a skill to amaze the old woman. 'Your dexterity is remarkable. Still, you must play accurately. Yes, my old ears are keen! Your tendency is to ornament and warp the phrases into the ways you know. Absolutely wrong! The Great Song becomes gibberish.'

Sexual activity among the slaves was encouraged, but couples were not allowed to form permanent liaisons. Etzwane occasionally saw Rune the Willow Wand across the compound where the women performed their own exercises, and one day during the period of 'free calisthenics' he took the trouble to approach her. She had lost something of her insouciance and nonchalant grace; she looked at him now without cordiality, and Etzwane saw that she failed to recognise him.

'I am Gastel Etzwane,' he told her. 'Do you remember the camp by the Vurush River where I played music and you dared me to knock away your cap?'

Rune's face showed no change of expression. 'What do you want?'

137

'Sexual activity is not forbidden. If you are so inclined. I will apply to the corporal and specifically request that –'

She cut him short with a gesture. 'I am not so inclined. Do you think I care to bear a child on this dreary gray hell? Go spend yourself on one of the old women, and bring no more blighted souls to life.'

Eztwane expostulated, citing one principle, then another, but Rune's face became progressively harder. At last she turned and walked away. Etzwane somewhat wistfully returned to his calisthenics.

The days dragged by with a slowness Etzwane found maddening. He estimated their duration to be four or five hours longer than the days of Shant: a situation which upset his natural rhythms and made him alternatively morose and nervously irritable. He learned the first twelve cantos of the Song, both the melodies and the associated significances. He began to practice basic communication, selecting and joining musical phrases. His dexterity was counterbalanced by an almost uncontrollable tendency to play notes and phrases as personal music, slurring here, extending there, inserting gracenotes and trills, until old Kretzel threw up her hands in exasperation. 'The sequence goes thus and so,' and she demonstrated. 'No more, no less! It conveys the idea of a vain search for crayfish along the shore of the Ocean Quagmire during the morning rain. You introduce random elements of other cantos to create a mishmash, a farrago of ideas. Each note must be just, neither under- nor over-blown! Otherwise you sing absurdities!'

Etzwane controlled his fingers and played the themes precisely as Kretzel had indicated. 'Good!' she declared. 'Now we proceed to the next canto, where proto-Ka, the Hiana, cross the mud flats and are annoyed by chirping insects.'

Etzwane much preferred Kretzel's company to the peevish admonitions of Polovits, and he would have spent all his waking hours practicing the Great Song had she allowed. 'Such diligence is wasted,' said Kretzel. 'I know the cantos; I can sing to the black ones in faltering First Style. This is all I can teach you. If you lived a hundred years you might begin to play Second Style, but never could you know the feeling, for you are not a Ka. Then there are Third, Fourth, and Fifth, and then the idioms and cursive forms, the converging and diverging harmonics, the antichords, the stops, the hisses and slurs. Life is too short; why exert yourself?'

Etzwane decided, none the less, to learn as best he could; he had nothing better to do with his time. Every day he found Polovits more detestable, and his only escape was to Kretzel. Or freedom in the hills. According to Polovits, the wilderness afforded neither food nor water, and Kretzel corroborated as much. His best hope of evading Polovits lay in the Great Song . . . What of Ifness? The name seldom occurred to Etzwane. His old life was vague; by the day it dwindled and lost detail. Reality was Kahei; here alone was life. Sooner or later Ifness would appear; sooner or later there would be a rescue – so Etzwane told himself, but every day the idea became more and more abstract.

One afternoon Kretzel became bored with the Song. Complaining of cankerous gums she threw the pipes to a shelf. 'Let them kill me; what difference does it make? I am too old to fight; I know the Song, so they stay my death, and I do not care; my bones will never know the soil of Durdane. You are young; you have hopes. One by one they will go, and nothing will be left but the bare fact of life. Then you will discover the transcendent value of life alone . . . We have been through much hardship; we

139

have known cruel times. When I was young they bred their copper warriors and trained them to spawn in human women, for what purpose I never knew.'

Etzwane said, 'I know well enough. The Roguskhoi were sent to Durdane. They devastated Shant and several great districts of Caraz. Is it not strange? They destroy the folk of Durdane, and at the same time capture them to use as slave warriors against their enemy.'

'It is only another experiment,' said Kretzel wisely. 'The Red Warriors failed, now they try a new weapon for their war.' She peered over her shoulder. 'Take your pipes and play the Song. Polovits watches for slackness. Take heed of Polovits; he likes to kill.' She reached for her own pipes. 'Ah, my poor, tortured gums! This is the nineteenth canto. The Sah and Aianu use raho fibers to wind rope and dig coral nut with blackwood sticks. You will hear both the schemes for blackwood and for rough wood employed in a rude scratching action, as is general usage. But you must carefully play the little-finger flutter, else the scheme is "visiting a place where the quagmire may be distantly seen" from Canto 9635.'

Etzwane played the pipes, watching Polovits from the corner of his eye. Polovits paused to listen, then turned Etzwane a flinty glance and continued on his way.

Later in the day, during calisthenics, Polovits suddenly exploded into fury: 'Crisply then! Do you detest exertion so much that you cannot put your hand to the ground? Never fear, I am watching, and your life is as fragile as a moth-shell. Why do you stand like a post?'

'I await new orders, Corporal Polovits.'

'Your kind is the most venomous, always with a glib retort just short of insolence! Don't indulge in dreams of glory, my Song-playing virtuoso, you won't evade the worst of it! I assure you of this! So now: a hundred high

140

leaps, for your health's sake; let them be agile, with a fine twinkling of the heels!'

In calmness and gravity Etzwane obeyed as best he could. Polovits watched with grim intentness, but could find no fault with the efforts. At last he turned and strode away. With a faint smile on his face, Etzwane returned to Kretzel's little office and practiced the nineteen cantos he already knew and learned the melody to cantos Twenty and Twenty-one from the reproducing machine. He would discover the semantic significance in due course.

Etzwane conducted himself with care, but Polovits was unrelenting. Etzwane's patience wore thin, and he decided to take positive action. Polovits, by some uncanny means, divined the fact of the decision and thrust his angular old face close to Etzwane's. 'A dozen men have thought to best me, and can you guess where they lie at this moment? In the great hole. I know tricks you never heard of! I'm just waiting for a single insurbordinate move, then you will learn the folly of proud attitudes on this sad world Kahei.'

Etzwane had no choice by hypocrisy. He said politely, 'I'm sorry if I have given offense; I want only to remain inconspicuous. Needless to say, I am not here by my own choice.'

'You waste my time with your witticisms,' bawled Polovits. 'I intend to hear no more!' He strode away, and Etzwane went to practice the Song.

Kretzel inquired as to his lack of zest, and Etzwane explained that Polovits was about to take his life. Kretzel gave a whinny of shrill laughter. 'That spleenful little dingbat; he's not worth the rumble of an ahulph's gut! He won't give you to death, because he's afraid to speak a lie. Do you think the Ka are fools? Come, I will teach

141

you Canto 2023, wherein the stave-cutters kill a stone-roller because he dented their moss. Then you need only play the eleventh phrase should Polovits so much as raise a finger. Better! Tell old Polovits that you are rehearsing the Canto of Open Inspection, and that you consider his conduct slack. To work. Polovits is of no more consequence than a bad smell.'

'Gastel Etzwane,' said Polovits, during the morning calisthenics. 'You move with the grace and agility of a pregnant grampus. I cannot accept those kneebands as accomplished facts. Has your well-known musical virtuosity rendered you absentminded? Well, then, answer! I count your silence an insolence. How long must I suffer your slights?'

'Not long at all,' said Etzwane. 'Yonder walks a Monitor; summon him. By chance I have here my pipes and I will play the Canto of Open Inspection, and we shall have justice.'

Polovits' eyes seemed to burn red. His mouth slowly opened, then snapped shut. He swung around and made as if to summon the Ka. As if by great effort he restrained himself. 'So then: he takes you and half this band of club-footed cretins to the hole; how do I gain? I only must start again with a group as bad. We are wasting time! Back to the calisthenics; once again the kneebends. Smartly now!' But Polovits spoke somewhat pensively and refused to meet Etzwane's gaze.

Kretzel asked Etzwane, 'How is Polovits now?'

'He is a changed man,' said Etzwane. 'His tirades have ended, and likewise his tantrums; he is now as meek as a grass-tit, and the drills are almost a pleasure.'

Kretzel was silent and Etzwane once again took up the pipes. He noticed a tear rolling down the brown folds of

142

Kretzel's cheek, and lowered the pipes. 'Has something occurred to distress you?'

Kretzel rubbed at her face. 'I never think of home; I would long since have been dead had I mourned. But one word stirred a memory and brought it to life; and I thought of the meadows above the Elshuka Pond where my family held a steading. The grass was high, and when I was a little girl I worked long burrows through the grass and surprised two tits at their nesting . . . One day I burrowed a long tunnel through the grass. When it broke open I looked up into the face of Molsk the Man-taker. He took me away in a sack and I never again saw the Elshuka Pond . . . I have no great time to live. They will mix my bones into this sour black soil, when I would once again be home in the sunlight.'

Etzwane blew a pensive tune on the pipes. 'Were many slaves on Kahei when you came?'

'We were among the first. They used us to build their Roguskhoi. I evaded the worst of it when I learned the Song. But the others are gone, save a few. Old Polovits, for one.'

'And in all this time has no one escaped?'

' "Escaped"? To where? The world is a prison!'

'I could take pleasure in doing general harm, if I were able.'

Kretzel gave an indifferent shrug. 'Once I felt the same way, but now – I have played the Great Song too many times. I feel almost a Ka.'

Etzwane recalled the occasion at Shagfe when the Ka captive had destroyed Hozman Sore-throat's asutra. What had triggered this spasm of violence? If all the Ka of Kahei could feel the same impulse, there would be no more asutra. Etzwane became conscious of how little he in fact knew of the Ka, of their way of life, their innate character. He put questions to Kretzel, who at once became cross and advised that he apply himself to the Great Song.

Etzwane said, 'I know twenty-two cantos; there are more than fourteen thousand yet to be learned; I will be an old man before my questions are answered.'

'And I will be dead,' snapped Kretzel. 'So then, attend to the mechanism; hear the double quaver at the end of the second phrase. This is a common device and signifies what is called "vehement assertion". The Ka are a brave and desperate people; their history is a series of tragic plights, and the double quaver expresses this mood, the challenge flung into the face of destiny.'

Polovits, the furious old fighting-cock, with startling abruptness had become a surly introvert, who gave minimum effort to the drills. The tension created by his old antagonism had collapsed; the drills became periods of droning boredom.

The mood, for Etzwane, infected every aspect of existence; he began to feel a disassociation, a sense of existence on two levels, inner and outer, and his mind, retreating into a subjective middle distance, watched the work of his body without interest or participation.

What of the Great Song? Each day Etzwane dutifully went to Kretzel. He played the cantos and memorised the significances, but the project began to loom vast and futile. He could learn the fourteen thousand cantos, and so become another Kretzel . . . Etzwane became wrathful, outraged by his own passivity. 'I defeated the Roguskhoi! I used my energy and intellect! I refused to submit! I must use these same resources to enforce my terms upon destiny!'

So he told himself, and, spiritually regenerated, plotted revolt, sabotage, a guerrilla operation, kidnap and holding of hostages, the capture of the bronze disk-ship beside

the compound, signals and communications . . . Each of
his schemes foundered on the same reef: impracticality.
In frustration he thought to organise a team of kindred
spirits, but encountered a discouraging lack of zest. Except
in one person, a gaunt and brooding man from the Sap-
rovno district who used the name Shapan, from a weed
with tenacious tendrils and fish-hook barbs. Shapan
seemed interested in Etzwane's views, and Etzwane began
to feel that he had encountered an ally until one day
Kretzel casually identified him as the most notorious
provocator of the camp. 'He's been the death of a dozen
men. He urges them into illicit conduct, then notifies the
Ka, and to what purpose other than sheer perversity I
cannot fathom, for he has profited not a whit.'

Etzwane became first furious, then disgusted with himself, then sardonically apathetic. Shapan seemed eager to
formulate new plots, but Etzwane feigned perplexity.

A clanging of gongs awoke the slaves while darkness still
pressed dank and heavy upon the camp. There were
flutings and the thud of running feet; emergency of some
sort was afoot. From the lumpy cupola atop the garage
sounded a wild ululation: the general alarm. The slaves
ran forth to find a transport ship at rest in the exercise
yard. The slaves stood back, murmuring doubts and
speculations.

From the ship came a dozen Ka, asutra clutching their
necks. Etzwane sensed haste in their conduct. Ka song-
speech, in the 'referential' First Style, fluted across the
compound. Again the ululating alarm sounded; the corporals ran forth and ordered their platoons; those who
had trained with weapons were marched to the transport
ship and up into a long, dim hold. The deck was dirty and
layered with filth; the air carried an abominable stench.
The slaves stood crowded together, one man's chin on

another man's shoulder, and the odor of sweating bodies added a sweet-sour overtone to the reek.

The hulk lurched and moved; the slaves held to stanchions or braced against the hull, or each other; there was no room to fall. Some became sick and commenced a lugubrious groaning; a few began to yell in anger and panic, but were silence by blows. The cries were muffled; the groaning gradually subsided.

An hour, or perhaps two, the ship moved, then jarred to the ground. The engines died; the ship was at rest. With open air so near at hand, the slaves became desperate and began to pound on the hull and to shout, 'Out, out, out . . . '

The hatch opened, admitting a gust of cold wind. The slaves cringed back involuntarily. A voice called, 'Everyone outside, in good order. Danger is at hand; the time has come.'

The slaves hunched out into blowing darkness. A pallid light winked off to the right; a voice called, 'March ahead, towards the light. Stay in line; do not straggle to either side.'

The miserable men stirred; without any particular volition they found themselves trudging along a soft, somewhat spongy surface towards the light. The wind blew steadily, driving a thin, cold rain. Etzwane felt like a man in a terrifying dream, from which he knew he must awake.

The column came to a halt before a low structure. After a wait of a minute or two, it continued forward, down a ramp into an underground hall, dimly illuminated. Drenched and shivering, the slave warriors stood pressed together, vapor rising fetid from their garments. At the far end sounded the fluting of a Ka; the creature mounted a bench, where he was joined by an old man, crooked of

146

body, with extraordinarily long arms and legs.

The Ka produced a set of First Style flutings; the old man spoke, his mouth a black gap at the back of his whiskers. 'I give you the meanings. The enemy has come in a spaceship. They have put down their forts; once again they intend to sweep across Kahei. All the wise helpers they will kill.' He pause to listen to the Ka, and Etzwane wondered who were the 'wise helpers'. Asutra? The old man spoke again. 'The Ka will fight, and you will fight with the Ka, who are your dominants. So you will be joined to the Song.'

The old man listened, but the Ka had no more to say, and the old man spoke alone. 'Look about you now, into each other's faces, because grim events are in the offing and many a man will never see another day. Those who die, how will they be remembered? Not in name nor in semblance, but by their desperate courage. A canto will tell how they went forth in lizard-cars and slid across the dark dawn to measure themselves against the enemy.'

Again the Ka fluted; the old man listened and translated. 'The tactics are simple. In the lizard-cars you are nameless destroyers, the simple essence of desperate rage. Let them fear you! What remains to you except ferocity? When you go, go only forward! The enemy holds the north moor; his forts control the sky. We strike from the ground –'

Etzwane cried out from the dark: 'Who is this "enemy"? They are men like ourselves! Should men kill men in aid of the asutra?'

The old man craned his neck. The Ka fluted; the old man played phrases on his double-pipes, then called to the warriors, 'I know nothing, so ask no questions; I cannot answer. The enemy is the enemy, no matter what his guise. Go forth, destroy! These are the words of the Ka. My own words are these: good luck to all of you. It is an

147

ill business to die so far from Durdane, but die we must, and why not gallantly?'

Another voice, hoarse and mocking, called out, 'Gallantly indeed we will die, and you can assure the Ka of so much; they have not brought us this far for nothing.'

A light flashed red at the end of the chamber. 'Follow the light; step forward then!'

Men milled and circled, none willing to be first. The Ka fluted; the old man cried, 'Out into the passage; go where the red lamp beckons!'

The men surged into a whitewashed tunnel and through a narrow portal at the end; here each man was gripped between two Ka while a third stuck a tube into his mouth and forced a gout of acrid liquid down his throat.

Coughing, cursing, spitting, the men stumbled out upon a pavement and into the watery gray light of the dawn. To either side lizard-cars stood in ranks. The men came slowly forward, and their corporals reached forth and turned them aside, towards a lizard-car. 'In you go,' Polovits told Etzwane in a toneless voice. 'Drive north, over the rise. The torpedo tubes are armed; torpedo the forts, destroy the enemy.'

Etzwane slid into the car; the lid slammed down upon him. He touched the thrust pedal; the car rumbled and hissed and slid off across the pavement and out upon the moor.

Ingenious and dangerous were the lizard-cars: not two feet high, supple and lithe to cling to the contours of the ground. Energy packs were carried in the tail; Etzwane knew nothing of the vehicle's range, but at the training camp they were refueled but seldom. Three torpedo tubes aimed directly forward; the dorsal surface supported a squat, swivel-mounted energy gun. The cars slid on nodes

148

of compression, and in favorable circumstances moved with darting rapidity.

Etzwane drove north up a slope padded with black velvet moss. To either side slid other lizard-cars, some ahead and some behind. The potion which had been forced down his throat now began to take effect: Etzwane felt a grim elation, a sensation of power and invulnerability.

He came up over the roll of the slope and retarded the speed-lever. The control failed to answer. No matter – or so his drugged mind assured him; forward and full speed; what other speed or direction was necessary? . . . He had been tricked. The knowledge eroded his drug-induced élan. He felt sudden prickles of anger. Not enough that they send him forth against 'enemies' he had never known! They also must ensure that he go to his death in haste!

A wide valley spread before him. Two miles away he saw a small, shallow lake, and near by three black space-ships. Lake and spaceships were surrounded by a ring of twenty squat black cones: evidently the forts which the slave warriors had been commanded to attack.

Over the hill came the lizard-cars, one hundred and forty in number, and none could be stopped. One of the cars in front of Etzwane swung about in a great semi-circle, and started back the way it had come, the man within waving, gesticulating, pointing. Etzwane and his rancor needed no further stimulus; he turned his own car about and drove back towards the base, yelling in crazy glee out the ventilation ports. One by one the other cars became infected; they veered and darted back the way they had come. On the ridge above crouched four mobile forts, observers within. These forts now slid forward, red lights flashing. Etzwane brought his torpedo sight to bear. He nudged the trigger and one of the forts spun up into the air like a fish breaking water, to crash back down on its side. The other forts opened fire; three lizard-cars became puddles of molten metal, but simultaneously the forts were struck and broken. From two of these clambered Ka, to run across the moor with great striding leaps; after them slid the lizard-cars, harrying, swerving, circling, and finally running down the Ka.

Etzwane waved his arm and bawled out the ventilation ports: 'To the base, to the base!'

Over the hill raced the lizard-cars. Instantly the weapon emplacements beamed glaring red rays of warning. 'Spread apart!' yelled Etzwane. He signaled with his hands, but none heeded. He aimed his torpedo tube and fired; one of the emplacements erupted. The remaining fortifications spat forth lances of energy, burning the lizard-cars at a touch, but other torpedoes struck home. In five seconds half the lizard-cars had become cinders, but the weapons were silenced, and the surviving lizard-cars raced back to the base unopposed. Someone fired a torpedo into the subterranean garage and the entire hill exploded. Turf, concrete, dismembered torsos, miscellaneity spurted high in the air and settled.

The base was a silent crater. The problem now was halting the lizard-cars. Etzwane experimented with the various controls, to no avail. He threw open the entry hatch, to actuate a cut-off switch. The motor died, the car slid to a halt. Etzwane jumped out and stood on the black velvet moss. If he were to be killed in the next minute, he would have died exultant.

The other men halted their cars as Etzwane had done and stepped to the ground. Of the hundred and forty who had set forth, half had returned. The drug still worked its effect; faces were flushed, with eyes prominent and brilliant, and each individual's personality seemed more concentrated, more distinct and powerful than before. They guffawed and stamped and recounted their exploits: ' – outlaws at last, with our lives not worth a twig – ' 'So, then: it's over the hills; into the far places! Let them follow if they dare!' 'Food? Of course there's food! We'll rob the Ka!' ' – vengeance! They won't accept our triumph; they'll drop down from the skies – '

Etzwane spoke: 'A moment; listen to me! Over the hill are the black spaceships. The crews are men like ourselves, from an unknown world. Why should we not go to greet them like friends and trust in their goodwill? We have nothing to lose.'

A brawny, black-bearded man known to Etzwane only as Korba, demanded, 'How do you know there are men aboard these ships?'

'I saw a similar ship broken up,' said Etzwane. 'The bodies of men were expelled. In any event, let us reconnoiter; we have nothing to lose.'

'Correct,' declared Korba. 'We live now from minute to minute.'

'One further matter,' said Etzwane. 'It is important that we act as a group, not a gang of wild men. We need a leader, to coordinate our actions. What of Korba here? Korba, will you undertake to be our leader?'

Korba pulled at his black beard. 'No, not I. You asserted the need and you are the man for the job. What is your name then?'

'I am Gastel Etzwane. I will take the responsibility unless someone objects.'

No one spoke.

'Very well,' said Etzwane. 'First, let us repair the cars, so that we may manage them more easily.'

'Do we need cars?' demanded a hot-eyed old man named Sul, who bore a reputation for disputatiousness. 'Why not move on our own feet and go where the cars cannot go?'

'We may have to range far for food,' said Etzwane. 'We know nothing of the country; the waste may extend a thousand miles. In the cars we have a greater chance of survival, and also the cars are equipped with weapons. We are dangerous warriors in the cars; without them we are a gang of starving fugitives.'

'Correct,' said Korba. 'If the worst occurs, as no doubt it will, we will make them remember us.'

The engine panels were lifted and the clamps removed from the speed controls. Etzwane held up his hand. 'Listen.' Faintly from beyond the hill came a fluctuating wail, of a weird, wild timbre to set the teeth on edge.

The men gave various opinions. 'A signal!' 'No signal; a warning!' 'They know we are here; they are waiting for us.' 'It is a ghost sound, I have heard it near lonesome graves.'

Etzwane said, 'In any case we now set forth. I will lead. At the crest of the hill, we will halt.' He climbed into his car, pulled down the hatch, and set off; the cars slid over the velvet moss like a troop of great black rats.

The hill swelled above them, then flattened, and here the cars halted. The men alighted. Behind them the moor swept down to the crater of the destroyed base and the distant morass; ahead spread the valley, with the pond, the spaceships, and the forts surrounding. About the pond stood a group of twenty men, performing some sort of work. The distance was too great to pick out their features or the nature of their business, but their motions conveyed a sense of urgency. Etzwane became uneasy; the air of the valley was heavy with imminence.

From the spaceships came another wailing call. The men at the pond jerked around, stood rigid a few seconds, then ran back to the ships.

On the hill Korba suddenly called out in awe; he pointed to the south where misty hills loomed up across

152

the dark overcast. Sliding into view from behind these hills came three copper-bronze disk-ships. The first two were of the ordinary sort; the third, an enormous construction, drifted up over the horizon like a copper moon. The first two slid forward with menacing purpose; the large ship drifted more slowly, low to the ground. From the conical forts around the lake came chattering white bolts of light, all striking the leading disk-ship. It gave off a blue coruscation, then bounded high into the sky and was lost to sight in an instant. The second disk-ship stabbed a bar of purple energy at one of the black ships. The forts threw out new energy bolts, but the black ship glowed red, then white, and slumped into an irregular molten mass. The bronze disk then dropped quickly behind a rise of the moor, apparently undamaged. The large disk settled upon the surface near by; its ports snapped open and ramps struck down to the moss. Out surged lizard-cars – twenty, forty, sixty, a hundred. They slid off towards the forts, streaks of black over the black moss, almost invisible and offering no target. The forts moved back towards the globe-ships, but the lizard-cars darted down the black velvet hillside and into torpedo range. The forts discharged bolts of white force; lizard-cars were shattered and flung high into the air. Others discharged torpedoes, and one after another the forts became fragments of torn metal. The lizard-cars hurled torpedoes at the black globe-ships, without effect; the impacts produced only spatters of angry red light. The two bronze disk-ships, the large and the small, lifted into the air and launched thick rods of purple incandescence towards the black globes. Overhead, assistance had arrived. Eight silver-and-white ships of complicated construction, long and slender, dropped down to hang over the black globes. The air flickered and vibrated; the purple bolts became a smoky amber-yellow; they dimmed and died as if the

153

source of their power had failed. The black globes rose into the air and sped off into the sky. They became dark spots on the gray clouds, then plunged through and were gone. The silver-and-white ships hung motionless for three minutes, then plunged away through the clouds.

The lizard-cars slid back to the large disk-ship. They mounted the ramps and disappeared within. Five minutes later, both copper disk-ships rose into the air and departed across the southern hills.

Except for the men on the moor, the panorama was empty of life. Beside the pond remained the exploded forts and the still molten black ship.

The men entered the lizard-cars and gingerly descended the slope to the pond. The forts were tangles of useless metal; the slumped black globe radiated so much heat that no approach could be made. There would be no food taken from this hull. Water however was near at hand. They went down to the edge of the pond. An unpleasant odor arose, which became more intense as they approached. 'Stink or not,' said Korba, 'I will drink; I have forgotten nicety.' He bent to lift up a handful of water, then jerked back. 'The water is full of swimming things.'

Etzwane leaned over the pond. The water swirled with the motion of numberless insect-like creatures, ranging in size from specks to things the length of his hand. From the pinkish-gray torsos grew six small legs, each ending in three tiny fingers. At one end black eye-specks peered from hairy cavities. Etzwane straightened up in disgust. He would drink none of this water. 'Asutra,' he said. 'Asutra by the millions.'

He looked around the sky. Black clouds swept low under the overcast, trailing skeins of rain. Etzwane shivered. 'This is a dire place; the sooner we are gone the better.'

One of the men said dubiously, 'We will be leaving water and food.'

'The asutra?' Etzwane grimaced. 'I'll never be so hungry. In any event they are alien life-stuff and probably poisonous.' He turned away. 'The spaceships may be back; we had better be gone before that time.'

'All very well,' complained old Sul, 'but where is our destination? We are doomed men; why make haste nowhere?'

'I can propose a destination. South beside the morass is the camp, the closest place for food and water.'

The men squinted at him in doubt and puzzlement. Korba demanded somewhat truculently: 'You want us to go back to the camp, when we are free at last?'

Another man grumbled, 'First I'll eat asutra and drink their filth. I was born a Graythorn of the Bagot race, and we are not the sort to enslave ourselves for food.'

'I said nothing of enslaving ourselves,' said Etzwane. 'Have you forgotten the weapons we carry? We do not go to eat slave food; we go to take what we want and to pay off some old debts. We follow the shore south, until we find the camp, then we shall see.'

'It is a far way,' muttered someone.

Etzwane said, 'We came by transport ship in two hours. To return we will ride two days, or three, or four, but there is no help for it.'

'Precisely right,' Korba declared. 'We may be killed by asutra lighting, but none of us expects long life! Let us go seek death on our own terms!'

'Into your cars, then,' said Etzwane. 'We drive south.'

They circled the pond and the smouldering globe-ship, then drove up over the black moor, where rows of glossy tracks indicated the way they had come. Down the long slope they slid, past the exploded base. Somewhere under the rubble, thought Etzwane, lay Polovits, his tyranny

155

completed, his face pressed into the mold. Etzwane felt a grim compassion, in which was mingled outrage for the wrongs done to himself and the human folk. He looked back at the lizard-cars; he and his fellows were as good as dead, but first they would harm their enemies.

The morass was close at hand: a limitless expanse of ooze, blotched with chalk-green scum. The cars swung south and proceeded along the edge of the moor. Clouds hung heavy and low; in the distance moor, morass and sky blurred together without discernible line of conjunction.

South slid the cars, a supple, sinister train, the men never looking back. During the afternoon they came to a slough of brackish dark water, of which they drank, despite a bitter aftertaste, and filled the receptacles within the cars; then, fording the slough at the very brink of the morass, they continued south.

The sky darkened; the evening rain fell, to be instantly absorbed by the moss. The cars proceeded through the dusk, which presently became darkness. Etzwane brought the column to a halt and the men climbed out upon the moss, groaning for their sore muscles and hunger. They stretched and hobbled back and forth along the line, muttering in gruff, hoarse voices. Some, noting how distinct was the division between the luminous ooze of the morass and the dead blackness of the moor, wanted to drive on through the night. 'The sooner we come to the camp the sooner we make an end to the matter; we will eat or be killed.'

'I am also in haste,' said Etzwane, 'but the dark is too dangerous. We have no lights and cannot stay together. What if someone becomes torpid and goes to sleep? Hungry or not, we must wait for day.'

'In the light we are visible to skycraft,' argued one of the men. 'There are dangers in both directions, but our bellies howl for food regardless.'

'We'll start as soon as the dawn gives light,' said Etzwane. 'To travel through the black night is folly. My belly is as slack as anyone's; for lack of anything better I plan to sleep.' He troubled to talk no further, and went down to the shore to look out over the morass. The ooze glowed blue in lines and reticulations, these slowly moving and forming new patterns. Flickers of pale light hung in the reeds and moved in wisps across the open spaces . . . At Etzwane's feet something scuttled across the mud; by its outline he saw it to be a large, flat insect, walking on a dozen pads across the ooze. He peered close. An asutra? No, something different, but perhaps in just some similar swamp had the asutra evolved. Perhaps even on Kahei, though the first cantos of the Great Song made no reference to asutra . . . Others of the group walked by the shore, marveling at the lights and the eerie solitude . . . Along the shore someone struck a tiny fire, using dried bits of moss and reed for fuel. Etzwane saw that several men had captured insects and were preparing to toast and eat them. Etzwane gave a fatalistic shrug. He was leader by the most tenuous of contracts.

The night was long in passing. Etzwane tried to find room to sleep within the lizard-car, then came forth and lay down upon the moss. A cold wind blew through the night, allowing him no real comfort. He dozed . . . Sounds of anguish awakened him. He rose to his feet and felt his way along the line of cars. Three men lay on the ground, retching convulsively. Etzwane stood a moment, then went back to his car. He could offer neither comfort nor help; indeed so close about them hung doom that the death of three men seemed of no great import . . . A misty rain slanted down on the wind. Etzwane once more entered the car. The groans of the poisoned men became less distinct, and presently were heard no more.

Dawn finally arrived, and three men lay dead upon the

spongy black turf: the three who had eaten insects. Without comment Etzwane went to his car, and the column proceeded south.

The moors seemed endless; the men drove the cars in a semitorpor. At noon they came upon another slough, and drank of the water. The reeds surrounding carried clusters of waxy fruit, which one or two of the men gingerly examined. Etzwane said nothing, and the men turned reluctantly away.

Korba stood looking along the moors to the south. He pointed to a far shadow which might be either a cloud or a jutting mountain. 'North of the camp rose a crag,' said Korba, 'perhaps that which lies ahead.'

'We have farther to go,' said Etzwane. 'The ship which took us north moved at a considerable speed. I suspect that two days of travel, or more, still lie ahead.'

'If our bellies will give us the strength.'

'Our bellies will take us there if the cars will do so. This is my main fear, that the cars will exhaust their energy.'

Korba and the others looked askance at the long black shapes. 'Let us move on,' said one of the men. 'At least we shall see the other side of the hills, and by luck Korba may have the accurate prediction.'

'I hope so too,' said Etzwane. 'Still, be prepared for disappointment.'

The column proceeded across an undulating black carpet of moss. Nowhere was there evidence of life; no motion, no ruined dwelling, no ancient post or cairn.

A brief storm struck down upon them; black clouds boiled low; a sudden wind came roaring out of the west ... In half an hour the storm had passed, leaving the air clearer than before. The shadow to the south was clearly a mountain of considerable mass.

Close upon the end of day the column breasted the ridge to look out over the panorama. As far as the eye

158

could reach appeared empty black moor.

The column halted: the men came forth from the cars to stare over the desolation ahead. Etzwane said briefly, 'We have far to go.' He reentered his car and slid away downhill.

A project had formed in his mind, and when darkness forced a halt he explained his plan. 'Remember the disk-ship which waits at the camp? I believe it to be a space vessel; in any case it is an object of great value, worth far more than the deaths of fifty or sixty men. If a ship is in fact still at the camp, I suggest that we capture it, and bargain our way back to Durdane.'

'Can we do this?' asked Korba. 'Will they not detect us and use their torpedoes?'

'I noticed no great vigilance at the camp,' said Etzwane. 'Why should we not attempt the maximum? For a certainty no one will help us but ourselves.'

One of the Alula said in a bitter voice, 'I had forgotten; so many events have come and gone. Long ago you told us of the planet Earth and mentioned a certain Ifness.'

'A fantasy,' said Etzwane. 'I too have forgotten . . . Strange to think! For the folk of Earth, did they know of us, we would be creatures of a nightmare, less than wisps of the swamp-light yonder . . . I fear that I will never see Earth.'

'I would be happy to see old Caraz,' said the Alula. 'I would think myself fortunate beyond belief and never grieve again.'

One of the men growled, 'I would be content for a chunk of fat meat.'

One at a time, reluctant to leave the warmth of companionship, the men went off to their cars and passed another dreary night.

As soon as dawn made the land distinct, they were under way. Etzwane's car seemed not as lively as before;

he wondered how many miles remained in its engine. How far ahead lay the camp? One day at least, three or four days at most.

The moss stretched ahead flat and soggy, almost one with the quagmire. Several times the cars passed pools of gray mud. Near one of these the column halted to rest and ease cramped muscles. The pools quaked with huge miasmic bubbles, rising with an unctuous suck. The periphery of the mud was home to colonies of jointed brown worms and running black balls, both of which submerged themselves in the mud at a sound: a fact which puzzled Etzwane; there seemed no natural enemy from which the creatures would be required to protect themselves. Etzwane searched the air: no birds, flying reptiles, nor winged insects. In the fringe of rotten black moss three or four feet back from the shore of mud he spied small burrows, from which issued the prints of small, three-fingered members. Etzwane examined the prints with frowning suspicion In the moss a small purplish-black shape moved back into concealment: an asutra, not yet mature. Etzwane drew back, alarmed and repelled. When races derived from such disparate environments as man and asutra, could there possibly be communication or sympathy? Etzwane thought not. A tolerance founded on mutual distaste, possibly; cooperation, never.

The column proceeded, and now one of the cars began to falter, rising and falling on its support nodes. The car at last sank down upon the moor and would go no further. Etzwane put the driver astride the most fresh-seeming car; once again the column proceeded.

During the middle afternoon two other cars subsided upon the moss; it was plain that a very few hours remained to any of the engines. Ahead rose another black hill, which seemed lower than that hill north of camp. If it were another hill, Etzwane thought they would never see the

camp, for none of the men had the strength to walk thirty
or forty or fifty miles.

They swung out close to the morass to avoid the
heights; even so the mountain met the morass in a pre-
cipitous bluff, over which they laboriously climbed.

Up towards the ridge moved the lizard-cars, groaning
and sagging. Etzwane led the way over the crest, the landscape to the south opened before them ... The camp lay
below, not five miles distant. A husky roar rose from fifty
dry throats. 'The camp; down to the camp! Food awaits
us; bread, good soup!'

Etzwane tottered out of his car. 'Hold back, you fools!
Have you forgotten our plan?'

'Why should we wait?' croaked Sul. 'Look! There is no
spaceship on the premises; it is gone! Even if there were,
your scheme is absurd. We shall eat and drink; all else is
now meaningless. On then, down to the camp!'

Etzwane said, 'Hold back! We have suffered too much
to throw away our lives now. There is no spaceship, true!
But we must make ourselves masters of the camp, and this
means surprise. We will wait for dusk. You must control
your appetite until then.'

'I have not come all this distance to suffer further,'
declared Sul.

'Suffer or die,' growled Korba. 'When the camp is ours,
then you shall eat. Now is the time to prove ourselves men,
not slaves!'

Sul said no more. Ashen-faced he leaned back against
his car, mumbling through dry gray lips.

The camp seemed curiously listless and desolate. A few
women moved about their duties; a Ka came briefly forth
from the far barracks. It walked aimlessly back and forth,
then reentered. No squads drilled upon the compound;
the garage was dark.

Korba whispered, 'The camp is dead; there is no one to stop us.'

'I am suspicious,' said Etzwane. 'The quiet is unnatural.'

'You believe that they expect us?'

'I don't know what to believe. We still must wait till dusk, even if the camp is empty except for three Ka and a dozen old women, so that they can't send off a message of emergency.'

Korba grunted.

'The sky is darkening already,' said Etzwane. 'In another hour the dusk will hide our approach.'

The group waited, pointing here and there at remembered corners of the camp. Lamps began to glow, and Etzwane looked at Korba. 'Are you ready?'

'I am ready.'

'Remember, I will attack the Ka barracks from the side; you enter the camp from the front and destroy whatever resistance appears.'

'The plan is clear.'

Etzwane and half the cars descended the flank of the hill, dark cars invisible on the black moss. Korba waited five minutes, then proceeded down the slope, approaching the camp across the old training compound. Etzwane's group, with cars dragging and bumping across the moss, drove up to the back of the lumpy white structure which the Ka used as a barracks.

The men lunged inside and swarmed upon the seven Ka they found in the single chamber. Astonished or perhaps apathetic, the Ka made only feeble resistance and were lashed immobile with thongs. The men, keyed up for a desperate battle and finding none, felt baffled and frustrated, and started to kick the Ka to death. Etzwane halted them in a fury. 'What are you doing? They are victims like ourselves. Kill the asutra, but do no harm to the Ka! It is purposeless!'

The men thereupon plucked the asutra off the Ka's necks and ground them underfoot, to the horrified moaning of the Ka.

Etzwane went forth to find Korba, who had already sent his men into the garages, the commissary, and the communication chamber, where they had discovered a total of four Ka, three of which they clubbed to pulp, lacking Etzwane's moderating presence. The men encountered no other opposition; they were masters of the camp, almost without effort. Reacting to the tension, many of the men became nauseated. Sagging to their knees they gave themselves to an agonised, empty-stomached retching. Etzwane, himself hearing strange ringing sounds in his ears, ordered the women of the camp instantly to serve hot food and drink.

The men ate, slowly, gratefully, marveling that the storming of the camp had gone with such facility. The situation was incredible.

After eating, Etzwane felt an overpowering drowsiness, to which he must not allow himself to succumb. Old Kretzel stood near by, and he called for her. 'What has happened to the Ka? There were forty or fifty in the camp; now there are ten or less.'

Kretzel spoke in a dismal voice. 'They departed in the ship. Only two days ago they went, in great excitement. Great events are in the offing, for better or worse.'

'When will another ship return?'

'They did not trouble to explain this to me.'

'Let us question the Ka.'

They went to the barracks where the Ka lay bound. The ten men Etzwane had left on guard were all asleep and the Ka were furiously working to liberate themselves. Etzwane roused the sleeping men with kicks. 'Is this the

163

way you guard our safety? Every one of you: dead to the world! In another minute you might have been dead forever.'

Old Sul, one of the men who had been left on guard, gave a surly response, 'You yourself described these men as victims; in all justice they should be grateful for their deliverance.'

'This is precisely the point I intend to make to them,' said Etzwane. 'Meanwhile we are only the wild men who attacked them and tied them with thongs.'

'Bah,' muttered Sul. 'I am unable to chop logic with you; you have the superior sleight with words.'

Etzwane said, 'Make sure the thongs are secure.' He spoke to Kretzel. 'Tell the Ka that we mean them no harm, that we regard the asutra as our mutual enemy.'

Kretzel peered at Etzwane in perplexity, as if she found the remarks strange and foolish. 'Why do you tell them that?'

'So that they will help us, or at least do nothing to hinder.'

She shook her head. 'I'll sing to them, but they will pay no great heed. You do not understand the Ka.' She took up her double-pipes and played phrases. The Ka listened without perceptible reaction. They made no reply, but after a brief silence made wavering, tremulous sounds, like the chuckling of baby owls.

Etzwane looked at them doubtfully. 'What do they say?'

Kretzel shrugged. 'They talk together in the "Allusive" Style, which is beyond my capability. In any event, I don't think they understand you.'

'Ask them when the ship will return.'

Kretzel laughed but obliged him. The Ka looked at her blankly. One warbled a brief phrase, then they were silent. Etzwane looked questioningly at Kretzel.

'They sing from Canto 5633: the "embarrassing farce". It might translate as a jeer: "What interest can this matter have for you?"'

'I see,' said Etzwane. 'They are not practical.'

'They are practical enough,' said Kretzel. 'The situation is beyond their understanding. Do you remember the ahulphs of Durdane?'

'I do indeed.'

'To the Ka, men are like ahulphs: unpredictable, half-intelligent, addicted to incomprehensible antics. They cannot take you seriously.'

Etzwane grunted. 'Ask the question again. Tell them that when the ship arrives they will be freed.'

Kretzel played her flute. A terse answer returned. 'The ship will be back in a few days with a new corps of slaves.'

Chapter 10

The mutinous slaves had gained themselves food, shelter, and a respite which all realised to be temporary. A certain Joro argued that the group should transport supplies to some secret place in the hills and hope to survive until they could dare another raid. 'By this means we gain another several months, and who knows what might happen? The rescue ships from Earth might arrive.'

Etzwane gave a bitter laugh. 'I know now what I should have known every moment of my life; that unless you help yourself, you die a slave. The fact is basic. No one is going to rescue us. If we remain here, the chances are good that we will shortly be killed. If we go out to hide upon the moors, we gain two months of wet clothes and misery, and then we will be killed anyway. If we pursue the original plan, at best we gain a great advantage and at worst we die in dignity, doing our enemies as much damage as possible.'

'The chances of "best" are few and of "worst" many,' grumbled Sul. 'I for one am fatigued with these visionary schemes.'

'You must do as you think best,' said Etzwane politely. 'By all means, go forth upon the moors. The way is open.'

Korba said curtly, 'Those who want to go, let them go now. The rest of us have work to do, and time may be short.'

But neither Sul nor Joro chose to leave.

During the day Rune the Willow Wand approached Etzwane. 'Do you remember me? I am the Alul girl who once befriended you. I wonder if you think warmly of me now? But I am haggard and wrinkled, as if I were old. Is this not true?'

Etzwane, preoccupied with a hundred anxieties, looked across the compound, trying to contrive a remark suitably noncommittal. He said, somewhat curtly, 'On this world a pretty girl is a freak.'

'Ah! I wish then I were a freak! So long ago, when the men reached to tweak off my little cap, I was happy, even though I pretended displeasure. But now, if I were to dance naked in the compound, who would look at me?'

'You would still attract attention,' said Etzwane. 'Especially if you danced well.'

'You mock me,' said Rune sorrowfully. 'Why cannot you offer me some consolation: a touch or a smiling glance? You make me feel squat and ugly.'

'I have no such intention,' said Etzwane. 'You may be assured of this. But please excuse me; I must see to our preparations.'

Two days went past, with tension increasing every hour. On the morning of the third day a disk-ship slid up the coast from the south and hovered over the camp. There was no need for alarms or exhortations; the men were already at their stations.

The ship hovered, hanging on a humming web of vibration. Etzwane, in the garage, watched with clammy sweat on his body, wondering which of many circumstances would go wrong.

From the ship came a mellow hooting, which after an interval reverberated back from the hill.

The sound died, the ship hovered. Etzwane held his breath until his lungs ached.

The ship moved, and slowly descended to the landing field. Etzwane exhaled and leaned forward. This now was the time of crisis.

The ship touched the ground, which visibly subsided under the mass of the ship. A minute passed, two minutes. Etzwane wondered if those aboard had perceived an incorrectness, the absence of some formality . . . The port opened; a ramp slid to the soil. Down came two Ka, asutra riding their necks like small black jockeys. They halted at the base of the ramp, looked across the compound. Two more Ka descended the ramp, and the four stood as if waiting.

A pair of drays set out from the warehouse: the usual procedure when a ship landed. They swerved to pass close to the ramp. Etzwane and three men came forth from the garage, to walk with simulated purposelessness towards the ship. From other areas of the yard other small groups of men converged upon the ship.

The first dray halted; four men stepped down and suddenly leapt upon the Ka. From the second dray four other men brought thongs; there would be only needful killing, lest they be left with a ship and no one to navigate. While the group struggled at the foot of the ramp, Etzwane and his men ran up the ramp and into the ship.

The ship carried a crew of fourteen Ka and several dozens of asutra, some in trays like that which Etzwane and Ifness had found in the wreck under Thrie Orgai. Except for the scuffle at the foot of the ramp, neither Ka nor asutra offered resistance. The Ka had seemed paralysed by surprise, or perhaps apathetic; there was no comprehending their emotions. The asutra were as opaque as flint. Again the rebel slaves felt the frustration of over-exertion, of striking out with all force and encountering only air. They felt relieved but cheated, triumphant yet seething with unrelieved tension.

The great central hold contained almost four hundred men and women. These were of all ages and conditions, but in general seemed of poor quality, spiritless and defeated.

Etzwane wasted no time upon the folk in the hold; he gathered the Ka and their asutra in the control dome and brought up Kretzel. 'Tell them this,' said Etzwane, 'and make sure that they comprehend exactly. We want to return to Durdane. This is what we require of them: transportation to our home-world. We will tolerate nothing less. Tell them that when we arrive at our destination, then we will make no further demands upon them; they may have their lives and their ship. If they refuse to take us to Durdane, we will destroy them without mercy.'

Kretzel frowned and licked her lips, then brought forth her pipes and played Etzwane's message.

The Ka stood unresponsive. Etzwane asked anxiously, 'Do they understand?'

'They understand,' said Kretzel. 'They have already decided what their answer will be. This is a ceremonial silence.'

One of the Ka addressed Kretzel in a set of careful First Style tones, delivered in a manner so offhand as to seem condescending or even derisive.

Kretzel said to Etzwane, 'They will take you to Durdane. The ship departs at once.'

'Ask if sufficient food and drink are aboard.'

Kretzel obeyed and elicited a reply. 'He says that provisions are naturally adequate for the journey.'

'Tell them one thing further. We have brought torpedoes aboard the ship. If they try to deceive us, we will all blow up together.'

Kretzel played her double-pipes; the Ka turned away without interest.

Etzwane had known many triumphs and joys during the course of his life, but never exhilaration such as now, on this journey back from the dark world Kahei. He felt tired but he could not sleep. He distrusted the Ka, he feared the asutra; he could not believe that his victory was final. Of the other men he felt confidence only in Korba, and he made certain that he and Korba never slept at the same time. To maintain a spirit of vigilance, he warned that the asutra were devious, that they did not readily accept defeat; privately he was sure that victory had been won. In his experience the asutra were impassive realists, unaffected by considerations of malice or revenge. When the Roguskhoi had been defeated in Shant, the asutra might easily have destroyed Garwiy and Brassei and Maschein with their energy bolts, but had not troubled to do so. Chances were good, thought Etzwane, that the impossible had been accomplished, and without the assistance of the ineffable Ifness, which added savor to the triumph.

Etzwane spent considerable time in the control dome. Through the ports nothing could be seen but dead blackness and an occasional streaming filament of spume. A panel depicted the outside sky; the stars were black disks on a luminous green field. A target circle enclosed three black dots, which daily grew larger; Etzwane assumed these to be Etta, Sassetta, and Zael.

Conditions in the hold were appalling. The cargo of men and women were ignorant of cleanliness, order, or sanitation; the hold stank like an abattoir. Etzwane learned that most of the folk had been born on Kahei and had known only the life of the slave camp. During the evolution of the Roguskhoi, macabre experiments had been part of their everyday routine; it had seemed the natural way of life. The asutra, whatever their virtues, displayed neither squeamishness nor pity, thought Etzwane, and perhaps these were emotions idiosyncratically human. Etzwane tried to feel compassion for the slave folk, but the stench and disorder in the hold made the task difficult. Once more on Durdane, these folk were destined for further misery. Some might wish themselves 'back home' on the black world Kahei.

The ship coasted through open space. Above danced the three suns; below spread the gray-violet face of Durdane. As the ship descended, familiar contours passed below: the Beljamar and the Fortunate Isles, Shant and Palasedra, then the vast world-continent Caraz.

Etzwane identified the river Keba and Lake Nior. As the ship dropped lower, the Thrie Orgai and the river Vurush appeared. With Kretzel's assistance he directed the ship down to Shagfe. The ship landed on the slope south of the village. The ramps descended; the passengers tumbled, staggered, and crawled out upon the soil of their home-world, each clutching a parcel of food and as much good metal as he could carry: enough to assure a comfortable competence on metal-poor Durdane. Etzwane provided himself with thirty rods of glistening red alloy from the engine room: enough wealth, so he calculated, to bring him once again to Shant.

Ever distrustful, Etzwane insisted that the Ka come forth from the ship and remain until the folk had dispersed. 'You have brought us here to Durdane, and now we are finished with you and your ship, but are you finished with us? I don't want to be destroyed by a purple lightning bolt that you discharge as soon as you have the capability.'

Through Kretzel the Ka responded, 'We don't care whether you live or die; leave the ship at once.'

Etzwane said, 'Either come out on the plain with us or we will remove your asutra, which you seem to revere so much. We have not suffered and hoped and striven to take foolish chances at the last moment.'

Eight of the Ka at last went out on the plain. Etzwane, with a group of his men, led them a mile up the slope, then dismissed them. They trudged back to their ship while Etzwane and his companions sought shelter among the rocks. As soon as the eight were aboard, the ship lifted into the air. Etzwane watched it dwindle and vanish, then within himself the knowledge came: he had really returned to Durdane. His knees felt limp; he sat down upon a rock, weary as he had never been before in his life, and tears flowed from his eyes.

Chapter 11

In Shagfe the advent of so many persons laden with
wealth had created dislocations. Some drank copiously of
Baba's cellar brew, others gambled with the Kash Blue-
worms, who still haunted the vicinity. Throughout the
night sounds of altercation could be heard: yells and
curses, drunken sobs and cries of pain; and in the morning
a dozen corpses were discovered. As soon as light came to
the sky, groups set forth for their ancestral lands, to
north, east, south, and west. The Alula, uttering no words
of farewell to Etzwane, departed for Lake Nior. Rune the
Willow Wand turned a single glance over her shoulder.
Etzwane, meeting the gaze, found it unreadable. He
watched them recede into the morning haze, then he went
to find Baba the innkeeper.

'I have two matters to take up with you,' said Etzwane.
'First, where is Fabrache?'

Baba replied in vague terms. 'Who is to trace the course
of that loose-footed man? The slave trade is ruined. Old
markets are gone and Hozman Sore-throat has disappeared; poverty stalks the land. As for Fabrache, when
he appears you will see him; he is not a man for pre-
dictability.'

'I will not wait,' said Etzwane, 'which leads me to the
second matter, my pacer. I desire that it be saddled and
made ready for travel.'

Baba's eyes protruded in wonder. 'Your pacer? What prodigy of imagination is this? You own no pacer at my stables.'

'But indeed I do,' said Etzwane in a sharp voice. 'My friend Ifness and I both left our pacers in your care. I, at least, now intend to resume possession.'

Baba shook his head in wonder and raised his eyes piously to the sky. 'In your own land odd customs may prevail, but here at Shagfe we are more practical. A gift once given may not be recalled.'

'Gift, you say?' Etzwane's tone was grim. 'Have you heard the tales told by the folk who brought you metal for cellar brew last night? How by our strength and will we won our way home to Caraz? Do you think that I am the kind of man to tolerate petty thievery? Bring me my pacer, or prepare for a remarkable thrashing.'

Baba reached behind his bar and brought forth his cudgel. 'A beating, is it? Listen to me, my cockscomb, I have not been Shagfe innkeeper without dealing a few beatings of my own, I assure you. Now leave these premises on the instant!'

From his pouch Etzwane brought the little weapon Ifness had given him so long ago: the energy gun he had carried to Kahei and back and never used. He pointed the gun at Baba's strongbox and touched the button. A flare, an explosion, a scream of horror, as Baba stared at the devastation which only a moment before had held a fortune in metal. Etzwane reached out, took his cudgel, and hit him across the back. 'My pacer, and in haste.'

Baba's fat face was lambent with fear and malice. 'Already you have done me out of a lifetime's earnings! Do you wish the fruits of all my toil?'

'Never try to cheat an honest man,' said Etzwane. 'Another thief might sympathise with your goals; as for me, I want only my property.'

174

In a voice nasal with rage Baba sent one of the yard-boys to the stables. Etzwane went out into the inn-yard, where he found old Kretzel sitting on a bench. 'What do you do here?' asked Etzwane. 'I thought that you would be on your way to Elshuka Pond.'

'The way is long,' said Kretzel, pulling the tattered cloak about her shoulders. 'I have a few bits of metal, enough to keep food in my mouth for a period. When the metal is gone I shall start my journey south, though surely I will never arrive at the grass meadows above the pond. And if I did, who would remember the little girl who was stolen by Molsk?'

'What of the Great Song? How many people of Shagfe will understand when you play your pipes?'

Kretzel huddled her old shoulders into the sunlight's warmth. 'It is a great epic: the history of a far world. Perhaps I will forget, but perhaps not, and sometimes when I sit here in the sun I will play the pipes, but no one will know the great deeds I relate.'

The pacer was led forth: a creature by no means as sound as that Etzwane had brought to Shagfe, with gear somewhat worn and makeshift. Etzwane pointed out these facts, and the boy brought him out sacks of meal and a bladder of cellar brew for the journey.

Standing by the side of the inn Etzwane saw a familiar face: it belonged to Gulshe, who watched his preparations with a lowering intensity. Gulshe would make an efficient guide, reflected Etzwane, but what of the times when Etzwane slept and Gulshe kept watch? The prospect caused Etzwane to shudder. He gave Gulshe a polite salute and mounted his pacer. For a moment he looked down upon old Kretzel, her head stored with wonderful knowledge. He never would see her again, and with her would die the history of a world . . . Kretzel looked up; their gazes met. Etzwane turned away, his eyes again full of tears. He departed Shagfe, and against his back he felt Gulshe's stare and Kretzel's farewell.

Four days later Etzwane rode over a jutting sandstone crest and looked down on the flowing Keba. Shillinsk, by his rough reckoning, should lie somewhat south, for he had lost his way crossing the Plain of Blue Flowers. He looked up the Keba shore and five miles south spied the Shillinsk dock. He turned the pacer down the slope and rode south.

The Shillinsk Inn was as he had remembered it. Neither cargo vessel nor barge was moored alongside the dock, but Etzwane felt no great impatience; the tranquility of Shillinsk was a thing to be enjoyed in itself.

He entered the inn to find the landlord polishing the surface of his counter with a bag of rottenstone and a greasy square of chumpa-skin. He failed to recognise Etzwane, for which Etzwane felt no surprise. In his ragged garments he was a far remove from that spruce Gastel Etzwane who had come to Shillinsk with Ifness.

'You will not remember me,' said Etzwane, 'but some months ago I came here with the sorcerer Ifness in his magic boat. You were the victim of an unpleasant incident, as I recall.'

The landlord grimaced. 'Do not bring such matters to my attention. The sorcerer Ifness is a man to be feared. When will he come for his boat? It floats yonder on the water.'

Etzwane stared in surprise. 'Ifness has not taken his boat?'

'Look through the doorway; you will see it, exactly as you left it.' And he added virtuously, 'I have kept the craft secure and unmolested, as I was charged.'

'Well done.' Etzwane was greatly pleased; he had watched Ifness at the controls; he knew the use of the

176

dials and also knew how to board the boat without suffering an electric shock. He indicated the pacer. 'For your trouble I hereby make you the gift of yonder pacer, with his saddle. I require only a meal and lodging for the night; tomorrow I sail away in the magic boat.'

'You will take it to Ifness?'

'In all truth, I can't imagine what has happened to him. I expected that he would have come to Shillinsk long ago and taken the boat himself . . . No doubt, if he requires either me or the boat, he will know where to find me – if he is still alive.'

If Ifness were still alive. Between Shagfe and Shillinsk lay a hundred dangers: chumpa, bands of crazy ahulph, robber tribes, and slavers. Ifness might have fallen victim to any of these, and all of Etzwane's hard thoughts might be unjustified . . . Should he go forth to seek Ifness? Etzwane heaved a long sigh. Caraz was vast. It would be an exercise in futility.

The landlord prepared a savory supper of river fish poached in a tart green sauce, and Etzwane walked out on the dock to watch purple dusk fall over the water. Shant and the city Garwiy were much closer than he had hoped.

In the morning he rowed out to the boat in a skiff and gingerly prodded the guard-switch with a dry stick. Then even more gingerly he laid his finger on the gunwale. No shock, no coruscation of sparks like that which had flung the landlord into the river.

Etzwane tied the skiff to the mooring line and cast off. The current caught the boat and carried it north and out into the stream. He hoisted the sail; Shillinsk receded, and became a line of toy houses on the shore.

Now: the critical experiment. He opened the console and examined the line of knobs. Cautiously he twisted the 'Ascensor'. Up rose the boat, gliding on the wind. Etzwane hurriedly lowered the sail lest a gust capsize him.

He tested the other knobs; the boat swung in a wide arc and flew east towards Shant.

Below passed the dove-gray plains and dark-green swamps. Ahead glistened the Bobol River, and then the great Usak.

By night Etzwane reached the east coast and the Green Ocean. A few flickering yellow lights indicated a shore-side village; ahead the stars reflected on the water.

Etzwane slowed the boat, so that it drifted, and slept; and when dawn came, the land of Shant loomed along the horizon to the southeast.

Etzwane flew high above cantons Gitanesq and Fenesq, then descended towards the Sualle. The towers of Garwiy could barely be seen: a handful of glowing jewels. The shores closed in; fishing boats worked in the distance. Etzwane dropped the boat into the water. He hoisted the sail, and with the wind at his back, drove with a bubbling wake towards Garwiy.

The wind presently slackened and the boat moved more slowly over the placid water. Drowsing in the warmth, Etzwane could find no occasion for haste; indeed, the prospect of docking the boat and stepping ashore aroused in him a curious mood of melancholy. The adventure would then be definitely finished; for all its misery and black despair, he had lived to his utmost capacity; he had augmented and enriched his life.

Across the halcyon water sailed the boat, and the towers of Garwiy reared above him like lords at a banquet. Along the shore Etzwane spied familiar sights: this building, that warehouse, and there the ramshackle old dock at which Ifness had moored his boat. Etzwane swung the tiller, the boat gurgled through the water. Etzwane dropped the sail; the boat coasted quietly to the pier.

Etzwane made the boat secure, then walked up into the

road and hailed a diligence. The driver looked him over with misgivings. 'Well, then, why do you stop me? I have nothing to give; go to the public hospital for your alms.'

'I want no alms; I want transportation,' said Etzwane. He climbed into the diligence. 'Take me to Fontenay's Inn, on Galias Avenue.'

'You have money?'

'Not in these garments. At Fontenay's you will be paid; accept my word for this.'

The driver flicked the pacer into motion. Etzwane called up to him, 'What has been happening in Garwiy? I have been away for months.'

'Nothing of any great moment. The Green and Purple have weighed us down with taxes; they are more ambitious with their schemes than was the Anome . . . I like air at my neck instead of the torc, but now the Green and Purple want me to pay for my liberty. Which is better: cheap submission or expensive independence?'

Through the dusk rolled the diligence, along streets which seemed quaint and small, dearly familiar and somehow remote. On Kahei, Garwiy had seemed a dream – yet it existed. Here in Garwiy, Kahei had become an abstraction – and it too existed. Elsewhere was the world of the black globe-ships with the human crews. He would never learn the actuality of this world.

The diligence halted before Fontenay's Inn; the driver looked truculently down at Etzwane. 'Now then, my money, if you please.'

'One moment.' Etzwane went into the inn, to find Fontenay sitting at a table enjoying a flask of his own merchandise. Fontenay frowned at the ragged apparition, then recognising Etzwane, uttered an ejaculation of astonishment. 'What is this? Gastel Etzwane in rags for a charade?'

'No charade, but an adventure from which I have only

179

now returned. Be so good as to pay off this importunate driver, then let me have a room, a bath, a barber, some fresh garments, and finally a good dinner.'

'Nothing could give me more pleasure,' said Fontenay. He snapped his fingers. 'Heinel! Jared! See to Gastel Etzwane's convenience!' Fontenay turned back to Etzwane. 'Can you guess who plays music on yonder bandstand? In half an hour he will arrive.'

'Dystar the druithine?'

'Alas, not Dystar! It is Frolitz and his Pink-Black-Azure-Deep Greeners.'

'This is good news,' said Etzwane from the depths of his heart. 'I can think of no one I would rather see.'

'Well then, make yourself comfortable. A merry evening lies before us.'

Etzwane bathed himself with zeal: the first warm bath he had known since departing Fontenay's with Ifness. He dressed in fresh garments, then a barber trimmed his hair and shaved his face. What of his sour-smelling rags? He was tempted to keep them for mementos, but threw them away.

He went down to the common room, to find Frolitz in conversation with Fontenay. Frolitz leapt to his feet and embraced Etzwane. 'Well then, my lad! I haven't seen you for months, and I hear that you have enjoyed a picaresque adventure! You always were the one for foibles and quixotries! But now, here you are, and looking – how shall I say it? – full of strange knowledge. What music have you been playing?'

Etzwane laughed. 'I started to learn a Great Song of fourteen thousand cantos, but mastered only twenty or thereabouts.'

'A good beginning! Perhaps we shall hear some of these tonight. I have taken on another man, a clever young Paganese, but he lacks elasticity. I doubt if he will ever learn. You shall have your old seat and Chaddo can work the sliding bass. What do you say to that?'

'I say, first, that I cannot play tonight; I would astound you all! Second, I am famished for a meal; I have been to Caraz and subsisted on porridge. Third, in regard to the future; it is a void.'

'Outside interests constantly interfere with your music,' declared Frolitz peevishly. 'I suppose you came to meet your old friend, whose name I forget. I have seen him often during the past few days; for a fact, there he goes now, to his usual table in the corner. Take my advice and ignore him.'

'The advice is good,' said Etzwane in a strained voice. 'Nevertheless, I must have a word with Ifness, and I will join you later.'

Etzwane crossed the room, to stand before the table in the corner. 'I am surprised to see you.'

Ifness looked up blankly then gave a brusque nod. 'Ah, Etzwane, you catch me at a hurried moment. I must take a quick meal and depart.'

Etzwane sank into a chair and stared into the long, austere face as if to bring forth Ifness' secrets by visual suction. 'Ifness, one of us must be insane. Who is it, you or I?'

Ifness made an irritated gesture. 'It would work to the same effect; in either case an equal disparity of opinion would exist. But, as I put forward, I –'

Etzwane spoke as if he had not heard. 'Do you recall the circumstances of our leave-taking?'

Ifness frowned. 'Why should I not do so? The event occurred at a place in north-central Caraz on a day I cannot precisely name. I believe that you departed in pursuit of a barbarian maiden, or some such thing. As I recall, I warned you against the project.'

'This was the general nature of the event. You went off to arrange a rescue operation.'

A waiter set a tureen before Ifness, who raised the lid, sniffed, then ladled forth a bowl of green sea-fruit soup. Ifness came back to Etzwane's remark with an abstracted frown. 'Let me see; what were the circumstances? They included the Alul tribesmen and Hozman Sore-throat. You wanted to organise a gallant expedition into the skies to rescue a girl who had struck your fancy. I pronounced such an effort impractical and even suicidal. I am glad to see that you were dissuaded.'

'I remember the matter from a different perspective,' said Etzwane. 'I proposed to capture the depot ship; you stated that such an acquisition would interest the Earth folk and that a rescue ship might arrive in a minimum of two or three weeks.'

'Yes, this was the case. I mentioned the matter to Dasconetta, who felt that such a step exceeded the capabilities of his office, and nothing came of it.' Ifness tasted of his soup and sprinkled a few flakes of pepper pod upon the surface. 'In any case, the eventualities were the same, and you need feel no more concern.'

Etzwane controlled his voice with an effort. 'How could eventualities be the same when a shipload of captives is taken to a far planet?'

'I speak in a broad sense,' said Ifness. 'As for myself, my work has taken me far afield.' He glanced at his chronometer. 'I have yet a few minutes. The asutra that I took here in Shant, and others, have been studied. You may be interested in what I have learned.'

Etzwane leaned back in his chair. 'By all means, tell me about the asutra.'

Ifness consumed his soup with slow, easy sweeps of the spoon. 'Something of what I will tell you is conjecture, some is induction, some observations, and some derives from direct communication. The asutra are a very old race, with an exceedingly long history. As we know, they are parasites evolved from a kind of swamp leech. They accumulate information upon the face of crystals inside their abdomen. These crystals grow and the asutra grows. A large abdomen indicates much stored wisdom; the larger the abdomen, the higher the caste. The asutra communicate among themselves by nervous impulses, or perhaps telepathy; an array of specialised asutra is capable of the most complicated intellectual tasks.

'It is a truism that intelligence develops during a time of gradually worsening conditions; so it was with the asutra. They had and have a high reproductive rate; each asutra produces a million spawn, which are oriented according to one of two modes and which must make juncture with an opposite mode to become viable. In the early days the asutra overpopulated their swamps and were forced to compete for hosts: a challenge which urged them to domesticate hosts, to build stables and pens, and to control their own reproductive rate.

'It is important to recognise the asutra dynamic, their basic psychic drive, which is the lust to dominate a strong and active host. This necessity is as fundamental as the force which turns plants to the sunlight, or prompts men to seek food when they are hungry. Only by recognising this lust to dominate can the activities of the asutra be understood even dimly. I must remark here that many, if not all, of our original theories were naive and incorrect. My researches, I am happy to state, have illuminated the truth.

'Because of their intelligence and their capacity to multiply this intelligence, and because of their natural pedacity, asutra history has been complex and dramatic. They have passed through many eras. There was an artificial period, during which they used chemical nutrition, electrical sensations, imaginary knowledge. During a time of lassitude, mechanisms created seas of nutrient sludge, in which the asutra swam. During another era the asutra bred optimal hosts, but these were conquered and destroyed by asutra on primeval hosts from the original slime. But these archaic hosts were moribund and nearly extinct; the asutra were stimulated to interplanetary adventure.

'On the planet Kahei they discovered an environment almost identical to their own, and the Ka were compatible hosts. The asutra assumed control of Kahei, which over the centuries became to them a second home-world.

'On Kahei they encountered a most unexpected and unwelcome circumstance. By subtle degrees the Ka adapted to the asutra, and slowly the roles began to shift. The asutra, rather than being the dominant member of the symbiosis, became subordinate. The Ka began to subject the asutra to undignified uses, as control nodes for mining engines, processing machinery, and other unpleasant tasks. In other cases the Ka employed arrays of joined asutra as computing machines or reference devices; essentially the Ka used the asutra to augment their own powers, rather than the other way around. The asutra objected to such arrangements; a war occurred and the asutra on Kahei were enslaved. Henceforth the Ka were the masters and the asutra the adjuncts.

'The asutra expelled from Kahei were anxious to discover new hosts. They came to Durdane, where the human inhabitants were as agile, durable, and proficient as Ka and far more responsive to control. Durdane was too arid for their own comfort; across two or three centuries they conveyed many thousands of men and women to their home-world and integrated them into their system of life. But they still coveted the world Kahei for its idyllic moors and delightful quagmires, and therefore launched a war of annihilation against the Ka, using men as their slave warriors.

'The Ka, never a numerous folk, were assured of defeat by attrition unless they could stifle the human assault. As an experiment the Ka contrived the Roguskhoi and sent them to Durdane to destroy the human race. As we know, the experiment failed. Next the Ka thought to use men as warriors against the asutra, but again the experiment met no success; their corps of slave warriors revolted and refused to fight.'

Etzwane demanded, 'How did you learn all this?'

Ifness made a casual gesture. He had finished his soup, and was now eating a plate of assorted meats and pickled fruit. 'I employed the facilities of the Historical Institute. Dasconetta, incidentally, is discomfited; I overwhelmed his pedantic inflexibility, and indeed took the matter before Coordination, where I found active endorsement of my views. The Earth-worlds cannot tolerate human enslavement by alien races; this is fundamental policy. I accompanied the correction force in the nominal capacity of adviser to the commander, but in fact directed the expedition.

'Arriving at Kahei we found both the Ka and the asutra exhausted and discouraged with the war. In the north country we halted an engagement of warships, then enforced a peace, which was hard but fair. The Ka were required to surrender all their asutra and to repatriate all their human slaves. The asutra abandoned their attempt to dominate Kahei and also agreed to return all human hosts to Durdane. The solution to a highly complicated problem was elegantly simple, and within a common zone of comprehension. So there, in a most truncated outline, you have the situation as it exists now.' Ifness drank from a cup of verbena tea.

Etzwane sat hunched in his chair. He thought of the

silver and white ships which had driven the Ka ships back from the black asutra globes. With a pang of bitter humor he recalled how defenseless and apathetic had been the training camp, and with what illusory ease he and his men had captured it. The spaceship which they had taken with such grim determination – it actually had come to take them back to Durdane. Small wonder the resistance had been so scant!

Ifness spoke in a voice of polite concern, 'You seem troubled; has my account distressed you in any way?'

'Not at all,' said Etzwane. 'As you say, truth destroys many illusions.'

'As you can apprehend, I was preoccupied with large causes and unable to attend to the captured Alula, who presumably once again wander beside the Vurush River.' He glanced at his chronometer. 'What were your own actions subsequent to our parting?'

'They were of no great consequence,' said Etzwane. 'After some small inconvenience I returned to Shillinsk. I brought your boat back to Garwiy.'

'That is good of you. Dasconetta sent a space car down to Shillinsk for me, which of course I used.' Ifness glanced at his chronometer. 'If you will excuse me, I must leave. Our association has spanned several years, but I doubt if we will meet again. I am leaving Durdane and I do not plan to return.'

Etzwane, slumping back in his chair, said nothing. He thought of far places, of flowing rivers and nomad clans. He remembered terror aboard the transport ship and the death of Karazan; he thought of black velvet moors and the purple-black morass; he recalled Polovits and Kretzel . . . Ifness had risen to his feet. Etzwane said, 'At Shagfe is an old woman named Kretzel. She knows fourteen thousand cantos to the Great Song of the Ka. The knowledge will die with her.'

186

.... some at your shop or newsagent or can be ordered direct from the publisher. Just tick the titles you want and fill in the form below.

VGSF, Cash Sales Department, PO Box 11, Falmouth, Cornwall.

Please send cheque or postal order, no currency.

Please allow cost of book(s) plus the following for postage and packing:

UK customers – Allow 60p for the first book, 25p for the second book plus 15p for each additional book ordered, to a maximum charge of £1.90.

BFPO – Allow 60p for the first book, 25p for the second book plus 15p per copy for the next seven books, thereafter 9p per book.

Overseas customers including Eire – Allow £1.25 for the first book, 75p for the second book plus 28p for each additional book ordered.

NAME *(Block letters)* ....

ADDRESS ....

....

....
